# The King & His Queen

Donna Fletcher

Donna Fletcher

This is a work of fiction. Names, characters, places, and incidents are either the product of the author's imagination or are used fictitiously, and any resemblance to actual persons, living or dead, business establishments, events or locales is entirely coincidental.

*The King & His Queen*
All rights reserved.
Copyright February 2017 by Donna Fletcher

Cover art
Kim Killion Group

Visit Donna's Web site
www.donnafletcher.com/
http://www.facebook.com/donna.fletcher.author

## Chapter One

Hemera hurried her cloak over her shoulders as she left her dwelling. She tilted her head back to look up at the sky and smiled. The first light of day was breaking on the horizon and she quickened her steps. She wanted to get to the forest and greet the dawn as she did most every day. She hoped to feel the bright rays of the morning sun upon her. Too often gray, thick clouds masked the rising sun.

The stronghold gate opened each day after the sun had completely risen, but that was of no consequence to Hemera. She often explored the small area of woods behind her dwelling that had once belonged to Paine, the King's executioner. For now, it was her home. It sat apart from the other dwellings that comprised the village within the stronghold as did the torture dwelling only a short distance away. The purpose? No one would hear the anguished cries of those being tortured. Thankfully, it had remained quiet since she had inhabited the adjacent home. Her curiosity had had her exploring the sinister dwelling, though she had been warned against going there. Seeing the instruments of torture, she could make no sense of such depravity. But then there were many things that made no sense to her.

The forest, however, she understood and embraced all it had to share with her. Not wanting to ever feel as trapped as she once did, she had searched for a way out of the stronghold, other than the main gate. She had found a slightly loose board in the tall, wooden fence that surrounded the stronghold and was hidden by the small area of woods behind her home. It had taken time and patience to work one of the boards free enough for her to slip past and secure back in place. No one would ever take notice of it, just as they did not take notice of the many other secrets in the stronghold.

Hemera secured the piece of fencing back in place and hurried along through the woods that were now as familiar to her as was the village. She would return before her sister Verity came looking for her. Verity and her husband Wrath, the King's commander warrior of his personal guards, would be too busy mating to pay any attention to her. She chuckled, recalling how she had entered their dwelling one morning to find Verity bouncing quite forcefully on top of Wrath. Hemera had been so surprised that she had simply stood there staring. That was until Wrath spotted her and she learned why his name suited him so well.

A slight wind swirled around her as she stepped away from the fence, bringing with it a chill and the scent of the forest. She smiled and sniffed the potent air. The earth's musky aroma was growing stronger. Soon the dark, rich soil would be eager to receive seeds, to birth new saplings, and provide for the creatures that called the woods their home.

She hurried along, eager to be well into the woods before the day dawned and the stronghold stirred to life. She stopped when light broke through the bare branches of the trees and tilted her head back to catch some of the sun's warmth on her face. Her hood fell away, unleashing her long, fiery red hair that, try as she might, could not be contained. Dawn always brought a smile to her face. Sunrise was pure magic, holding the promise of another day and all it had to offer.

One could never tell how long the sun would last. The heavens seemed to have a mind of its own, changing so suddenly that one never knew what to expect from sunrise to darkness. Lately though, she had been seeing signs of change in the woods. Hues of green and yellow grass were sprouting and tiny buds were beginning to make themselves known on the trees.

Hemera sighed with a smile. The sun kissed her face with its warmth and made her even more eager to seek the solitude of the forest and see what it had to show her today. She turned her attention to her surroundings and took a path that was not yet truly a path, having yet to be worn down by footfalls or horses' hooves.

Her glance darted about, keeping a keen eye on where she stepped and her surroundings. She had always been light in her steps and watchful, skills that had served her well. Particularly now, having no wont to happen upon any of the sentinels the King kept stationed on the outer boundaries of the stronghold. Guards had spotted her a few times and reported her to the King. The King, in turn, had chastised Verity for not keeping watch over her sister.

Why the King thought Verity should be responsible for her baffled Hemera. She was capable of tending herself. Besides, she kept to herself out of choice. Solitude was more to her liking, since more often than not, she found people uninteresting, and men completely puzzled her.

"A snow tear," she said excited and dropped down on her knees beside green leaves sprouting from a small patch of snow that had yet to melt.

Soon a bud would emerge and a drooping white flower would spring from it. She had named the flower snow tear since it often bloomed from a lingering patch of snow and its drooping appearance made it appear saddened that the snow was melting.

She welcomed the leaves with a gentle stroke of her finger. "It is good to see you."

A sudden noise had her head shooting up and her eyes turning wide. Several red squirrels were racing along the ground and spiraling up the trees. It was mating time for them, but it did not appear as if the squirrels were engaged in the routine of playfulness before mating. It appeared more like they were scurrying to get away from danger, perhaps from hunters or a larger animal.

Hemera got to her feet, though remained crouched, looking about, pleased the forest animals had alerted her to possible danger. She kept crouched down as she made her way behind a formation of boulders, to wait and listen.

She kept herself aware, always aware, knowing the problem with the Northmen was far from over. King Talon may have ordered Ulric, son of Haggard, Chieftain of the Southern Region of the Northmen, to leave Pict shores, but Ulric was not one to obey orders. He barely obeyed his father. Why should he submit to King Talon's demands?

No, the Picts had not seen the last of Ulric.

King Talon had unified all the Pict tribes, though not without bloodshed. He had made them a stronger force against Pict enemies. Some, however, continued to disagree with the unification, and more strongly the

# The King & His Queen

fact that the King, after two marriages, had failed to produce an heir to the Pict throne. Some believed he never would, especially since both previous wives now carried their new husbands' bairns. Opinions were growing stronger that King Talon should surrender the throne to a man who could produce heirs and secure the future of the Picts.

A third marriage had been arranged and was soon to take place. If the future queen did not bear the King a child, then there would be an outcry for him to renounce the throne. If not, the throne would surely be taken from him.

Light footfalls caught her attention. They were coming her way. She remained where she was, not moving, not making a sound. As she heard them pass near to where she was hiding, she waited until she was sure the person was a good distance away, then she peeked past the boulder, keeping low so as not to be seen.

Hemera peered past the many trees, now glad for the barren branches that were only beginning to show signs of budding and briefly caught sight of a figure draped in a cloak, the hood drawn up. She recognized the black cloak, but not the dull black color of most garments. This was a rich black cloak, the wool dyed in bog mire with oak twigs and chips to keep the color deep and steadfast. It was the unique color of the King's personal guard.

What was one of the King's personal guards doing out here alone, so early, in the forest?

Hemera watched and waited until the lone figure completely disappeared from sight, then she waited until she heard the animal's scurrying about in play before emerging from behind the boulders.

Hemera smiled. The threat had passed and the squirrels felt safe once again. She watched as the male squirrels frantically chased after the females, eager to mate and sire progeny. Her smile faded as her brow drew together. Why had one lone figure frightened them so badly? Or had the figure not been alone?

She would think on it. Something she often did when an answer was not directly forthcoming. Not now. Now she would enjoy the woods while she could. She continued on, the woods growing denser with her every step. It would be a good place to forage for plants and food throughout the moon cycles.

Something caught her eye on the ground and brought her to an abrupt halt and she crouched down to get a better look. Footfalls had left their shadows in patches of snow and the wet soil. There was something about them that had her staring, tilting her head, and viewing them from different angles. Three people of varying bulk had met here and she would not be surprised if one had been the cloaked figure she had seen walking toward the stronghold. Had that figure found a secret way in and out of the stronghold as she had done?

Hemera stared in the distance, her thoughts churning. Was someone inside the stronghold plotting with the King's enemies and was it one of his own personal guards? She would have to tell him about it. It meant his safety and the safety of the stronghold.

She turned, having lingered long enough in the woods. Verity would be looking for her soon for them to take the morn repast in the feasting house together, while Wrath spent time with King Talon. She quickened her steps, deciding to return through the front gate rather than the spot in the fence. It was more of a direct path to the feasting house and she had no doubt that Verity was already there waiting for her. If she did not appear soon, Wrath would have warriors searching for her. She stopped at the edge of the woods that opened onto the clearing in front of the stronghold. She was a distance away and she wondered if the King's warriors would question her. They were diligent in their task, keeping a watchful eye on all who left and returned. And being she had already been taken to task by the King for walking in the woods alone, they might make note of her return and question when she had left.

A quick thought came to mind and she hurried to gather small broken branches. It was common to see women returning to the stronghold with armfuls of broken branches. The branches were used to keep fire pits going when large flames were not necessary. Hopefully, the familiar sight would have the King's warriors paying her no heed. If not, there was little she could do, but face the consequences. Something she had become familiar with often throughout the years.

With sure and steady steps, Hemera made her way toward the stronghold gate. She stopped suddenly when the guards frantically began waving their hands for people to move aside, clearing the gate entrance. One guard waved quite forcefully at her and hearing horses' hooves behind her, she quickly obeyed.

It could be only one person who demanded such attention—the King.

Hemera turned to see him bearing down on the stronghold and he was a sight to behold. He looked as though he was riding into battle rather than returning home. A deep scowl attempted to mar his fine features, but failed. His perpetual glare added a look of assured power. He was to be obeyed or else. His body, lean, though strong with muscle, exuded even more power. She had heard talk that he could snap a man's neck with little effort and swing a sword with even less effort. She wondered if it was more myth than truth. His dark garments added to the mystery surrounding him, making him appear more sinful than righteous.

She wondered if he was truly either.

At this moment, though, she believed sinful was the correct choice.

His black stallion pounded the earth and the King leaned lower over his horse and to the side as he drew closer to her and when his arm shot out, she realized too late his intention.

His coiled arm snagged her around the waist, the strength of it rushing the breath from her and sending the armful of sticks she held flying.

## Chapter Two

Talon dropped her to sit sideways in front of him on his horse. Her arms quickly clamped around his neck and she buried her face there as well. He held her firm, her full breasts pressing against his chest and the scent of her flooding over him. She forever smelled of the savory pine trees and the ripe earth, ready for planting.

*Would she nourish his seed when no other woman could?*

He forced the sudden and absurd thought away and grew annoyed at the unexpected stirring in his loins. He had no interest in this woman. She had proven to be more a nuisance than anything and she failed to obey him at every turn. So where had the strange thought come from?

Talon slowed his horse as they approached the open gates and entered the stronghold at a tempered pace. Activity came to a halt as all in the village stopped to stare at him. Some failed to hide their shock, their mouths agape, while others' eyes rounded so wide that he thought for certain they would burst from their heads.

"Return to your chores now!" he called out, his powerful voice leaving no doubt he was to be obeyed.

The people were quick to submit, stealing glances the King's way and, though Talon saw, he did not correct the offenders. They would be the ones who would watch and let others know that the King looked after Hemera's safety and nothing more.

It did not surprise Talon to see Verity standing outside the feasting house, Wrath at her side. Someone must have hurried to let her know her sister rode with the King, since she wore a look of worry, and well she should. He brought his horse to a stop in front of the couple, his arm tightening at Hemera's waist to keep her from sliding off the horse.

Hemera felt the sharp tug that gripped her middle. She also felt the protectiveness in it. The King was keeping her safe, seeing that she remained unharmed and, at that moment, she felt safer than... She could not remember the last time she felt as safe as she did now.

Reluctantly, she let her arms slip down from around his neck, though she was not ready to remove her face from where she had kept it tucked in the crook of his neck. He had a scent about him that she found appealing. What it was, she did not know, but she would like to.

"Hemera!" Talon snapped.

She raised her head and her brow narrowed slowly. His fine features were even finer, seeing them so close. His dark, slim brows arched perfectly over eyes that were a deep color of blue that rivaled the mighty sea. Her skin paled next to his warm color and it was unmarred, except for the drawing that ran down the one side of his face, the swirling lines reaching out to brush his cheek.

Her eyes roamed his face with far too much curiosity, and she was far too beautiful for him to stare at her with equal curiosity. Frustrated, he said, "How often have I warned you not to walk in the woods alone?"

Her brow furrowed as she tilted her head slightly and, after a moment, she said, "I believe it was five warnings."

He drew in a breath to keep hold of his temper. He had to continually remind himself that she was slow to understand. Anger, warnings, threats were wasted on her.

"Verity, tend your sister!" he ordered without taking his eyes off Hemera.

"Why do you burden my sister with an unnecessary chore?" Hemera asked. "I do not need tending. I can look after myself."

Talon planted his face closer to Hemera's. "You do need tending when you fail to obey my orders."

After a brief hesitation, she said, "Not the ones that make sense."

Verity rushed forward, Wrath following closely behind her.

King Talon's hand shot up again, halting them.

"You question my reasoning?"

"How can I not question it when there is fault to it?"

"Let me take her," Wrath said, hurrying around his wife and reaching up for Hemera.

"Keep her from me," Talon ordered as he shoved her gently off the horse into Wrath's arms.

Verity stepped forward, taking her sister's arm and rushing her into the feasting house.

Talon watched them, wondering how the two sisters could be so different, not only in nature but appearance as well. Verity was a beautiful woman, but she could not compare to Hemera. Her beauty stunned the eye. Verity' hair was as bright as the sun while

Hemera's hair was the color of fiery flames and appeared just as untamable, like her nature.

He shook his head. What was it that kept his thoughts on her?

"Bring Broc to me," Talon ordered Wrath after dismounting. "He assured me he would make certain that Hemera did not leave the stronghold alone. He has failed me and I want to know why."

Wrath went to do as the King ordered while one of the King's guards led the King's horse away.

Talon entered the feasting house and before turning to go to the High Council Chambers, he looked to see Hemera sitting between Verity and Anin at one of the many tables. He hoped the two women would be able to keep her contained, though he doubted Hemera could ever be contained.

He turned and stopped after one of the two personal guards that stood at the chamber's doors when occupied, opened it. He glanced from one to the other. "Guard the feasting house doors and do not let Hemera leave unless someone is with her."

They both nodded and went to do as ordered.

Talon left the door open after entering the room. He wanted to discuss the problem of Hemera with Broc and also Wrath and see it done, then move on to more important matters. There was the Northmen to consider and after ordering Ulric off Pict land, he knew it was not the last he would see of him. Besides, there was still the matter of Northmen joining forces with those looking to see Talon dethroned.

Many voices had been heard during the talks to unify the tribes under one rule. Talon's voice had been the strongest. He had made many see how by uniting, instead of warring against one another, they could defend their land against foreign invaders successfully. If they remained divided, they would eventually be conquered and become nothing more than slaves.

Those that refused to see the wisdom of his words had continued to harbor resentment against him and the Unification. To make matters worse he had failed to produce heirs with his last two wives and secure the future of the Pict reign. The situation then had grown far worse than he thought possible. He had arranged marriages for his last two wives and both were now heavy with their husbands' bairns.

Talon went to the head of the table and before taking his seat, he filled a vessel with wine. He took a generous swallow, then shook his head. His appetite for mating was ravenous. How was it that he could mate with so many women and his seed never take root?

"My King," Wrath called out as he and Broc entered the room.

"Sit," Talon ordered, but offered no drink. He would have an explanation first. "Tell me how Hemera got past your guards."

"Hemera did not get past them. She never left the stronghold through the gates," Broc said, standing firm, his wide shoulders drawn back.

Though Broc seemed to be sure of his words, Talon gripped his vessels tighter and asked, "You are sure of this?"

"I am, my King. The men were warned and told there would be no second chance if they failed to make it so. Several of the warriors just now informed me that when they saw Hemera approaching the gates, they intended to stop her and hold her until she could be turned over to me."

"She could have slipped past with her hood pulled up," Wrath suggested.

Broc shook his head. "No. All hoods must be left off when leaving or entering the stronghold, whether man or woman."

"An order instituted after Hemera had slipped out that way a few times?" the King asked.

A sharp, annoyed nod had Broc admitting to being tricked. "It is not easy keeping track of Hemera. One moment she is there and the next she is not. I do not know how she moves from place to place so fast."

"And so quietly," Wrath added.

"Has she surprised you at an inopportune time?" Talon asked with a slight grin.

Wrath's temper flared when he admitted, "More than once."

Broc laughed quietly, it ending quickly when Wrath's dark eyes turned an irate warning on him.

"Have there been any complaints about Hemera?" Talon asked.

Broc shook his head. "Not one, but few know her. She is often with Verity or Anin, otherwise she keeps mostly to herself."

"Is she treated poorly by others?" Talon demanded, not one to suffer fools lightly.

"None would dare," Broc said, nodding toward Wrath.

"She is my wife's sister," Wrath said as if no other words were needed.

"Perhaps a husband can be found for her," Broc suggested.

"Are you volunteering?" Talon asked.

"No! No!" Broc said, shaking his head frantically. "I would not be a good husband for her. She needs someone quiet and understanding of her ways."

"Broc is right," Wrath said. "A warrior would never suit Hemera. A quiet man, one who works the soil, would suit her well."

"Find some men who would be willing to take Hemera as a wife," Talon ordered. "And I will decide who is best for her."

Wrath was hesitant. "Maybe I should speak with Verity about this first."

"I gave an order," Talon said. "Now sit and drink. We have much to discuss."

Wrath nodded, knowing the King would say no more on Hemera, though Wrath knew his wife would have much to say when she learned of the King's plan to see Hemera wed.

Wrath and Broc sat and Paine soon joined them.

Talon had not called a High Council meeting. He wanted no one but the three men present when the issue of the Northmen possibly joining those disgruntled Picts, wishing to seize the throne from Talon, was discussed.

Traitors had already been exposed in the stronghold and had quickly met their deaths. It was the one who led the traitorous group that Talon intended to find. The longer it took, the more damage was done, and the better chance there was of the Unification of Tribes being dissolved, and the Pict tribes being plunged into chaos. Talon could not let that happen. Too many good men and women had died so that the tribes could unite and work as one to keep foreigners off Pict soil.

"Word comes that there is no movement," Paine informed them. "Some wonder if the threat has passed, but I wonder if the quiet means that the threat grows stronger."

Talon respected Paine's opinion and his strength. He was a warrior few would go against, his large size intimidated and his body drawings, covering all but his face, frightened most. That he once was his executioner also had had many fearing him. But Talon also called him friend, having known him and having fought beside him before he was claimed King.

"This will not end until the leader is found and executed for all to see," Wrath said.

The door flew open before Talon could speak, and Hemera entered as if it was not at all unusual for her to do. One of the King's personal guards hurried in behind her, his face crinkled with dismay and worry for not having caught her before she reached the Council Chamber door.

Talon bolted to his feet, forcing the three men at the table to stand, though a harsh demand to 'sit' had them doing so quickly. He waved the guard off, his blue eyes burning with anger as he turned to Hemera, "What have I told you about entering this room?"

"To knock before I enter, which I did. Did you not hear the knock?" Hemera asked innocently.

"Knock and wait until I bid you to enter," Talon reminded with a sharpness that stung even his ears.

She gasped lightly, her eyes going wide. "I forgot that, as I forgot to tell you something important before we parted ways."

Talon brought his fist down hard on the table, annoyed that she could so easily dismiss his command.

"You cannot enter this room at will, Hemera. This room is now forbidden to you. You can never enter it again."

Hemera's wide eyes narrowed in question. "Why?"

Wrath shook his head while running his hand over his face, Broc lowered his shaking head, and Paine's lips curled in a slight smile.

Talon took quick strides and came to stop in front of her. That she had not budged or flinched at his hurried approach made him realize she simply did not understand the severity of her actions and words.

He calmed himself as much as he could before he spoke. "I cannot have anyone simply entering Council Chambers while important matters are being discussed."

"Of course not," she said as if horrified by the notion. She placed her hand on his shoulder.

Wrath, Broc, and Paine could not hide their shock, their eyes turned wide and a mouth or two fell open. No one, absolutely no one touched the King without permission.

Hemera took a step closer to Talon. She went up on her toes as she brought her mouth close to his ear.

The three men looked even more horrified, except for Paine, another slight smile touched his lips, since it appeared as if she kissed his cheek.

Hemera's lips almost brushed his ear as she said, "You must be careful who you trust."

Her warm breath felt like a fine feather tickling his ear and it sent a jolt to his loins, arousing him. Her red hair whispered delicately across his cheek as she stepped away, the soft strands taunting his flesh. Then there was that familiar scent about her that stung the nose, pine and earth, but that was not all. There was another scent as well, something he could not place, and the urge to step closer and drink deeply of it had him taking a quick step back away from her.

"That was your important message?" Talon asked his glance settling on her fiery strands that seemed in stark contrast to their delicate softness.

She looked at him oddly, appearing as if she did not understand the question. "Why would I speak of something important in front of others after what I just told you?"

"Paine and Wrath are my most trusted warriors and Broc has proven his loyalty time and again. You may speak freely in front of them."

"That may be true," she said, "but it would not be wise."

"Are you saying I am not wise?" Talon asked, barely holding on to this temper.

"Aye, in this situation you are not wise."

Wrath jumped to his feet. "I will—"

"Sit!" Talon ordered without looking at him.

Wrath was quick to obey and catching a smile on Paine's face, he shot him an angry look, which only caused Paine's smile to widen.

Giving no thought to wait for permission to speak, Hemera continued. "Your trusted warriors are trusted for a reason and surely understand of what I speak and certainly feel no insult by my request. They can wait outside the door. It will not take long for me to say what I have come to tell you, then you may resume your meeting and inform them of my news if you choose to."

"You disregard my order, touch me without permission, then tell me what should be done and you find nothing wrong with any of that?" Talon asked the question more of himself, reminding him of her limited ability to understand.

Hemera tilted her head and stared at the King. She was reminded of what her father had often told her. *Others do not see things as you do, even the wisest of men.*

"I meant no offense," she said softly.

Talon felt something he rarely ever did—guilt. She offered forgiveness, though she did not understand why. She had believed she was offering help and he had responded with anger.

"I will give you only a moment," he said and the smile that lit her lovely face almost had him catching his breath, though he caught it before it could pass his lips. She was far too beautiful to leave on her own. She needed a husband to look after her. Or did she need a husband to protect her from him? "Leave us," he ordered and the three men left to wait outside the closed door.

Talon folded his arms across his chest. "Have your say and be done with it."

"While in the woods, I spotted one of your personal guards or one who wore the cloak of your personal guards."

"My personal guards walk in the woods for various reasons," he said, wanting to make things as clear as possible to her so that she would not bother him with nonsense again.

"Why would one of your personal guards meet with others in the woods, away from prying eyes, if it was not to keep the meeting a secret?" She gave him no time to answer. "Would you not know of the meeting ahead of time? Would you not be the one to give permission for the meeting? Unless of course you know the meeting took place and I assumed wrongly." Again she did not wait for him to respond. It was not necessary. The way his brow tightened was enough of a response. The King had not been aware of the meeting. "I will see what more I can learn, since few pay heed to me and speak as if I am not there."

Talon grabbed her by the shoulders and yanked her close. A mistake since her full breasts brushed his chest. He had only had a woman this morn when he woke and she had left him satiated. Though if he was truthful with himself, he would admit he was never left completely satisfied. There was a part of him that he feared would never be assuaged. Still though, his body should not have grown so easily aroused. Annoyance at his reaction had his tongue more curt than he intended. "You will do no such thing. You will leave this be."

Hemera shook her head slowly, his words leaving her puzzled. "Who then will you appoint to see if there is a traitor among your personal guards? If anyone close to you, any of your trusted friends, begin to question your personal guards, the culprit will be alerted and take precautions not to be discovered, and worse, continue to betray you."

Again his tongue was curt. "It does not concern you."

She gasped lightly when a thought struck her. "Anin. She will touch each of your personal guards and tell you what she learns." She nodded slowly. "It would be the easiest thing to do," —she shook her head—"but not the wisest."

"You question my wisdom in this matter?"

"If you only wish to discover who among your personal guards betray you, then your decision is a wise one. If you wish to discover how deep the betrayal goes then is not your wisdom flawed? Surely that guard has informed others of Anin's abilities and he himself knows the wisdom of sharing what he learns, but not being told anything of what is planned."

Silence took hold of Talon as he made sense of her reasoning, something he never would have expected.

Hemera glanced to each of his hands where they gripped her shoulders. "You are quite strong."

Talon dropped his hands off her, though made no move to step away from her.

"Do as you will," —Hemera held his eyes with hers— "you are King."

He did not need reminding of that, though she did. She had to obey his rule just as everyone else did. "And a King is obeyed."

"Aye, sadly enough, even when he is wrong."

"Are you telling me I am wrong?" he asked with a flash of temper.

"You anger easily."

"It is easy to do with you," he spat.

"So I have been told."

The sadness that suddenly filled her eyes had him reining in his anger. He had to remember she was slow to understand. She did not make sense of things as others did, though there were times she made more sense than most. She was a puzzle to Talon and he did not know what to do with her.

"I have told you what I came to say. I will take my leave now and trouble you no more."

"Hemera," he said, stopping her as she turned to

go. "Keep a watchful eye and alert Wrath to anything questionable." A chore would keep her occupied and away from him.

"I will keep watch."

There was something in her tone that gave Talon pause. Who exactly would she keep watch over?

She had almost reached the door when a thought struck him. "Hemera!"

Her name so sharp on his lips brought her to an abrupt halt and she turned with a flourish.

"How did you get out of the stronghold? And do not waste your breath in a lie. I know you did not leave through the gates."

## Chapter Three

A knock sounded at the door, then a shout was heard. "An important message has arrived, my King."

Hemera hurried to open the door and as Wrath, Paine, and Broc hurried in, Hemera slipped out, though not before sending the King a smile. A shiver raced through her when the color of his deep blue eyes churned like a raging sea before a deadly storm. He was not done with her. He would have his answer.

Verity called to her from where she and Anin sat in the feasting hall and waved her over. Her sister would want to know what happened, since she had warned Hemera against disturbing the King while in the Council Chambers. It had made no sense for such important news to wait and she had paid her sister's words no heed. Anin had offered no advice and Hemera wondered if there were things Anin knew since first laying hands on her arm that she had yet to share with Hemera.

"Did all go well?" Verity asked anxiously, reaching out to take Hemera's arm and gently tugging her to sit on the bench beside her.

Hemera did not want her sister to worry. Verity had worried enough about her since their arrival on Pict soil, a few moon cycles ago, and she certainly had suffered enough while they had been enslaved by the Northmen. Verity had Wrath now and she was happy. Hemera could well look after herself. Her time with the

Northmen had taught her that.

"Aye, all went well," Hemera assured her sister.

"King Talon was not angry with you for interrupting his meeting?" Verity asked.

"His snarl is not as bad as it appears."

"I do not agree with that," Anin said. "I still fear him."

"You laid hands on him?" Hemera asked and was surprised when Anin nodded. "I did not think he would allow it."

"He did not allow it. I touched him without permission." Anin shivered, rubbing her arms to chase the sudden chill.

Hemera was quick to ask, "What did you feel?"

"Potent strength and unimaginable power."

"Both will serve him well as a King," Hemera said.

"There was also a smoldering passion that seemed to remain strong and steady in him."

Hemera nodded. "A strong passion would benefit a King."

Anin shook her head. "The passion I felt might be more of a deterrent than a benefit for him."

Verity kept her voice to a whisper. "There is talk that no one woman can satisfy him and with so many different women having shared his sleeping pallet, it makes one wonder."

Hemera lowered her head in thought. It was odd that the King would join with so many women and not sire one bairn. Usually the woman was always blamed when an heir was not sired, but with the King's two previous wives now with child the blame could not be placed on them. Was it truly the King's fault? Was he unable to sire a bairn?

"Hemera. Hemera."

Hemera raised her head.

"Lost in thoughts again?" Verity asked as a servant placed a bowl of meats on the table.

"More brew?" the servant asked.

"We have plenty, Simca," Verity said.

Though Verity maintained a smile, Hemera saw a shadow of concern in her sister's eyes as she turned toward her. Verity had always been protective of Hemera, never knowing what Hemera had suffered to keep her sister safe. But that mattered not now. She and Verity were finally free and Verity need not worry about her anymore. Now if only she could convince Verity of that.

"Busy thoughts," Hemera said with a grin. "Was there something you said I should know?"

Anin nodded. "It was something I said that your sister felt you should hear."

"About King Talon?" Hemera asked and turned, having heard a stirring behind her. She saw no one, though wondered if the shadows in the corners could be hiding someone. When she turned to Verity and Anin to see them both nodding in answer to her, she tapped a finger to her lips for them to speak low.

Hemera and Verity leaned in closer as Anin kept her voice to a whisper, "What troubled me the most when I touched the King was that I felt I was of no consequence to him. What happened to me, punishment or death, he cared not."

Hemera was all too aware of how ruthless those who ruled, or wished to rule, could be. She had seen it among the Northmen tribes and it seemed to be the same here. Was King Talon heartless or was he a King who kept his heart shielded so that he could rule his people with strength and courage like another ruler she knew?

"Could his reaction have been due to the situation at hand at the time?" Hemera asked.

"I had not given that thought at the time and I had little experience of laying my hands on someone then." Anin frowned. "I also was to be queen, until Paine and I were found sleeping naked together, though nothing had happened between us."

"So you betrayed the King," Hemera said.

"No, I did not betray the King." Anin shook her head firmly, though it eased as she appeared to think on Hemera's accusation. "In a way, I suppose I did, since I lost my heart to Paine."

"It is good it happened," Hemera said with a shrug.

"Hemera, do not say such a thing!" Verity scolded sharply.

"Why?" Hemera looked puzzled at her sister. "It was good it happened or else too many would have suffered for what was not meant to be. Anin would be stuck with the King, a man who cared nothing for her, and Paine would suffer every day knowing the woman he had given his heart to was in the arms of another man."

Anin smiled and patted Verity on the arm. "Hemera is right. No worse fate could have befallen me than to be forced to wed the King. So it was good it happened as it did."

Hemera wondered if King Talon had seen it that way. Had he thought of Paine and Anin and how they had lost their hearts to each other when he had made his decision not to accept her as his queen? Or had he cared only for himself? If he had, though, would he not have had Paine and Anin executed or at least punished severely? Another thing for her to think on.

The women talked a while longer, but Hemera's thoughts kept drifting. She wished for some solitude so that she could think on things that would not leave her alone. The problem was getting out of the feasting hall alone. She had seen how alert two of the King's personal guards, who stood at the feasting house doors, had become when they thought she approached them on her way to the Council Chambers. They intended to stop her. They had become confused and had reacted too slowly when she hurried past them to the Council Chamber's doors and were too late to stop her from entering.

She turned to Verity and waited a moment until she finished talking with Anin. "Walk me out of the hall so that the guards do not stop me. I wish to seek the solitude of my dwelling."

"In a moment, Hemera, if you please, Anin is advising me on my visions."

Hemera got annoyed, not at her sister. It was not her fault, it was her own for being caught outside the gates. Verity could benefit from Anin's guidance when it came to her visions. She was trying to gain more control of them, instead of the visions having control of her.

Hemera waited, with little patience, realizing her sister and Anin were lost in their discussion and Verity was not close to leaving. She got up, letting her sister know she was going to warm her hands at the fire pit.

After a few moments, her hands warmed, though it was not the true reason for her being there, she saw that the two guards on duty at the front door were no longer watching her. She made her way into the shadows along the wall and toward the doors. She stopped in the shadows nearest the doors and waited.

She smiled when the doors opened and both guards hurried to the Council Chamber's door, one to open it and one to step inside to announce the arrival of the members of the High Council. It was just the distraction she needed to slip out unnoticed.

Once outside, she hurried off to her dwelling.

~~~

"I want to know how these men are getting past my sentinels!" the King demanded, his fist coming down on the table so hard the wood creaked.

"Someone is feeding them information," Paine said.

Talon had kept Wrath and Paine after the High Council meeting had ended. He had chosen to inform Wrath and Paine, but not the Council of what Hemera had told him just for the very reason Paine had stated. Someone in the stronghold was feeding information to the enemy.

"I cannot believe any one of your personal guards would betray you," Wrath said, having become indignant when told of what Hemera had witnessed. "Hemera could be wrong in what she saw."

"Hemera sees more than most," Paine said with a grin at Wrath.

Wrath scowled, knowing Verity probably told Anin about Hemera walking in on them while they had been mating. "Because she is in places she should not be."

"Does no one keep a watchful eye on her?" Talon demanded.

"Is she not free like others?" Paine asked.

"Others do not have her penchant for being in places she should not be," Wrath snapped.

"Still, is she free or not?" Paine argued.

"She is free to obey my rules," Talon reminded and gave a wave of his hand. "That is enough about Hemera we need to be more concerned that a traitor walks among us. See what you both can uncover, but let no one know what you are about. It is not only the traitor I want, but the one the traitor reports to." Talon stood. "We are done here."

Wrath and Paine got to their feet and followed the King out of the room.

Anin tried to hurry to her feet, her rounded middle making it difficult to move too fast. Verity went to help, having already gotten to her feet.

"Stay as you are, Anin," Talon ordered.

Paine sent him a grateful nod as he went to his wife's side and leaned over her to stroke a loving and protective hand over the bump that held his child.

Wrath went to Verity, though she drifted into his arms before he reached her and splayed his hand over her middle.

"Something you have failed to tell me, Wrath?" Talon asked.

Wrath looked to his wife and she smiled. "Verity only confirmed it this morn. At harvest time, Verity will give birth."

Anin squealed with joy and Paine slapped Wrath on the back.

"I am pleased for you Wrath," Talon said, his

stomach turning tight. He wished to hear such words from his future queen soon after they wed, if the woman ever arrived, and if his seed ever took root.

"Hemera will be thrilled," Anin said.

Verity quickly searched the room for her sister, having been so deep in conversation with Anin, she had forgotten all about her. She squeezed her husband's hand after her eyes roamed the feasting hall and Hemera was nowhere to be seen.

Verity's actions told Talon all he needed to know. He turned to the two guards at the door, his voice powerful as he demanded, "Did Hemera get past you both?"

The two guards glanced around the room just as Verity had done, everyone else following their lead as if somehow Hemera would suddenly appear.

Verity finally spoke up, evident that Hemera was not there, though her voice quivered. "Hemera is probably at her dwelling. She had asked me to take her there, but I got lost in conversation with Anin."

"It is not our fault your sister sneaks away," Wrath assured her.

"Wrath is right." King Talon turned to the two guards at the door, his voice booming as he called out, "It is their fault. Wrath, see to their punishment."

"I will see to my sister," Verity said.

Talon's head snapped around, his eyes glaring at Verity. "No, I will see to your sister."

## Chapter Four

"Hemera! Hemera!" Talon called as he approached her dwelling. Seeing no signs of her, his anger mounted. He stopped and cast a glance around. His brow narrowed, wondering if he was in the right place. Was this the executioner's home?

It looked nothing like he remembered it, but then there had been no reason for him to be here. The heavy snow, all but gone now, had brought a quiet to the stronghold and most of the villagers spent their times inside as had he. He had had a variety of women warming his sleeping pallet, though he had allowed none to stay the night. He had no wont of being wrapped around a woman until dawn. He preferred his solitude.

He glanced around again. Half broken crocks were placed around the front of the dwelling with tiny buds peeking out of the soil. An outside fire pit burned brightly with two small benches sitting to either side of it and a pleasant scent wafted out of the flames. On the door of the dwelling was painted a symbol, a Northmen symbol, Talon was familiar with. There was a straight line with two lines extended up from each side. It resembled a person with his arms reaching up to the heavens. The symbol offered protection against enemies.

Who, though, was Hemera's enemy?

"Sit and warm yourself. A chill has caught the air

and I fear we may have more than a sprinkle of snow tonight."

Her enticing scent drifted over him as she walked past him and sat on one of the benches, holding her hands out near the flames to warm them. He wondered if it was her blazing red hair that smelled so inviting. He thought how easy it would be to take hold of her and bury his face in her wild curls and see for himself.

He was brought back to his senses when he realized that she was sitting while he stood.

"You sit in my presence?" he asked with a sharp demand.

"It is unkind of you to make another stand because you do not choose to sit."

"Kindness is not something you will find in me."

Hemera cocked her head, her eyes studying him for a moment before she asked, "What would I find in you?"

Talon took a step closer, the heat of the fire drifting over him. "I am King."

She scrunched her face and shook her head. "No. Somewhere within you is Talon the man, not the King."

"Talon is no more. I am King and you need to remember that." The warmth of the fire had him sitting and holding his hands out to the flames. His breath caught when his eyes settled on her over the tops of the flames that seemed to flicker and sway beneath the soft roundness of her chin, highlighting her graceful features. As he watched, he grew annoyed, for the flames appeared as if they kissed her softly and the way she smiled, so content, made it appear that she favored their touch.

"You do not let me forget you are King."

Was that sorrow he heard in her voice? He shook his head as if needing to shake sense back into himself. "And well you should not. I remind you too often to obey me. Need I keep a guard on you at all times?"

"Am I a prisoner?" she asked, slipping her arms inside her cloak and rubbing them.

*I could keep you warm.* The unexpected thought startled him and he snapped at her. "No!"

"Then why would I need a guard and why do you think I need to be watched?"

"Because you are too slow-minded to understand things and I do not wish to see any harm befall you. So you will obey me or you will have a guard trailing you wherever you go." Talon knew his words were unkind, but it seemed it was the only way to make her understand.

His remark was met with silence. She sat there staring at him and he wondered if his words had hurt her or she simply did not understand.

"Do you have any other body drawings besides the one on your face?" she asked.

Silence struck him this time, along with anger, but he tempered it, reminding himself that she was not like others. "My body drawing does not concern you, obeying my every word does." He stood and spoke calmly and slowly. "Will you obey me Hemera or do I have a guard follow your every footfall?"

Hemera stood, though remained silent.

Talon gave a nod, her response in her action, standing since he did. He looked to the heavens, a bit bleak with grey clouds. "No snow will fall, Hemera, rain perhaps, but no snow." He turned to leave.

"Talon, you keep me safe," she said as if it

surprised her.

"I will always keep you safe, Hemera." *Even from me*, he thought as he turned again.

"Talon."

He turned again.

"It will snow."

A slight smile caught at the corners of his mouth. "Rain, Hemera, rain."

"If it does snow will you grant me permission to find out who it was I saw wearing one of your personal guards' cloaks?"

"A wager?"

She smiled. "If you dare?"

"You will leave the matter be—"

"If you win, aye, I will," she finished.

"It will rain, I am sure of it. You have your wager, Hemera." He turned and took only a few steps when he stopped and without turning around, called out, "I am King, Hemera, and you will address me as such."

"Aye, my King."

Talon walked off, annoyed at his own command. He favored the way she seemed to caress his name as it fell from her lips. It was why he had not stopped her when she first said his name. He wanted to hear her say it again and it annoyed him that he would not hear her say it again. For that reason alone he would keep his distance from her. Or was it that he found himself thinking things about her that he never should think? Either way, he would make sure to see little of her.

*Unless she won the wager.*

The thought had him stopping abruptly and a scowl marring his fine features. Those walking nearby him hurried off and others in his path kept their distance.

He shook his head. It was not cold enough for snow. It would rain. The snow had passed and there would be no more. The tiny buds in her broken crocks proved that as did the trees that were beginning to bud. He shook his head again. There would be rain. He was right. He was always right.

~~~

Hemera returned to the bench after Talon was out of sight. It would snow tonight, a light coating, nothing more. It was a welcoming nod to the land as it awakened from its slumber. She knew the land well. It was part of her. It spoke to her. It had been no risk for her to wager with the King. It had been a way for her to get him to agree to her plan to search for the culprit in the woods.

It had not bothered her when he had called her slow-minded. She had been called far worse and in a far more offensive way. He had spoken truthfully, at least what he thought the truth. She could not fault him for that. No, that had not disturbed her at all. What had troubled her was the way he sometimes looked at her and how she was beginning to feel when he did.

Then there had been the overpowering thought that she wanted him to stay with her and talk more. Why had her insides twisted in knots as he walked away? Why had she felt the need to tell him that he kept her safe?

Her father had told her when she was a wee bairn that she should never trust a man that men lied and schemed to get what they wanted. He told her to keep her own council and trust her instincts.

Somehow she felt she could trust Talon, the man.

Whether she could trust the King was another matter.

~~~

King Talon looked around the crowded feasting hall that echoed with talk and laughter from the warriors and their families enjoying the evening meal and companionship. Wrath, Verity, Paine, and Anin shared one of the tables and he would have liked to join them, not as King but as a friend, and that was no longer possible.

"With the snow gone, the future queen will be able to begin her journey here and arrive within a moon cycle," Gelhard said.

Talon turned a stern look at the man sitting beside him. "You are sure she comes from a line of women who have delivered fine sons to their husbands?"

"She has five older brothers and her grandmother birthed six strong sons. Her family stock is strong and if she does not give you—" Gelhard stopped abruptly.

"Say what everyone believes, Gelhard, that it is my fault no heir has been sired, that my seed is no good, that I am not the potent King everyone believed me to be."

"It will be different with Daria of the Fermour Tribe," Gelhard assured him

"The Fermour are more farmers than warriors, are they not?"

"True, but her brothers are strong men who do well with weapons when necessary."

"What you are telling me is that this Daria is the only woman you could find whose lineage produces more sons than daughters."

"She is a good, obedient daughter and sister. She will serve you well as queen."

"I suppose that is all that matters," Talon said, turning away from Gelhard and wondering why Hemera's lovely face should flash in his mind. He forced his thoughts elsewhere. There were too many important matters for him to think on than to let Hemera trouble his thoughts.

If he did not quell the opposition soon, it would not matter if he sired an heir or not, the throne would be taken from him and the Pict Tribes would once again be thrown into battling each other. After all the men and women who had suffered and had given their lives for the Pict Tribes to unite, Talon could not let that happen.

Talon caught the sudden movement of Verity out of the corner of his eye. She had stood abruptly and Wrath had followed suit, his hand firm on her arm. They seemed to be arguing and he had an idea of what it was about.

Surprisingly, Paine was sitting with an arm around his wife and a smile on his face. Paine was not one to smile easily, though since he had joined with Anin, his smiles were more frequent. This smile was different. It was almost as if he knew something that others did not and he was enjoying the secret.

Talon was surprised when Verity yanked her arm free from her husband's grasp, though he was not surprised she headed his way. Wrath would let Talon deal with his wife's anger over hearing that he was having a husband found for Hemera, especially since Wrath did not bother to follow her.

"Forgive me, my King, may I have a word with you?" Verity asked.

Talon turned to Gelhard and, without a word, the man excused himself and left the two alone. He turned back to Verity, though he did not offer her a seat. It was wiser she remembered who she spoke with. He nodded for her to continue.

"Wrath tells me that you plan to find Hemera a husband."

"One suited to her," Talon clarified, wondering if any could truly suit Hemera.

"I beg you, my King, to rethink your plan," Verity pleaded, a slight tremor to her voice.

"Why?" Talon asked curious.

Hemera prefers being on her own. She has no wish to marry."

"She needs someone to look after her."

"I look after her."

"Not well enough. Besides, you will have a bairn to look after soon enough and probably more bairns to follow. You will have no time to keep watch over Hemera. A husband will solve the problem."

Verity shook her head. "Hemera will never agree to it."

"It is not her choice."

Verity nipped at her lower lip as if holding back her words and shut her eyes for a moment before finally speaking. "She will leave here if you force a marriage on her."

Talon shook his head. "There is no place for her to go. This is her home now and I will see her kept safe."

"You cannot keep Hemera safe. No one can."

Talon rose quickly to his feet, bringing Wrath to his wife's side just as quickly, but before Talon could voice his anger that Verity should think him incapable of keeping Hemera safe, his eyes caught sight of several warriors entering the hall. Snow covered the hoods and shoulders of their cloaks.

"It is snowing?" Talon shouted.

Silence filled the room as all heads turned to the warriors.

One spoke up. "Aye, my King, the ground will be covered by morn at the way it is falling."

"Damn," Talon muttered and grabbed his fur-lined cloak off the bench beside him, rounded the table, and hurried out of the hall. He turned on the two personal guards that followed behind him. "Return to the feasting house now!"

If only he could get Hemera to obey as quickly and without question as his guards did.

~~~

Hemera stood outside her door watching the snow fall and waiting. He would come. He had lost the wager and she had no doubt that he did not like to lose. The snow looked heavy, but the flakes were light and the wind strong, making it appear worse than it was. It was also a late snow, buds already breaking through the soil and on the tree branches, which meant it would not last long on the ground.

The King would come and he would not be happy.

She tucked her cloak more tightly around her and squinted as she attempted to see through the swirling flakes. A large shadow suddenly rushed through the swirling snow at Hemera and she took a quick step back.

The King had arrived.

The wind whipped his cloak behind him, making him appear as if he had wings and his long dark hair blew around his head while the drawing on the side of his face made it appear as though a shadowy hand had claimed hold of him.

Talon stopped directly in front of her.

"I won the wager," she said with a smile before he could say a word.

He grabbed hold of her chin and did something he never expected to do.

He kissed her.

## Chapter Five

Shock froze Hemera and by the time she regained her senses, Talon had ended the kiss, shoved her away from him, turned, and disappeared into the swirling snow.

Her fingers went to her lips, still warm and sensitive. It was then she realized that she had tensed when he kissed her, but her lips had not. They had responded to his demanding ones. She had felt the hunger in his kiss and was surprised at her own ravenous taste for him. The more he had demanded, the more she willingly gave, the more she enjoyed the kiss.

She had not stopped him when his tongue had forced her lips apart and entered her mouth. Her tongue had welcomed him and his demand softened, his tongue cajoling, and a warm tingle had wrapped around her. She had felt a familiar comfort, one she felt only when embraced by the forest, and she did not know what to make of it.

That was when he had ended the kiss and pushed her away, then disappeared. She wondered if he had been sorry he had kissed her or if the kiss had disappointed him. It had not disappointed her, an unexpected thought, but then the kiss had been unexpected. Had it been so to him as well? If so, why had he kissed her? A more surprising thought was that she hoped he would kiss her again.

She shook head and entered her dwelling, hanging her cloak on the one of the two pegs by the door to dry.

She went to the fire pit to warm her hands that were cold from the chilling wind, though the rest of her had been warmed by his kiss.

Her fingers once again went to her lips to touch them lightly. It was almost as if she could still feel his lips upon hers, his kiss had been so strong, so memorable. She had never been kissed. Talon had been her first, but she had not been his first. She would be wise to remember that and wise not to let him kiss her again.

There could never be anything between her and the King, and she would have no man dictate to her. She had suffered enough of that and she would suffer no more of it.

Hemera gave a firm nod and spoke to the empty room. "There will be no more kisses from the King and no husband to tell me what to do."

~~~

Talon walked around the village, angry with himself for kissing Hemera, though more angry that the kiss had been more enjoyable than any he had ever had. And he had wanted to do more than just kiss her. His swollen manhood attested to that.

He should go and appease his hunger with one of the women who always lingered nearby in the evening and were always willing to please the King. He had no favorites, anyone of them would do. The thought annoyed him even more. He had never felt complete satisfaction with any woman. He had always been left with a lingering ache and nothing, he did or a woman did, had ever appeased that relentless ache.

*What if Hemera could?*

He was a fool for thinking such an unwise thought. He should have never kissed her. He had not planned to kiss her, but when he saw her there, her red hair blowing wildly in the wind, the snowflakes kissing her cheeks, her nose, her lips, jealousy had surged up in him and he had responded to it. Where it had come from, he did not know. He only knew that his lips were the only ones meant to touch hers.

"I must see her wed," he muttered and his words sent his anger soaring. He fisted his hands and with heavy footfalls turned toward the feasting house.

The feasting hall was empty except for Wrath and the two guards waiting on the second floor outside his private chambers.

Talon stopped as Wrath approached him. "Find Hemera a husband right away."

Wrath grabbed the King's arm as he went to walk away. "What have you done, Talon?"

Talon looked to Wrath's hand gripping his arm, then to him, a deadly warning in his eyes.

Wrath apologized quickly. "I am sorry, my King—*my friend.*"

Talon shook his head. "It is not what I have done. It is what I will do if a husband is not found for Hemera."

Knowing Talon would never take a woman against her will, Wrath said, "She would not be willing."

Talon gave a brief laugh. "She would be more than willing."

"This cannot happen."

"I agree. Find her a husband." With that, he stormed past Wrath.

"I will send a woman to you."

"Do not bother," Talon shouted and climbed the stairs.

He stripped off his garments and climbed into his sleeping pallet, hoping sleep would claim him quickly. While solitude was often his friend, this evening it was his enemy. It tormented him with thoughts of Hemera.

Though she had tensed in his arms, her lips had welcomed him with an intensity that had surprised and pleased him. She had responded as if she had been waiting forever for him to kiss her. Or had he wanted to believe that? Had she responded so eagerly because it had been too long since she had been kissed? How many men had kissed her? How many had joined with her?

The annoying thoughts had a low growl rumbling in his chest.

He tried to chase thoughts of Hemera away and being a disciplined warrior, he eventually did and sleep eventually claimed him.

*Her hair faintly brushed his face, the silky soft strands sending a shiver through him before her lips settled over his, strong and demanding, as his had done to hers earlier. He reached out, his hand cupping the back of her neck, holding her firm, keeping her locked to him.*

*The kiss grew more frantic, then she suddenly tore her mouth away from his, though he fought to keep her lips on his.*

*"I want more," Hemera whispered and brought her mouth down on his neck to nibble along it.*

*He moaned when her teeth nipped at his flesh, sending a stinging pleasure racing through him. His moan rumbled when her lips trailed down along his chest and swirled her tongue around his nipple before suckling on it. She continued on, trailing down along his middle, kissing and nipping until his moan sounded like a roar in his ears when she finally took his hard manhood into her mouth.*

*It was like nothing he ever felt before. Every part of his body sparked with an intense passion that continued to build and build and build until he thought he would surely die from the pleasure and be happy about it.*

*The passion intensified. Soon he would explode. Soon he would climax like never before. Soon he would finally feel satisfied. Soon the relentless ache would be gone.*

Talon woke to find his hand pleasuring himself and not Hemera's lips, and he had no choice but to finish. He tossed the blanket off himself and swung his legs off the sleeping pallet to sit on the edge and finish what he wished Hemera had truly started, though he got little satisfaction from it.

He went to the bucket of water kept near the fire pit when done and cleaned himself. He could not recall the last time he found it necessary to pleasure himself. He had always found a willing woman and now being King, there seemed to be an endless stream of willing women.

Talon returned to his pallet, resting his arm behind his head. His future queen would be here soon, perhaps she would satisfy him.

*Hemera will satisfy you.*

Several oaths flew from his mouth at the thought. She was an innocent or was she?

He shook his head. It did not matter. It would not

be right to join with her. She deserved better than to be one of the King's endless streams of women. He would see that she got a good husband and it would be done, for he would not touch another man's woman.

His hand went to push against his middle, his insides feeling as if they were being twisted into endless knots. He let several more oaths fly, then swore over and over that he would keep his distance from Hemera, until finally sleep once again claimed him.

~~~

"Hemera. Hemera."

Hemera looked up from where she sat on the bench in front of the fire pit to see her sister waving as she approached. She stood and with a forced smile walked over to greet her. Verity was not there for a visit. She was there to find out why she had not seen Hemera for the last three days. And that would not be easy to explain to her sister.

Hemera had been busy watching each one of the King's personal guards, trying to determine if any one of their sizes or their gaits were recognizable. None proved familiar. That had gotten Hemera thinking that it was more likely that someone had borrowed one of the guards' cloaks without him realizing it. She had tried to speak with Talon about it, but she had been turned away every time she attempted to see him. She finally came to the conclusion that he was avoiding her, which got her wondering if it had something to do with the kiss.

Verity hurried her arms around her sister and hugged her tight. "I have missed you. Why are you keeping your distance? Are you not feeling well?"

"I should be asking you how you are feeling since you are with child."

"You heard," Verity said, feeling contrite. "I wanted to tell you before the news spread, but I have not seen you for the last three days."

Hemera shook her head. "I did not hear the news from anyone. I knew you were with child for some time now. I was waiting for you to realize it and tell me and," —Hemera shrugged— "I could wait no longer." She hugged her sister. "I am so thrilled for you and so excited about becoming an aunt."

When they parted, Verity asked, "How did you know?"

Hemera shrugged again. "Signs. You shied away from food in the morn. Some foods made you pale or you would make a face at them." She demonstrated by wrinkling her nose dramatically, which had Verity laughing.

"You should have told me."

"No, it was for you and Wrath to know first."

"I am glad you are happy for me and I will be just as thrilled for you when you are wed and with child."

Hemera gave a hardy laugh. "Never will I wed."

A frown gripped Verity's face and she paled.

"You are not well," Hemera said concerned and hurried Verity to one of the benches by the fire pit and made her sit. "I will get you a warm brew."

"No," Verity said, reaching out and taking Hemera's hand. "I am fine, sit with me."

Hemera sat. "Something troubles you."

"Aye, even more so now that I know that you knew I was with child and failed to tell you when you should have been the first to know after Wrath. We have not kept things from each other and I do not want to start now."

Hemera felt her stomach lurch. She had kept things from her sister, but her silent tongue had been born out of necessity. "You have something to tell me that you fear I will not like?"

Verity nodded. "I do not want you to hear it from someone else and since the search has already begun, tongues are wagging."

Hemera cocked her head and wrinkled her brow. "What would a search have to do with me?"

Tears gathered in Verity's eyes and since she had suffered much at the hands of the Northmen without shedding a tear, it had been another sign that had Hemera thinking Verity was with child.

Verity took hold of her sister's hand and she hesitated a moment as if unwilling to speak, then the words rushed from her mouth. "King Talon has ordered a husband to be found for you."

## Chapter Six

Hemera remained silent, staring at Verity.

"The King will find you a good husband and you will be happy like I am," Verity said, hoping to help her sister accept her fate when she would have preferred to protest it, as she had done with Wrath when she had learned that the King was adamant about a husband being found for Hemera immediately. And Wrath had agreed. He also had agreed with the King that a husband would serve Hemera well. He would protect her and keep her safe.

Verity had disagreed most strenuously. She wanted someone who would care for her sister, a man who would willingly give his heart to her. She wanted for Hemera what she had with Wrath and Anin had with Paine.

Verity raised her chin, not realizing the weight of her thoughts had brought it nearly to rest on her chest, when she felt Hemera's hand on hers.

"This troubles you," Hemera said softly.

Tears rushed up to pool in Verity's eyes. "I do not want to see you forced to wed."

"I will not wed," Hemera said. "I want no husband."

"The King—"

"Will be disappointed he does not get his way," Hemera said with a smile.

"The King always gets his way," Verity warned.

Hemera laughed and gave Verity's hand a squeeze. "Not this time."

"You need to take this seriously, Hemera. The King will see you wed and you will not be able to stop him."

"I can and I will." Hemera's smile faded. "We have been through much, you and I, and I did not see us escape only to be forced once again into a life I have no wont of." She squeezed her sister's hand once more as her smile returned. "Do not worry on it."

Verity continued to try to make her sister understand. "The King's word is law."

Verity sighed softly when Hemera glanced at the fire, drifting off into her thoughts instead of responding to her. Her sister did that often. They would talk and suddenly Hemera would grow silent until she once again spoke.

"All will be well," Hemera said, turning her eyes on Verity.

Verity could not help but smile at the familiar words that had always made her feel better and oddly enough often things had worked out for the better. This time, though, Verity was not so sure.

A sudden thought brought a smile to Verity's face. "I know what we can do. We can have Anin touch the men that are interested in being your husband and see which one best suits you." She jumped up. "The King surely would not object to that." She reached down and grabbed Hemera's hand. "We will go speak with Anin right away."

Hemera stood. "You go and speak with Anin. I have no wont to be around anyone right now."

Verity gave her sister a tight hug, then stepped

away. "You are upset and rightfully so. I will speak with Anin." Verity smiled widely. "You are right. All will be well."

Hemera watched her sister hurry off happier than when she had arrived. It was always good to see her happy. She had done as much as she could to keep her sister safe while they were captives of the Northmen. As the years passed she had planned and waited for the time they would make their escape. The moment Verity had told her about her visions of Wrath, Hemera knew the time was right.

Verity was free and safe now. Unfortunately, Hemera never would be.

She looked around, making sure no one was in sight, and hurried into the wooded area that stretched a distance behind her dwelling. She needed the comfort of the forest beyond the stronghold fence. That was where she would find the peace she so desperately sought.

It took her no time to escape the confines of the stronghold and enter the welcoming peace of the woods. A chilly, gentle wind had the tree branches swaying, sounding like a soft whisper to Hemera. There was little crunch beneath her feet as she walked, the ground still damp from the snow that had dissipated the day after it had fallen. Red squirrels scampered around the tree trunks, chasing after one another in play. Birds took flight from tree to tree, calling out in their distinct voices. Mating time was not far off and some of the birds' plumage would begin to change in preparation.

Hemera had missed her time here in the forest. It was not that the Northmen's forest had not welcomed her, but here, on Pict soil, was where memories of her mother were the strongest.

She followed the now familiar path toward a spot she had discovered shortly after settling in her dwelling that had become her favorite place to go when she needed comfort. Whenever she stepped into the secluded area, she immediately felt the forest embrace her.

*Like Talon's arms had done when she rode on his horse with him.*

The thought brought her to such an abrupt halt that she almost stumbled. She did not need such intimate thoughts about Talon—the King—yet he would not leave her mind. He seemed to have taken root there and no matter how many times she tried to pluck him out, he returned.

She hurried off. He was one of the reasons she had sought the peace and solitude of the woods. Here her thoughts were clearer. Here was where things made more sense to her. Here was where she felt cared for the most.

A few more steps and she would be there. She stopped abruptly again when she saw that the squirrels suddenly halted their play and she caught sight of a grouse scurrying off to take flight. Something had disturbed the calm in the forest.

Before she could turn, a familiar, demanding voice shouted at her.

"What are you doing here alone?"

Hemera turned to see the King headed toward her with quick strides. He wore his usual ill-temper on his handsome face. Black-hide coverings were fastened at his broad shoulders and covered the front of his long, dark shirt that fell to well above his knees. His legs were wrapped in the same black-hide and the hilt of his sword could be seen behind his shoulder, where it was strapped to his back.

His tongue was curt when he stopped in front of her. "Answer me!"

She saw no reason to lie to him. "I wanted some time in the woods alone."

He leaned a bit closer to her. "Did I not make myself clear that you were not to come here alone?"

"You always make yourself clear."

He threw his hands in the air. "Yet you fail to listen to me."

"You walk the woods alone."

"That is different."

Hemera shrugged. "How is it different?"

"You dare question me?" Talon was pleased when she drew her head back quickly and her eyes widened as if startled. Finally, she comprehended that she had erred.

"As I have said before, how can I not question something that makes no sense?"

That she was more shocked and believed he had failed to understand her had him shaking his head and leaning in closer to warn. "You do not question the King."

Hemera's eyes caught on his lips as they gave potent power to each of his words, but she barely heard them. It was his lips as moist and powerful as they had been when he had kissed her that she was drawn to. A sudden tingle washed over her, raising the flesh on her skin.

With his temper short and seeing her staring as if she paid no heed to him at all, he demanded. "Do you understand me, Hemera?"

With a slight cock of her head and scrunch of her brow, Hemera asked, "Why did you kiss me?"

He had asked the same of himself repeatedly and had failed to answer as he did now.

"Your silence tells me you do not know why."

Her tone did not accuse, it was more curious and that annoyed Talon all the more. "We will not discuss this." He turned and took a quick step away from her, then turned just as quickly around, pointing a finger at her. "And do not ask me why."

"Then tell me why you have ordered a husband to be found for me?"

So the wagging tongues had reached her and yet she spoke with curiosity and not a bit of anger, which annoyed Talon even more. "You need someone to look after you."

She sighed, his words proving tiresome. "You waste your time. I will not wed."

Her response should have angered him, but instead he felt a sense of relief and that disturbed him even more. That she should not want to wed would leave her free and that could prove troublesome. He had to make her understand that marriage was the best thing for her, though again he questioned if it was best for her or more so for him.

"You will have a choice of a few men," he offered, thinking it might appease her.

She laughed softly. "It makes no difference. I will not wed."

Wind captured her laughter and swirled it around him like a gentle hug before carrying it off in a whisper. The slight shiver it sent through him had him realizing that there was something he needed to make clear and she needed to understand. Strong in demeanor and tone, he said, "I am King and my word is law."

Her blank stare made him wonder if she had understood anything he had said. She caught him unware when she turned and walked away from him, paying him no mind, and he followed after her, annoyed that he did so. He was King and he followed after no one.

She sat on a tree trunk that had toppled over from decay and now lay prone on the ground. His tongue was ready to give her a good whipping for far too many transgressions, starting with walking away from him without permission and sitting when he stood. Seeing her eyes focused on the distance, staring at what, he did not know, he held his tongue and lowered himself down beside her.

Her brow scrunched, as it often did when it seemed as if she was not there. He wondered where her mind took her at those moments. Expressionless or not, nothing distracted from her beauty. She even wore a frown well and her untamed red hair was much like her, it did as it pleased.

Would she be untamed and wild when mating? She had been untamed in his dream. He cursed silently and turned his head away, annoyed at his thought. He could not and would not join with her. It would not be proper.

Hemera turned to him, forcing him to turn as well. "Who did you meet in the forest?"

"I met no one." Angry he had answered her, he snapped. "Do not question me."

"You did not have to respond, though why else would you be in the woods alone without your personal guards? That reminds me, it was not one of your personal guards that I saw in the woods that day."

"How did you reach that assumption in such a short time?" he asked surprised and a bit concerned that she should realize his reason for being in the woods alone.

She had been eager to tell him what she had discovered and without thinking, she reached out and gripped his arm. "I have been watching your personal guards the last three days, the way they walk, the pace of their gait. None match the person I saw in the woods. Someone must have snatched a cloak, without one of your guards knowing it, and used it to disguise himself."

That she should have the presence of mind to follow his guards around and study them made Talon wonder if Hemera was not as slow as everyone believed her to be...different perhaps, but slow?

"The problem is that your personal guards leave their cloaks where anyone could snatch them up and if they are left elsewhere your guards take no notice when retrieving them."

"How would you know that?" He shook his head. "Did you snatch my guards' cloaks and leave them elsewhere for them to find?"

She gave his arm a slight squeeze as her face lit in a smile. "I did. Tilden was the only one who scratched his head and looked about when he found his cloak a short distance from where he had left it. The others guards snatched their cloaks up and paid no thought to where they had found them." She frowned. "Wrath is not going to be pleased when you tell him this."

"You have not mentioned this to him?" he asked, trying to ignore the light touch of her hand on him and finding it difficult. There was something different about the way she touched him, almost as if it was the most natural thing for her to do, and he had no wont to stop her.

"It is not my place."

How was it she understood that and not that she was to obey him?

Her smile returned and she squeezed his arm again. "I intend to keep an eye on all and see if I can spot a familiarity in someone's gait and of course to see if anyone disturbs the woods with their threatening presence."

"I forbid you to do anything more about the incident in the woods and I forbid you to come to these woods alone," Talon decreed. "If I or anyone else catches you here alone, I will see you locked away until you obey me." Talon was surprised when she shut her eyes and lowered her head to rest on his shoulder.

"Please do not do that to me, Talon. I was kept a prisoner far too long. I need the freedom and comfort of the woods to survive. Please understand. Please do not take this from me."

Her soft plea felt like a piercing sword to his chest, splitting him in two. He had given no thought to her time with the Northmen or what they had done to her and his anger flared.

He took hold of her chin and forced her head off his shoulder to look up at him. "What did the Northmen do to you?"

"I will not speak of it."

"You will tell me," he demanded, his anger mounting.

"No, Talon, I will not tell you," she said softly.

Her warm, sweet breath whispered across his lips like a tender kiss, teasing the spark of passion that forever burned in him. That mattered not. He could not let it. He would have his answer. Before he could speak, she did.

"I do not want to relive the pain." She slipped her chin out of his hand and once again laid her head on his shoulder, turning her face into the crook of his neck. She felt safe there, protected, as she had the other day when on his horse with him. She had not felt this protected in—she could not remember when. And it was so wonderful to feel that safe again.

Talon's arm went around her, tucking her against him. She needed comfort and he would not deny her. It was odd sitting there in the quiet of the forest simply holding her. He never simply sat and held a woman. His time alone with a woman was spent mating, rarely anything else. Yet at this moment, he wanted nothing more than to hold and comfort her.

He brought his hand up to gently stroke her neck and he felt her body sigh against his. "One day, Hemera, you will tell me."

"Aye, Talon, one day I will tell you," she agreed quietly.

Aye, she would. He would see that she did, but for now he would simply hold her.

After a few moments, Hemera slipped out of his arms. "You will be missed if you do not return soon."

Talon stood and extended his hand. "You will return with me and you will cease looking for the traitor in the forest."

Hemera bounced up, ignoring his hand. "It is said you are a fair King, are you not?"

"I believe I am," he said proudly.

"I won the wager," she reminded with a grin and a playful poke to his chest.

He almost swore aloud, having forgotten about it, and he was a man of his word. "You will be careful," he said grudgingly. "And you will report any findings only to me. No one else is to know what you are up to."

She laughed softly. "You do not want anyone to know you lost the wager, do you?"

He grabbed hold of her hand and began walking. "You will show me where you sneak out of the stronghold."

"Only if you show me where you sneak out."

Talon stopped abruptly. "You are tempting fate."

Shh," she whispered with a finger near her lips, "fate will hear you."

Talon leaned in close to her. "Fate follows my command."

She smiled. "Then we have nothing to worry about. Our fate is secured."

A bird call followed by a second one had Talon turning his head to listen. Two more followed.

"Your friends search for you," Hemera said and seeing the question on his face explained. "Their bird calls are skillful, but miss the true melody, but that serves you well for then you can distinguish their calls from the true sound." She wet her lips with her tongue and mimicked the sharp call.

Talon waited to hear Wrath and Paine respond, but there was only silence.

"They cannot recognize the true sound." She nodded. "Call to them. You will see. They will answer you."

Talon turned and mimicked the bird, though after hearing Hemera, he caught the difference in the call as he did. One call followed another and Talon turned, expecting to see Hemera grinning or hear her soft laughter.

But she was gone.

## *Chapter Seven*

Hemera made her way back to her dwelling and after adding more wood to the fire pit, she laid on her sleeping pallet, her thoughts heavy on Talon—the King. She needed to remind herself of that again and again. He was King and she really should not have touched him the way she had, and yet it had been instinctive. Laying her hand on his arm, resting her head on his shoulder seemed as natural to her as the breaths she took.

It was odd, so very odd, that she should feel comfortable enough to be so familiar with him. She had even enjoyed sitting in the woods with him, so much so, that she had not wanted to leave his side. She had wanted to remain there with him...until their time together had been interrupted.

Even now, she wished they were still together, talking, sitting close, just the two of them. She shook her head. There were more important things for her to dwell on then such nonsense like how the King himself had managed to escape the confines of the stronghold without anyone knowing.

One thing she had learned was that men in power always had secret escape routes to use when all else failed them, though she doubted that was what Talon had intended for his secret route. He was not a king who would desert his people. He would die fighting alongside them. No, the intended purpose of his secret exit from the stronghold was much like hers. It allowed him to escape and be alone for a while or to meet with someone he wanted no one to know about.

But who was he meeting with and why?

Secrets could cause more problems than they were worth and yet sometimes secrets proved necessary. It was a lesson she had learned well.

Hemera rolled off her sleeping pallet and onto her feet. She would not waste time in thought. She had things to do. Besides trying to discover the identity of the traitor in the stronghold, she intended to prepare a patch of land for seedlings that she planned to collect from the forest. She intended to also plant various seedlings around the dwelling so that the whole area would burst with abundance of color and fragrance from planting time through to harvest.

She left her dwelling, her mind finally off Talon, though not his familiar woodsy scent. It lingered on her garments, tickling at her nose and her senses. Would he never leave her?

*Did she want him to?*

The startling thought had Hemera hurrying off to get her planting tools. Busy hands would still a busy mind, as her mum had once told her and, at the moment, she would prefer a still mind.

Hemera got to work digging and by the time she heard her sister shouting her name, she looked to see that she had finished turning over the soil on half of the garden. She was pleased with her efforts and smiled, pointing out her accomplishment to her sister as Verity approached.

"Look what I have done," Hemera said with pride. "I will have a fine garden to plant my seedlings."

Hemera frowned when she saw that Verity was not smiling. "What is wrong?"

"You will not be here to harvest the crop. By then you will be residing with your new husband."

Hemera dismissed her words with a reminder. "I told you, I will not wed."

"This place is too far removed from other dwellings for you to make this your home. You need to be closer to other people," —Verity reached out and laid a hand on her sister's arm— "closer to me."

"I am not that far from you and we see each other often. Besides, Wrath takes up much of your time as it should be." Hemera patted her hand. "Regardless of what others expect of you, Verity, it is not necessary for you to look after me."

"You looked after me, protecting me from the Northmen, making my lot with them easier."

Memories Hemera preferred not to stir had her saying, "Not easy enough."

"Not true," Verity insisted. "Memories of our time with the Northmen have haunted me of late and I recall how you would ask me how I fared when we were granted permission to visit and how any problems I had would disappear soon afterwards. You knew all that went on with me, yet I know little of what went on with you at the hands of our captives."

"It is no good to dwell on the past. It is now, this moment we share, that matters most."

"Aye, it is," Verity agreed, "and it is about you this time. I want you to be happy."

Hemera smiled. "I am happy more than you know, Verity."

"How can you be happy in a place of such

suffering?" Verity asked with a nod at the larger dwelling not far from them. "Brutal suffering went on there."

"No more though, it is quiet now." Her voice filled with excitement as her smile spread wide. "This whole area will find peace and happiness once the seedlings start sprouting and blooming. Also, I have given thought to what I can do with that dwelling so that it is not thought of as a place of horror any longer."

Verity was pleased to see her sister happy and she did not want to steal that happiness from her, but how could she let Hemera go on thinking this place would remain her home when that would not happen.

"Hemera, even if you do not wed, you would not remain here. This was meant as a temporary dwelling and due to the harsh snow that was here when you first arrived your stay here was longer than intended. A smaller dwelling would be found for you and this place would go to the next executioner."

Hemera seemed to ponder her sister's words before saying, "Why would another executioner be needed? The King has Anin now. With her ability to know what people feel and think with one touch of her hand certainly would prove far more accurate than torture."

"I do not know the King's reason. I only know what Wrath has told me." Verity shook her head. "Enough of this talk. Come with me to visit Anin. We will speak of happier things and have a brew while Wrath and Paine are busy at the grievance meeting."

"Grievance meeting? That is today?" Hemera asked, not having given it thought since she had no grievance to take to the King...until now.

"Leave the digging and come with me," Verity

urged.

"Let me finish what I must and then I will join you."

"Please do," Verity urged again.

"When I finish," Hemera assured her and gave her a hug.

When Hemera could see her sister no more, she shook dirt and debris from her cloak before entering the dwelling, then she quickly washed the dirt from her hands and freshened her face before hurrying off.

~~~

Talon sat at the table in the feasting hall, listening to a litany of complaints from various villagers. Wrath and Paine had come searching for him to let him know that people were already lining up to bring their grievances to him to settle. Wrath suggested that he might want to start earlier than planned or it would be well after dark before he finished.

Wrath also warned him about taking to the woods alone, reminding him that it was especially dangerous now with an elusive enemy out there who was trying to unseat Talon from the throne.

"I beg you not to drive me to madness," Wrath had pleaded. "Take your guards with you when you go, since I know I will not be able to stop you completely from seeking the solace of the woods."

"Do you trust me, Wrath?" Talon had asked.

"It pains me that you should even ask that," Wrath had said.

"Then no more needs to be said," Talon had responded.

Through it all, Paine had never said a word until they had reached the feasting house. Then he had taken a moment to whisper to Talon, "I trust you, my King, but do you trust the one you met in the forest?" When Talon had sent him a questioning glare, Paine responded, "Yours were not the only prints in the soil."

"I know not what to do, my King?" the painfully thin woman standing in front of the table before him asked, wringing her hands.

While his thoughts had wondered, he still had heard the woman's plea. Her husband had taken ill recently and was not strong enough to work the land. She had traveled here alone, leaving her husband in the care of their only bairn, a young daughter. It had taken her since the first light of dawn to arrive here on time for the grievance meeting that took place each moon cycle when the moon was the fullest.

"My daughter helps me tend the animals, but our parcel of land is large and I fear I will not be able to till all the soil and prepare it for planting." She continued to wring her hands nervously. "If we cannot plant a full field, we will have barely enough to pay our share to the stronghold at harvest and none to keep us fed through the next cold."

Talon turned to Ebit, his Crop Master, standing to the side along with the other members of the High Council. "Ebit, send field servants to Ruth and William's farm to till and plant the seeds."

"Forgive me, My King," Midrent said, stepping forward, "but William and Ruth are already in arrear of payment to the stronghold."

Ruth paled and her hands began to shake.

"Do you suggest I not help them because they have

not paid their full tariff?"

"It is your law, my King," Midrent said with a bow of his head. "I am here to serve your law."

"Wise response, Midrent," Talon said and turned to Ruth. "Why did you fail to pay your full share?"

"William takes ill often and I try to do what I can—" Ruth held her tongue as soon as the King raised his hand.

Whether William was prone to illness or simply lazy, Talon did not know, but with Ruth thin to the point of frailness, it had Talon believing that she was starving herself to keep her family fed.

"Conor!" he called out and a lad yet to reach the cusp of manhood hurried through the crowd. His mum and da had died, leaving him alone. His da had told him with his dying breath to go to the King that he would see him cared for and that was what he had done, arriving before the snow settled in. "You have a family now. Ruth and William will take you in and you will help work their land."

Conor stared at the King a moment before daring to say, "Truly?"

Talon looked to Ruth.

With a smile, she reached out and took the lad's hand. "Truly, Conor. You are the son of Ruth and William now."

Conor grinned, looked to the King, and bobbed his head. "I am grateful, my King."

Talon turned a warning glare on Ruth. "Hear me well, woman. If I learn that Conor is mistreated in any way, you and your husband will suffer for it." Talon was pleasèd that Paine, though no longer his executioner, stepped forward, his threatening presence adding to the warning.

One look at the double-sided battle axe gripped in Paine's hand and Ruth paled again. "We will care for him like our own."

Talon ordered Ebit to send extra food for Ruth and her family before he dismissed her with a wave and the next person stepped forward. It went on like that for a while, some grievances petty, some difficult, and others mere nuisances. He dispatched each one, some feeling they were treated fairly, others disgruntled, but then he could not please everyone and he had no intentions of trying. His decision was law and the people had no choice but to abide by it.

The feasting hall was nearly empty, only four villagers left on line, it would not be long before this was done. Talon reached for his vessel, a servant hurrying to fill it for him before he looked over at the next person and was about to give permission for him to speak when he thought he caught sight of fiery red hair sticking out wildly from behind the back of the last man in line.

He tilted his head slightly to the side and as he did, Hemera eyes peeked at him from behind the man's one shoulder.

Talon did not know what she was up to, but he was not happy to see her there on the grievance line. He nodded at the man in front of the line to speak and listened to his complaint while his mind wondered about Hemera. Wrath would see her soon enough, though he would have no recourse. Talon had made it law that anyone could seek a grievance from the King and would not be removed from the line unless the person was causing harm to others. Wrath would only be able to stand there and watch.

Talon dispatched the man's complaint with ease and the man after him. That was when Wrath caught sight of Hemera. He appeared ready to step forward when Paine's hand shot out, stopping him. It was the reminder Wrath needed. He stayed as he was, though the anger in his eyes showed that he was not pleased.

Hemera stepped forward after the man in front of her took his leave. The feasting hall was nearly deserted, most having left after the King had ruled on their grievances and looking to seek the shelter of the dwelling with dusk settling over the land. She kept a tight rein on her tongue, eager to speak, but needing to wait for permission from the King to do so.

While Talon did not care to see her on the grievance line, he was pleased to see her again and that he felt that way annoyed him.

With a curt tongue, he demanded, "What grievance do you bring to me?"

"I would like what others have...a permanent dwelling," she said.

It was an easy complaint to resolve for Talon. "You will have a permanent dwelling when you wed."

Hemera did not plan on arguing. She planned on getting the executioner's place as her own. "If by chance I do not wed, will you grant me the executioner's property?"

"Need I remind you that fate is mine to command," he said, letting her know she had no choice in the matter.

"Then what should it matter to grant my grievance?"

Talon heard the challenge in her tone and he could

not let it pass. "The executioner's property will become your permanent dwelling if you do not wed." Her lovely face lit with a beautiful smile and he felt his insides tighten not to mention the stirring to his manhood.

"I am most grateful, *my King*," she said with such joy and a clap of her hands, like a bairn who had just received a wonderful gift, that had all the members of the High Council, but Wrath and Paine, smiling with delight.

Talon stood and walked around the table to stand in front of her, the breadth of him blocking her from being seen by the High Council.

"Your fate is sealed," he said for their ears alone.

She leaned in close, going up on her toes to whisper, "Be careful what you command of fate, she just may give it you." She stepped back. "My sister waits." And off she went.

Annoyance plagued Talon, though he was not sure if it was because she took her leave without waiting for his permission to do so or because her words suggested that he may be sorry he commanded that she wed.

What annoyed him even more though was that he had the overpowering urge to go after her, scoop her up over his shoulder, carry her off to his sleeping chambers and mate with her again and again and again.

Talon turned, his strong voice carrying throughout the feasting hall. "Wrath, see that you find Hemera a husband before the moon turns full again!"

## Chapter Eight

The High Council meeting was coming to an end and Talon was not at all pleased with what Gelhard had to report. He had dismissed Ebit and Midrent, both having had little to say which pleased him since it meant things were going well with the crops and tariff. Ebit was busy seeing that the fields were being made ready for seeding. Midrent was busy preparing for the annual tariff collection, which would take place at the Pict Gathering held once every twelve moon cycles when the sun remained longest in the sky.

Wrath, Paine, and Broc had given their reports but Talon had ordered them to remain. He wanted to know how the hunt for a husband for Hemera was going. It had been several days since his encounter with Hemera at the grievance meeting and he wanted to see this issue resolved immediately. Even more so with what Gelhard had to report.

"You are telling me that the future queen has fallen ill and will not be able to travel for at least another moon cycle?" Talon asked, perturbed by the news.

Gelhard gave a quick nod. "Aye, my King."

Talon glared and his temper sparked. "Is this woman prone to illness?"

"Not from what I have been told. Her mother's mother still lives. She seems to come from strong stock."

"Yet she is ill and it will take another moon cycle

for her to grow well and journey here."

Gelhard's head jerked in another nod.

"If she does not arrive as planned this time, she will not be my queen," Talon decreed.

"I would not be so hasty to dismiss her, my King. As much as you may not want to hear it, you need this union more than she does."

"He is right, my King," Wrath said, agreeing with the older man. "You cannot wait any longer to wed. To ease the trouble that is brewing amongst the discontent, you should have a queen by your side for the Pict Gathering."

"Preferably rounded with child," Gelhard added.

What he needed was a wife to distract him from Hemera. Thoughts of her had plagued him relentlessly since their time alone in the woods as did a churning ache to talk with her again, feel her head on his shoulder, her hand resting on his arm, and the sweet scent of her drifting over him. Those thoughts troubled him more than the desire to mate with her. Never before had he enjoyed simply speaking with a woman, but then never had a woman challenged him as Hemera did.

After having agreed to another wager with her, he wondered if he had been too hasty in his decision and that annoyed him all the more. He never questioned his decisions. He was confident in his judgments and never gave thought to them once made. That was not proving true with Hemera.

He shook his wandering thoughts away and returned his attention to the meeting. He looked from Broc to Paine. "Do either of you have anything to say about this?"

"I agree with Wrath and Gelhard," Broc said.

"Tongues are wagging more often about there being no queen and now with this delay..." He shook his head. "I fear the wagging will increase and not in a good way."

Gelhard bobbed his head in agreement, a worried look in his sharp eyes.

Paine spoke up. "Fate will decide for you."

He found himself repeating the words he had said to Hemera. "I command fate."

"You command fate for others, not yourself."

Talon brought his fist down on the table so hard that it sent it swaying. "You doubt my command?"

Paine glared at him. "I have always spoken the truth to you whether you liked it or not."

Talon could not argue with that. Never had a lie spilled from Paine's lips. He turned to Gelhard. "She has a moon cycle. If she has not arrived by then...it is in fate's hands."

Gelhard nodded, his eyes sparking, pleased with the King's decision.

"Stay, Gelhard, you may be of help with what I have to say," Talon ordered and Gelhard gladly remained seated as Talon addressed the issue to be discussed. "What progress has been made with finding a husband for Hemera?"

Broc scratched at the nape of his neck. "Not much interest has been shown."

"No one?" the King snapped annoyed. What fool would not step forward to wed a beautiful woman like Hemera?

"No one I or you would approve of," Wrath said.

"Bower has been asking me about Hemera," Paine said.

Wrath turned a nodding head on Paine. "Bower is a

good man and is a skilled bow maker. He might be a good husband for Hemera. What has he said to you?"

"He told me he searches for a wife and that Hemera is pleasing to look upon and keeps a good tongue, but others have warned him that she is slow to understand and will be more of a hindrance than of help."

"That seems to be the problem with most men. They fear she would understand little of being a wife and mother," Broc said.

Paine shrugged. "That is easily solved. I told Bower to speak with Hemera and decide for himself. He agreed."

"Why did you not tell me this?" Wrath accused. "You know Verity would want to know of this and prepare her sister."

"I only confirmed this with Bower before coming here. Besides, it is better Bower approaches Hemera without her knowing his interest," Paine argued. "He would come to know her better that way."

"How do you know that?" Wrath demanded with a glint of anger.

Paine retaliated. "I know Hemera better than you, having spent time with her while we were with the Wyse Tribe."

"Enough," Talon ordered with a clipped anger that seemed to accent his every word. "If Bower is the only one showing any interest then let him speak with Hemera, and continue the search."

"I may know of a prospect or two that would be interested. Neither lives here in the stronghold. They tend their own crofts. One has never been wed and the other recently lost his wife in childbirth," Gelhard said.

Wrath shook his head and spoke up. "Verity would not want her sister living far from her. I would prefer to keep the search confined to the stronghold, at least for now."

Gelhard looked to the King, he having the final word.

"Do as Wrath says. The sisters have been separated enough," Talon ordered, though wondered if that was the true reason he had agreed with Wrath. That he questioned himself again had his temper igniting even further. "See this done, enough time has been wasted on it."

All but Paine nodded. He sat there smiling.

"Have we heard anything from the warriors sent out to discover the identity of the leader of those who oppose me?" Talon asked.

Broc, being commander of the King's warriors answered, "Nothing new. Whoever it is keeps his identity well-hidden and followers loyal. But we keep a good watch. We will find him and put an end to his opposition."

A rapid knock at the door had Talon shouting out with annoyance. "Enter!"

Tilden, one of Talon's personal guards hastily apologized. "I am sorry for the interruption, but there is a problem in the field and Ebit requests your immediate help."

"What kind of problem could Ebit have that requires the King to intervene?" Talon asked more perplexed than annoyed. In all the times Ebit had been Crop Master, he had never requested help from the King when in the field. It seemed incredulous that he should do so now. Until a name popped into his head the same time it spilled from Tilden's lips.

"*Hemera.*"

Talon stood, bringing the other men to their feet. "The meeting is finished, see to your duties."

Wrath kept step with Talon and reached out to snatch both their cloaks off the pegs on the wall before walking out the door.

Gelhard hurried behind them, though turned away once in the feasting hall to go see to his duties as did Broc once outside. Paine followed a few steps behind the King and Wrath, a slight smile tempting the corners of his mouth.

There was a crowd of field servants blocking one of the fields as Talon approached. They scurried out of his way when he shouted, "Return to your chores now!"

Talon halted abruptly when he saw what they had been staring at.

Hemera was lying in the middle of the tilled field that was ready for planting, her untamable red hair fanning out around her head and her arms spread out from her sides, as if in sacrifice to some god. She wore no cloak, only a long, brown wool shift, gathered at her trim waist with a knotted, leather belt. Her leather foot coverings were worn to the point of providing little protection. Annoyance jabbed at him like a stick to his side and his hands fisted.

Wrath went to step past the King.

Talon's strong command stopped him. "I will handle this."

Talon took quick strides to where Ebit stood beside Hemera.

Relief flooded Ebit's face and he spoke as soon as Talon came to a stop on the opposite side of Hemera.

"Forgive me, my King, for disturbing you, but I did not know what to do. Hemera refuses to remove herself from the first of the fields ready for the seeds that must go in today."

Hemera glared at Ebit. "He will not listen to me. The seed will either die or not grow well if planted here."

Ebit shook his head at her. "I am Crop Master. I know what I am doing."

"Then you should know that the soil is too ill to accept the seeds."

"She speaks foolishly," Ebit said.

"The soil needs nourishment and time to grow strong again. You cannot plant here now," Hemera insisted.

"Please, my King, this field must be seeded now," Ebit all but pleaded.

"Get up, Hemera!" Talon ordered sharply and stretched his hand out to her.

Hemera knew she could not defy the King, especially in front of others. She had learned all too well what happened when she defied authority. She reached out and took hold of his hand. He yanked her to her feet as easily as if he plucked a seedling from the ground.

Talon released her once she was steady on her feet, though he did so reluctantly. Her hand was chilled and he wished he could warm it for her. "You will stay away from the planting fields," he ordered with an abrupt snap of his finger near her face.

Hemera squatted down and thinking she was going to stretch out on the soil again, Talon reached for her, grabbing hold of her arm and yanking her up once again. She winced when she turned to face him and he realized that he had grabbed her harder than he had intended. He dropped his hand off her.

"What did I tell you?" he demanded, knowing every eye was on them, waiting to see what he would do for disobeying him.

"I will follow your command, but first I beg of you to feel the soil. It cries in distress when it cannot nourish the seeds it is given. Listen to it...it will speak to you."

Talon caught Ebit shaking his head, a look of sorrow in his eyes for the poor foolish-speaking lass.

Hemera stepped closer to Talon and reached out and took his hand to gently place the soil she held in it and close his fingers around it.

Gasps were heard as she did, for she had not been given permission to touch the King and once again they all waited to see what he would do.

"Feel it. Listen to it," she urged with a whisper.

Talon wanted to believe her, if not for anything but that others would not think less of her or think her foolish or mindless. He was aware that those around him waited to see what he would do and he wondered himself.

"My sister speaks the truth."

Wrath turned and, seeing his wife approach, reached out to stop her from walking past him. He was not surprised when Verity pushed his arm aside. He was, however, surprised when she skirted his attempt to snatch her around the waist. His anger flared, more so when he caught the smile on Paine's face and the way Anin stepped willingly into his outstretched arm.

Anger rumbled in Wrath's chest as he caught up

with his wife when she came to a stop beside the King.

"My sister knows the soil well. She coaxed many a seedling to grow when others could not."

"Forgive me, my King," Ebit said, "but this is a vast growing field, not a woman's plot of seedlings."

"A small plot or a whole field, my sister still knows the soil well," Verity argued, ignoring the pokes to her side from her husband.

Talon was about to silence the bickering pair when Hemera's gentle whisper reached his ears.

"She speaks to you."

Talon was well aware that if one watched closely the trees, plants, animals, and clouds offered help. The signs were there and it was not wise to ignore them. Ebit knew the planting signs well and had produced more abundant crops but also scarce ones. His choice who to trust was obvious...until he felt a sadness rush through his hand that held the soil. He looked at the dark soil and it almost felt as if it sighed. He looked to Hemera.

"The soil tells you that it is not well enough for planting. Once it heals, the soil will welcome the seeds again," she whispered.

Did she know of what she spoke or were her words nonsense?

"Please, my King, the field must be planted now if the people are to be fed," Ebit pleaded.

"What happens if what my sister says proves true? Then there will be no food for the people when the lands turns dormant and the cold descends on us once again," Verity said.

Talon had a duty to see his people fed. He had always trusted Ebit's knowledge, but what if Hemera actually knew something that Ebit did not? He dropped the soil from his hand and brushed both hands together to rid himself of what had remained and a sudden chill ran through him. He caught the shiver and stopped it before it could surface. The strange occurrence had helped him make his decision.

"Plant half this field, Ebit," Talon ordered.

Ebit unwisely protested. "You cannot mean to listen to a slow—"

"You defy your King?" Talon said with such a forceful anger it sent a shiver through the crowd.

Ebit shook his head. "Nay. Nay. Forgive me, my King. I will see it done immediately."

Talon turned his attention on Verity. "Speak when not given permission again and you will spend time in a prison chamber."

Wrath stepped forward.

"You will join her if I hear a protest from your mouth," Talon warned.

Verity hurried to take hold of her husband's arm and even more hastily offered an apology. "Please forgive my foolishness, my King. I meant no disrespect. I wished only to protect my sister."

"From what?" Talon snapped. "Her own foolishness?"

Verity wisely held her tongue.

"Teach your wife the wisdom of knowing when to keep silent," Talon ordered, "or the next time she will suffer for it."

Wrath nodded, his anger too close to the surface to trust himself to speak.

"I will hear it from your lips," Talon demanded in a near roar.

"Aye, my King," Wrath said with a shout that was laced with anger.

Talon took a step toward Wrath, his anger as palpable as Wrath's.

Hemera saw fear catch in her sister's eyes and she hastily stepped between the two men and raised her voice to drift over the crowd that had grown larger. "What is my punishment, my King, for doing far worse than what my sister did?"

Talon glared at her. "Three days in a prisoner chamber might serve you well or perhaps the sting of a switch would serve you better." When she stared at him speechless, her eyes wide, he waited. He would not be tricked again into believing that his threat had actually frightened her into possibly obeying his rules when she was thinking something entirely different.

Gasps filled the air when Hemera's hand reached out and rested against the King's chest.

Fury rose up in Talon not only that Hemera had disobeyed him again, but that he would have no choice but to see that her punishment reflect it.

He was about to push her arm off him when he saw her face turn as pale as freshly fallen snow.

"Please no," she begged in a soft whisper before her body went limp and she fell forward into his arms.

## Chapter Nine

Talon caught Hemera's limp body, his arms closing protectively around her. Without thought or consequence, he scooped her up and rested her tightly against him.

"Hemera!" Verity cried out.

Anin stepped forward and placed a hand on Verity's arm, stopping her from going to her sister while looking to the King. "Please, my King, bring Hemera to my dwelling so Verity and I may tend her."

Talon nodded and keeping Hemera tucked firmly against him, he called out to the servants and those who had gathered out of curiosity, "Return to your chores or I will see more punishments enforced."

Everyone scurried away and whispers drifted overhead as thoughts were exchanged over Hemera's fate.

Talon felt a powerful dread gnaw at his insides as Hemera's head lolled against his chest and her body remained lifeless. He had learned to rein in his fear, to never let it take control, but it had gripped him so fast when Hemera collapsed against him that he had no time to fight it off. Now it squeezed him unmercifully like a giant hand that refused to let go. He fought it, struggling mightily to free himself. He was King. He ruled. Nothing ruled him. He would not permit fear to take root in him.

He felt Hemera begin to stir in his arms, her face

turning slightly to press against his chest and her body regaining strength. She struggled to wake while the fear he had resisted began to dissipate.

She turned her head away from his chest with some effort and tilted it back slowly, her eyes fluttering as they fought to open.

"You are safe. I have you, Hemera," he whispered.

Her words came slow to her lips. "Do...not let...me...go...Talon"

His response rushed from his mouth in a firm whisper, "*Never!*"

Her head dropped against his chest, her face turning to rest there once again.

"This way, my King," Anin said.

It was good that she did, since Talon was about to bring his lips to kiss the top of Hemera's head. He shook his head as he entered the dwelling, not understanding how he seemed to be unable to stop himself from reacting without reasonable thought to this woman.

Anin and Paine's dwelling was larger than most since Paine now held the council's seat of Master Builder. It was two rooms instead of one and Talon recalled how he had designed it along with the previous Master Builder, Bodu, who had betrayed him and suffered the ultimate punishment—death.

Talon walked over to the long cloth, hanging from above the door to the sleeping chamber and pushed it aside with his shoulder and entered. He was reluctant to place Hemera on the sizeable, raised sleeping pallet and leave her to the care of the women. But he had no choice.

She was not his and the thought irritated him.

He laid her gently on the raised pallet and as he stepped back, her eyes opened and her hand instinctively reached out to him. He went to grasp hold of it, once more without thought, but Verity hurried around him, taking hold of her sister's hand.

"I am here, Hemera. I am here with you," Verity said, a tremor of fear in her soft voice.

He thought he saw disappointment in Hemera's eyes or was it because he felt it himself? He stepped to the side, near to where Wrath and Paine waited. He did not intend to leave. He had questions for Hemera.

"You should be wearing your cloak," Verity scolded, pulling the blanket at the bottom of the pallet up and tucking it around her sister. "The air is chilly today."

"And the soil has grown ill," Hemera said.

Verity ran a gentle hand over her sister's brow. "Worry not about that now."

Hemera's head finally cleared of the fog that had taken hold of it and she looked around. "This is not my home."

Anin stepped forward. "Mine was closer so the King brought you here."

Hemera tried craning her neck to look past the two women and when she failed to spot the King, she called out, "You need not have Anin touch me to tell you what you wish to know. All you have to do is ask me." She dropped her head back on the soft pallet with a sigh.

Talon stepped in from the other room. "Leave us and wait outside."

Verity looked to her sister, reluctant to leave her.

"I will be fine," Hemera assured her.

Anin tugged at Verity's arm and she grudgingly

turned. Both women went to their husbands and shortly after the front door could be heard closing.

Talon walked over to the sleeping pallet and looked down at Hemera. Color had returned to her face, a slight heat rising high on her cheeks. She did not look ill. She looked as beautiful as ever.

Annoyed at his thought, he demanded, "Are you feeling ill?"

"No, I am not feeling ill."

"Then why did you faint?"

She gazed off a moment, lost in a memory, then shivered. "Fright of severe punishment."

"Punishment of your own making. You persistently disobey and disrespect me—"

"Only when necessary."

"You do it again," he said, shaking a finger at her. "You interrupt the King."

Hemera struggled to get up.

Talon leaned down, shaking his finger close to her face. "You will stay put until you are well enough to get up."

"I want to sit up," she said and once again struggled to do so.

Talon slipped his hands under her arms and with a gentle yet strong heave brought her to a sitting position. His hands slipped loose as soon as he saw she could sit on her own and as he pulled them away, his fingers accidently stroked the sides of her full breasts. Their soft fullness flared his desire and he stepped away, silently berating himself for not having satisfied himself with a woman for a while now.

"I do not always think of you as King," she admitted softly, as if revealing a secret.

"If not King, then what?" He shook his head. "Hold your tongue. I do not want to—"

"Friend," she said with haste.

Talon clenched his hand, shaking it in front of her. "Again you disobey me, and we are not friends. I am your King."

"Talon is my friend."

"We are one and the same."

"No, you are not. There is Talon and then there is the King"

Talon let his hand drop to his side, though it remained clenched, but not tightly.

"The King can be friends with no one," Hemera said. "He has a duty to fulfill."

"True," he said pleased she finally grasped what he was saying, though made sure to clarify it, "which means we can never be friends."

"Too late, we already are friends." She continued on so fast he had no chance to correct her. "I almost forgot. There is more to tell you about the traitor we hope to find. I continue to keep watch on your personal guards' cloaks when I can and the other day I took note of one. When I returned to the spot later, the cloak was gone—"

"The owner returned for it," Talon said as if the explanation was simple.

"Not so," Hemera corrected. "The owner had returned as well to find it gone. He asked me if I had seen it. I informed him that I saw it there earlier. He told me that this was not the first time this had happened. It had happened twice before, which means the culprit continues to use the cloak of your personal guards to meet with your enemy. You should order

Wrath to see that your guards keep better watch over their cloaks. The culprit would be left to find another way to sneak out of the stronghold and it might just be enough for him to make a mistake and reveal himself."

Talon wondered how her mind seemed to grasp some things quickly and others things not at all. But she was right, he would need to speak with Wrath. "With being so busy searching out the traitor, how did you wind up lying in the planting field?"

"Bower mentioned it when—"

"Bower spoke with you?" Talon asked his tongue sharp and his annoyance obvious. He had only given permission at the High Council meeting a short time ago for him to do so. Then he recalled how Paine had already told Bower to speak with Hemera. The man certainly had not wasted time.

"Is there reason Bower should not speak with me?" she asked. "He is a kind man and a skilled bow maker. His features are plain, but pleasant and though his body is thick, it is hard with muscle, which tells me how hard he works at his craft. He offered to fashion me a bow and I offered to tell him what wood to look for to create a stronger bow. I thought you would be pleased since I would not be going into the woods alone...Bower would be with me."

Talon's shaking finger shot out at her again along with his temper. "You are not going anywhere. You have a punishment to face."

Hemera stared at him and her face began to pale.

"Do not think fainting again will stop your punishment," he warned.

"Will you let me serve my punishment in a prison chamber?" She lowered her head. "I am not very good with pain."

She had survived a slave to the Northmen. How could she not deal with pain? "Then grow strong and bear it, for life does not come without pain." He turned to go, saying as he did," You will have my decision by dusk and your punishment will be served in the morn."

Hemera threw the blanket off her and swung her legs off the pallet once she heard the door close. She did not want to think about her fate. She wanted to go and seek solace in the woods.

She was on her feet when Verity entered with tears in her eyes. Anin followed close behind her.

"I cannot believe he will punish you," Verity said, hugging her sister, then with her hands on Hemera's shoulders, eased her down to sit on the pallet. "You need to rest."

"I need to go home," Hemera said and stood, placing a gentle hand on her sister's arm. "Do not worry so. We have faced far worse. I will be fine. And it is not right for me to impose on Anin any longer."

"You do not impose, though I think home would bring you what you need right now," Anin said and her hand rushed to her rounded middle. "My daughter grows in strength like you have, Hemera. You are a strong woman and fate will not fail you."

Hemera laughed softly. "Did you not know that the King commands fate?"

Anin smiled and patted Hemera's arm. "Then the King will not fail you."

Hemera left, wondering over Anin's words and went to the one place that never failed to comfort her...the woods.

~~~

The King wore a scowl. He did not know he wore one as he walked through the stronghold, but others saw it and moved out of his way. His strides were strong, his shoulders thrown back, and his hands fisted. He appeared ready to fight and everyone wondered who the unlucky recipient would be.

Talon stopped at the bow maker's dwelling. Bower was so engrossed in refining a newly made bow that he did not hear the King approach.

"Bower!" Talon snapped annoyed the man paid him no heed.

Bower jumped, the bow falling to the ground. "Forgive me, my King, I did not know you were here."

Talon was there for one thing. "You spoke with Hemera earlier."

Bower bobbed his head. "Aye, my King, I did. Paine said I should when I inquired about the search for a husband for her. She is a beautiful lass and seems pleasant enough." He scratched his head.

"Something troubles you about her. Tell me," Talon ordered, seeing that the man looked reluctant to say more.

Bower did not hesitate to obey the King. "I offered to make a bow for her and she offered to show me what trees would produce the strongest bows. My father and his father before him were bow makers and they have taught me since I was a wee bairn. I know what it takes to make a fine bow, but she told me I was using the wrong trees to make my bows. Now I hear she has told Ebit the soil was not fit for planting." Bower shook his head. "She is also slow to speak sometimes and other times she does not seem to grasp what I say."

"Then you are no longer interested in taking her as a wife?" Talon asked, annoyed for feeling pleased rather than disappointed.

"No, my King. Oddly enough, I enjoyed the time I spent with her and I would like to come to know her better before I make a decision. As I said, she is a pleasant woman to be with and a woman like that is not easy to find," Bower said with a grin.

Talon had an overwhelming urge to reach out and strangle the man, but he forced his clenched hands to remain at his sides.

"Am I permitted to continue to speak with her in hopes of a possible union, my King?"

Again he wanted to strangle the man, but he said as he turned, "Aye, but do not let it interfere with your chores."

"I am grateful, my King," Bower said with haste, but the King was already a distance from him.

Talon's temper grew and his scowl along with it as the thought of Hemera joining with Bower filled his head. The idea that Bower—good man that he was—would touch Hemera intimately, infuriated Talon. And it was the very reason why he had to encourage their union.

He stopped suddenly, hearing a growl behind him and turned.

"Your angry snarls are frightening everyone, including Bog," Paine said with a nod to the black wolf growling beside him. "Enough, Bog, the King is in a foul mood this day." The wolf quieted, though kept his eyes on the King.

"Bower spoke with Hemera," the King said.

"That makes you angry?"

Talon stifled the *aye* that wanted to rush from his lips and instead said, "Hemera makes me angry. She obeys none of what I command, speaks without permission to me and places her hand on me without permission. She needs to be punished."

"Then let her punishment show it," Paine said as if the solution was easy. "I will take the switch to her. How many would you like me to deliver to her back? Ten? Twenty?"

Talon turned silent, the thought of Paine striking Hemera's smooth back over and over, leaving gashes and welts, some that no doubt would scar, had his insides roiling.

"Or you could put her in the prison chamber for three sunrises, no less, since it is the least amount of time required when sent there. It is a tight space and will be cold, the sun not hot enough to warm it yet." Paine shrugged. "Either way she must be punished, the people will expect it after what she did in the planting field today."

Talon knew he was right, which only fueled his anger more. Hemera's disobedience could not be allowed to go unpunished. Not after she had displayed it for all to see.

"I would use the switch on her. It will be done and over quickly," Paine advised and he looked down at his side upon hearing a deep growl. "Bog does not agree, but then he favors Hemera and will have to be locked away while she is punished or he will not hesitate to protect her. Shall I use the switch on her?"

"You are no longer my executioner."

"Would you want someone else delivering the

blows to her back?"

Talon felt like roaring out his rage. He did not want to see this done to Hemera and yet he had no choice. He had never been reluctant, uncertain, or regretful when handing out a punishment, until now.

"Ten blows, no more, to her back on the morn," Paine ordered and turned and walked away.

Anin appeared from around one of the nearby dwellings and approached her husband. His arm went out as soon as he saw her and she, as always, drifted into his embrace.

"You are feeling well?" he asked and gave her brow a kiss.

"I am, though I believe our daughter will be a mighty warrior like her da, her kicks are so strong."

Paine rested his hand protectively over his wife's rounded middle. "I will teach her well."

"I heard what you said to the King," Anin said, covering her husband's hand with hers. "Why do you torment him?"

"Why ask me when your touch tells you why?" Paine said with a quick kiss to her cheek. He was growing accustomed to her feeling and knowing things when she touched him. He kept no secrets from her, so it did not matter. He especially enjoyed it when they mated, for she felt his pleasure along with hers.

"I am practicing what my grandmother taught during our recent visit there. How not always to feel what others are feeling when I touch."

He nipped at her ear, whispering, "I like when you know what I feel."

Anin closed her eyes and smiled, her husband's desire flaring her own.

"You should rest," he whispered in her ear.

"Only if you join me."

Paine turned her around in his arms. "You will get no rest then."

"Promise?"

"You are a wicked woman." Paine laughed.

She poked him in the chest. "And you are wicked for tormenting the King."

"He needs tormenting."

Concern rested in her furrowed brow. "You cannot mean to take a switch to Hemera."

Paine kissed her quick. "You know as well as I do that the King will never allow it."

"I do not know that. He is a stubborn man."

"He more wise than he is stubborn," Paine argued. "Mark my words he will rescind his edict."

"I hope he does, for Verity will not stand by idle and see her sister beaten and... neither will I."

Paine's eyes shot wide, then his brow narrowed to a scowl and his arm hooked snug around her waist as he stepped closer to her. "Listen well, wife, you will not put yourself and our daughter in harm's way."

Anin eased out of his arms, resting her hand over her rounded middle. "What is there for you to worry about when you believe the King will rescind his order? I must see to an errand. I will see you later." She turned and walked off, leaving a scowl on Paine's face.

~~~

Hemera had barely settled the loose fence board in place and emerged from the small wooded area behind her dwelling when Verity and Anin appeared. From the worried look in her sister's eyes she knew Verity had brought alarming news.

Hemera did not need to hear it to know what it was... her punishment had been decided.

"Ten strikes of the switch on the morn," Verity said.

Hemera stepped away from her sister before she could hug her, the words echoing in her head like a resounding bell.

"I will beg the King for mercy," Verity said.

"You will waste your breath," Hemera said and shook her head, turning away from the two women. "Please go. I wish to be alone."

"I cannot leave you—"

Hemera went to her sister and took her hand. "You can, you will, and you must not do anything that will bring you harm."

"We have been through much together. I will not see you go through this alone," Verity insisted.

"You bear no burden in this, Verity, and you will leave it be. You have the bairn you carry to think about. Now go and worry on it no more." Hemera turned away once again.

Verity watched her sister enter her dwelling and she wanted to rush after her and hold her tight, keep her from harm, keep the switch from striking her back. They had suffered much together while with the Northmen and she did not want to see her sister suffer this alone.

An arm wrapped around Verity's shoulder, feeling like a warm blanket that was much needed on a cold day.

"All will be well. Do not worry."

Verity took solace in Anin's words, but then she had little other choice.

~~~

Talon lay on his sleeping pallet, wishing his chaotic thoughts would settle and he would slip into the oblivion of sleep. Not that it would matter, since deep sleep rarely claimed him. The endless battles he had fought had taught him to always remain alert even in sleep. Enemies could lurk anywhere, though this time he was his own enemy.

He could not get the feeling of how helpless he had felt when Hemera fell limp against him. He had reacted instinctively, his arms going around her to protect her and keep safe. There was also the troubling thought that she did not do well with pain. How had she survived her time with the Northmen if she could not bear pain? With the way she spoke or acted without first thinking, surely the Northmen had found reason to punish her at times.

His thoughts had him bolting up in bed. Hemera was not a weak woman. Why would she say she was not good with pain? Unless...

Talon hurried off the bed and into his long, open tunic, belting it at his waist. He wore nothing else but his foot coverings. He went to a section in the wall, furthest from his pallet, and eased his finger into what appeared to be a small hole and, with a lift, the section of the wall opened. He slipped around the narrow door, closing it behind him. He took narrow steps down and lifted another small toggle when he got to the bottom and stepped out into the dark night.

He had not planned the secret exit. It was done by one of his warriors, an older one who had since met death with valor. He had shown it to Talon when it was finished, explaining to him that a King always had to have a private exit for those private times. He had not fully understood the man's reasoning, but in time he had learned what he meant, and even more so this night.

The stronghold was quiet, all asleep, except the guards who were on alert and who he avoided, the shadows providing cover as he moved among them with ease. Once in the area of the executioner's dwelling, he need not worry. It sat so remote from others that no guards were present anywhere near it. And this night he was grateful for that.

Talon did not bother to knock once at the door. He flung it open and was not surprised to see Hemera pacing by the fire pit. She stopped abruptly and her eyes took on the glare of an innocent animal, knowing there was no escape... it had been caught.

He shut the door and stepped further into the room and though the fire pit separated them, Hemera took a step back as if the distance would offer her more protection.

His intent was not to frighten her, but to learn the truth. "Show me your back," he ordered.

Hemera stared at him, frozen where she stood. She could not. She would not do as he commanded. She did not refuse him, she simply did not respond to him.

He took a hasty step forward and she instinctively took another step back.

"I will strip you myself if you do not obey me."

What choice did she have? Let him strip her? Leave her feeling vulnerable. Nay, she had not lacked courage in front of the Northmen, she certainly would not lack courage in front of the King.

She wore only her shift and to show him her back she had to remove it. She had to stand naked in front of him. She raised her chin and turned, presenting her back to him as she gripped the sides of her garment and began to remove it.

## Chapter Ten

Talon stood rigid, his eyes on Hemera as she slowly lifted the garment. The back of her legs bore not a single mark on her lovely pale skin. Her backside was the same, as it came into view. Not a mark on it, smooth, taut, and round. The thought of caressing it, squeezing it, kissing it, was enough to stir him to arousal.

As the hem of the garment reached her waist, she suddenly yanked it up and over her head, grasping it to her chest and her whole body grew rigid.

Talon stood there stunned, unable to move or speak, his eyes wide, and his anger quickly turning to rage.

Her back was covered in scars that had left welts and gorges from what could only have been a brutal or several brutal lashings. Fury rose in him as he imagined the hand of the man, who had delivered her torture, come down again and again on her lovely smooth back. He could almost feel every blow she suffered and feel the never-ending pain as she was struck again and again, helpless to do anything.

He took slow steps to her, his eyes focused on her back and the suffering she had endured. He did not think her body could turn more rigid, but it did. She stood as stiff as the trees she favored spending time with in the woods. He stood there staring at her scars, seeing how they crisscrossed one another and he knew for sure that she had suffered more than one lashing.

His hand reached out and touched her back gently. She startled.

"I will not hurt you," he said, his whispered breath stirring the strands of her long, red hair. He gathered her hair in his hands, the feel of her wild curls softer than he expected and as he placed it over her shoulder to rest on her chest, he caught a whiff of pine. She carried the scent of the forest upon her and it reminded him when he would take to the earth floor at night to sleep. The familiar scent would welcome him and wrap around him like a woman who had long missed him and was eager for his return.

His fingers faintly traced the many scars, going from one to another as if his tender touch could make them disappear.

Hemera closed her eyes, his gentle touch feeling much too good. The way he purposely touched each mark on her back made her feel that he actually cared for her. She lingered in the thought, finding it pleased her.

His other hand went to rest at her waist as his hand continued to caress her back while question after question rushed to his lips, but they died there. This was not the time for questions. He leaned down to whisper in her ear. "I will never let anyone hurt you again."

His warm breath tickled her cool skin and she shivered, though it was more of a tingle.

Talon felt her quiver and knew it was not from a chill, for his body had tingled along with hers. He told himself not to do it. He warned himself to step away, but her bare, silky smooth neck beckoned his lips.

*One taste. Just one.*

He brought his lips down on her neck, softly and inquisitively, and tasted. He shut his eyes against the pure, intoxicating pleasure.

One taste would never be enough.

His kisses grew more ardent. Never had he found the taste of a woman as appealing as Hemera. It was as if he drank of a rare brew that he could not get enough of.

She shuddered, drawing her shoulders up as a soft sigh escaped her lips. That she enjoyed his lips upon her only encouraged him, and his kisses soon turned to nips, and she shuddered once again. And he turned hard.

*Stop now. Right now*, a voice in his head warned.

He did not listen.

He continued to nibble along her neck while his hand slipped around the front of her and with one sharp tug at the garment she grasped to her chest, it fell from her hand, and dropped to the floor. His hand slipped beneath her breast to cup it, feeling its full softness and squeezing it gently, and a strange thought entered his head, one he never had before when with a woman. He thought how much he would enjoy feeling her breasts heavy with milk for their child.

She drew him out of his musings when she dropped back against him with a soft moan. She hungered for more just as he did.

His fingers grazed her nipples, already puckered from passion and his hands went to her waist to turn her and taste the tiny buds, hard and ready for his tongue to enjoy.

He stopped when she looked up at him, eyes full of passion, ready to surrender to him. If she did, what then? What would be left for her? She would be his woman, no more than that. Never more than that.

He pushed her away and she almost stumbled, but he paid her no heed. He swerved around and left the dwelling, closing the door strongly behind him. His strides were angry, his temper mounting and he wished he was in the heat of battle right now, for he would strike down warrior after warrior and still not assuage his rage.

He should have never gone to her, never touched her, never kissed her. Now he hungered for her like a starving man. Never had he felt desire rip at him, tear at every part of his body as it did now. Never had he wanted a woman as badly as he did Hemera. He was insane with the need for her. It was not good. He could not surrender to it. He would not surrender to it.

An image of her naked rose in his mind, her pale body soft and supple. Her arms reached out to him, inviting him and urging him to join with her. She climbed on top of him and he could almost feel himself slide snug inside her. She felt as if she was made for him and him alone.

*Mine.*

For the first time ever, Talon lost a battle. He turned and hurried to her dwelling, swung the door open and swung it closed with just as much strength. Hemera had not moved from where she had been standing and he went to her, shedding his foot coverings and his garments as he did.

His arm shot out as he got close and he coiled it around her waist to yank her against him and before he brought his mouth down on hers in a hungry kiss, he commanded as if making it law, "*Mine!*"

No response came to Hemera's mind. She wanted nothing more than his lips and hands upon her. She would try to make sense of it all later or perhaps not. Perhaps she would enjoy it and not think on it like she did most things.

Her arms went around his neck and she was soon lost in the kiss.

His hand settled on her scarred back and he felt her tense. He tore his mouth away from hers reluctantly and held her eyes with his own. "Never deny your scars. Wear them proudly for they attest to your immense courage and strength."

Her heart surged not with desire, but happiness, something she had not felt since she had been young. She smiled as she said, "You are kind."

"If I were kind, I would deny my need for you."

"Never will I deny my need for you, Talon," she whispered as her lips met his.

Many women had professed similar words in the heat of passion, though none had ever dared to call him kind or by his name and none had ever touched his heart and twisted it into knots as Hemera just did.

Talon's hand drifted down along the curve of her back, to slip further down over her backside. The soft roundness invited a tender squeeze as he pressed her closer against him. His rigid manhood settled against the triangle of fiery red hair between her legs, making him more eager than ever to join with her.

His hands cupped her backside and he lifted her, her legs instinctively locking around his waist. He walked over to the sleeping pallet, not taking his lips off hers. He lowered her down, her arms remaining around his neck as if she refused to be separated from him. He felt the same. He wanted to have her close, always close to him.

She spread her legs as he settled on top of her, willingly offering herself to him, but he would not have this moment pass quickly. He wanted to savor her, claim her with his touch and his lips before he settled inside her to claim her completely.

Talon ended the kiss, his brow resting on hers as he steadied his breath. "I will know all of you."

Hemera's brow wrinkled, not sure what he meant, then he began to kiss along her neck, raising bumps along her flesh and sending a teasing tingle between her legs. Her mind suddenly quieted and she felt herself drift off on a cloud of pleasure and she relished it.

Talon felt the moment of her surrender, not so much to him, but to herself. She was no longer thinking, only enjoying and feeling her give in to her desires fired his own pleasure.

He kissed along her stomach, his playful nibbles leaving small red spots upon her pale skin, his hand continued to roam over her in a gentle caress. When his fingers settled over her delicate nub nestled in the thatch of fiery red hair between her legs and she moaned long and hard, he thought she would come there and then. He would not allow that, not until he was deep inside her.

"Talon," she said in one long breath.

He planted his hands on either side of her and with one push lifted himself off her.

"No! Do not leave me," she begged, grabbing his arms, her fingers digging into taut muscle.

"Never," he said and lowered his head to tease her sensitive neck with his lips and teeth.

She shivered, gasped, and moaned so loud, he feared she would wake the village, so he brought his mouth down on hers and she fed on his kiss as if it was the last they would ever share.

His own need soared and he shifted so that the tip of his manhood slipped slightly into her.

Both her hands dug into his arms, his flesh too hard to do any damage, as she bucked against him and he slipped further inside her. Her red hair blazed around her as she lifted her head, planted a quick hungry kiss on his lips, then threw her head back on the pallet, letting out a long moan.

He was about to slip further into her, not wanting to rush and cause her pain, when suddenly her legs came up to lock around him as she quickly lifted her bottom up off the pallet, driving his manhood into her.

She cried out, her breath catching before a sigh of pleasure followed.

She could wait no longer and either could he. He thought to take her gently at first, but she thought otherwise. She demanded and so did he.

He set a fast, hard rhythm and she matched it, their bodies slamming against each other. He lowered his head and caught her lower lip with his teeth, dragging along it slowly, before releasing it and driving his tongue into her mouth as he drove into her again and again.

She slipped her hand around to the back of his neck, cupping it tightly, forcing his mouth to remain on hers, wanting to taste deeply of him, and as she did she felt her need for him growing ever stronger. It was not long before she broke away from his lips and took deep breaths, her chest heaving, and once again she latched onto his arms and moaned.

"Talon! Talon!"

His name grew more frantic on her lips, and he closed his eyes and listened to its powerful cadence. He felt the strength of it reach deep down inside him and tug harder and harder and harder.

"Talon!"

His eyes shot open and he not only watched her climax, he felt it as well and then his own climax gripped him and tore him apart like never before. He never felt such tremendous pleasure. It crashed over him like a thunderous wave, tossing him around, rolling him over and over, again and again, until he thought he would die from the exquisite pleasure.

He collapsed on top of Hemera and her arms slipped around him, squeezing him tight, and he felt the last strands of his mighty climax hover for a moment then, with a shiver, slip away.

After a few moments, he lifted his head from where it lay next to hers and kissed her brow. He pulled back, planting his hands on either side of her head, and saw her green eyes so bright with tears, though not one had fallen, that they startled the senses.

"What is wrong? Did I hurt you?" he demanded with a scowl, angry that he may have caused her pain.

Hemera shook her head and smiled. "Not at all, you brought me more joy than I knew was possible."

"Then you will be a very joyful woman by morn," he said and kissed her and with a quick turn and an arm around her shoulder, Talon slipped off her, taking her with him to rest against him.

He was familiar with the way she would grow silent and simply stare now and again before she responded. So he waited in silence while she lost herself in thought.

"Did you find our coupling pleasing?" she finally asked.

He turned on his side to face her, his hand going to rest at the curve of her waist. "So pleasing that I think I will never get enough of you."

"Good, for I feel the same," she admitted happily and snuggled against him.

His hand fell on her back and he was reminded of her scars. "Who did this to you?"

"What difference does it make, it is done."

"It makes a difference to me. I will see the man who did this to you suffer beyond measure."

She placed her hand gently on his cheek. "Will you make yourself suffer when you deliver the same punishment to me on the morn?"

Anger flared in his blue eyes. "You left me little choice. My laws must be upheld or they will be meaningless, then chaos will reign. Now tell me who gave you these scars." His sharp command left no room that he was to be obeyed.

"Please not now, Talon," Hemera said. "This precious time we spend together is not meant to open old wounds."

"You will tell me one day," he said, agreeing that it was not the time to drudge up painful memories for her.

"One day," she said on a yawn.

"Rest, you are tired and we have most of the night ahead of us," he said, leaving her side for a moment to retrieve the blanket crumpled at the end of the pallet. He placed it over them and after easing Hemera against his side, he tucked it around her.

Hemera lay beside him silent in her thoughts. She could not recall ever feeling as satisfied and peaceful as she did at this moment. Times had been difficult, but here at this moment she felt something she had never thought she would feel again... hope.

The warmth of his body next to hers and hearing his heart beat gently against her ear lolled her into a welcoming slumber.

Talon held Hemera close, feeling the moment her body surrendered to sleep. He had warned himself to keep his distance from her and yet, here with her sleeping in his arms, he was glad he had paid no heed to his warnings. She belonged right where she was... she belonged to him.

*Mine.*

Never had he felt the satisfaction he did when coupling with Hemera. Never had he experienced a climax that left him satisfied, not looking for more, actually satisfied. And never had he felt such pleasure holding a woman in his arms afterwards as he did with Hemera. He never wanted to let her go. He wanted her with him always and the thought that that could never be pained his heart.

He glared at the ceiling, annoyed with his thoughts. He would not let her go, but was it fair to have her live in the shadows, never fully being part of his life? The alternative of her not being part of his life in any way was much worse.

He had seen the spot of blood on her thigh when he had reached for the blanket. He was her first and he would be her last, for he would allow no other to touch her.

She startled in his arms and he was quick to soothe her with gentle caresses along her back and she settled quietly. Her scars once again reminded him of what she was to suffer on the morn and he cursed himself. He could not put her through that again. He would not put her through it again. What he would do, he did not know, but he would not see her suffer that way again.

He shut his eyes and let his thoughts drift with possibilities and soon his eyes grew heavy and he fell asleep. He found himself in a dream, one that pleased him.

*Hemera lay on top of him, her lips busy kissing at his neck, along his shoulder, down on his chest, taking her time at each spot to kiss, nibble, and nip playfully. When her hand settled on his manhood to explore, he felt himself grow hard and grow even harder as her innocent touch ignited a fiery passion in him and her innocent exploration would have him bursting in her hand.*

His eyes suddenly shot open to see that it was not a dream and that he was ready to come. He sat up, grabbed her around the waist, tossed her down on her back, locked both of her wrists in his one hand, so she could not do anymore damage before he could enter her, then he drove into her in one hard thrust.

That he would not last long angered him. That he felt an immense climax building pleased him. That he saw the same pleasure in Hemera's eyes touched his heart. They came together in an explosion of sheer pleasure and when it was done, they lay with labored breaths in each other's arms; silent, satisfied, and sleepy.

It was shortly after they joined for a third time that

Talon said reluctantly, "I must leave."

Hemera felt a tug in her chest. She did not want him to go, but he had to. He was King and could not be found here in her dwelling.

With great reluctance, he left her side and slipped into his garment and pulled on his foot coverings. He returned to the sleeping pallet and leaned down over her to kiss her.

Her arms went around his neck and she kissed him soundly, fearful she would never know the pleasure of his lips again.

Talon pulled his lips away from hers and whispered, "Later."

Hemera smiled, pleased that he would return to her.

He stood. "For now, no one can know what we do."

"I understand."

"We will talk later," he said, knowing he would have to make things clear to her of what could and could not be between them.

"As you say."

Talon walked to the door and turned before opening it. "You will not suffer the switch to your back today."

Hemera sat up. "You must punish me if you want to keep your peoples' respect."

"I am aware of that," he said, "so you better be on time to the feasting hall this morn to receive your punishment."

## Chapter Eleven

Hemera hurried to dress after Talon left. The dawn would break soon and she wanted to be off into the woods just as it did. There was a secluded, small pool of water she had come across when exploring the forest. She thought of it as her private bathing spot. The water was cold and she was hoping it would warm enough when the sun turned hot so that she could actually bathe in it. For now, it served as a way to keep herself refreshed.

She opened the door to find Bog waiting there for her. She lowered herself to his side and gave him a good rub behind the ears and lavished kisses on him. "Did Paine send you to protect me, knowing I would not stop going into the woods?" Bog licked her face and she laughed softly. "Come along, it will be good to have company."

Bog followed her, squeezing through the fence after her and keeping at her side. As they walked along, the sun rose brightening the sky. Hemera did not worry that Talon might have sent someone to follow her. It would not be wise of him to do so and it would have people gossiping. The thought that she and Talon would have to keep their distance from each other hurt her heart.

It was strange to feel as she did for him. She cherished her solitude and yet she wished he was there with her. She enjoyed talking with him when he was not dictating to her, but he was King so she understood his authoritative nature. Mostly though, she immensely enjoyed when he held her, kissed her, and mated with her. Never had she felt such pleasure and never had she felt... what did she feel for Talon? The question troubled her and with no answer forthcoming, she pushed it from her mind.

Bog drank from the small pool while she knelt to cup water in her hands to refresh her face. She winced as she did, feeling a slight discomfort between her legs. She was sore and the cool water would certainly dull the ache. If she took off her foot coverings and hoisted her shift, she could lower herself enough for the cold water to soothe her.

With a quick release of her cloak and hasty removal of her foot coverings, she lifted her shift high, bunching it in her hands and tucking it tightly against her middle before stepping cautiously into the pool. She gasped as a chill raced through her when the cold water grabbed at her ankles like icy hands. It took a moment for her to gather the courage to dunk down enough for the cold water to dull her soreness. The freezing sharpness of the water had her hurrying to escape the pool and in her haste, she lost her footing. She went down hard and fast, hitting the side of her head on a stone. It stunned her, almost knocking her out.

Bog was at her side immediately, dragging her by the shoulder to the shore. She lay there, gathering her senses while admonishing her own foolishness. She should have known better than to have gone into the pool. Or to linger after her feet had turned numb. It was her own fault.

The wolf was poking her with his nose and she

knew what he was trying to tell her. Get up and get warm. Something he needed to do as well, since he had braved the cold water to rescue her. She staggered to her feet, threw her cloak around her and, grabbing her foot coverings, she and Bog hurried off.

She stopped abruptly, having thought she heard something—a sound foreign to the forest— and the fur on Bog's back went up. She picked her way quietly along behind tall bushes that kept the small pool secluded, and listened. She heard voices not too far off and she motioned, with a finger to her lips, for Bog to remain quiet.

The chill that had grabbed hold of her body was beginning to numb her limbs and if she did not get moving soon and warm herself, she would be in danger of surviving or possibly losing a limb. She had seen it happen to those unwise of the way of nature.

She crept along behind the bushes and stopped when she finally heard a voice clearly.

"You have done well. We will talk again soon."

Footfalls were the only thing to follow the man's remark and Hemera could not take the chance and be seen or she could risk losing her life. However, it did not stop her from taking a cautious peek. Once again she caught the back of one of the King's personal guards' cloaks, a good distance away. Peeking in the opposite direction revealed nothing, though not trusting that the person the traitor had met with could still be lurking about, Hemera took a different path home.

She hurried into her dwelling, Bog on her heels, and she stoked the fire pit to heat the room more. Bog had shaken some of the wetness off him along their return trip home and now settled down close to the fire pit to warm himself. She had wrung her garment out and laid it on the edge of the fire pit to dry and hurried into the only other garment she had to wear. It was threadbare in places and patched in other places, but it would have to do.

She draped her cloak around her shoulders, grateful for the generosity of Anin's grandmother since she had lost her cloak after arriving here.

"Stay and get warm, my friend," she said to Bog. "I will leave the door ajar so you may leave when you wish."

Bog acknowledge her with a yawn, his eyes closing before he rested his head on his paws.

Hemera rushed through the village, drawing stares from all she passed. It was not until she joined her sister at the table she shared with Anin that she realized the stares had nothing to do with their concern for her forthcoming punishment. It was her appearance.

"What happened to you? Your hair is wet and how did you get that bruise to the side of your head?" Verity's eyes were wide with concern as she rushed to her feet and to her sister's side.

Hemera did not want her sister worrying. "A minor accident. Nothing more." She avoided further questions by saying, "I am hungry."

With an arm around her sister, Verity guided Hemera to a spot on the bench beside Anin, then sat to Hemera's other side. "The King will be here soon, so hurry and eat before..." Verity turned teary eyes away from her sister unable to bear the thought of what she would suffer.

Hemera's words echoed what she had often said to assuage her sister's fears through the years they had spent as captives of the Northmen. "All will be well, we—"

"Are free now," Verity said with a smile, remembering her sister's encouraging words. Always ending it with, *we will be free one day*. And here they were finally free.

Hemera barely finished a piece of bread when everyone rushed to their feet... the King had arrived.

King Talon entered the room from the High Council Chambers, Gelhard at his side, and Paine and Wrath making their way from behind him to join their wives at the table. Curious stares at Hemera from them both had each of them, in turn, looking to their wives, but neither offered an explanation.

"Sit!" King Talon ordered with a dismissive wave. He was busy talking with Gelhard who walked at his side.

Paine looked across the table at Hemera as he sat. "You went to the woods. Tell me Bog was with you."

"He was and he was of great help. He is sleeping in my dwelling."

"Attention!" Gelhard called out and a hush fell over the hall.

The King took the seat at the middle of the long, narrow table facing all the other tables in the feasting hall.

Hemera's hand went to her middle, having felt a strange flutter when her glance fell upon him. Stranger still was the tug at her heart that made her want to run into his arms and hug him tight. She lowered her head, her glance falling on the food on the table that no longer appealed to her, her mind heavy with thought.

"Hemera, step forward and receive your

punishment," Gelhard announced.

Verity poked her sister with her elbow when she did not move, then gave her a nudge when she still did not move.

"Hemera!"

Her head shot up at the sound of Talon's demanding voice, shattering her thoughts.

Verity helped her sister off the bench and gave her hand a squeeze as she whispered, "I am here for you."

Hemera made her way to stand in front of Gelhard who looked her up and down for a moment, shook his head, then stepped aside.

Talon's glare grew as his brow scrunched tighter and tighter. He rose and walked around the table to stand in front of her, his hands clenched together behind his back.

She did not look up at him. She could feel his anger. It burst in great waves around her, drawing her in, tumbling her around, as she fought for breath and balance. Next thing she knew, his hand gripped her arm.

"My High Council Chambers now!"

Gelhard stepped forward. "My King—"

"Not a word, Gelhard, or her punishment will be yours," the King warned and Gelhard stepped back in silence. He propelled Hemera down the middle of the feasting hall, all eyes following them.

Hemera watched as one of the King's personal guard, standing in front of the Council Chamber's door, stood aside and opened it.

"Let no one enter," Talon ordered the guard.

The door closed and Talon let her go to grab her by the shoulders and give her a slight shake. "What happened? Who gave you that bruise?"

"Why are you angry?" she asked softly and eased her shoulders away from his hands to step closer, wrap her arms around his waist, and rest her head on his chest with a sigh. "I have missed you."

Talon's insides twisted in knots and he closed his eyes as his arms wrapped around her. He could feel the chill in her body even through both their garments. He took firm hold of her and refused to let go. He closed his arms tightly around her so that the heat from his body would melt her chill away. He had missed her far more than he thought possible, but he would not tell her that. It would not be fair.

*Home.*

How was it that she felt at home in his arms? She had not felt that since... far too long.

Talon opened his eyes, scooped her up in his arms and walked to one of the long benches at the table and sat, settling her in his lap and keeping her close, so that his heat could continue to soak into her body and warm her.

He took hold of her chin with his one hand and turned her face to examine the bruise at her temple more closely. "Tell me," he said, an ember of anger marking his words.

Hemera kissed his lips lightly.

"You play with fire when you do that, woman," Talon warned, feeling his body flaring to life and it annoyed him since there seemed to be no controlling himself when around her.

"I miss your lips on mine," she said and kissed him ever so gently.

"Hemera!" Talon warned sharply, forcing his lips

away from hers.

"I went to the woods," she began.

His temper sparked in his eyes. "I have warned you—"

"I was not alone."

His brow shot up, jealousy rearing its head.

"Bog went with me," —she was quick to say— "he dragged me out of the pond when I fell and hit my head on a rock."

Talon felt a vicious stab to his heart. It pierced him so sharply that he wanted to roar with the pain—the pain that he could have lost her.

Hemera gripped his arm, her eyes turning wide with a spark of excitement. "The traitor made another appearance in the woods and he was not alone. I heard a man praise the traitor for a task well done."

That news twisted Talon's middle in knots. She was forever placing herself in harm's way and it had to stop or endless worry for her would drive him mad. How to do that, though, was a question he had yet to find and answer to, especially since she had won the wager they had made and he had been forced to keep his word.

"When I peeked past the bushes, I saw the back of one of your personal guards' cloaks, though the person was too far away for me to see anything clearly. I saw no one else when I peeked further around. Still, I took a different path home just to be safe."

"You should not have been in the woods in the first place and however did you fall in the small pond?"

"I was sore from our frequent mating last night and hoped to ease the discomfort with the chilled water."

*Guilt.* How was it that this woman could so easily

make him feel guilty when he had rarely if ever felt guilty before she had entered his life?

"Are you feeling better?" he asked, hoping she healed not only because he did not wish to have her suffer, but also because he was looking forward to coupling with her again tonight. And guilt struck him again for even thinking it.

"The cold pond water took the ache away since I soaked in it longer than I intended," she said with a soft laugh.

He brushed his lips over hers and though it pained him to say it, he said, "I will not visit with you tonight so that you may continue to heal."

She gasped and threw her arms around his neck, shackling herself to him. "Nay, you cannot do that. My body aches for you now. I cannot bear to think how I will feel if it is not until the morrow that we join once again."

Her eagerness to join with him stirred an ache in him and he grew aroused. He had to stop this now.

Her words echoed his thoughts. "If we do not leave here soon, I will spread myself naked on this table for you."

Talon had her off his lap in an instant, the image her remark had created too vivid in his mind to ignore.

"Back into the hall," he ordered sharply and turned to walk to the door, then stopped and returned to her. He cupped her face in his hands and kissed her, his tongue delving into her mouth as he imagined her spread naked on the table, his manhood thrusting into her.

He tore his mouth away from hers and said, "Tonight you will not sleep." He turned and walked to the door.

Before he could open it, she said from behind him, "Will you be up to it?"

He turned and when he saw her smiling, a smile easily came to his lips. "Is that a challenge?"

She leaned close to him and whispered, "A hope."

He swung open the door, not trusting himself to remain there with her a moment longer and walked out for her to follow behind him. All eyes once again were on them and Hemera kept her head down, fearful the smile she kept locked away would escape.

She came to a halt as Talon took a stand in front of the long table and raised her head to look at him, keeping her lips pursed tight to keep herself from smiling.

Gelhard hurried to stand off to the King's side as the punishment was announced.

"Hemera, I have amended your punishment. You will work with the cook for five sunrises doing whatever chore assigned you."

## Chapter Twelve

"There were tracks where you said there would be, though they were too marred by animal prints to be able to follow," Paine said, filling his vessel with wine from the flask on the table, then handed it to Wrath seated across from him.

Wrath spoke as he filled his vessel. "That area by the pond is difficult to keep watch over. It is dense with trees and foliage even at this time when buds are just sprouting."

Talon listened to his friends, having sent them to inspect the area Hemera had told him about and see if they could find anything.

"If there is one traitor in the stronghold, there could be more," Wrath warned. "What troubles me even more though is how long this traitor has been among us and how close he may be to you, Talon."

"I agree," Paine said. "You must remain vigilant to all around you and trust few."

"You know me well enough, Paine, to know that I trust no one beyond you and Wrath."

*Hemera.*

Her name tolled in his head. He trusted her. There was no doubt in that and why he believed it so he could not say, although perhaps, it was because she spoke with honesty, whether one wanted to hear it or not.

"We do not know what kind of damage this traitor is doing. He needs to be caught so that we can find out what he knows," Paine said.

"He has been successful in avoiding detection so far and I wonder why that is," Talon said.

"He blends with others," Paine suggested.

Wrath offered his opinion. "He shows himself to be no different than others here. He makes us believe he is one of us. How, when everyone looks the same, do we find the one that is different?"

The three men grew silent, giving the difficult question thought.

A hard tap at the door had Talon, bidding the person to enter.

Tarnis, one of the King's personal guards entered the Council Chambers. "Forgive me, my King, but the cook says it is important and that he must speak with you immediately."

*Hemera.*

The name entered all three men's minds.

Talon waved his consent and when the cook entered he was quick to ask, "What is the problem, Nock?"

Nock twisted his hands in front of his thick waist. He was shorter than most men with a thatch of red hair on top of his head and the sides shorn, defining him part of the servant class. His pudgy face was pleasant to look upon, particularly since he smiled all the time, though he was not smiling now.

"I beg you, my King, please remove Hemera from my cookhouse."

"Why?" Talon demanded with a sharpness that startled Nock and had sweat beads breaking out along his brow.

Nock kept a cautious tone to his words. "Hemera

pays no heed to my commands. She makes changes without my consent and—"

"What changes?" Talon asked curious.

"She tells me that scraps of food should not be dropped on the floor for the dogs to scavenge. She placed baskets at various spots by the cutting table and instructed my servants to deposit the scrapes in them. She chased the dogs outside and refused to let them back in, telling the servants to dump the food scraps outside for them that the dogs would learn to wait for them."

Talon noticed the smile that caught the edges of Paine's mouth. Come to think of it, Paine had been smiling a lot whenever Hemera's name was mentioned.

"Hemera also had the servants scrub the cutting table with heated water that she added herbs to and told them to do it after each cutting of the meat." Nock shook his head. "Then she tells them that vegetables should be cut on a separate table from the meat and sees a table prepared for it. When I threaten that I would see her whipped for her failure to obey me, she told me that I did not have the authority to make that decision."

"Hemera is right," Talon snapped. "You do not have that authority."

"Forgive me, my King, I know that I do not, but I was so frustrated with her that I did not know what to do." He ran his shirt sleeve across his sweaty brow. "She also had leaves of a plant I am not familiar with added to the stew that cooks and I fear how it will taste, or that it may poison everyone."

Wrath spoke up. "How has she accomplished all this in such a short time?"

Nock shook his head again. "I do not know.

Everyone seemed to follow her lead without question, though she did explain that the changes would make for better tasting food."

"Then we will see if she is correct when the evening meal is served," Talon said.

Nock twisted his hands tighter. "Please, my King, I fear—"

"Hemera's punishment stays."

"But, my King—"

"I will hear no more from you, Nock," Talon ordered sternly.

Nock bobbed his head. "As you say, my King, but there is one more thing."

"What is it?" Talon snapped annoyed.

"Hemera insisted that the size hole in the cookhouse dwelling was not adequate enough for the smoke to escape."

"I will have Paine look at it," Talon said.

Nock sighed heavily. "I told Hemera the same, but she believed it was too important to wait for Paine to have a look."

Talon hurried to his feet. "What did she do?"

"Hemera is on the roof, widening the hole."

Talon cursed and marched toward the door, Paine and Wrath following quickly behind him and Nock moving nervously out of their way to wait and trail behind them.

Talon's heart slammed against his chest when he caught sight of Hemera up on the thatched roof, on her knees, with a saw in her hand.

"Hemera!" Talon cursed himself when she startled and stopped herself from falling over and off the roof.

"You might want to try talking more calmly to

her," Paine suggested and received a scowl from Talon that stabbed at him like a sharp knife, though did not penetrate... a smile being his shield.

Talon came to stand a short distance away from the ladder leaning against the roof. His voice remained strong, though he did not bellow at her. "Get down from there now, Hemera."

"I am not finished yet," she said and returned to her task, her head looking as if it disappeared down the hole.

"You are finished!" Talon ordered with a shout.

"I do not think she heard you," Paine said and locked his lips tight to prevent himself from laughing.

When the King headed around the dwelling, Wrath jabbed his friend in the arm. "You are not helping the situation."

Paine released his laugh. "No, I am not, but I am enjoying it."

Talon entered the cookhouse and the servants scurried to a corner. He looked up at the hole to see Hemera's face almost sticking through it. "You are finished!"

"Nay, I am not," she said, her head tilting a bit to the right. "I little more off this side and I should be done."

"You are done now! Paine will see to the rest."

The servants in the corner cringed at the King's forceful tone.

"I will be done quickly enough."

The servants cringed again, hearing her defy the King.

Talon stormed out of the cookhouse and returned to the ladder, placing his foot on the bottom rung.

"My King, let me," Wrath said, stepping forward, fearful for Hemera.

A threatening glare had Wrath halting his step.

Talon climbed the ladder quickly, stopping on a rung when the middle of his chest met the edge of the roof. "Come here now, Hemera!"

Hemera turned with a smile. "I have no need of help. I am finished."

Talon raised his hand and summoned her with one finger.

Hemera cautiously eased her bottom along the roof until she reached him.

"The saw," he ordered his hand stretched out to her. She handed it to him and he dropped it to the ground. "I am going to place you over my shoulder and carry you to the ground."

Hemera stared at him, tilted her head, stared some more, then strained her neck to look over the edge. "That would not be wise."

"Why?" he asked annoyed that he did.

"The ladder will not hold both of us."

"The ladder is sturdy enough," Talon said and held his hand out to her.

"It is worn with time and you would do well to climb down, for it surely feels your bulk," she warned with concern.

"You try my patience."

Hemera leaned closer to whisper, "I worry for you and a crowd gathers. Do you truly wish your people to see their King crash to the ground?"

"We will not crash to the ground," he said his patience growing shorter. "Now come here to me."

Hemera moved closer. "If I am right, and we crash

to the ground, will you suspend my punishment?"

"This is one wager I will win and gladly gloat when I do."

Hemera smiled and moved closer. "Do not let me land on my head when we fall."

He looped his arm around her waist. "It is my hand that will land on your backside after we climb down." He eased her over his shoulder and stepped one rung down. He was about to take another step when he heard the snap and felt the ladder give.

In a split moment, Talon yanked Hemera off his shoulder, wrapped his arms around her, and twisted his body so that he would take the brunt of the fall.

Talon felt the jolt to his back as he hit the ground hard. Hemera landed secure and safe in his arms on top of him.

Wrath and Paine were at their sides, Wrath helping Hemera up and Paine offering his hand to the King.

Talon brushed it aside. He needed no help and he would never show weakness in front of his people.

"Hemera!"

Talon heard the fear in Verity's voice before he saw it in her eyes and he swerved around to look at Hemera. Blood was pouring from her mouth, down her chin, and onto her garment. He rushed to her side.

Hemera brought her torn sleeve to her mouth to try and staunch the flow of blood. She needed to stop the bleeding, stop it from dripping down her throat, stop the taste of it. Stop the memories of the last time she had tasted blood on her lips.

Hemera paid no heed to those around her, trying desperately to dispel the memories that roiled her stomach unmercifully.

"She needs the healer," Verity cried as she hurried to her sister's side.

It was not Verity that Hemera looked to when she felt herself about to heave or who she reached out to.

Talon grabbed hold of Hemera's hand, hurried his arm around her waist, and rushed her around the side of the cookhouse, ordering the others to, "Stay where you are."

His arm went around her middle as she bent over and her insides released all that was in there. When there was no more left to come out, Talon ripped the torn sleeve off her arm and wiped her mouth, then eased her up to rest back against him for a moment before lifting her in his arms.

He came around the cookhouse and issued orders. "Get the healer, a fresh bucket of water," —he looked to Verity— "and a clean garment for her."

With Talon having dispersed the crowd that had gathered and the cookhouse not far from the feasting house that was now empty, few if any saw him carry Hemera inside and into the Council Chambers.

Talon wanted to lock everyone out of the chambers and tend Hemera himself, but that could not be and he was glad Paine followed in not far behind them, or he would have been much too tempted to do just that. He carried two buckets of water, one full and the other half full. Paine knew, just as Talon and Wrath did, that Hemera would need to rinse the blood from her mouth repeatedly until the bleeding stopped. Mouth wounds always bleed profusely, but more often than not, stopped in good time.

Talon no soon as sat her on the bench, when voices were heard approaching the room.

Hemera hurried to take hold of his hand and gave it a tight squeeze, her eyes begging him not to leave her.

His heart felt as if it would explode from his chest, he ached so badly to give her what they both wanted... time alone together. Instead, he offered her what he could.

"Later," he whispered and he was glad to see her smile, though got angry when she winced from the pain and blood that ran from her mouth.

Verity rushed to her sister as soon as she entered along with Anin. Bethia, the healer, followed soon after.

Gelhard followed them in and waited by the door, a frown on his face.

Talon reluctantly left Hemera, walking out of the room in forceful strides and Gelhard hurrying to keep up.

Paine and Wrath caught up with the two men in the feasting hall.

"She is a problem," Gelhard said. "No matter what is done with her she continues to be a problem. She needs a husband to keep her in tow. Join her with Bower and be done with it."

Talon stepped toward Gelhard. "I do not recall asking for your advice."

"But I give it nonetheless, as a good High Counselor is expected to do. I only ask that you give it thought, my King, for when the future queen arrives, it will be she who requires your attention and not a witless woman." Gelhard bowed his head and hurried off before the King could make his annoyance known.

Paine stepped forward. "Shall I inform Nock that Hemera will not return to the cookhouse until tomorrow?"

*If I am right, and we crash to the ground, will you suspend my punishment?*

Her words had returned to haunt him as did his. *This is one wager I will win and gladly gloat when I do.*

"Tell Nock that I have granted his request. Hemera will not be returning to the cookhouse."

"You will amend her punishment again?" Wrath asked worried that his wife would once again be concerned for her sister.

"I will find something that will keep her out of trouble," Talon said.

Paine laughed. "Good luck with that."

~~~

Talon sat at the long table in the feasting hall not touching the food in front of him. He wanted the evening done, well at least this part of the evening. The rest he would spend with Hemera. She had challenged him earlier, asking if he was up to mating tonight. He had never thought she might not be, but that did not matter. He wanted time with her, to hold her close, feel her warmth, drink in her sweet scent.

"I guess Nock was wrong about us all being poisoned and Hemera was right. The food was tastier than usual," Paine said, sitting down beside him.

Talon had not tried the stew, though he did now, scooping up a chunk of meat with bread. It was tasty and he suddenly found himself hungry.

"Are you saving yourself for your new queen?" Paine asked.

Talon leaned back in his chair with a glare that

would have had most men shivering.

Paine continued speaking. "I have noticed that you have not taken a woman to your chambers in," —he rubbed his chin, tilted his head, and scrunched his eyes as if thinking— "for some time now."

Talon's glare deepened.

A flicker of humor sparked in Paine's eyes as he smiled and said, "Who is the woman you keep hidden from everyone? And do not bother to tell me I am wrong. Everyone knows you do not go long without a woman. If I see it, then so do others."

Talon leaned forward, planting his face not far from Paine's. "It is not yours or anyone else's concern."

"Your future queen may think differently."

Paine's words had Talon's temper flaring at the thought of not being with Hemera.

"Do I need to come between you two?"

Talon looked to see Wrath standing in front of the table.

"Curious eyes are beginning to drift your way since it appears as if the executioner and King are arguing," Wrath said, keeping his voice low.

"Paine is no longer my executioner," Talon said with a curt tongue.

Wrath turned a questioning glare on Talon. "Is he still your friend?"

"Always," the King said without hesitation.

"It is as a friend I shared my opinion," Paine said all trace of humor gone. "Be careful, Talon, it will not be you who suffers for your overindulgences."

Talon thought on Paine's words as the evening wore on endlessly. What did it matter what the future queen thought? Their union was for one reason and one reason only, for her to produce an heir to the Pict throne. She probably would be grateful he had another woman so she would not have to suffer his touch.

What of Hemera, though? She would be relegated to the shadows, never able to walk by his side for all to see that he cared for her.

*Cared.*

Did he truly care for her? He had cared for no woman he had joined with over time. He treated them well, satisfied them, but care? Once he parted from them he had given them no thought until the urge to mate struck him again.

Hemera was different. He could not get her out of his mind. She was there all the time and he found himself having to catch a smile from surfacing for no reason except that he had thought of her. Oddly enough that had been before they had coupled. She had entered his head often and for no reason. He did not know what it had been about her that he had been drawn to... her peculiar nature perhaps, her stark honesty, her lovely lips, her body that curved so nicely?

He forced his thoughts away from her since he was beginning to grow aroused and looked over the feasting hall. Paine and Anin were talking and laughing with Wrath and Verity while other warriors did the same with their wives and single warriors were trying to entice single women to their sleeping pallets for the night. Broc had been having success lately with Simca, but then she pleased herself with many of the warriors as some of the women were wont to do.

He had done the same many times with the willing women, yet now he found himself wanting only one.

*Hemera.*

He was growing impatient for the evening to end. He needed the village asleep for the night so that he could finally go to Hemera. No one could see him. No one could know.

Heaviness captured his heart and flared his anger. He stood abruptly, rushing everyone to their feet and taking quick steps he climbed the stairs and disappeared into his sleeping chambers.

There he waited impatiently and when all seemed quiet, he opened his door and stepped out past the two guards who kept watch at his door until morn. He walked to his private chamber and took a glance down at the feasting hall. He could not see all of it, but what he did see pleased him.

It was empty. He could go to Hemera now.

"Let no one disturb me," Talon ordered the guards as he entered his sleeping chamber and once the door closed he took the secret passage down and stepped out to be swallowed by the shadows of the night and make his way to Hemera.

## Chapter Thirteen

Hemera sat on the edge of her sleeping pallet, her lip quite sore. She had suffered such an injury more than once, her tooth having jabbed into her lower lip from a hard blow to her mouth. It would bleed profusely at first, then stop, and then need time to heal, the soreness lingering. While she had experienced it before, this time was different. This time her injury would prevent her from kissing Talon until it healed, which left her with a heavy heart. She enjoyed kissing him and the feelings that followed, and she so wanted to explore those feelings more.

She was eager for his arrival tonight and hoped any moment he would walk through the door. That she missed him as much as she did continued to surprise her. Her solitude was something she cherished and yet now she cherished time with Talon more.

A sudden chill sent gooseflesh running over her and though the fire roared in the fire pit, she added a bit more kindling. She also wrapped one of the blankets around her naked body. Her garment had been unsalvageable between its worn spots and the blood that had stained it. She had only one garment now, but somehow she would find a way to rectify that.

Her impatience had her pacing by the fire pit, its crackles and heat soothing and it made her aware of the many aches left to her from the fall. She needed rest, but she needed Talon more and the thought that he came before all else halted her pacing. How could someone make such a difference in her life in such a short time?

The door suddenly opened and Talon entered and for a brief moment, no more than a blink of an eye, Hemera's heart caught in relief. He had returned to her. She let the blanket fall and went to him.

Talon hurried forward to meet her, his arms circling her, bringing her close, feeling the slight chill of her flesh and wrapping himself around her to keep her tucked safe and warm against him. She belonged there in his arms, in his bed, always beside him and he almost flinched when he felt a piercing stab at his heart that it could never be.

"You are chilled," he said and lifted her in his arms and carried her to place gently on the sleeping pallet.

Hemera moved, leaving enough room for him to slip in beside her. She was about to protest when he stepped away from the pallet, fearful that he did not intend to join her, but stilled her words when she watched him quickly shed his garments.

He climbed in beside her and took her in his arms once again, his hand drifting down along her back, caressing the scars that flared his anger every time he touched them. He would have his revenge against the person who had beaten her unmercifully and he would see him suffer far worse before taking his life.

Hemera enjoyed his touch more than she could say. It was tender yet strong, caring yet sensual, and she had missed it in the short time they had been separated.

She tilted her head up off his chest. "You suffered no wounds in the fall?"

"No more than an ache or two, and they trouble me

little," he admitted, having suffered far worse falls and bruises. "Lips bleed more than they need to when inured. Your lip will heal in time."

"It has before and it will again."

His hand at her back moved to her waist and gave it a tender squeeze. "What do you mean it has before?"

"I have suffered such an injury a few times before."

"How many times?" he asked curious and concerned it had been no accident but a forceful blow.

"Three maybe four," she said.

"Tell me," he ordered.

"Not now," she said on a sigh. "We have little time together and I do not want to waste it on memories better left alone."

She was right. They had precious little time together to waste. "There will come a time when—"

"I will tell you," she said softly and brought her lips to his neck to nibble on.

Talon almost stopped her—almost—but her teeth nipping at his flesh stirred his passion that had already risen to the surface. He lay still, his eyes closed, and let her have her way, let his passion soar.

He felt her gasp in the sudden tautness of her body against his before he heard it. His hands took hold of her shoulders, easing her away from him. He cursed aloud when he saw blood running down her mouth.

"I will clean the blood from you," Hemera rushed to say, seeing the anger in his eyes.

Talon had her on her back so fast that her eyes looked as though they would pop from her head. "You will stay put," he ordered and left the bed to return with a cloth and the fresh bucket of water her sister had left near the fire pit.

Hemera lay quiet as he saw to cleaning the blood from her mouth, dunking the cloth and rinsing it after each gentle stroke. His every touch was thoughtful, almost as if he was fearful of somehow harming her.

"You should not have been on that roof," he scolded.

"You should have listened to me," she reprimanded.

His hand stilled. "Are you saying I am at fault?"

"Aye, I told you the ladder would not hold us both."

"If you had listened to me when I told you to get down off the roof—"

"I was not finished," she interrupted.

Talon leaned his face close to hers. "You were finished when I told you that you were finished."

She tapped him on the nose. "But I was not finished and I could not leave the chore undone."

"You can when the King orders you to do so," he argued and grabbed her finger so she could not tap his nose again.

"It was a nonsensical order. It was much wiser to finish what I had started, since I was already on the roof." She scrunched her brow. "I do not think Nock likes his task as cook."

"All were given preference to chores of their choosing when possible."

"Not Nock," she insisted.

Talon went to disagree, but a quick kiss from her silenced him, though brought a wince from her.

"You will not kiss me," he demanded with a sternness that had her frowning. Guilt rushed up to stab at him and he found himself explaining before he could stop himself. "Until your lip heals you will not kiss me." Her frown remained and he leaned down to kiss her cheek. "I will lavish your body with enough kisses for us both." That brought a smile to her face. He kissed her other cheek. "You will promise me you will stay off roofs." She stared at him and he waited, knowing she was thinking and would not speak until her thoughts were clear.

It was not long before she said, "I cannot promise you, for I know not what the future holds. If something necessitated my climbing up on a roof, I would not want a promise holding me back, especially a promise I made to you." She could not stop a yawn from surfacing or the wince that followed it.

"You need rest," he said.

"I need you," she whispered and pressed her cheek to his, wishing she could kiss him, but her blood already stained his neck. She took the cloth from his hand after reluctantly moving her face away from his and tenderly wiped her blood off his neck. She kept her eyes on his as she stretched her arm out, until her hand hung off the edge of the pallet and she let the cloth drop, hearing it splash in the bucket of water, then she placed her hand upon his chest. "Mate with me."

He wanted more than anything to stretch over her, keeping his body just above hers as he slipped slowly and deliberately into her and once snug inside her, he would take her nipple in his mouth and tease it with his tongue. He wanted nothing more than to do that, but her puffy, red lip, the tiredness that dimmed her lovely green eyes and another yawn warned that she was not up to mating.

He did not want to deny her or himself, but he also wanted what was best for her and at the moment it was not mating. He stayed as he was sitting beside her and ran a slow, gentle hand over her cheek and down along her neck.

"You are tired and should rest a while. We have time," he said in a soft whisper.

Hemera sighed, his touch more caring than carnal. "Not enough time," she argued on a yawn.

Talon smiled at her fight to keep her eyes open as he continued stroking her face and neck, his plan of lulling her to sleep proving successful. "Plenty of time," he whispered. "Close your eyes at least for a few moments."

"A few moments only," she said as her eyes fluttered closed.

Talon continued caressing her until he was certain she slept soundly. He sat there staring at her, thinking how he had never denied himself or a woman pleasure, and though he ached for her, had grown hard with the need for her, his first concern was for her well-being.

He cared for this woman more than he should. He could try and deny it, but to what purpose? Fear had gripped him like never before when the ladder had broken and sent him and Hemera tumbling. His only thought was of keeping her from harm.

With a faint touch, like a feather delicately brushing over flesh, he ran his finger over her injured lip. That he had not succeeded tormented him. He had hit the ground hard, sending a jolt through his body, but he had given it no thought. His only concern had been for Hemera.

He had known little caring in his life, his mum

having died when he was young and his father a hard task master. His da had taught him many things that had served him well and he had insisted Talon was meant for greater things and that the time would come when he would rule the Picts. He had warned him to guard his heart against caring too deeply, for a caring heart never ruled wisely.

Memories had Talon leaving Hemera's side and standing near the fire pit. He had guarded his heart well and his father's words had proven wise. No decision had proven difficult to him...until Hemera. No amount of guarding his heart had mattered. She had managed to chip away at every wall and shield he had constructed. Since her arrival several moon cycles ago, her innocent and honest nature had challenged him at every turn and to his surprise he had begun to enjoy their encounters. He had actually found himself looking forward to them, a warning sign he should not have ignored.

Talon turned and looked at Hemera sleeping peacefully. Even with her swollen lip, she was beautiful even more so having suffered her injury without complaint and still wanting to kiss him when it pained her to do so. She was an extraordinary woman, though some thought otherwise. They thought her slow in mind and while there were times she took the time to think on things, her mind was far from slow.

He turned away from her. He should have never touched her and if he had not allowed his heart to rule him, he never would have touched her. It was not a difficult decision. He should leave her be before someone discovered they had mated or worse...that he cared for her.

"Talon."

His name was a bare, yet urgent whisper on her lips and he did not hesitate... he went to her. He slipped in beside her and she snuggled and settled quietly against him as his arms wrapped protectively around her.

He rested his cheek on the top of her head, the familiar sweet scent that always permeated her rushing up his nose and pleasing his senses. He could fight it all he wanted to, but in the end it would always remain the same.

*Mine.*

Hemera belonged to him and he would never let her go.

~~~

Hemera woke and rubbed the sleep from her eyes to make sure what she saw was not a dream. Talon was hurrying into his garments. "You are leaving?" she asked upset. "We have not mated."

A twinge of guilt hit him as he finished dressing. "I slept far too late. Dawn is almost upon us."

Hemera threw the blanket off her.

"Do not come near me!"

His stern order halted her and brought a frown to her face.

"I want you as badly as you want me, but I want our secret to remain a secret more badly than anything or else our time together may come to an abrupt end."

"What difference does it make if it is known that I am the woman who warms your sleeping pallet? I have no plans to ever wed and if you grow tired of me or I grow tired of you, we can part ways."

Talon gave not a thought to his actions, he went to her, grabbing her arm and lifting her to her knees. "You are mine and will always remain mine."

Hemera did not know why his words sent a thrill through her when he could not possibly know what the future held for them.

"You will get no sleep tonight when I return," he said and hurried to the door. Her naked body was much too distracting and much too inviting. He had to leave or he risked mating with her and risked them being discovered.

"That is too long to go without you." She grew silent, turning her head to the fire pit to stare at the flames.

Talon had to leave, he could not stay watching her naked, kneeling on the sleeping pallet, her back arched slightly, her breasts thrusting forward, her nipples hard—he turned his head before turning his whole body and reaching for the door.

"Meet me at the pond just after mid-morn," she called out to him.

He swerved around. "You are not to go into the woods alone."

She smiled. "I cannot wait until tonight to feel you inside me. Meet me at the pond."

His anger, desire, frustration came out in a growling rumble. "Do not disobey me on this." He turned once again and finally left the dwelling.

Talon stalked the shadows that were quickly fading with the light that suddenly peeked in the sky. If he did not quicken his steps, he would soon be discovered and while none would know of his time with Hemera, there would be questions of how he left his sleeping chambers without being seen.

He made it through the hidden door just as light

sprung over the land and, not long after, he left his sleeping quarters to take his morning fare in the feasting hall for all to see him. Gelhard joined him shortly after he sat.

"How proves the skies this morn?" Talon asked.

"Pleasant enough. Do not forget the High Council meeting at mid-morn."

*Meet me just after mid-morn.*

Talon shook his head, trying to chase her tempting words away.

"There will be no High Council meeting this morn?" Gelhard asked.

"No... aye," Talon said, shaking his head again. "There will be a council meeting. My thoughts were on another matter."

"Is all well, my King?" Gelhard asked his voice a whisper.

"Everything is fine, Gelhard," Talon assured him.

Gelhard cleared his throat.

"Have your say and be done with it so I may enjoy my meal," Talon ordered, familiar enough with the man to know his throat clearing was a sign of his hesitation to approach a matter.

Gelhard spoke bluntly. "You have not taken a woman to your sleeping pallet in some time."

Talon's blue eyes burned bright with annoyance. "That does not concern you, Gelhard."

"Forgive me, my King, but it does when there is damaging gossip."

"What is being said now?"

"Some fear you are ill, not having produced an heir, and now having no interest in coupling," Gelhard explained.

"I am surprised they are not complaining that I grow soft since I changed Hemera's punishment."

"That is one thing they seemed pleased with," Gelhard said with a nod. "The people thought it good of you to spare her such an ordeal since she has a slow mind and does not understand things. The people also think it is good of you to find her a husband that would see to her care."

That annoyed Talon more than the people thinking him ill, especially since he could not rescind the edict he had put forth. How he would stop it, he did not know. He did know that Hemera would not wed anyone.

Right now Gelhard needed reassuring. "All is well with me. There is no cause for alarm. I await my future queen with great impatience."

Gelhard cleared his throat again.

"Do not tell me there is a further delay with the future queen's arrival."

Gelhard spilled it out fast. "She is still not well enough to travel."

"This does not pose well for her. I want a strong woman. A fearless woman. A woman to match my strength and courage."

"That is not possible, my King. Such a woman does not exist."

*Hemera.*

Talon bit his tongue, keeping from saying her name aloud. A sudden thought came to him. She was of Pict blood, why not wed her?

*No one would approve.* His own answer annoyed him.

They believed her slow-minded and her mother had

birthed two daughters, no sons. She would not be considered a good candidate to be queen, and his enemies would use her against him.

"Continue your search for a queen," Talon ordered with anger bubbling inside him.

"What of the one already chosen?" Gelhard asked.

"I will meet with her and see if she is fit to be queen. In the meantime, you will search for another woman to take the other's place if she should prove unworthy."

"A wise choice, my King," Gelhard said.

"A necessary one," Talon corrected.

Talon discussed a few more issues with Gelhard and when the High Council members began arriving Talon and Gelhard convened with them in the High Council Chambers. Several matters were discussed and decisions made. No progress was being made on finding out the leader of the group who opposed the King.

Talon hoped he would hear from some of the men he had planted in various places to see what they could learn, especially Vard. He was a trusted warrior of Egot, chieftain of the Ancrum Tribe and Talon's uncle. Vard had infiltrated one of the opposing groups and the last time Talon had spoken with him, he had been close to meeting the head leader. It had been some time since last he had heard from him and hoped the loyal warrior was well and unharmed and that he would receive a message soon.

"Many are pleased to see that Hemera and Bower are spending time together. He will make her a good husband and keep her in tow."

Talon turned to Ebit, having heard what he said to

Gelhard. He fought down the anger that rushed up and almost choked his words. "You saw Hemera and Bower together?"

"Aye, my King, they went for a walk in the woods." Ebit smiled. "Hemera had hold of his arm and Bower wore a pleasant smile. They are a good match."

Talon stood suddenly, his chair almost tumbling over if Gelhard had not grabbed it quickly. "This meeting is done. I have matters to see to."

No one took note of the King's sudden dismissal. He was wont to do that at times. What did surprise them was that he stormed out of the Council Chamber before any one of them did. Usually he was the last to leave or he would spend time alone in the chambers, working on one of his many building projects.

Talon ordered the two personal guards assigned to him for the morn not to follow him. "You will wait here." When Tarnis went to speak, a quick raise of Talon's hand silenced him. "I will hear no excuses and I will give none. Do not follow me."

Talon made his way through the village, ignoring the unusually bright sun and the touch of warmth in the air. He also paid no heed to the people who bobbed their heads respectfully while rushing out of his path. It was obvious to them that their King was in a foul mood, his hardened frown and scrunched brow confirming it.

He had had an escape exit made in the fence and a storage dwelling built in front of it to make it easier for him to take his leave when he wished or if escape became necessary. Escape was now necessary.

Talon's strides were quick and determined as he made his away along in the woods. He thought he knew where Hemera would be and he followed his instincts.

As he got closer to the area, he thought he heard laughter.

That she should be enjoying herself with another man infuriated him. That she was in the woods when he had forbidden her to come here enraged him even more. But that anger did not come close to the rage that filled him when he spied Hemera and Bower a short distance ahead, rolling around on the ground together.

## Chapter Fourteen

"You must lie on your back and study the branches overhead if you are to know which ones will serve you well," Hemera explained. "The young sturdy branches will make the best bows, but you cannot just take your axe to a branch and cut it from its source of life without asking permission. Everything here in the forest has a voice and will tell you all you need to know if you listen carefully."

"You believe the forest speaks to you?" Bower asked, his brow wrinkling in confusion.

"Everything speaks to us," she said and patted the ground. "Put your hand on the earth and see what it says to you."

Bower hesitated, feeling foolish, but surrendered to her whim or it could have been her exuberant smile that had him yielding.

"Feel its chill? By now you must feel it in your body as well, the layer of pine needles beneath us not sufficient to protect us from the cold the ground continues to harbor." Hemera suddenly cocked her head to the left, something catching her eye. Her arm swung up from her side and pointed. "There that branch where the squirrel sits. It will make a bow fit for a king."

She scrambled to get to her feet and lost her footing. Bower tried to hurry to his feet to help her, but instead he bumped into her legs, causing her to completely lose her balance and topple over. His hand shot out, trying to grab her and stop her from slamming against the ground, but rapid momentum dragged him along with her and sent them both into a roll.

"What goes on here?" The thunderous roar sent the nearby animals scurrying, birds fleeing the trees, and Hemera and Bower falling over each other.

Nostrils flaring, jaw tightening, anger ready to burst in flames from his eyes, Talon took hasty steps over to the entangled couple, his hand closing powerfully around Hemera's upper arm and yanking her away from Bower to stand beside him, though he gave her no choice since he kept tight hold of her.

"Get up!" Talon ordered Bower and the man hurried to his feet, not able to hide the tremble that quivered his body. Talon attempted to keep the deep anger out of his voice, but his snarling timbre sounded much worse. "Explain your actions!"

"Bower made a gallant attempt to stop me from falling," Hemera said.

Talon snapped his head to the side to look at Hemera and, seeing twigs and pine needles sticking out of her hair flaming as red as a setting sun, grew furious that another man had laid hands on her. "I did not ask you and did I not order you to stay out of the woods?"

"Alone," Hemera reminded, "and I obeyed. I did not go into the woods alone. Bower escorted me."

Talon had negotiated peace with various tribes, arranged trading agreements with leaders of foreign lands, settled endless disputes amongst his people, yet this supposedly slow-minded woman had managed to outwit him at every turn.

"Bower has been kind and gallant," Hemera said.

It was not what Talon wanted to hear. He was

looking for an excuse to order Bower to stay away from Hemera and here she stood, defending the man.

"And Hemera has been most gracious," Bower said in her defense.

"See to your chores, Bower," Talon ordered sharply and was surprised when the man hesitated to take his leave. "You hesitate to obey me?"

"I wait to escort Hemera back to the stronghold," Bower was quick to explain.

Talon was impressed that though the man was obviously fearful of him, he had not allowed his fear to stop him from protecting Hemera even from the King himself. But Talon was King and he owed no explanation to anyone. His sharp response reflected that. "Leave us!"

Bower bobbed his head, turned, and with quick strides was soon gone from sight.

"Why are you angry at Bower?" Hemera asked. "He was doing what you gave him permission to do, seeking my company with thought of marriage."

Talon brought his face close to hers and with a harsh whisper said, "Do you actually think I would ever let you wed anyone?"

Hemera stared at him a moment before she gave a slight shake of her head. "That matters not, since I have told you often I will not wed."

"If I command it, you will," he said, as if pronouncing it an edict.

She stared at him again and shook her head more strenuously this time. "That makes no sense. You all but tell me you will never let me wed and now you say if you command it I must obey. And do you realize that your grip is painful to my arm?"

Talon dropped his hand off her as if her flesh suddenly scorched him. He almost apologized but held his tongue. He was King. He apologized to no one.

"The forest often has eyes and ears we cannot see. We should go to the secluded pond where little can be heard or seen."

Talon walked ahead of her in response and Hemera followed.

Once in the safety of the secluded area, Talon pulled Hemera into his arms and kissed her gently, mindful of her wound. He meant it to be a quick kiss, but once his lips touched hers all was lost. She was familiar in so many ways to him that when her arms wrapped around him, it felt as if she had welcomed him home, and he never wanted to leave.

He moved his lips to her neck as he slipped his hand inside her cloak, running them down along her back, imagining her naked in his arms. His hands went to her backside and gave her soft bottom a gentle squeeze as he maneuvered her to fit against his arousal.

She whispered in his ear, "I have missed you terribly. Do not make me wait to have you inside me."

Her words fueled his desire as quick as a flame to a wick and he bit back the oaths ready to spew from his lips that she should fire his loins so easily. His passion controlled him when it came to Hemera and that could prove dangerous, yet at the moment, he did not care. His only thought was of burying himself inside her and bringing them both to pleasure.

Hemera kept her lips closed tightly to keep a moan from rushing out and ringing through the forest as Talon's hands cupped her bottom, lifting her. She forced another moan from surfacing when he braced her against the trunk of a tree. She hurried her hands to help him get her garment out of the way before her hands went to push his tunic up.

She turned her head to the side, closed her eyes, and fought to keep her moans from escaping. The tip of his manhood sunk into her wetness as his teeth came down on her exposed neck and his teeth sunk into the soft flesh to tease it with sensual nips

Her eyes flew open and she let out a sudden gasp.

Talon's head shot up, hearing the fear in Hemera's voice. The shock on her face had him following where her eyes focused.

It was a body, a short distance from them, the man's eyes staring lifeless in their direction.

Talon moved away from her, adjusted his garment and ordered, "Stay here."

Hemera shook her head and grabbed hold of his hand.

Talon did not argue with her, though he kept her tucked partially behind him as they approached the body. Pine needles, sticks, and decayed leaves covered the lower part of his body. The upper part of his body had been left exposed and it revealed the awful torture he must have suffered before finally dying.

Talon fisted his hands, not realizing he held Hemera's hand until she winced. He did not let go of her, though he eased his grip.

"You knew him?" she asked.

"Aye, I knew him," Talon said.

"Talon!"

Talon shoved Hemera behind him, the bushes rustling as someone made their way through them.

"Wrath," Talon said once the man emerged.

"Am I the commander of your personal guard or not?" Wrath demanded, laying eyes on Talon and giving him no chance to respond. "If so, then I expect the King to follow the rules he, himself, has set forth. Otherwise, why bother to have personal guards. Need I remind you how dangerous it presently—" Wrath stopped abruptly when he caught sight of the body.

"Vard," Talon said. "Summon the men I know you brought with you and see that his body is taken to the executioner's chamber and have Broc meet us there. I want to know how his body got here without one sentinel seeing it."

Wrath stepped away from them and with his hand braced to the side of his mouth, he let out a strange call.

"Wrath," Talon said with a curt snap.

Wrath looked to the King and spoke before Talon could. "I should not have spoken to you as I did, my King. My concern for your safety had me speaking foolishly, though after finding Vard this way, I am not sorry that I came in search of you, *my friend*."

Talon gave a nod, accepting his apology. "Did Bower tell you where we were?"

"He did. He was worried that Hemera may be punished for something that he claims was his fault."

"Bower is a good man," Hemera said.

"I am glad to hear that, Hemera, for he would make you a fine husband," Wrath said.

"Have one of my personal guards escort Hemera to her dwelling," Talon commanded.

"As you say, my King," Wrath said and went to speak to the warriors that began emerging from behind the bushes.

Talon turned to Hemera, wanting desperately to

take her in his arms, but instead shielding her from curious eyes with his body and keeping his voice low for only her to hear. "Are you all right?"

She turned a gentle smile on him. "I am good. I have seen tortured bodies before, though I was not expecting to see one here in this peaceful spot."

"You have seen tortured bodies? I would ask you where, but I believe your answer would be as usual—I will tell you one day—and I have not the time to argue with you. You will go and remain in your dwelling until I come to you."

"Aye, my King," she said with a bob of her head.

*Obedient.* She was never obedient, but there was no way she could misconstrue his command. He turned and Wrath approached with a warrior.

Talon was glad it was Tilden. The young warrior was the newest member of his personal guards and while all of the warriors were highly skilled, Tilden set out to prove himself worthy every day. He had erred before he was appointed to the King's personal guards and ever since he had gone beyond his duties to right his wrong. Hemera would be safe with him.

Wrath kept his attention on the King as he spoke, "Tilden will take Hemera to her dwelling and then fetch Paine."

Talon nodded and watched, his heart growing heavier and heavier with each step she took away from him. He would keep her close all the time if he could. She may have gasped at the shock of seeing a dead body not far from them, but she had suffered no crying fit nor did she turn away from it. She also had remained at his side when he had gone to take a closer look. She had courage and he admired that. Though, he did wonder how it had come to pass that she had seen tortured bodies. What had she been made to do when she was a slave to the Northmen? One day she would tell him. He would make sure of it or so he kept telling himself.

~~~

    Hemera wanted a closer look at the body. She had thought she had seen familiar torture marks on him and she wanted to take a closer look and see if she was right. If she was, it would mean that Northmen had been involved in the torture. That would mean that Northmen still lingered here in Pictland and were involved with the leader of the group that wished to defeat the King. It was important for Talon to know that.

    She watched Tilden as they walked. You would not think him a mighty warrior, being short and slim, but he was wiry, cords of muscles pressing tight against his garment, and he walked with strong confidence, his steps determined. She could rule him out as the person she had seen in the woods wearing a cloak of the personal guards.

    Tilden spoke not a word until he stood at the open door of Hemera's dwelling and waited for her to enter. "Be sure to latch the door."

    Hemera smiled and nodded. "I will be sure to do as you say." And she did, waiting several moments before opening the door and peeking out. When she saw that he was gone, Hemera hurried to the executioner's chamber. The light from the open door sparked the horrors of the place and so as not to be swallowed by them, she left the door open.

She waited in a spot a short distance from the door where light did not intrude on the shadows. Talon would not be happy when he found her there, but she had not disobeyed him. He had told her to wait in the executioner's dwelling. He had not specified which dwelling.

Hemera did not have long to wait, though it was not Talon who entered first...it was Paine.

"What are you doing here?" Paine asked, catching a movement to his left upon entering and surprised to see it was Hemera.

She saw no reason not to be honest with him. "I was with the King when the body was found and I would like a closer look at it."

"Why?" Paine asked as he proceeded to light candles around the room.

Hemera stared as little by little the torture devises were exposed and she could not stop a shudder from running through her. It brought back memories of times she preferred to forget.

"It is not a pleasant place. You should leave."

"I must see for myself."

"What must you see?" Paine asked.

Voices approaching the door kept Hemera from answering and she moved further into the room, nearer to what shadows were left where she could remain unnoticed for now.

Two warriors carried the body in and placed it on the torture table. They left when they were finished, though Hemera saw them take positons on either side of the door outside. The King entered next followed by Wrath and Broc.

Talon spoke with a biting sharpness that stung. "Do not give me excuses, Broc, I want results or you will be removed as Warrior Commander. That Vard's body should be left so close to the stronghold without anyone noticing is a failure on your part."

"I regret failing you, my King. Sentinels patrol that area more heavily since tracks were discovered just beyond the pond, but nothing suspicious has been reported. I will question each warrior myself and see what was missed."

"This body was not in the woods long," Paine said as he looked over the dead man. "The animals have yet to feast on it. It is also a message to you, my King. Your enemies let you know that whatever this man knew they now know, since no one could withstand such torture and hold his tongue."

Talon looked to Broc. "I want answers by nightfall." He turned to Wrath. "Go with him and let me know if he is failing his command."

Wrath nodded and followed Broc's determined steps out of the dwelling.

"What else can you tell me?" Talon said to Paine.

"I believe she can tell you more," Paine said and bobbed his head toward the shadows.

Hemera stepped forward as Talon turned.

His anger or was it sheer frustration that rose up and had his hands itching to throttle her? "You disobey me again? I ordered you to wait in your dwelling."

"This is one of the executioner's dwellings, so I did obey you."

Talon stared at her as she so often did to him. It was not that he was at a loss for words, it was that he was trying to understand how she outwitted him so often.

Paine broke through his thoughts. "She is right."

Talon turned slowly to glare at him. "Did I ask you for your thought?"

Paine said nothing, though he smiled.

"We can discuss whether I obeyed or disobeyed you later. It is more important that I share with you what I believe I saw," Hemera said and walked over to the dead man and remained silent as she looked him over.

Talon joined her, keeping close to her side.

"Have you seen anything like this?" she asked Paine, pointing to various wounds along his body.

"Only once when I was far north."

Talon looked from Paine to Hemera. "They are the mark of the Northmen?"

Hemera nodded. "It is a slow, agonizing torture, letting one of their birds of prey pluck at the body until..." She turned, burying her face against Talon's chest.

Talon wrapped an arm around her, knowing he should not demonstrate such caring, but unable to stop himself. If Hemera was familiar with this, then it meant she had seen someone suffer through it and once again he found himself wanting to do harm to the culprit.

"The Northmen are still among us and are working with my enemies," Talon said, looking to Paine. "Go and inform Wrath and Broc and see that a High Council meeting is convened immediately."

Paine nodded and left the dwelling.

As soon as he did, Talon took Hemera by the arm and hurried her out of the door and to her dwelling, his two personal guards following and taking up posts at the door as he entered with Hemera.

Once the door shut behind him, Talon took Hemera into his arms, holding her tight against him.

Once again, she buried her face against his chest, feeling safe and secure in the protection of his powerful arms. She imagined them bands of metal that no one could rip away. No one could take her from him. No one could do her harm when locked in his embrace.

Talon lifted her in his arms and walked to the sleeping pallet and sat, keeping her tucked close against him. "One day you will tell me everything about your time with the Northmen."

"Not today," she whispered with a shiver.

"Not today," he confirmed and kissed her temple.

"You will come to me tonight?" she asked hopefully.

"Nothing will keep me away."

A knock sounded at the door and reluctantly Talon sat Hemera on the sleeping pallet and before stepping away from her, he lowered his head to steal a much too quick kiss from her lips, before whispering, "Later."

He went to the door and stepped outside when he saw Wrath and the anger that twisted his face into a simmering rage. "What is it?"

"Two of the sentinels were found dead."

## Chapter Fifteen

Talon informed all at the High Council meeting of the three deaths and issued orders that no one was to enter the woods alone and for more sentinels to be posted on the outskirts of the stronghold. But it was learning that Vard, who they had all met one time or another, had been tortured by Northmen that had each one of them anxiously speaking out.

"Have more Northmen joined with our foe?"

"How could a Pict be so disloyal to fight beside a Northman?"

"Have more Northmen descended on Pict soil?"

"This could mean war with the Northmen."

"Silence!" Talon demanded, his fist coming down hard on the table, quieting the room instantly. "Vard had infiltrated the enemy camp and was close to discovering who led the group."

Brows shot up in surprise.

The King continued. "There are things that go on that you are not made aware of for obvious reasons. The more people who know of a secret mission the less likely it is to succeed. How Vard was discovered puzzles me for only I and one other person knew of his mission and that person I trust with my life."

All eyes looked to Wrath and Paine, knowing the two men were like brothers to the King. Neither man said a word or showed any sign of revealing which one knew of the mission.

"The enemy walks among us in the stronghold," Gelhard said.

"Could it be more than one person?" Ebit asked anxiously.

"How do we find this culprit?" Midrent asked.

"Stay alert and if you see anything you feel is suspicious come to me," Wrath said.

"Other steps will be taken, but not discussed," Talon added.

"A wise decision," Gelhard agreed with a nod.

Talon doubted Gelhard would agree with his next decision. "You are to suspend the arrival of the future queen until further notice."

Gelhard's obvious annoyance had him stumbling over his words. "That is...you should...I strongly advise you to reconsider."

"I have spoken, Gelhard, and you will see it done," Talon said and cast a stern eye on all those at the table. "You will not share that news beyond these walls. If I hear one gossiping tongue mention it, everyone here will lose their seat on the council. Is that understood?"

All heads nodded.

"Broc, I know you are eager to see to the changes we discussed. Keep me apprised of how things go. You are dismissed," Talon said.

Broc gave a nod and hurried out of the room.

"Midrent," Talon said, addressing his Tariff Collector. "Cancel all tariff collections until further notice. I will not chance having you suffer at the hands of our enemies or chance the tariff stolen to aid the enemy. You are dismissed to see to the task immediately."

Looking relieved, Midrent nodded and took his

leave.

Talon directed his attention to Ebit. "How far are you along on your planting?"

"We have several more fields to seed."

"I will assign more warriors to the area for protection," Talon said and Ebit nodded. Talon dismissed him and waited, knowing Gelhard was impatient to speak.

"My King, I strongly advise you to reconsider your decision about the future queen. Her arrival is imperative now. The more you delay in taking a wife, the more your enemy will stoke the fire of dissatisfaction against you."

"If you recall, Anin was once a possible future queen and found her life in danger. If not for Paine, she would not have survived. I will not see another future queen suffer a similar ordeal. Marriage will wait until this matter is settled to my satisfaction."

Gelhard did not give up. "It is not only the marriage you delay, but an heir to the Pict throne and that could prove dangerous."

Wrath agreed with the man. "Gelhard is right. The people want to know that the Pict throne is secure."

"A throne is never secure. There is always someone who believes he deserves the throne more than the reigning King," Talon said.

"That might be true, but an heir provides the people with a belief that the present King's reign will continue," Wrath argued. "If there is no heir, the people worry over who will replace you and if he would be a wise and just King like you."

"The King's decision is wise and should stand," Paine said. "It would be foolish to take a chance with the future queen's life. The only solution is to see this matter resolved quickly so that the King can get busy making many bairns and securing his sovereignty."

"My decision stands. Only when this matter is finally put to rest will I give permission for the future queen to travel here," Talon said, sending Gelhard a warning scowl after hearing his annoyed snort. "See it done, Gelhard."

"As you wish, my King," Gelhard said with a nod, his annoyance with the King's decision still obvious as he marched stiffly from the room.

"There is another important matter that must be discussed, my King" Wrath said.

Talon filled his vessel with wine. "You are angry with me for going into the woods without the protection of my personal guards."

"Three deaths is a good reason for me to be angry and that we had discussed this before and you had agreed to follow your own rule," Wrath argued. "Whatever possessed you to go into the woods alone?"

Talon was quick with an excuse. "I needed to think."

"Your guards would have respected your privacy and kept a safe distance, but would have been there if needed. You cannot take such risks, Talon. It is not fair to your people."

"You are right, but tell me this" —Talon leaned forward, his arms braced on the table— "are you certain that every one of my personal guards can be trusted not to betray me?"

Paine joined in. "When two previous High Council members were found to be traitors to the King, I would say no man beyond this room can be trusted. What troubles me more is that whoever it is here among us in the stronghold that betrays the King has incited others to do the same. The question begs then how many among us are traitors?"

"Another good reason that you will go nowhere without your personal guards," Wrath ordered as if he were king.

"If some changes are made," Talon said and raised his hand to silence Wrath when he appeared ready to argue. "No guards outside my sleeping chamber's door. They can position themselves down in the feasting hall, since anyone would have to go through there to reach my chamber. It will afford me at least some privacy."

"I can agree to that," Wrath said.

Talon continued. "Instead of two guards tailing me, I want one as my shadow while in the stronghold, two or more when outside the stronghold. It leaves you to assign some of my guards to patrol the stronghold and see what they can find out."

Wrath voiced his concern. "With a traitor or traitors among us, having only one guard with you worries me."

Paine laughed. "Talon has conquered every opponent on the practice field and you worry if he can protect himself?" Paine gave another short laugh. "I am sure he can keep his opponent at bay until we come to his rescue."

Talon's commanding tone settled it. "Good. It is done."

"What of Hemera?" Paine asked.

Talon lowered his vessel without taking a drink. "What about Hemera?"

"Her punishment. Will she continue in the

cookhouse?"

"I have not decided yet and I will hear no more about it now," Talon was quick to say, stopping Paine before he could say anymore. "Leave me now. I want to think and plan on ways to rid us of this traitor."

Wrath and Paine took their leave.

Once outside, Paine said to Wrath, "You are going to have one of his guards follow him without him knowing it."

"His safety is my responsibility."

"He will find out. What then? Are you prepared to face the consequences?" Paine asked.

"He will not find out."

"Talon sees more than you think and knows more than you think. It is why he is King," Paine reminded him and looked to say more, but shook his head stopping himself.

"You hold your tongue on something. What is it?"

Paine looked around. "Not where there are so many ears to hear. My dwelling, Anin went with Verity to see how Hemera is doing."

"Tell me," Wrath said, his concern having grown in the silence between them before they had reached the dwelling.

"Everyone wonders if there is something wrong with Talon since no one has seen him take a woman to his sleeping pallet in some time."

"You tell me something I already know."

"Then you already know that he never goes long without a woman," Paine said and smiled when he saw Wrath's eyes light with surprise.

"He has a woman." Wrath shook his head. "Why keep her a secret?"

Paine shrugged. "It could be anything. A short liaison he wants no one to know of or he believes others may frown upon the woman he has chosen or with his impending marriage he feels it is best to keep it quiet."

"That was why he went into the woods alone. He was meeting a woman," Wrath said with the excitement of finding an important piece to a puzzle. "Bower and Hemera prevented their meeting. Hemera may have seen a woman in the woods. We should talk with her now." Wrath did not wait for Paine to agree, he hurried off, knowing his friend would follow him.

~~~

Hemera stood by her dwelling, her hands clenched at her sides. Warriors came and went to and from the torture chamber. The body of the two warriors had been placed inside with orders that they be examined for any signs of torture before being presented to their family. The wife of the one dead warrior wept in the arms of the brother of the other warrior who had died. Many wanted to know more about what happened. There was worry that the stronghold could be invaded by the enemy and they were all in danger.

Did they not realize that the enemy purposely did this to make them doubt that the King would keep them safe? They had to stay strong together to defeat the enemy or the enemy would destroy them from within. How did they not see what the enemy was doing?

"They should leave. There is nothing they can do here," Hemera said, turning to her sister. "You should go too. You see that I am fine. There is no reason for you to be here."

Anin reached out, hoping a gentle touch would calm her.

Hemera pulled away, not wanting Anin to know how she felt. "Do not touch me."

"What goes on here?" Paine asked sharply, taking hasty strides to his wife's side.

"She is agitated, perhaps too many people disturbing her usual quiet," Anin whispered to her husband and patted his arm that circled her waist to rest on her rounded middle.

"Let us go inside," Paine suggested, feeling relieved his wife was in his arms. "Wrath has a question for you, Hemera."

Hemera shook her head. A confined space would not help her. She longed for the solitude of the woods, the soft whisper of the trees, the gentle melody of the birds, the feel of the rich earth beneath her bare feet. There in the silence she could think more clearly.

Wrath saw the worry for her sister in his wife's pinched brow and in the way she gripped her own hands so tightly. He rested a tender hand on her shoulder and whispered, "It will be all right." He went to take a step closer to Hemera.

She jumped back away from him. "No more questions. I have answered the same over and over. There is nothing left for me to say."

"Just one," Wrath said.

"Nay, no more," Hemera said, shaking her hand in front of him, warding him off. Why did they continue to ask when the answer would always remain the same?

Verity reached out and slipped her hand in her husband's, tugging him back to her side. "She is upset and I wish I knew why. Please leave her be."

Wrath surrendered to his wife's wishes and bothered Hemera no more.

Hemera did not understand her own frustration. She disliked crowds, but she coped with them when necessary. For some reason this crowd, that seemed to be growing more hostile, disturbed her greatly.

Wrath turned and, seeing the sizeable crowd that had gathered, gave a nod to Paine.

Paine eased his wife toward Verity. "Go home, now." When she looked ready to argue, he leaned close to her ear and whispered, "Do not argue with me on this, wife."

Wrath did the same with Verity, only his anger flared when she protested leaving her sister.

Hemera spoke up. "Do as Wrath says, Verity, unrest grows in the crowd and you have a bairn inside you to worry about."

Wrath was grateful to Hemera since Verity listened to her words of warning and turned away reluctantly, with Anin, though not before saying to her sister, "I will see you at supper in the feasting hall."

Hemera gave a nod, though she had no desire to be in a crowded hall this evening, listening to the grieving and complaints of what took place today. That would solve nothing.

"They should leave. This does no good."

This time Paine ordered sternly. "Go inside."

Verity heard his strong voice as she and Anin walked off. She stopped and turned. "Leave her be, Paine."

Wrath rolled his eyes and shook his head.

"She would do better inside her dwelling," Paine said.

"That is for her to decide," Verity said, leaving Anin's side and marching straight to her sister.

Hemera backed away. "Leave. Go now. It is better for you to be away from here."

"I agree with Hemera," Wrath said. "Go now!"

Verity scowled at her husband and he scowled right back, walking over to her. "You will listen to me, wife."

Hemera watched as everything seemed to collide at once. Her sister argued with Wrath. Anin and Paine exchanged words and the crowd seemed to roar with anger, at least to her they did. The discord was too much and reminded her of the night she and Verity had been taken from their village. People screamed, fires burned, and she could do nothing to stop it. Would the Northmen come for her again? Would they take her from Talon? The thought gripped at her heart and filled her with fear

"Silence!"

Hemera caught her breath as Talon's powerful voice sliced through the noise and silenced it. Her eyes turned wide and fear began to crawl over her like little bugs nipping at her chilled flesh.

"Return to your chores now or suffer for it," Talon roared. "There is nothing to see and nothing to fear." The crowd spread as he marched to the front and stopped in front of the grieving wife and brother. "Avena, your husband Bard and, Hollins, your brother Tumason died brave deaths defending our people. Hold your head high in honor of the courageous warriors they were and walk with pride in their memory. They will be prepared for burial and brought to your dwellings for all to pay their respects this evening.

Tomorrow they will be buried with the dignity they deserve."

That the King honored them by addressing them by their names and speaking the fallen warriors' names pleased the two grieving people and they bobbed their heads in respect to the King and, holding on to each other, walked away. The crowd followed behind them in dead silence.

Talon was grateful to Tilden who had made him aware of the situation and had assembled all of his personal guards to follow the King. They now walked behind the people, making certain no straggler remained behind.

Talon turned to Wrath and Paine, neither men looking too pleased, but that did not matter to him. What troubled him was Hemera. Her face was deathly pale, her eyes as round and wide as the moon when full in the sky, and her body taut and anxious, fighting the urge to run into his arms.

As he approached the group, he ordered, "Leave, and you," —he pointed to Hemera—"come with me. We have your punishment to settle."

He brushed past Verity as Wrath pulled her away before she could protest and Anin who turned and took her husband's arm to walk off, and reached out to take hold of Hemera's arm and rushed her inside the dwelling.

## Chapter Sixteen

The door closed and Hemera collapsed in Talon's arms, her head dropping against his chest and her arms going around his waist. Talon's powerful arms closed tight around her, her body's quivers shuddering against his hard muscles. She was not one to submit to fear, so what had made her fearful?

He held her, saying nothing, letting his strength seep inside her and chase her tremors away. When they were all but gone, he scooped her up and went to the sleeping pallet to sit with her, settling her in his lap.

"Where does this fear come from?" he asked in a whisper and before she could answer he kissed her lips, eager to not only taste her but to return a soft blush to them. He eased his mouth off hers and was glad her lip had healed some and was pleased it had plumped a gentle red, and when she laid her head on his shoulder, he knew no response would be forthcoming. "More memories you do not wish to recall?" He felt her nod and lifted her chin, forcing her to look at him. "I will not wait for you to tell me one day. You will tell me now."

She stared at him and the words spilled eagerly from her lips as if she needed to be rid of the memories. "The people, the noise, the arguing reminded me of the evening Verity and I were taken by the Northmen. With Northmen in the area, I feared they would come and once again take me away... away from you."

Her brow crinkled as if her own words surprised her.

His words did not surprise him, though the catch to his heart did. "I would kill anyone who would try to take you from me. I will remind you again—you are mine. No one takes what is mine."

She shivered, recalling another time someone had said those exact words to her. *No one takes what his mine.*

"You are safe here with me. You will always be safe with me. There is no reason the Northmen would come for you. You are a Pict. You are home. You are mine." His lips came down on hers and proved how possessive he was of her. It was not a gentle kiss like before. This one claimed her, branded her, made it clear that no one would come between them.

He gripped a handful of hair at the back of her head and yanked her head back. "No one will ever take you from me."

His lips settled on hers once again and Hemera let herself be swept away in the power of his kiss. It consumed her, ravished her, and vanquished her fears. She almost cried out her disappointment when he ended the kiss and rested his brow to hers as he fought to steady his breathing and to speak.

"I cannot stay," he said through labored breaths. He suddenly lifted her and sat her on the sleeping pallet before walking away.

Hemera was reminded of this morn when he had done the same, walked away, and she wished things could be different. She wished he could stay as long as he pleased, visit her as long as he pleased, and couple with her as often as he pleased.

Talon turned away, seeing the disappointment in her frown and his own disappointment evident in his scowl.

"My punishment," she said, getting him to turn around.

He swerved around. He had used the punishment as an excuse to be alone with her after having seen how upset she had been. He was glad for the short time he had had with her, though ached for much more with her and, like her not wanting to be separated from him, he did not want to be separated from her. It was a feeling foreign to him and yet so potent it consumed his senses.

"Your punishment is mine as well for I must take my leave and I want nothing more than to strip you of your garments and plunge into you again and again until we both are spent with satisfaction and exhaustion. Then we would rest and do it all again."

Sadness filled her eyes and her shoulders slumped. "Aye, it is a most painful punishment to endure. I hope it will not last long."

"I hope to come to you tonight, but I must pay my respects to the fallen warriors families and spend time with my people, reassuring them that all is well and they are safe."

"Your duty comes first. I will wait for you, but if I fall asleep wake me," she urged her soft smile as enticing as her lush lips still plump from his kiss.

"With pleasure," Talon said, a smile teasing the corners of his mouth, and not trusting himself to give her one last kiss, he took his leave.

~~~

Hemera lay awake unable to sleep. She shivered and wrapped the blankets more tightly around her, wishing Talon was there his, body snug around hers. The dark had brought cold with it that would leave frost on the ground by morn and a wind that seeped through the dwelling. Though she made sure the fire pit would burn strong until morn, there was still a chill to her naked body that only Talon could heat.

She hoped that his duties would not keep him from coming to her this evening. She needed to feel his powerful arms settle around her, hug her tight against him, feel his strength that rippled through every muscle in his potent body. Mostly though, she wanted to feel him slip inside her and join with him as one.

A soft sigh escaped her lips and she turned on her side and stared at the flames roaring strong in the fire pit. She had been trying to make sense of the fear that had consumed her earlier. She had been frightened, but also angry when the Northmen had yanked her sister out of her arms and threw her into the arms of another Northmen before reaching down and grabbing her and tucking her under his arm.

Her fear then had been nothing to the terrifying feeling she had experienced earlier when the thought of being ripped away from Talon had hit her. The pain had been unbearable to the point where she had thought she would collapse. He had become part of her and if ever they should separate, she worried that she would not survive, not want to survive without him.

It was a strange feeling, one she had never felt before. She had worried for her sister while with the Northmen, but she had made sure that Verity had been protected. Talon was King. There was little she could do to protect him and she wondered how much he could actually do to protect her.

Marriage, to her, was a necessity to most and a duty to others. Few if any wed because they felt *tuahna* toward one another, a caring so deep it stole the heart and never let go. It was rare or perhaps not as rare as she thought since her sister had found it with Wrath, and Anin had found it with Paine, and her mother had found it with her father, though fate had warred against them.

Had the terror she felt today been because she was losing her heart to Talon? Or had she already lost it and had yet to realize it? And what would she do if that was so? Would she be able to watch him wed, know that he would join with his wife as he did with her? Her stomach roiled at the thought.

"Stop! Stop! Stop!" she ordered her thoughts.

She had survived more pain than she thought she ever could. She would survive this. No matter what she would survive. A tear fell from her eye and she brushed it away. Tears did no good. She had learned that a long time ago.

Courage and strength had been her shield and her sword, a gift given to her long ago, and one she would always cherish.

She forced her thoughts silent and listened to the melody of the wind outside her dwelling and let it loll her to sleep, an inkling of hope that Talon would come to her strong in her heart.

~~~

The hand was cold that touched her bare shoulder and woke Hemera and when the blanket was pulled down, she smiled and turned ready to greet Talon as he climbed in the sleeping pallet beside her.

Her smile vanished and she grabbed for the blanket when she saw that it was not Talon standing over her.

It was Hollins, brother of Tumason, the sentinel that had been killed, and he held a long, thin dagger in his hand. With his other hand, he yanked the blanket away from her, leaving her naked.

While he had pleasant features, anger had distorted them until he looked more demon than human, his dark hair having been whipped wild around his head as if the wind had battered him and his eyes bulged with a murderous glint. He was slim, though there was strength to the grip he had on his dagger and it had grown his muscles taut beneath the sleeve of his shirt.

Hemera drew back as he stepped closer, her bare back hitting the wall and she shivered, whether from the chill coming from the wall or fear of what he intended to do to her, she did not know.

"I know who you are," he whispered with a sneer.

It was not his foul breath that roiled her stomach, but his remark. She stared at him.

He tapped the side of her head. "Do you understand what I say, dimwit?"

Once hurtful words stung her as hard as a physical blow, but her father had been the one to gift her with a shield of courage and a sword of strength, and he had taught her how to use both.

"Ulric has plans for you. You will be the one to defeat King Talon and end his reign."

Her heart hammered against her chest that she could hurt Talon that way. She held her shield strong as she probed carefully to find out what Ulric had planned. "I have no such power."

"No, you have no power at all," Hollins said, waving the dagger dangerously close to her face. "You are nothing but a slow-minded woman and how fitting it is that one such as yourself will bring down the mighty King Talon."

"You make no sense," she said.

Hollins stuck his face right in front of hers and sneered. "It is you who makes no sense. Ulric will see you dead and see that it is blamed on King Talon. Your battered and abused body will be found in the woods, since all know how much you favor the woods, and the person from the stronghold who finds you will weep as all learn that it was with your dying breath that you let it be known that it was King Talon who brutally attacked you after you denied mating with him." His sneer grew. "I will be the first of many men who will leave the evidence of his brutality."

"No one will believe it. The King can have any woman he wants." She hoped she could keep him talking until Talon arrived.

*Please, Talon, please help me. I need you. Please, wind, hear me and take my plea to him.*

One good thing was that he thought he had time to do as he pleased with her. That her dwelling was far enough removed from others that no one would hear what went on, so he would not be in a hurry. She had to keep him talking.

Hollins laughed. "Everyone knows he has had no woman lately and believe he must be in desperate need of one. When he found you alone in the woods and you refused him, he took what he wanted. The person who tells the tale will make everyone at least doubt and that is all that is needed since King Talon's end is already near."

She shook her head. "King Talon will not lose the throne."

"He will," Hollins demanded, "although this plan to grab you would have gone easier if my useless brother had joined with me. I had no choice but to kill him, when he tried to stop me, and Bard as well when he tried to help Tumason." He shoved the dagger near her face once more. "Now spread your legs for me and if you think of screaming—"

His blade struck her face so fast she barely had time to turn away so that the blade caught the edge of her chin instead of her cheek.

"You will suffer more of that."

~~~

It was late when Talon arrived in his sleeping chamber and he debated about going to Hemera. He wanted to go, but they would have little time together before he would have to leave her again. She was probably already asleep and they both had had little sleep lately, not that he needed much, but she did.

*Talon!*

He shivered from the sudden chill that swept through his chamber and he swerved around, expecting to see Hemera standing there. When he did not, his flesh rose along his arms and the back of his neck and he knew something was wrong. He was out through the secret passage, running through the stronghold, not caring if anyone saw him.

The wind hurried along with him, propelling him, urging him and all the while he heard Hemera call anxiously to him over and over and over.

~~~

Hemera appeared as if she was about to do as he asked when she suddenly grabbed the blanket, flung it over the dagger, and gave Hollins a hard shove with her foot, sending him stumbling to the ground. She grabbed the other blanket and hurried to the end of the sleeping pallet, hoping to get out the door before he could right himself.

She nearly made it when a yank at her ankle had her falling so hard to the ground that all her breath escaped her and as she fought to get it back, Hollins collapsed on top of her.

## Chapter Seventeen

The door flew open and Talon rushed in as Hemera struggled with Hollins to keep his blade from coming down on her cheek. A terrifying roar ripped through the air, chasing the wind that had entered with him out the door and turning Hollins stiff with fear.

Hemera did not see Talon's hand grip Hollins by the back of the neck, he moved so fast, but she saw him yank the shocked man off her, grab Hollins' hand that held the dagger and in one swift motion bury the dagger in Hollins' throat.

Talon watched as the man choked on his last breath. "You are fortunate I killed you so fast or your suffering would have been endless." Talon tossed his lifeless body out the door as careless as one would discard a useless carcass.

Hemera had scrambled to her feet, and hearing shouts and running footfalls, reached down to grab the blanket to wrap around her.

Talon reached it before she did and draped the soft wool blanket around her shoulders and as he let it fall down around her, she trembled.

"*Talon.*"

She drew his name out in a whispery plea that had him gripping the ends of the blanket tight in one hand, while anger raged through him for what she had suffered. His arm circled her waist and as he responded to her plea and brought his lips came down on hers, Tilden came barreling through the open door.

Talon snapped his head to the side, his eyes glaring with such rage that Tilden took a step back. His arm tightened protectively around Hemera as she lowered her head and kept her face buried against his chest.

Tilden kept his eyes on his King. "Others are not far behind me, my King."

Talon gave the young warrior a nod for the warning and reluctantly walked Hemera over to her sleeping pallet and sat her down on it. He lowered himself to rest on bended legs in front of her and his rage swelled to a roar in him when he saw the blood at her chin.

"They arrive," Tilden warned and stepped outside the door.

Wrath entered first, then Paine.

"You are unharmed, my King?" Wrath asked.

"I am, but Hemera is not," Talon said. "Send for the healer."

"I do not need the healer," Hemera said. "I can see to the wound myself."

Talon went to reaffirm his order when she placed her hand gently on his arm.

"Please, my King. The healer is not necessary."

"Hemera! Hemera!"

Hemera shut her eyes a moment, hearing her sister's anxious shouts. She did not want to see anyone. She wanted to be alone with Talon, tight in his arms, where she would be safe. She opened her eyes to see Wrath stopping his wife at the open door with a strong arm to her waist.

Talon felt the struggle inside Hemera for it mirrored his own. He wanted to be alone with her, hold her tight, ease her fear, though he saw little of that in her. She was strong. She had fought Hollins... the thought struck him like a fist to his jaw. He wanted to ask her if Hollins had had his way with her, but not in front of others.

It was a brief moment but Hemera caught the flash of fury as Talon's body grew so taut she thought he would snap in two and that his jaw would crack. The fiery question in his eyes as they ran over her body had her realizing what troubled him.

It was her sister who helped her reassure Talon when she could not.

"Tell me he did not hurt you, Hemera. Please, my King, please let me know my sister is unharmed," Verity begged.

"I am well, Verity," Hemera said. "King Talon arrived before Hollins could do me any great harm."

Talon fought the urge to pull Hemera into his arms, he was so relieved to hear her words. Instead, he grudgingly stood, giving Hemera's leg a light squeeze as he did and even more grudgingly stepped away from her and gestured for Verity to enter.

"He did hurt you," Verity said, her eyes welling with tears when she saw the blood.

"It is nothing, barely a wound. You will see when you help me clean it," Hemera assured her.

"When Verity is finished, you will tell me what happened here, Hemera," the King ordered.

Hemera went to respond when she caught the familiar look in her sister's eyes when she was about to have a vision. "Wrath," she called out, but Talon was closer and he caught Verity in his arms before she could collapse to the ground.

Hemera hurried off the sleeping pallet, making way

for her sister as Wrath took his wife's limp body from the King. He sat on the pallet, holding her, talking to her, assuring her that he was there with her and that she was to return to him soon.

It warmed Hemera's heart and eased any worry she had for her sister to see how much Wrath cared for and protected her while she was in the throes of one of her visions. She had warned Verity when they were with the Northmen and she had had her first vision not to tell anyone about them. If she had, she would have been sent away to live with the older seers and Hemera had feared if that happened she would have never been able to rescue her.

Verity's eyes fluttered open and once they were fully open, the King demanded, "What did you see?"

Verity shook her head gently, the corners of her eyes crinkling. "I am not sure."

Talon was not satisfied with her answer and took an abrupt step forward, Hemera thrust herself in front of him. He bumped into her, sending her toppling forward. Instinct and familiarity with her had him grabbing her hips to steady her and a collective silence filled the room.

He released her and with a bite to his words warned, "Watch where you step!" His anger was evident to all and eyes quickly turned away from the King. He grew even more angry and not at Hemera as everyone thought. He wanted this secret, this farce to end. He wanted everyone to know that Hemera was his woman and whoever found fault with it be damned.

"Tell us what you saw," Hemera encouraged her sister.

"Hemera in the woods," Verity said. "Someone

called to her. That was all."

"A man or a woman? Was she frightened? " Talon probed.

"A man and I saw no fear on her," Verity said and eased out of her husband's arms. "I will think on it and see if there is anything else that may be important. But now what is important is for me to tend my sister."

Wrath's hand went to rest on his wife's middle, reminding her of their bairn she carried. "Are you sure you do not need to rest after having the vision?"

Verity shook her head. "I am not tired, though I will rest after I finish with Hemera."

That pleased Wrath and he kissed her cheek, bringing a smile to her face.

The tender moment between the couple annoyed Talon. He wanted that with Hemera and he wanted it here and now when she needed him. She needed comforting and attention now, yet she was giving it to her sister.

"Hurry and see to Hemera so that I may question her," Talon ordered his tongue so sharp it pricked at everyone's skin. He took leave of the dwelling, his steps as curt as his tongue.

Wrath and Paine followed behind him.

Once the door shut, Hemera joined her sister to sit on the sleeping pallet. She took her hand in hers and feeling the chill rubbed it between her two warm ones. They sat like that in silence for several moments, Hemera warming Verity's other hand as well.

"You know me well," Verity said, breaking the silence. "Better than I know you."

Hemera laughed. "I do not even know me. I confuse myself." She took hold of Verity's one hand.

"Though, I do know that your visions are clearer than they once were. Tell me what you saw that you wanted no one else to know?"

"I believe what I saw was for your ears alone. You were in the woods when it was lush with growth. You turned when you heard the sound of a man's voice and," —Verity hesitated— "you were softly round with child."

~~~

Broc had arrived with warriors and after Talon ordered him to remove the body and to see to posting extra guards inside the stronghold, he joined Wrath and Paine, waiting to the side of the dwelling.

"What were you doing here so late?" Wrath asked Talon.

"You question me?" Talon asked, glaring at Wrath.

"Why is it I must constantly remind you that I am responsible for your safety? You, yourself, agreed to it. I follow your rules," Wrath argued.

"I wanted another look at Vard," Talon said not in itself a lie, since he had intended to have another look at the body. "It can be discussed later, away from others. Right now I want to find out what happened here."

"That will have to wait on Hemera, since the only other witness is dead," Paine said, "and it does not bode well that it was one of our own. It leaves doubt that there are others among us who mean us harm."

"Find out who Hollins has been seen with and talked to. Track where he has gone recently. Find out everything about him and his brother and that stays between the three of us," Talon ordered.

Wrath and Paine nodded.

The door to the dwelling opened and Verity summoned her husband with a wave. "Hemera is ready to speak with the King," she told her husband. "I will take my leave and go rest, Hemera insists upon it, and I gave my word to you."

"I am glad you obey me," Wrath said and with a snap of his hand summoned Tilden.

"For now," Verity said with a sweet smile

Wrath had no chance to respond, Tilden stepped beside him. "See that Verity gets safely to our dwelling."

Verity's steps were slow as she walked away and Wrath was glad that Tilden quickly offered her his arm and that she took it. He could now see to his duties without worry over her. He stepped to the side of the door, letting the King know he could enter.

Questions spilled rapidly from Talon, not only anxious to find out what happened to her, but to try to end this ordeal with enough time for him to return and share the remainder of the night with her. Even if he could steal only a few moments with her, he wanted to steal them.

A yawn prevented her from answering quickly and Talon realized the toll the attack had taken on her. The skin beneath her eyes had darkened some. The wound on her chin, now clean of blood, was not as bad as he had first thought. Though, that did not stop Talon from wanting to kill Hollins all over again. He was pleased that she was sitting up in the sleeping pallet, wearing a worn shift, a blanket tucked around her lower half, and another draped over her shoulders like a shawl. Her red hair was its usual wild self and the green of her eyes had dimmed a little. She needed rest.

"I will tell you all that happened, my King, and what Hollins said to me," she offered, fighting down another yawn. Verity's tender care had soothed her so much that she was ready for sleep.

"Tell me and be done with it, for you need rest after such a troubling ordeal," Talon said.

It was a troubling ordeal that she wished was done, but she knew it had only begun. "Hollins told me that Ulric has plans for me." She took a moment to gain strength to say what he had said next.

Seeing her hesitate, Talon took a step closer to her, clenching his hands at his sides, fearful he would reach out and take her in his arms, comfort her, protect her, care for her like he cared for no other. "You are safe."

She doubted she was safe, but for the moment she allowed herself to believe so. "Hollins told me that I would be the one to defeat you and end your reign." The shock of her words showed on Wrath and Paine's faces, not so Talon. He remained stoic, not a change to his expression.

She continued. "Ulric intended to see me dead and see that it was blamed on King Talon. My fondness for the woods would help Ulric with his plan. All know how much I enjoy my time spent there, and there is where my beaten and abused body would be found. A traitor among us in the stronghold would find me and tell all that with my dying breath that it was King Talon who brutally attacked me because I refused to mate with him. Hollins intended to be the first of many men who would leave evidence of his brutality on me." She shook her head. "I told him that no one would believe that about King Talon."

That Hemera would defend him while threatened with dreadful harm made him realize that there was much more to this woman than he knew. And he wanted to learn all he could about her. It also had him wishing that he had not killed Hollins. He wished that he was still alive so that he could rip the man apart limb by limb and make him suffer for what he had put Hemera through.

"Hollins laughed and told me that everyone was aware that the King had had no woman lately, so he must be in desperate need of one. The person who found me would relate the tale I supposedly told before dying that the King found me alone in the woods and when I refused him, he took what he wanted. Hollins insisted that at least it would put doubt in the mind of the King's supporters and that was all that was needed to end King Talon's reign since it was already near its end anyway."

She took a needed breath and shook her head. "I told him King Talon would never lose the throne. Hollins grew angry at my words and angry that his plan to grab me would have been easier if his brother Tumason had joined in the plan with him. He killed his brother when he tried to stop him and Bard as well."

Talon realized then what Hemera had done. She had kept Hollins talking, waiting for him to arrive and rescue her. His insides churned, recalling that he almost had not come to her.

*Never. Never again would he leave her unprotected.*

"You will have a guard by you at all times from this moment on," Talon said and shook his hand at her when she went to speak. "It is done."

Hemera bit back a retort. She would have her say when they were alone, if they could ever be alone now. With a guard constantly on her, how was Talon to come to her at night?

Talon turned to Wrath. "Go and get Tilden. Assign him the evening shift. He is still trying to prove himself worthy of his new position as one of my personal guards and has been extra vigilant. He will do well guarding her in the evening when an attack on her is more likely."

Wrath nodded and left the dwelling.

"You can go, Paine," Talon said dismissing him, intending to have a few moments alone with Hemera.

"A word outside, my King?" Paine asked and went and opened the door as if not giving Talon a chance to refuse.

The door barely closed behind Talon when he snapped at Paine, "What is it?"

"I am not blind and either is Wrath, Talon," Paine said, letting him know he spoke to him as a friend and not his king. "I know you do not go without a woman. Remember, a secret cannot stay a secret for long when it grows beyond what you intended it to be. It will be discovered. What then?"

Wrath and Tilden arrived, leaving no chance for Talon to respond, nor did he intend to. He was too busy wondering if Paine knew that he had made Hemera his woman or if he did not know the identity of the woman. Either way, something would have to be done about the situation soon.

Talon entered the dwelling and to his annoyance Wrath followed him in. He stopped when he saw that Hemera lay sound asleep. She was curled on her side, the blanket having slipped off her shoulder, leaving it bare and no doubt chilled. He wanted to go over and cover it, tuck the blanket around her. He almost shook his head. What he really wanted was to climb in naked beside her and take her in his arms, hold her close against him, warm her, and keep her safe.

"It is good she sleeps. She has been through much and should rest."

"She is a brave woman," Talon said.

"That she is," Wrath agreed. "Verity told me how Hemera always found a way to get to her after the Northmen had separated them. She was sure Hemera had suffered for it, but still she defied the Northmen to get to her sister. Hemera also assured her that one day they would escape and return home and that the hope her sister had instilled in her had helped her to survive."

Talon would have to talk with Verity, though it would not be easy since the woman feared him far more than she should, and see what else he could learn about Hemera.

"Two of your guards wait to escort you to your sleeping chamber and Tilden is already at his position outside the door. All should be fine," Wrath said. "You should retire and rest yourself, my King."

Talon nodded. He should rest but not in his chambers, here beside Hemera. He stepped outside reluctantly, not that he let anyone see it.

"Go to your wife, Wrath. I want a few words with Tilden," Talon ordered.

Wrath looked to Tilden and to the two guards that stood to the side, confident the King was protected, he gave a nod and took his leave.

Talon stood in front of Tilden and kept his voice

low for only the young warrior to hear. "What did you see?"

"Only what you want me to, my King," Tilden responded his own voice a near whisper.

"Keep her safe.

"With my life, my King."

Reluctantly Talon took his leave, Paine's warning echoing in his head. Paine was right. The secret would not stay a secret for long. What then?

The answer was simple to Talon. Hemera belonged to him and he would let no one take her from him.

## Chapter Eighteen

Hemera sat on the edge of the sleeping pallet, her mind churning. That she and Talon would not have this night together disturbed her. Even if she only got to sleep in his arms for a short time, it was better than not being with him at all.

She began to pace around the fire pit and as she did a plan began to form. She remembered shortly after her arrival here, seeing Talon emerge one evening from behind several bushes that grew close to one side of the feasting hall. Curiosity had gotten the better of her and one day she explored the area and found a door that one would never find or think was there—a secret door.

It had taken a bit of a struggle but she had managed to unlock the door and climb the stairs. She had been surprised to find herself in Talon's sleeping chamber. Upon hearing several voices below, she had stepped out of the room to find the feasting hall crowded. She was not spotted until she was on the stairs and had received a few strange looks, but no one had given thought to her presence there.

She stood, having made up her mind. She would go to Talon. Her only problem was getting past Tilden. It took only a moment for a thought to strike her and she hurried to brew a concoction of leaves. The drink would make Tilden drowsy enough for him to fall asleep and hopefully he would remain asleep until after she returned.

Tilden seemed grateful for the brew and guilt nudged at her as she watched him drink hardy of it as she closed the door to her dwelling. She snatched her cloak from the peg and after slipping it on, she placed her ear against the door. She smiled when after a while she heard a light snoring.

She eased the door open and was pleased to see Tilden sitting on the bench beside the door, his head resting back against the wall, and a light snore coming from his mouth that hung open. That he had been weary to begin with had helped in having him fall asleep.

With light steps, she hurried off to the secret door.

~~~

Talon paced his sleeping chamber, fighting the urge to return to Hemera and at least hold her close until she slept. He shook the persistent thought from his mind before he surrendered to it and forced his musings elsewhere.

He needed to speak with some of the chieftains of the various tribes, especially those who were his closest allies, those who had encouraged him to unite the Pict tribes and bring peace to the land. Not that Talon believed there would ever be peace. There would always be someone who sought power and dominance or in some cases revenge.

There were those who had not wanted the tribes to unite, hatred for each other having grown strong, but with foreign invaders threatening the Pict shores, it was either force unification or lose their land and their freedom. Together they would survive. Divided they were sure to be conquered. Unfortunately, there were still those who felt strongly against unification and their opposition was mounting. He had to put a stop to it before it spread and war once again raged across the land.

Talon slipped out of his garments and stretched out on his sleeping pallet. This land was home to him. It was his heritage. He recalled his mum telling him tales of this land and how it had welcomed their ancestors here when they arrived long ago. The land shared its abundance, providing them with food and shelter. He had enjoyed hearing the myths, though he had discovered they had not all been myths. He, himself, had gotten to meet what he had thought a mere myth...the Giantess. She guarded the forests and all within them. He had thought to show his prowess to his warriors by entering her special domain and disproving her existence or conquering the myth.

He had failed, though not in the eyes of his warriors. They believed him invincible after having survived confrontation with the Giantess. It was her revenge that gave credence to the rumors that he could wield his sword against a mountain of men and satisfy a handful of women in one night. She had cursed him for daring to challenge her by increasing his prowess with more than just his sword. His thirst for women had increased until it seemed he was never satisfied... until Hemera.

She satisfied him like no other woman could. His thirst now was for her and her alone and she seemed as hungry for him as he was for her.

He closed his eyes and shook his head as he felt himself grow aroused. He only need think of Hemera and he found himself wanting her.

His eyes suddenly flew open and he lay still, not moving a single muscle. Had he heard a soft creak? He had been too deep in thought to be sure. He lay there listening and once again he heard it. He recognized the sound.

It was the door to his secret passage—opening.

He slipped silently off his sleeping pallet and padded across the wooden floor so lightly that not a sound was heard. He positioned himself behind the door, waiting. No one knew of this door but he and the man who had built it and he was dead. The person who had learned of it would rue his discovery, for he would not live to see another sunrise.

The door continued to open slowly and Talon wished he had added more wood to the fire, the room having grown dark, making it more difficult to see who entered. He would have his hands around his throat soon enough.

The culprit stepped past the door and Talon's hands lunged for his throat.

Bright red hair blazed before his eyes as slim hands frantically tore at his.

Talon released Hemera so quickly she stumbled back, gasping for air.

Oath after oath flew from his mouth as he reached out and grabbed her arm. "Easy. Breathe slowly." Her eyes remained as round as full moons, though they shined bright green. "Slow," he urged again.

Hemera gripped his other arm and did as he said, breathed slowly, her fear abating. He had shocked her when his hands landed around her neck, squeezing tightly. She had been so excited about seeing him that she had not given thought he would think her an intruder, possibly someone there to kill him.

She stumbled over labored breath to say, "I shou—should ha—ve an—announced myself."

"Do not try and speak until you can breathe properly," he scolded, more annoyed with himself than her for causing her harm. "How do you know about this passage?" He shook his head. "Never mind. Do not speak yet."

He stripped her cloak off and helped her over to the sleeping pallet to sit. She took tight hold of his hand after he sat beside her and that she should seek solace from him after what he had done to her had guilt rising up to jab repeatedly at his insides.

Finally her breathing calmed and a faint smile surfaced. "I needed to be with you."

His tongue was ready to chastise her for her foolish actions and to demand she tell him how she had learned of his secret door, but he said none of that. He lowered his mouth to hers and kissed her.

It did not take long for them both to shed their garments, their hands busy helping each other until finally they both stood naked in front of each other. When Hemera shivered, Talon hurried to stoke the fire and add more wood.

Hemera was climbing into the sleeping pallet when he turned and went to her, grabbing her at the waist and pulling her back against him. His hands splayed across her stomach, gently kneading her soft flesh before roaming further down.

She shuddered and her head fell back against his chest when his thumb teased the small numb nestled in the triangle of red hair and sending it pulsating. She let out a small gasp when his hands moved further down between her legs, and one of his fingers slipped inside her.

He nibbled along her ear. "You are always ready for me as I am for you.

She moaned when he rubbed against her, his hard manhood poking her backside.

His hand drifted up ever so slowly over her stomach in a faint swirling motion and her whole body burst with a tingling passion that seemed to devour her until it finally reached her one breast. She continued to moan as his fingers circled her breast with deliberate slowness and when he reached her taut nipple, he gave it a hard squeeze.

Talon yanked her head back and caught the gasp that rushed from her lips with a kiss that demanded. He did not know why or perhaps it was because of what she had suffered at another man's hands, but he had to claim her. Make her realize without a doubt that she belonged to him.

"Mine," he said briefly moving his lips off hers, then claiming them again in a kiss that left no doubt that he meant it.

Hemera could barely breathe when the kiss ended and her body could barely stand to wait another moment with the steady, teasing, rhythm of his finger inside her, she was going to come.

"I cannot wait." That she heard herself beg, she did not care. "Please, Talon. Please."

She gasped when he bent her over the sleeping pallet, her hands going to brace herself on it. Then she let out a long moan when he entered her from behind in one swift thrust.

Talon groaned as he buried himself deep inside her and felt her close tightly around him. He was close to coming himself, but he held back. He would make her come more than once before he came himself.

Hemera dropped her head forward and let herself feel and delight in every hard thrust. Even the slap of flesh against flesh excited her beyond reason. And it would not be long before... her moan grew louder.

He stopped suddenly and his hand went to cover her mouth. "If you moan any louder the guards will hear and this will end."

She nodded and clamped her mouth tightly shut after he removed his hand and resumed his mighty thrusts. It was not easy keeping quiet with the way he was making her feel. How he had tempted and teased her and fired her passion until she wanted to scream aloud with pleasure and with what she knew would follow.

"Talon," she whispered with a heavy breath, drawing nearer and nearer to that moment of exquisite release. "Please. Please," she begged and with two deep plunges, she burst so hard that she had to clamp her mouth tightly to stop from screaming with pleasure. She felt as if her whole body exploded in unending satisfaction. It poured from her over and over and she never wanted it to end. When the rippling pleasure began to fade, Talon startled her by pulling out of her, scooping her up and dropping her on the pallet to drop down on his knees between her legs, lift them over his shoulders and enter her again.

That he could spark her passion again before it completely faded had her gripping the blanket beneath her and fighting hard to keep from crying out as her body burst to life once again.

Talon climaxed with her this time and with an immense pleasure he had never felt before, but then that seemed to be the way with Hemera. Their coupling grew more and more satisfying each time they joined together.

He dropped down over her after the last of their shudders rippled away and rolled off her onto his back, his hand reaching out to take hers. They lay beside each other, their breathing labored, their bodies wet, and the scent of mating heavy in the air.

"I have never felt anything so wonderful," Hemera whispered.

"I will make sure you feel wonderful often," he said a slight smile tempting his lips at the thought of how much they would enjoy each other.

Hemera turned on her side. "Have you felt this way before?"

He rolled on his side, aware that she was truly asking if other women pleased him as well as she did. He ran his finger lightly over her lips. "Never. Only with you have I felt extreme pleasure."

Hemera sighed. "I am glad I came to your sleeping chamber."

Talon turned a light scowl on her. "You will tell me how you found out about my secret entrance and how you got passed Tilden."

"First answer me a question?" she asked, placing a gentle hand to his chest.

"One," he said with a nod.

"Are you glad I am here?"

His scowl faded and he shook his head before lowering it and kissing her lips lightly. "More than I care to admit."

Hemera smiled. "I am glad to hear that, for there is no other place I want to be."

"And no other place I would have you." He kissed her again, his scowl returning, though not as deeply as before. "Now tell me."

She grimaced as she said, "Please do not punish Tilden. I gave him a brew that made him sleepy and being he was already tired, he fell asleep easily. It is entirely my fault and I feel terrible for doing it to him, but my need for you overpowered my good sense."

"I will consider your plea," he said. "Now tell me how you learned of my secret door."

Hemera told him how she had come across it after seeing him emerge from the bushes one day.

"So that is how you appeared on the stairs that day in the feasting hall," he said. "It has always puzzled me."

"I am glad I found it," she said, snuggling close against him. "Now I can use it to visit you."

"You will not use it. It was meant for me and me alone. I forbid you to use it."

"Why? When it would make it so much easier for us to be together," she argued.

"I take a chance when I use it. To have another use it would only be inviting discovery."

Hemera sighed disappointed. "As you say, but if an emergency should arise—"

"It would have to be a dire one. You will not use it again."

"How will I return to my dwelling?" she asked.

"I will escort you back through the secret passage and have a word with Tilden."

Her eyes pleaded with him.

"Tilden will get what he deserves...a heavy dose of guilt and humiliation in front of his King for being duped by a woman."

"I am grateful he will not suffer because of me."

Talon laughed. "He will suffer more than if I raised my hand to him."

Hemera cringed, understanding the young warrior will feel that he failed his King, a far worse punishment to one of the King's personal guards than a beating.

They fell asleep in each other's arms, woke, and enjoyed the pleasure of mating slowly before dozing off again. They woke shortly before sunrise and hurried to Hemera's dwelling where Tilden paled so badly upon seeing Hemera approach with the King that he almost dropped in a faint.

Hemera went to apologize to the young warrior when Talon ordered, "Go inside and wait for me." She did not dare disobey him again and with a nod to him, she did as he commanded.

Tilden stood stoic, ready to accept his punishment, fearing the worse, dismissal from the King's personal guards, a position he took great pride in.

"You will take no drink or food from Hemera ever and you will continue to protect her with your life, always," Talon ordered. "You also have my permission to knock on her door and if she does not answer, you may enter and make certain she is within."

"Aye, my King. I will keep a more vigilant eye on her."

"It will not be an easy task, but if you manage to do it, you will rank the highest among my guards and have my utmost respect."

Tilden's chest broadened. "Have no doubt, I will not fail you, my King."

"I am pleased to hear that," Talon said for he knew the young warrior would do anything now to keep Hemera safe.

Talon entered the dwelling to find Hemera curled up on her sleeping pallet asleep. He pulled the blanket over her and kissed her cheek lightly.

He turned and walked out of the dwelling, ignoring the twinge to his heart and how it grew as he got further and further away from Hemera.

## Chapter Nineteen

Hemera was lost in her thoughts. It had been seven sunrises since last she had seen Talon and she had missed him more and more each passing day. No one would say where he had gone. She had woken the morn after she had snuck off to Talon's sleeping chamber to find him gone, and a guard following her every step.

She was upset with both and worse was that she could not seek the comfort of the woods. With a guard always near, she could not sneak through the opening in the fence, not that she would, though it probably had been a concern of Talon's. With Ulric still having plans for her, she would be foolish to place herself in harm's way.

Her hand went to rest at her middle. If her sister's vision proved true, which they always had, she would be carrying Talon's bairn... the King's bairn. The thought brought a smile to her face. She would give Talon what no one else could. It was another reason she would not chance going into the woods. She would not only be placing herself in harm's way, but possibly the heir to the Pict throne.

If she was softly round with child when Verity had seen her and the land had been lush with growth as she had said, then it would mean the bairn would be born when the land began its sleep, possibly when the first snow fell. It would mean that Talon's seed had already taken root and was flourishing inside her.

She smiled, the thought pleasing her. Her smile vanished when further thought had her wondering if people would doubt Talon was the father. No one knew they had mated. Would everyone believe it a ruse?

A scrunch of her brow had her wondering why his seed could flourish in her and not his two previous wives who now were near to giving birth to their new husbands' bairns. Why her and not the other two women? If she questioned it, would others do the same?

She shook her head. She could not worry over something that was yet to be.

She stepped outside her dwelling to greet the morn and see the clouds restricting the sun, letting it shine through only at their whim, and to see that a guard was ready to follow her wherever she went. Her solitude had been disturbed and she could not bear it much longer, especially when Talon returned. They would never have any time alone together if they both were forever watched.

She had been spending more time on finding out who in the stronghold was involved in the plot to unseat the King. Unrest had settled over the people and Hemera could not blame them. If Hollins, one of their own, had betrayed them who was to be trusted?

"It is over."

Hemera was not the only one stopped abruptly by the sharp retort. Others had stopped and sent a curious glance at Broc. Seeing that he had drawn attention, he grabbed the servant, Simca he had spoken to by the arm and hurried her off to the side of a nearby dwelling.

It seemed obvious that Broc was ending whatever had been between them and Simca looked none too pleased.

She continued on as did the others and a smile brightened her face as it did her sister's when they caught sight of each other. A quick hug was exchanged before they walked off, arm and arm, and it was not even a moment later that Simca ran past them, tears staining her flushed cheeks.

"I believe Broc and Simca are no more," Verity said, keeping her voice low and shaking her head. "It is her own fault."

"Why do you say that?" Hemera asked, thinking how she would feel if Talon told her it was done between them. She had not given such a possibility thought. She had joined with Talon with no preconceived notions. He was King and would have a queen one day and she would... what? What would she do if he did not want her anymore? She had found herself missing him terribly since his departure and it only grew worse the longer he was away. What would it be like if he was done with her like Broc was with Simca? How would she cope with this unexpected and growing ache while separated from him?

A small gasp nearly slipped from her lips when a sudden thought hit her.

She had lost her heart to Talon or perhaps he had stolen it. What was she to do? She had never given the prospect thought, never believed such a thing would happen to her. She favored her solitude and yet she ached for Talon's return, ached that they never be separated this long again.

"Did you hear me, Hemera, or do your thoughts wander?" her sister asked accustomed to her sister's mind straying.

"My thoughts hold me captive," Hemera admitted.

Verity patted her sister's arm. "We are captives no more."

That was not completely true. Talon held her heart captive and she would never be free, but she said none of that to her sister. "Tell me again."

"Simca gives her favors to many men, staying faithful to none, then becomes angry when a man no longer wants her. Wrath dealt with her anger once."

Hemera turned surprised eyes on her sister.

"We were not together yet." Verity's brief laughter fell around them softly. "He was trying to avoid his attraction to me.

"That brought a smile to Hemera's face. "I remember the visions you had about him. It helped in the decision to escape, knowing there would be someone there to care for you."

"And you," Verity said with an excited smile. "There is someone who will soon care for you or has he already?"

Hemera shook her head. "What are you saying?"

Verity lowered her voice. "According to my vision, you will be with child shortly and I heard about how King Talon found you having fun in the woods with Bower that day and you have been seen with him a couple of times in the days since King Talon's departure." She gave her sister's shoulder a nudge with her own. "Bower is a good man and I would be happy for you."

"Bower is a good man," Hemera agreed, "but not the man for me. His time with me is spent talking about the tree branches that are best to craft fine bows. I have made it clear to him that I expect or want no more than friendship from him."

"Then who could it be that would steal your heart so suddenly?" Verity asked, chewing at her bottom lip in thought when suddenly she stopped walking, her eyes turning wide. "Someone has already stolen your heart."

Hemera's first thought was to deny it, but that would only make her sister wonder more and since her vision she would be curious about anyone who looked Hemera's way. It would be better if her sister knew there was someone just not the identity of that someone.

"I was not ready to share it yet," Hemera said.

Verity could hardly contain her excitement. "I am thrilled to hear it. Who is it? I want to meet him and Wrath will want to meet him. However did you keep it from us? I am so happy for you." She threw her arms around Hemera and squeezed tight.

Hemera could not help but think if her sister would be this happy if she knew who it was.

"Tell me all about him," Verity said, taking hold of Hemera's arm once more to continue walking.

"He is more than I believed him to be and all that I want."

Verity stilled her steps, a gentle smile gracing her lips. "You have lost your heart to him. Has he done the same?"

Hemera shook her head. "It is all new. I am still learning how I feel."

"You will never fully comprehend it all and that is the joy of losing your heart. Now tell me who it is. I am impatient to know."

"Not yet," Hemera said and started walking again.

"Hemera—"

"Please, Verity, let me have this to myself just a

while longer," Hemera pleaded, wishing she could share it with her sister yet knowing that was not possible.

Verity gave it thought for a moment and not hiding her disappointment, finally agreed grudgingly. "A *little* while, no more. I want to know that this man is good for my sister."

"I feel safe with him."

Verity gasped, a hand going to her chest. "I feel that way with Wrath." A sudden frown caught her face. "If you want no one to know, how have you met with him since the guards have been assigned to follow you?"

Leave it to her sister to realize that, though Hemera provided an honest response. "We have not been together since the attack."

"You must miss him."

"Terribly," Hemera said.

"Hmmm," Verity said with a cock of her head. "I wonder if we can do something about that."

~~~

Talon was never so glad to see the burning torches atop the stronghold fence as he rode through the gates, darkness having long claimed the land. He had been gone far too long. It had been imperative that he meet with several chieftains in the surrounding area. He needed to speak with each one of them to see for himself if there was any thought of disloyalty and a surprise visit from the King was one way that proved effective, discussing various concerns was another. They all had voiced concern that Northmen continued to roam Pict land and worried about a possible war with the northern savages. Another grave concern to them was the lack of an heir to the Pict throne. A throne with no heir was ripe for conquest, the more heirs the stronger the sovereignty.

That was the one concern that troubled him the most. Hemera had not left his thoughts since he had departed the stronghold. There had been times when thoughts of her consumed him and he had had to chase her away and when he did, he missed her intruding on his musings. He could not wait to see her, hold her, and couple with her.

Women had approached him while away, but he had no interest in them. His only thought was of Hemera and how he felt when they joined as one. He had no desire for any other woman than Hemera and he was sure no other woman could prove as satisfying as her. He wanted Hemera and only Hemera.

What then did he do about a queen?

"Go to your wives," Talon ordered Wrath and Paine a short distance into the stronghold. "The High Council meeting can wait until morn."

The two men gave respectful nods and hurried off. He could not blame them. If he were free to go to Hemera, he would not waste a moment. He would be there now with her.

*Not so*, he thought. She would be with him in his sleeping chamber. There would be no more sneaking or secrets. All would know she was his woman and that could prove a problem. While he saw her strength, others saw weakness, and none would think her fit to be queen.

Talon brought his horse to a halt at the feasting

house and after a young lad took the animal, he decided he did not want to wait to see Hemera. He would not be able to stay, but at least he could lay eyes on her and know she was safe and let her know he would be returning later. He turned and walked off, one of his personal guards following.

~~~

    Hemera had left her dwelling before Tilden took his post just after dusk, wearing Verity's hooded cloak. Tilden was one of Talon's more astute guards so when Verity suggested they change places, giving her time to sneak off and meet with the man she favored, Hemera had been quick to agree, though it had to be before Tilden took his post or the task would prove more difficult. Not that she would meet with anyone. Though, it would give her the chance to move about the stronghold without a guard, remaining mostly in the shadows undetected, while seeing or hearing anything that would help discover the identity of the cloaked figure or who else might be a traitor to the King.

    She had watched, hoping she might catch movements similar to the person she had seen in the forest wearing one of the King's personal guards' cloaks, but she had had no luck. With nothing else catching her eye, she decided to return to her dwelling, having been gone long enough and not wanting to take the chance of getting caught. She took only a few steps when she spotted the guard, Tarnis who had been at her door when she had taken her leave.

    His steps were hurried and he cast anxious glances about, as if making sure no one paid him heed or followed him. Hemera decided to trail after him since his actions seemed odd to her. Why would one of the King's guards appear secretive?

She followed along in the shadows her steps quiet, a skill she had acquired out of necessity while with the Northmen. He was near to the front of the stronghold when a sound distracted her for a mere moment and when she turned, he was gone from sight. He was there one moment and gone the next. She stood, listening. Barely a moment past when she heard laughter—a woman's laughter. Whispers followed, then it turned silent, though not completely. She could hear them kissing and the fumbling of their garments as they hurried to couple.

Hemera turned away, disappointed it had proven to be nothing of importance. She had explored enough. She needed to return to her dwelling. She had barely taken a step when shouts filled the air and she rushed to duck behind a nearby dwelling, not sure what had caused the commotion.

Suddenly the air resonated with the heavy pounding of a drum—the King had returned.

Hemera hoisted her long cloak all set to run when Tarnis suddenly stopped right in front of where she had taken cover. If darkness had not settled, he would have seen her and if he was not hastier in attending to his garments, she feared discovery, especially since Wrath also had returned and would be looking for his wife.

When Tarnis finally scurried away, Hemera paused before leaving her hiding nook, waiting to see if the woman would follow him, and she did.

It was Simca and she called out to Tarnis, chasing after him and disappeared into the darkness.

Hemera continued to wait after hearing more

footfalls passing by until it finally turned quiet. She went to hurry off when a shadow rushed by, turning her still.

Her curiosity had her stepping out of her hiding nook quietly and when she caught sight of the shadow a short distance away she realized what had piqued her interest. The figure had the same gait as the one Hemera had seen in the woods. The figure was also wearing the black cloak of the King's personal guards.

Hemera did not hesitate... she followed the figure.

~~~

Talon was pleased to see Tilden guarding Hemera's dwelling. He would say nothing of his visit now or later when he returned. He need not explain his presence there, but thought it best to say something since curious eyes had watched him head this way.

"Hemera is here? I want a word with her."

"Aye, my King, Hemera is inside," Tilden said.

Talon opened the door before Tilden could and stepped inside. She lay on her side, the blanket completely covering her. He wished he could slip in naked beside her, wrap himself around her and... he reached out and gently touched her shoulder and was about to lower his head and steal a kiss when she turned.

"Verity?"

"My King?"

## Chapter Twenty

"Where is Hemera and what are you doing here?" Talon demanded as Verity scurried to her feet.

Verity was so stunned to see the King in Hemera's dwelling and that he had placed his hand on what he had thought was Hemera's shoulder that she was at a loss to respond. All she could do was stare at the King.

"Find your tongue, woman, and tell me what goes on here!"

His stern, sharp voice vibrated through her and before she could respond, the King walked to the door and threw it open.

"Tilden! Where is Hemera?"

The guard entered the dwelling, a baffled look on his face as he saw Verity but no Hemera.

"Did you see for yourself that Hemera was inside when you took your post?" Talon demanded his tongue remaining sharp.

"Aye, my King, I rapped on the door and when I received no answer, I entered and saw," — he glanced at Verity—"who I thought was Hemera sleeping and did not wish to disturb her."

"Who stood guard before you?" Talon asked.

"Tarnis and he did say that Verity had paid Hemera a visit and was returning later."

Talon's deep blue eyes glared as hot as the flames in the fire pit when he turned to Verity.

Verity paled. She had feared the King from first

meeting him. He had not been kind and she did not believe him kind. Many claimed he was a fair King, but fairness and kindness did not always work hand-in-hand.

"Where is Hemera?" Talon demanded.

Verity's limbs grew weak as she fought to find the words to speak and nearly dropped on the sleeping pallet with relief when Wrath walked through the door. She reached her hand out to him as he hurried around the King to her side, his arm going around her. She let her body rest against him and his arm tightened around her.

"What is wrong? Are you ill? Is it the bairn?" Wrath asked anxiously, his worry over his wife mounting.

Talon answered, certain fear had stolen Verity's voice. "What is wrong is that she is here and Hemera is not, and she has yet to explain why."

Wrath looked to his wife, concern in his eyes but also a spark of annoyance. He knew Verity well. She would do anything to help her sister and he worried that was what she had done. "Tell me."

Talon nearly cursed aloud when he saw how Verity paled even more and went limp in Wrath's arms. He was quick to order, "Sit with her before she collapses altogether."

Wrath was grateful to Talon for realizing the toll the situation was taking on Verity and that was his first concern. His second was that if his wife was this upset, then she worried not that she angered the King, but for her sister who no doubt was doing something she should not be doing.

Wrath kept a firm arm around his wife as he sat

with her tucked against him, and repeated, "Tell me."

~~~

Hemera tracked the dark cloaked figure silently through the woods, keeping a safe distance and her steps silent. She had asked for help from the forest upon entering it and as always the forest never failed to help or guide her.

After a short distance in, it was apparent that the cloak figured was well acquainted with the forest. He stepped without fear and with much confidence. He had to have done so often to be so familiar with it. There was something else that had churned Hemera's thoughts. The figure had followed close behind Tarnis and wore the cloak of the King's personal guard, so could it be a woman she followed? Or in his haste had Tarnis simply forgotten his cloak and the traitor had snatched it up?

An owl hooted, halting Hemera's steps and she listened. She heard nothing and realized the cloaked figured had stopped walking. Hemera continued with cautious steps, retreating to the protection of the darkest shadows that shifted and changed with the glow of the half moon and the clouds that raced by it.

She took a few more steps, listening for any sound when a squirrel suddenly ran in front of her, bringing her to an abrupt, but silent stop. She listened and hearing voices treaded lightly along the forest's ground to get closer so she could hear what was being said. She kept her hood up over her red hair, not wanting a spark from the moon catching it and alerting anyone to her presence.

When she could finally hear clearly, she settled

against the safety of a thick tree trunk that had been there long before the Picts settled here. The old tree sheltered her against harm and she felt safe in its protection.

"Hollins failed his mission?"

The voice was low, but the forest carried it enough so that Hemera could hear it, though not distinguish it.

"He did and now that the King knows his enemy is after the slow-minded one, he has ordered his personal guards to watch over her."

"None of them can be tempted to go against him?"

"No, I would not even try. His personal guards are faithful to him. We may have to change plans."

"Ulric will not be happy."

"Why is it so important to him?"

"I do not know or care as long as he helps us take the throne."

"We must hurry. A guard will pass this way soon."

"How goes the plan with the future queen?"

"The poison is working well. She will be dead soon enough and the search will have to begin again. With unrest over the King's failure to secure an heir and the trouble with the Northmen, we will taste victory soon."

"That is good to hear."

"Is the King still without a woman?"

"He is and his appetite has waned for any woman, and tongues wag wondering what is wrong with him. It helps our cause, for he continues to grow weaker in the eyes of the people. I have no more to tell you. We must leave now or be caught."

Hemera stayed where she was, unmoving, letting the old tree and the shadows protect her. She waited until the cloaked figure passed her, then she followed after him, hoping to finally learn his identity.

She had only taken a few steps when a strong hand clamped down on her shoulder.

~~~

"Repeat that," King Talon ordered.

Wrath would have said the same if Talon had not, since he did not quite believe what Verity had said.

"Hemera has been seeing a man, she has come to care for, but she wishes to keep it secret since it is new and the feelings unfamiliar to her. With always having a guard on her, it has become impossible for her to meet with him, so I offered to change places with her so that she may have some time with him this evening."

"She did not tell you who this man is?" Wrath asked.

Verity shook her head. "No, though I told her she could not keep it a secret for long. I want to know who it is that has captured my sister's heart and if he is good for her."

"So do I, though if it is Bower, I would approve. He is a good man," Wrath said.

"She is a friend to him, no more than that, and she has made it quite clear to him."

"She truly cares for this man she has been seeing?" Talon asked, wanting to know what Hemera had confessed about this man—about him.

"I believe more than she realizes," Hemera said. "Her eyes brighten when she speaks about him and that she missed seeing him was obvious. I thought you might be relieved, my King, to know she has found someone who cares for her and she could possibly wed, as you wish."

"Does he care for her?" Wrath asked. "Why does he not step forward? What stops him from claiming what he feels for her? Or is it that he is ashamed to be seen with her?"

*Or was it that he was King and could never claim her as his rightful wife?* Talon thought and Wrath's words disturbed him. What disturbed him more was that since he was the man they spoke about, where then had Hemera gone?

~~~

Hemera ran as fast as she could, letting the forest and its creatures guide her steps. She did not dare lead the enemy to the secret opening in the stronghold gate. The thought gave her mind pause. Was the opening known to the enemy? Had the traitor in the stronghold shared that knowledge with his cohorts?

She had to get back to the stronghold and tell Talon what she had learned and she had to tell him of not only the opening in the fence the traitor had slipped through, but her own as well. And what if there were more openings? The enemy could attack the stronghold from within.

A strong whisper from a towering tree halted her racing steps and she quickly ducked behind its thick trunk. Footfalls hurried past her, but she could not take a chance and see if it was the King's warriors and seek help, since she was not sure who to trust.

~~~

"I never thought of that," Verity said upset. "Hemera is a good, kind person. That someone would be ashamed to be seen with her never entered my mind."

Wrath did not like seeing his wife upset or that someone could be taking advantage of Hemera. "Do not worry, Verity, I will find out who this man is and his intentions towards Verity."

"It may be too late," Verity said, recalling her vision and suddenly regretting that she had not told all of what she had seen. She had told her sister she would say nothing, but now, thinking on it... what if Hemera cared for a man who cared nothing for her?

"What do you mean?" Talon demanded.

Verity jumped at the King's sharp tongue and wondered if her silence would be more harmful to her sister than if she confessed the truth. "I gave my sister my word."

Talon heard a niggling of doubt in her voice. "Will keeping your word benefit or harm her?"

"The King is right, which helps Hemera more... the truth or silence?" Wrath asked.

Verity did not want to betray her sister's trust, but she had to consider what was best for Hemera. She had seen no man in the vision with her. She had stood in the woods alone. Would this man dessert her? Leave her alone, carrying his bairn?

The thought upset her so much that she said, "When I saw Hemera in the woods, she was softly round with child, which means she is either already with child or soon to be."

Talon almost stumbled back from the impact of Verity's reveal. After all this time could it possibly be true? It took all his strength to keep from showing his shock and even more strength not to let himself feel joy, at least not until he could confirm it.

"We must find Hemera," Talon said anxious to ask Hemera about this and even more anxious to know she was safe.

Wrath stood. "On your word I will order a search of the stronghold."

Broc rushed in the dwelling before Talon could give Wrath permission and with labored breath said, "Enemy warriors have been spotted in the woods," — he took a quick breath— "Hemera has been seen there as well."

Verity gasped, her hand pressing against her chest.

"I will see Hemera safe," Talon said to Verity and turned to Wrath. "Get Paine, we go into the woods."

~~~

For a brief moment, clouds allowed the half-moon to peek through and Hemera caught a hasty glimpse around. Seeing no one, she waited until another cloud slipped over the moon before taking cautious steps from behind the tree. A chilled wind whipped around her, reminding her that she had lost her cloak, a tree snagging it as she ran. She had dared not stop for it. She hugged herself for warmth and kept her footfalls light as she made her way through the dark, once again depending on the forest to guide her.

She was not that far from the stronghold, though she would have to enter through the opening in the fence by her dwelling since the gates were closed. She wondered if her absence had been discovered. Surely,

Wrath would search for Verity once he saw that she was not in their dwelling and he would look first at Hemera's place. And what of Talon? Would he seek her out right away or wait until the stronghold slept for the night?

If he missed her as much as she missed him, would he not find a reason to come to her right away, at least for a brief visit until he could return to her later? But he would not find her...he would find Verity. What then?

She pushed the disturbing thoughts from her mind. This was not the time to worry over it. She needed to think only on returning safely to the stronghold. She continued keeping her steps cautious, listening for any unusual sounds or warnings from the forest.

*Hurry!* The wind suddenly urged, swirling around her.

As she hurried her steps, she heard footfalls a distance behind her and when their pace turned rapid, she knew whoever it was had spotted her and was now after her. She did not hesitate and she did not glance back...she ran.

~~~

Talon wanted to scream out for Hemera when he entered the woods along with Wrath and Paine and a contingent of his warriors, but he stopped himself. It would be a foolish thing to do when his enemy lurked about.

The warrior who had spotted Hemera and tried to stop her and return her safely to the stronghold had quickly sought help once the darkness had swallowed her and he could no longer follow her tracks.

When Talon had been handed Verity's cloak that she had lent her sister, a fear like never before raced through him and squeezed at his heart until he thought it would burst. She was in the woods, alone in the dark with his enemies lurking about. If they found her... his one hand clenched the handle of his sword he held at the thought of what she would suffer. And fear prickled his flesh as his anger soared.

Talon turned to Paine. "Where is the wolf?"

"I have called Bog, but he has not answered. He took off for the woods just before we entered the stronghold."

Talon silently cursed the animal. The wolf had befriended Hemera and he was hoping the animal could track her scent. He stepped forward and led his warriors into the woods.

The search seemed endless to Talon, though it had not been long since they had begun. He had to quell the rising urge to shout out to her with every step he took. He had to find her. He would not rest until he did. Whether she carried his bairn or not, did not matter at the moment. He wanted Hemera safe in his arms.

~~~

Hemera raced with all the speed she could muster, but whoever followed had more and from the sounds of his footfalls he was getting ever closer. She would not make it. He would catch her. She would never see Talon again and she thought her heart would shatter from the pain.

*Shout out to him!*

It was a familiar voice to Hemera one she had

heard throughout the years whenever she was in peril, and she had listened to it without question just as she did now.

"Talon! Talon! Talon!"

The wind picked up her scream and sent it whipping through the trees like a thunderous roar and racing over the land to reach Talon.

~~~

Talon's heart felt as if it burst when he heard Hemera frantically calling out to him. He did not hesitate, he ran. He paid no heed to Wrath and Paine who called out to him with alarm. He was faster than the both of them, faster than any of his warriors and they knew it. He would reach Hemera before they did and that was their worry.

He did not care. The only thing that mattered was Hemera.

Talon vaulted over fallen, decaying trees, cleared large boulders in two easy steps, and ran as swiftly as the deer. Anger erupted in his blue eyes turning them such a deep blue that they appeared as black as the night when he came upon Hemera running for her life, three men following close behind her.

Her eyes turned wide, fear heavy in them.

The three men fanned out behind her when they saw him and all three grinned as if their greatest wish had come true.

Talon ran even faster, holding his sword high and letting out a roar so fierce, the men stumbled in their tracks.

He reached Hemera before they could and as he

grabbed her arm and flung her out of harm's way, Bog burst through the trees and plunged his fangs into the back of one warrior's neck before he could stop the ferocious wolf.

Talon ducked and swung his sword as one of the two remaining warriors went to swing his weapon. The sharp blade and the ferocity of his swing nearly split the man in two. Fear hesitated the last man, seeing both his fellow warriors fall so quickly and as he brought his sword up, Talon's blade came crashing down on his wrist, severing his hand from his arm.

The man fell to his knees screaming as Talon kicked the sword, the hand still attached to the handle, away from the man.

"Guard!" Talon ordered Bog and the wolf took an attack stance in front of the man, his snarling mouth and fangs covered with blood.

Talon hurried to Hemera as she stumbled to her feet a bit dazed, though when she caught sight of him, she ran to him. His one arm circled her waist, drawing her up against him, keeping his sword tight in his other hand.

"Are you hurt?" he asked, dirt marring her one cheek and her fiery red hair speared with several pine needles.

She shook her head and two pine needles dropped from her hair. "I am good."

Hearing that, he did what he had been aching to do since the day he left the stronghold. He kissed Hemera. It was a demanding and quick kiss, his lips strong on hers that gave eagerly in return. He forced himself to end it far too quickly. He needed to keep his wits about him should more culprits be lurking about.

Hemera had yearned for his kiss since he had been gone and this brief one would never do, but it would have to wait. His men had to be close behind him and they could not find them in an intimate embrace.

She laid her head on his shoulder, taking a moment to linger in his arms, feel the warmth and strength of his body embrace her before she would have to step away from him. When she heard the thunder of footfalls ponding the earth, she reluctantly went to step away from him.

His arm locked around her possessively. "You will stay where you are."

Hemera could not move if she wanted to, his arm feeling like an iron shackle around her waist. He had no intentions of letting her go.

She listened as the footfalls drew closer. Any moment the warriors would be upon them. She turned her face up to his to remind him that they could not be found like this, and his lips came down on hers.

## Chapter Twenty-one

The intensity of the kiss shivered Hemera deep down to her bones. She realized then that it was not Talon who kissed her... it was the King. It was meant for all to see. He was claiming her as his woman.

Hemera rested her brow to his shoulder to catch her breath when he ended their kiss and he spoke as if he was setting forth an edict and woe to anyone who challenged it.

"*Hemera is mine.*"

She raised her head and looked upon the sea of faces to see eyes turned wide on some, mouths agape on others, while a few shook their heads. The only anger she saw stirring was in Wrath's eyes and Paine was the only one who wore a smile.

Wrath approached the King, his strides strong and his jaw set tight, as if fighting to hold his tongue.

"Later I will hear what you have to say, Wrath," Talon ordered when his commander warrior was a short distance from him. "See that the prisoner is taken to the torture chamber and sear his stump. I want him alive long enough to tell us what he knows. Also, have the warriors scout the area to make certain no one else lingers about."

Wrath gave the King a sharp nod and as he looked to Hemera, he saw Talon's arm tighten possessively around her waist. "You are unharmed?"

"I am. How does my sister fare?" Hemera asked,

assuming they had discovered Verity where Hemera should have been.

"She is good, though concerned about you and will be more so when she learns..." Wrath let his words trail off. There was no need saying what was obvious to all.

"I will go to her as soon as I return to the stronghold," Hemera said eager to assuage her sister's worries.

"You will go when I permit it," Talon said and felt her whole body stiffen as tight as a taut bow string.

Wrath saw Hemera's reaction and a smile curled at the corners of his mouth as he turned and walked away to join Paine who was already seeing to the prisoner.

"I was wondering when you would see the humor in all this," Paine said with a low chuckle.

Wrath lost his smile to a sudden scowl. "The question is what will the King do with Hemera?"

Paine shook his head. "Do you not know your wife's sister at all? It is not what the King will do with Hemera that should concern you, but what Hemera will do to the King."

~~~

Verity was waiting at the gate for her sister's return and when Hemera saw her, she rushed off before Talon could stop her. The sisters hugged so tight, Talon did not think anything could pry them apart.

Talon went to them, his glance settling on Hemera. "Go to the feasting hall and have your say with your sister, for when I arrive there we will talk. I will not be long, so be quick about it."

Hemera hugged him, shocking Verity and the few

who looked on. "I am grateful." She grabbed Verity's hand and tugged her along, forcing a hasty pace.

"You cannot hug the King like that." Talon heard Verity scold her sister, then she added, "And what were you doing in the woods?"

Talon spoke with Wrath and Paine with regard to the prisoner, Broc busy having taken part in the search for other enemy warriors. "See to searing his wound, then chain him to the wall for the night and leave him to think on what the morn will bring. Leave four guards outside around the chamber and two inside. Switch them periodically with no set times. When you finish, come to the High Council Chambers so you may hear what Hemera has to tell us."

The two men went to do as the King bid and Talon headed to the feasting hall.

~~~

"The King? The King is the man you have been meeting? The man you favor?" Verity asked, shaking her head in disbelief.

Hemera nodded and went to speak.

Verity grabbed her arm and whispered, "You carry the King's bairn?"

"It is too soon to tell, though I suppose if you saw me round with child, then it must be so."

"He will not claim you as his queen," Verity said anxiously.

Hemera drew her head back startled. "I have given no thought to being queen."

"You would not want to see him wed another, would you?"

The thought upset Hemera and a pain so sharp speared her heart that it almost stole her breath.

"Besides, you will give him what no woman has been able to, an heir to the Pict throne. It will help confirm his right as the Pict King and end the unrest among our people. His enemy will no longer be able to deny his ability to rule."

"You told him about seeing me soft with child?" Hemera asked not surprised when her sister nodded.

Verity squeezed her sister's arm lightly. "I was worried he would deny you the man you favored, when he made it known it would be his decision who you would wed."

Hemera glanced down at the table, her thoughts straying. Was that why he had openly claimed her... his woman? Would Talon have done so if there was no bairn? He had not known for sure if there was, but then he trusted Verity's visions.

Verity's soft words of regret broke through Hemera's thoughts.

"I am sorry, please forgive my foolish tongue."

Hemera slipped her arm around her sister. "It is my fault not yours. You only wanted to protect me. I should have been truthful with you."

The door to the feasting hall opened and the King walked in. His guards followed behind him and spread out through the feasting hall as he approached the table where Hemera and her sister sat.

The two women stood and gripped hands tightly.

"Do not bring my sister pain," Verity said with a strong lift of her chin.

Though she quivered when she spoke, Talon was pleased to see that Verity had not let her fear stand in the way of protecting her sister. Still, he was King and could not let her dictate to him.

He crossed his arms over his chest and said, "You threaten your King?"

Hemera nudged Verity to take a step back, leaving enough room for Hemera to partially stand in front of her sister. "We protect each other and that will never change."

Talon glared at Hemera. "Everything changed the moment I claimed you mine." He snapped his finger at her. "Come with me."

Hemera turned to her sister and with a hug and a whisper said, "Wait here and we will talk more. There is much I must tell Talon."

Verity nodded and reluctantly released the grip on her hand, fearing as she did that she was losing her sister. There was a tender familiarity in the way Hemera had spoken the King's name, as though she spoke it often. It made Verity wonder how long the King had been intimate with her sister.

Hemera followed Talon to the High Council Chambers and was relieved to see Anin enter the feasting hall and hurry to Verity. It pleased her to know her sister would not be alone.

The door to the Council Chamber no soon as closed, then Hemera found herself in Talon's arms and his lips on hers. She relished the way he kissed her with such power and intent. He would not be denied and though it seemed that he demanded, he more coaxed her into responding, not that she needed coaxing. She was eager to kiss him any time she could. She missed his lips, the taste and strength of them.

She draped her arms around his neck and was

about to press harder against him when he tucked her closer and she felt him hard and ready against her.

She eased her mouth away from his, no easy task, since he refused to let her go, but she managed and whispered in his ear, "It has been too long since last you were inside me. I miss having you there."

Talon's groan rumbled deep inside him and he silently cursed as his manhood demanded relief. He wanted Hemera so badly that nothing else seemed to matter at that moment. The only thing he cared about was burying himself inside her and claiming her over and over and over, so that no one could dispute that she belonged to him.

He shoved her away, though it was the last thing he wanted to do. "We need to talk before..."

"We couple," she finished, though added, "numerous times."

"Enough!" he said and turned away from her. He needed to get control of himself. There were things that needed to be discussed, issues that needed settling, and—he jumped when he felt her hand rest tenderly against his back. He could almost feel her warm flesh straight through his garments and it made him yearn even more to feel her gentle touch upon his naked flesh.

"There is much I must tell you. Later we can make up for the time we have missed together," she said softly.

He turned and cupped her face in his hands. "That we will." Just as he was about to give her a quick kiss, an angry voice could be heard on the other side of the closed door.

"I command you to let me in now!"

Talon flung the door open to see an angry Gelhard

shaking his finger at one of the guards.

Gelhard turned away from the guard to enter the room. "How dare he keep me from entering after—" Gelhard did not hide his distain when his eyes fell on Hemera. "It is true."

Hemera took a step back, the man's scowl so angry that it contorted his face, making him appear more like a demon.

Gelhard swerved around, turning his scowl on Talon. "You cannot be serious. You will be thought a fool if you claim this witless woman as your own."

"If you want to keep your tongue, Gelhard, I advise you to watch it carefully," Talon warned his anger tangible.

The tips of Gelhard's ears turned red with fury, his eyes grew wide and his lips twitched.

Hemera stepped in. "This is no time to argue. The future queen is being poisoned."

"What nonsense does your witless tongue speak?" Gelhard demanded, his tone as harsh as a father reprimanding a misbehaved bairn.

Paine and Wrath entered as Talon ordered, "I warned you, now you will lose your tongue. Paine, *see it done!*"

Paine and Wrath stood shocked by his command.

Hemera shook her head. "That is a senseless command."

Paine smiled, Wrath ran his hand over his face, and Gelhard stared at Hemera, his mouth hanging open.

"You let your anger speak," Hemera said, shaking her head at Talon. "How will Gelhard serve you if he cannot speak? He is your High Counselor. It is his task to advise you wisely."

"He loses his tongue for speaking harshly to you, and I owe you no explanation," Talon said annoyed, wondering why he had even explained.

"Of course he speaks harshly. I sound the fool to him. After he hears the whole of it, he will think differently and I am sure he will offer an apology." Hemera turned to the short man who had paled as white as the clouds that filled the sky on a sunny day. "What say you, Gelhard?"

"Aye," Gelhard said with a nod, "I need to hear the whole of it."

Talon ordered them all to sit and Hemera to speak once they did.

She explained what she had heard. How the future queen was being poisoned and would die soon if word was not sent to her family.

Talon listened to her every word, thinking all the while what danger she had placed not only herself in, but if she should be carrying his bairn, then the future Pict King. The thought that it could possibly be true, that their child was growing inside her this very moment had him feeling all the more protective of her. And all the more reason to make certain she did not go off on her own again.

Talon turned to Gelhard. "Go make arrangements for someone to leave at first light and give warning to the Fermour Tribe and let them know they have a traitor among them and that he is poisoning Daria."

Gelhard looked hesitant to leave the room and Hemera could not blame him. The King was dismissing him, not allowing him to remain and hear what else Hemera had to say. It was obvious the King was letting him know he did not trust him or that Talon was still angry with the man for the way he had spoken to her.

"As you say, my King," Gelhard finally said and took his leave, wearing his worry heavily on his stooped shoulders.

"Tell us the rest," Talon ordered as soon as the door closed.

"You need not worry about any of your personal guards betraying you," Hemera said, excited to share this particular news with him. "The traitor talked about how he would not dare go near your personal guards that they were all faithful to you." She continued, letting him know that the pair had spoken about the unrest over the King's failure to secure an heir and how they felt they would taste victory with the help of the Northmen.

The three men kept their eyes on her when she abruptly stopped speaking. She tilted her head and scrunched her eyes, then broke the silence suddenly. "The traitor has a good knowledge of how faithful your personal guards are, which could only mean that he holds a positon that gives him access to the King." — Hemera turned her head— "or Wrath."

Wrath nodded. "Since I lead the King's personal guards."

"You would know things others would not," Hemera confirmed. "Think on whom you see often and who has asked more questions than others, or perhaps someone who simply lingers nearby and watches."

Wrath nodded again, his thoughts already stirring on possibilities.

"This information remains with us alone," Talon ordered.

Paine looked to the King. "You do not suspect

Gelhard, do you?"

"Gelhard is not the traitor," Hemera was quick to say. "He is more faithful to the King than anyone realizes. It is why he questions the King so often. Gelhard makes him see possibilities, problems that lie ahead with decisions he may make. It wins him no favor, but his position as High Counselor to the King is more important than being favored by others."

Her acute observation of Gelhard amazed Talon. If she was slow-witted, how did she understand the very reason why he had chosen Gelhard as his High Counselor? There was more to Hemera than he had been told or perhaps no one ever realized.

Talk continued, though Talon brought the discussion to a quick end when Hemera yawned. "We are done for the evening. Go home with your wives and we will talk and plan more on the morrow."

To Talon's dismay, Hemera hurried out of the room first, leaving the men to follow. He was not surprised to see she went to her sister when he followed her out. He was glad to see that the feasting hall was empty, but then it was late and all were where they should be. The prisoner was under full guard and more sentinels patrolled the stronghold. All was safe. It was time for everyone to take their leave.

Talon stood at the bottom of the stairs as Wrath and Paine gathered their wives.

"We will see Hemera safely to her dwelling," Verity said, standing in front of her sister as if shielding her from the King.

"Hemera stays with me," Talon commanded and silence hung so heavy in the air that the only sound heard was the spit and crackle of the fire in the fire pit.

Hemera broke it as she stepped around her sister and approached Talon. "For tonight," she said and walked past him and climbed the stairs.

Verity and Wrath looked on in surprise while Anin smiled softly and Paine held back laughter, especially when Talon hurried up behind Hemera, scooped her up, and carried her off to his sleeping chamber.

## Chapter Twenty-two

After entering the room, Hemera coiled her arms around his neck as soon as he set her on her feet. Her lips found his and her kiss showed him how much she had missed him, missed being alone with him, missed his touch, missed coupling with him.

Talon's hands sat at her waist. They ached to strip off her garments and join with her, having thought nearly of nothing else while away. But there was something he needed to know before they spent the remainder of the evening enjoying each other.

Reluctantly, he ended the kiss and asked, "Do you carry my bairn?"

Hemera shook her head. "It is too soon to tell, but if my sister's vision is true, then the bairn does grow inside me now."

His heart pounded in his chest that it might be so. "When will you know?"

"Not long after the moon turns full."

He had not meant to speak his thoughts aloud, or perhaps he did. "Why you and not my previous two wives?"

"A question many might ask if it should prove true. I imagine some would even question if the bairn is truly yours."

His anger flared. "They would not dare."

Hemera smiled and softly caressed the anger lines bunched between his eyes. "I am pleased to know you never gave that thought."

"Why would I? I saw your virgin blood and know you have been with no other than me."

"But will others be as sure as you or will their tongues tell tales?" she asked a sudden worry filling her.

A shudder of concern ran through her and he drew her closer into the crook of his arm. "It does not matter. When the bairn is born, he will look like me and any doubt will be laid to rest."

Silence fell over her along with a frown that Talon was about to chase away with a kiss when she said, "What if I give you a daughter?"

"You will give me a son first," he said, sounding more confident than demanding.

"How can you be sure?" she asked, though felt pleased that he did.

"You are too stubborn to do otherwise," he said with a brief laugh.

Hemera was about to argue when she abruptly shut her mouth, tilted her head in thought, then after a few moments said, "You are right, I would be. It is a son you need and a son I shall give you."

"Stubborn," he said and lowered his mouth to hers.

"Something we share," she managed to say before his lips touched hers.

The knock at the door had them both groaning with anger.

"Forgive the disturbance, my King," Tilden said from the other side of the door. "It is important."

Talon went to the door and opened it. His threatening glare warned Tilden to speak fast and be done with it.

"The prisoner says he must speak with you now. It is about the Northmen. Paine will meet you at the torture chamber."

"I will be right there," Talon said and closed the door. He went to Hemera and yanked her into his arms, wanting desperately to keep her there. "I must go, but when I return I want to see you naked in my sleeping pallet. I have ached to have you naked in my arms since we parted. I missed the feel of your soft, delicate skin, and I have hungered for the sweet taste of you." He kissed her quickly and let her go just as hastily and left the room with the same suddenness.

Hemera stood shocked by his abrupt departure, though more curious over what the prisoner had to say about the Northmen. Possibilities ran through her mind and she decided that while she wanted nothing more than to be there naked in Talon's sleeping pallet upon his return, she wanted even more to hear what the prisoner had to say. The question was could she do both?

She had no doubt she could and with that thought in mind, she went to the secret door in Talon's wall and made her way down the stairs. Once at the bottom, she eased the door open and peered out to make sure no one was about, then she took off for the torture chamber.

The darkness covered her swift steps, though she need not worry since no one was about and that made her task much easier. She managed to creep close enough to the one side of the dwelling that had no guard. She braced her ear against the wood and asked the worn wood to let her hear what was being said inside.

"A drink. Please a drink."

Talon nodded to Paine and he partially filled the vessel beside the near empty bucket not far from the prisoner and held it to his mouth. He drank hungrily, groaning afterwards from either the pain of his seared wound or pain from hanging from the shackles at his arms and legs that bound him tightly to the wall.

"Speak," Paine ordered, throwing the last of the drink from the vessel in the prisoner's face.

The man lapped at the drink splashed around his mouth and looked to Talon. "I will tell you something I know of the Northmen," —a cough choked off his words— "something I heard in secret." He coughed again.

Talon said nothing, he stared at the man. He did not trust him and wondered what this was truly about.

"No one knows I heard." He gagged more than coughed this time. "I heard and I know. It will help defeat you once and for all." A cough took hold that refused to let go and the prisoner struggled through it until he barely had a breath left. Blood began to drip from the side of his mouth and when he coughed, he spit blood.

Paine looked to Talon. "He has been poisoned."

The prisoner laughed, blood spewing from his mouth. "By your hand."

Paine looked to the bucket.

"We are among you." He choked on the blood that spilled from his mouth. "Hemera will be the one to end you." He gasped and fought for breath, as if someone was choking the life from him.

Worry gripped Talon's insides. He nodded to Paine and left the dwelling, his only thought to see that Hemera was safe in his sleeping chamber.

"Too late," the prisoner gagged. Too la—" His head dropped down.

"For you," Paine said and turned away, leaving the man to take his last dying breaths alone.

Hemera moved cautiously away from the dwelling after hearing Paine speak and the door to the dwelling open and close. As she made a wide berth around the dwelling, she saw that Paine was alone and it struck her then that she had not heard Talon speak for some time before Paine's last words. Had Talon left before Paine?

The thought had her racing off to reach Talon's sleeping chambers before he did.

~~~

Talon took the stairs two at a time, eager to see that Hemera was safe and even more eager to find her naked in his sleeping pallet. Before he reached his door, he slipped off his foot coverings. He opened and closed the door quietly in case she was asleep and stripped off his garments ready to join her. He went to the fire pit to add more logs and light to the room, wanting to see every beautiful part of her body that he intended to touch and kiss.

Since she had made no sound or heard her stirring, he looked forward to caressing her awake. The fire sparked and the flames grew brilliant and when they did, Talon saw that his sleeping pallet was empty.

~~~

Hemera fastened the door shut behind her, securing it tight so that no one would see from the outside that a door existed. While she wanted to rush up the stairs, she had to take them cautiously with no light to guide her. When she reached the top, she opened the slim door slowly and slipped in, pleased the shadows hugged her, and closed it quietly behind her.

Hearing not a sound, she breathed a sigh of relief that she had made it to the room before Talon...until she stepped into the light.

Talon stood near the sleeping pallet stark naked, his arms folded over his solid chest, his long, muscled legs spread slightly apart and his manhood aroused and growing more so when her eyes fell on it.

"You disobey me again," Talon said annoyed, though relieved she had returned.

How did she defend herself when he was right? Why even try? She chose silence and she chose to shed her garments, her need for him soaring with him standing naked in front of her.

"You will not distract my anger by removing your garments," he warned, knowing what she was up to by how slowly she revealed every part of her naked flesh. "You deserve to be punished." Her response was to turn her naked backside to him as she leaned over to place her garments on the bench. He wanted to reach out and grab hold of her taut, round bottom, bend her over, and plunge into her swiftly, but he stopped himself.

She would not get out of this punishment. He would win this time.

Hemera stretched her arms slowly above her head, her plump breasts rising high as she reached higher, locking her wrists together. "Punish me then."

His manhood betrayed him, stiffening so hard he almost let out a loud groan. His anger at his body's own betrayal had him saying. "We will not couple." He almost cringed at his foolish edict.

Hemera lowered her arms and stared at him a moment, then shaking her head she walked over to him. "Your anger speaks." She rested her hand on his chest. "Let your heart speak."

His arm snaked around her waist and he yanked her up against him, flesh meeting flesh and nothing ever felt so good to him. "You vex me, woman."

"I do not mean to vex you just as I did not mean to lose my heart to you, but I did. It is yours. It belongs to you now, please be careful with it."

Talon's own heart thundered in his chest. Never had words had such impact on him and never had words meant so much to him. Though his own words failed him, he did not fail to respond. He brought his mouth down on hers and kissed her, not a sweet, tender kiss, but one that claimed the heart she had freely given him, tucking it away deep inside him and forever keeping it safe.

His hands went to cup her bare backside and as he lifted her, she brought her legs up to wrap around him. He walked them to the sleeping pallet, never taking his lips off hers and dropped down with her on the thick stuffed pallet.

His plans to take his time, go slow, savor every inch of her was lost to a distant memory. His only thought was to bury himself inside her, claiming her once again, leaving no doubt to himself or her, or anyone that she belonged to him.

She tore her lips away from his and he grew annoyed until her whisper rushed from her lips.

"I cannot wait. I have been too long without you."

Her hand reached down, working its way between them to take hold of his manhood. "Hurry, before your mighty kisses make me come."

A shiver ran through him as she urged him with a tug toward her entrance. He brushed her arm away before slipping his arm beneath her waist and moving her further up on the pallet so that he could enter her easily and slowly... and he did.

His groan of pleasure echoed hers and at that moment he knew without any doubt that he had lost his heart to her. He was where he belonged, where he always wanted to be...with Hemera, forever united.

"Please, Talon," she begged with a soft intensity. "I need you."

He kept his thrusts tempered while Hemera moved more anxiously against him. She was near to coming and he wanted her to so that he could make her come again soon after. He knew exactly how to make certain that she did. He lowered his mouth to her one nipple and teased it with his tongue.

Hemera thought she would die from the pleasure racing through her. Talon's tongue worked magic wherever it touched her. It stirred a flame that always seemed to be burning deep down inside her for him, one that would never extinguish, would always need to be fed, one that would burn forever for him.

"*Talon*," she pleaded as that flame grew ever stronger.

Talon brushed his lips over hers and ordered, "Come for me."

Hemera cried out as he thrust into her harder and she exploded with pleasure that rushed through her, claiming every bit of her body and her senses and as it began to recede, Talon moved inside her demanding more. Once again she felt her pleasure building and she smiled as she dropped her head back and groaned with the sheer joy of feeling her passion mount once again.

Nothing was more satisfying than seeing that look of pleasure and bliss on Hemera's face as he brought her once again to the edge of climax. It heightened his own pleasure, but then he needed only to look on Hemera and his body stirred with desire.

Her sighing groan and his aching need had him realizing he would not last much longer. He would burst soon enough, though he would make sure Hemera did as well. All thoughts faded as his passion took hold and he set a rhythm that soon had Hemera gripping his arms and her passionate cries filling the room.

She burst with pleasure once again and Talon joined her, tossing his head back and groaning as wave after wave of pure passion coursed through him.

Hemera's arms went around him as he dropped down on her and with labored breath whispered, "Welcome home, my King."

*My King.*

The stark reminder had him rolling off her and taking her in his arms to rest against him, though more so to keep her there, where he wanted her, where she belonged.

It also had him saying, "We are bound, you and I, and nothing can ever break that bond—*nothing*."

"I will always be yours."

That she said it without a bit of doubt pleased him, though it still disturbed him that she would never truly be his, truly belong to him unless she was his wife.

Her yawn and the way she snuggled closer against

him had him reaching for the blanket bunched at his side and he covered them both.

"I am glad you are home. I missed you so much," Hemera said, laying a hand on his chest while her head rested comfortably on his shoulder.

"So you have told me often since my return," he said, keeping his arm firm around her, wanting her as close as he could get her.

"And you will hear it often so that whenever we are apart you will know how much I ache for your return." She sighed and tapped his chest. "Now tell me, who do you think poisoned the prisoner's water?"

He grabbed her chin with two fingers and turned her face up to look at him. "Did I not order you to remain in this room?"

"Did you truly expect that I would?"

"I am King," he said, wondering if he was reminding himself more than Hemera.

"Aye, you are."

Her few soft words resonated loudly in his head. He was King and he could do as he pleased.

Her yawn had him releasing her chin and as she settled comfortably against his shoulder once again, he knew what he would do.

He would make Hemera his queen.

## Chapter Twenty-three

The thought of making Hemera his queen simmered in Talon's mind for several days and more so at night when she slept in his arms. He wanted her there always. He would accept no other woman in his sleeping pallet and the more he thought on it, the more he came to realize that he could have no other woman as his queen.

It was difficult for him to grasp how a woman like Hemera had worked her way into his heart and try as he might to ignore it or admit it, she had. His heart was lost to her and surprisingly he was glad for it. Not that he would let anyone know. After all he was King and needed to show strength, not weakness. But had Hemera not told him that it took courage to care, to lose one's heart?

Talon heard footfalls approach the opened High Council Chambers's door and cleared his thoughts, though Hemera refused to leave. She lingered there, poking at him with memories that tugged at his heart and tempted his manhood.

Gelhard entered, closing the door behind him.

Talon could see by the intent look in his eyes and firm set of his mouth that Gelhard had something to say to him. He had something to say since he had learned that Hemera was sharing Talon's sleeping pallet, but he had held his tongue. It appeared he was not going to hold it any longer.

"My king," Gelhard said with a respectful bow of

his head. "As your High Counselor, I feel I should speak with you regarding Hemera."

Talon kept his posture taut and his words sharp. "Have your say, Gelhard, but measure your words well."

"People are whispering and wondering why a mighty King takes a," —Gelhard paused when he saw the King's eyes flash an angry warning— "woman *unlike* others to his sleeping pallet."

"Let them whisper and wonder, it does not concern them."

"It does," Gelhard objected strongly. "You are their King. You have led them with courage and wisdom. You have brought relative peace to this land and tribes have thrived because of it. They wish a long reign for you so prosperity and peace may continue. That is why they wish to see you wed and heirs born."

"They will have it. Begin plans for the wedding," Talon ordered.

A smile spanned the whole of Gelhard's face, vanishing in an instant when next Talon spoke.

"I will wed Hemera."

Gelhard stared at him a moment unable to speak and when he finally did, he did not measure his words wisely. "You cannot be serious. You cannot wed a slow-minded woman who pays no heed to your every word and who the people find foolish and ignore. It is bad enough you mate with such a woman, but make her queen?" Gelhard shook his head. "It cannot be allowed."

Talon rose slowly to his feet. "You *dare* to tell the King it cannot be allowed."

Gelhard realized his mistake and quickly lowered

his head. "Forgive me, my King." He raised his head. "Please, my King, think of what you do. Hemera's mum gave birth to two daughters, not one son, so would Hemera even give you an heir?"

He wished he could tell Gelhard that she already carried his child, but Hemera had yet to confirm that and until it was certain, he would say nothing.

"You may be pleased with your choice, but the people will think differently."

"It is not their decision."

Gelhard continued to plead. "What if she does give you a son and your son is as slow-minded as her?"

Talon glared at Gelhard. "You truly believe Hemera is slow-minded?"

"Is it not obvious?" Gelhard asked stunned that the King should even question it. "What of her heritage?"

"The chosen queen must be born of a Pict mother. Hemera's mum was from the Alpin Tribe."

"How do you know that for sure?" Gelhard questioned. "She has spent many years with the Northmen. She knows more of their ways than she does Pict ways. Should you not at least find out more about Hemera before you make her your queen?"

Talon was reminded of why he had made Gelhard his High Counselor. The man made him aware of issues that might arise over any decisions the King pondered. He also was reminded of how often Hemera avoided telling him of things that had happened while she was with the Northmen.

*One day, but not now.* That had been her answer. No more. It was time for her to tell him.

Gelhard's brow wrinkled and he tapped his finger to his chin. "Minn was from the Alpin Tribe. I recall her not knowing anything about an attack on the Alpin Tribe by the Northmen. It is a shame she returned to the Imray Tribe or we could have spoken with her about it."

"Send for her and see what she has to say," Talon ordered.

Pleased by the King's command, he gave a firm nod.

"You will also spend some time with Hemera each day and come to know her."

Gelhard could not hide his surprise or annoyance. "What am I to do with her?"

"I am sure you will take the time to get to know her and find reasons I should not wed her or perhaps she will surprise you and you will find reason to agree with me that she will make a good queen."

Gelhard nodded slowly as his eyes lit with opportunity.

The man expected to find fault with Hemera. Talon thought otherwise, but it did not matter, since in the end Hemera would be his queen.

~~~

Hemera was busy planting seeds she had begged off Ebit, not that she had to beg him. It seemed now that it was known she was the King's woman, everyone treated her differently. They acknowledged her with a nod or a smile, but they also whispered about her, not that they had not done so before, they just did it more frequently now.

It did not bother her. People were wont to talk. It was the way of things in a tribe. Besides, they were curious about her and the King. She returned smiles and nods when she caught them and some women even stopped to speak with her.

She stepped back when the last of the seeds were planted and admired the garden she had enlarged days before. She would have good crops when the weather warmed and when harvest came.

She washed her hands in the bucket she kept near the rain barrel and cast a glance along with a smile around her home. She had come to care for this place. It had brought her solace when she so badly needed it and it was here she had joined with Talon.

Nights now were spent with Talon in his sleeping chamber, but her days were spent here. Sometimes Talon would stop by and they would wind up inside, Talon ordering his guard that they were not to be disturbed.

Things finally were good, though she did miss the woods terribly, but the time would come when once again she would be able to go there. For now, she was content and for the first time in a very long while she was happy.

Though, the matter of the prisoner that had been poisoned still plagued her. She knew Talon had ordered Wrath and Paine to see what they could find out and had ordered her not to interfere. The water had been brought from the cookhouse. Servants had been questioned but nothing out of the ordinary had been discovered. It was all rather strange as to how the poison had gotten into the bucket of water.

She thought back to her time at the cookhouse and how servants would come and go, Nock, the cook, not keeping mind of things. Anyone could have poisoned the water before it had reached the torture chamber, leaving an unknowing worker to deliver the fatal drink.

Hemera decided to take a walk to the cookhouse and look about to see for herself if anything seemed out of the ordinary.

She had gotten to know all of Talon's personal guards since they took turns guarding her. Each were different yet the same when it came to guarding her. They all kept a watchful eye on her and not one of them would accept food or drink from her, Talon's orders.

Gerun was guarding her today. He was thick in body and solid as a tree trunk. She felt sorry for anyone who attempted to run into him.

"I go to the cookhouse, Gerun, perhaps Nock will share some fine food with us."

That brought a smile to the usual stoic Gerun.

Hemera was surprised when Gelhard approached her and she stopped, tilted her head and stared at him.

Her strange ways unnerved Gelhard. He thought her a poor soul with little sense. It had to have been her beauty that caught the King's attention and a queen needed more than beauty to reign beside a king, especially King Talon. Gelhard hoped the King would lose interest in Hemera as he did other women he had mated with, given time. He needed to delay the King from wedding Hemera or learn something about her that would convince the King he was making a mistake before he foolishly wed the wrong woman.

"A moment of your time," Gelhard said, fighting to produce a pleasant smile as she continued to stare at him. "I wanted to let you know that if you need anything—now that you are spending time with King Talon—you only need ask me." He had tried to keep the distain out of his voice, but it had crept in.

"I am grateful for your offer, but there is nothing I need. I have all I want and all that is necessary."

"I thought perhaps there was something you favored while with the Northmen and I could be of help in providing it for you," he said, pleased with himself for finding an opening to speak with her about her time with the Northmen.

Hemera scrunched her brow and she saw that Gerun did as well. "Why would I want anything that would remind me of my time spent with the Northmen?"

Gelhard shrugged. "You spent many years there. You must have taken comfort in something."

"Freedom," Hemera said without hesitation. "I took comfort every day knowing that one day it would be my last day there and my sister and I would finally be free."

"It must have been hard being held captive for so long."

Hemera stared at him again, though this time it did not appear as if she truly looked at him. Her eyes held a more faraway look and Gelhard wondered what she was actually seeing.

Hemera shook her head, chasing past memories she did not wish to recall and not wanting to speak with Gelhard and continue to be reminded of her time with the Northmen, she turned and walked away.

Her actions shocked Gelhard and he hurried up alongside her. "The memories must still be painful for you."

"You waste your time if you expect me to tell you about my time spent with the Northmen," she said without glancing at the man.

He stumbled, caught off guard, never thinking she would realize what he was doing, but now that she had. "Why? Do you hide something from us?"

"Everyone hides something, Gelhard, even you."

He grew indignant that she could think to accuse him of such a thing. "I have nothing to hide. I am faithful to my King. And you will address me properly. I am the High Counselor."

"The very thing you hide. You should let Talon know how much you fear losing that respected and important position."

His eyes registered his shock, turning so wide Hemera feared they would burst from his head. Tired of him trying to extract information from her and wanting to think only on the problem of the poisoning, she hurried her footsteps, hoping he would realize she had nothing more to say to him.

Gelhard would not be ignored, he rushed to keep up with the annoying woman.

Hemera shook her head when she saw that little had improved at the cookhouse. Instead of keeping a designated area to dump the scraps for the dogs, as she had arranged, servants were simply tossing them out the cookhouse door.

"Stop that," Hemera yelled at a worker who went to throw a basket of scraps from the open door, and the man stilled. "Over there," she said, pointing to an area a distance from the cookhouse.

She saw that he was about to ignore her, but he stopped when Gelhard stepped forward and reluctantly went and dumped the basket where Hemera had told him to.

Hemera looked about, disappointed that Nock had paid little heed to the suggestions she had made and continued to run the cookhouse so poorly. It was no wonder that someone could so easily poison the water that had been given to the prisoner.

She was not surprised to see Nock, hurrying out the cookhouse door shortly after the worker had returned inside from dumping the scraps. Nock headed straight for Hemera with a hunk of bread in his hand.

"High Counselor," Nock said with a respectful bow of his head to Gelhard.

He nodded in return and lifted his chin toward Hemera, hoping she noticed how properly Nock had addressed him.

"I have brought some freshly baked bread for you to try." Nock broke a piece off and handed one to Gelhard before giving a piece to Hemera.

"I am grateful, she said, taking it and breaking a small piece off to taste. No soon as the flavor hit her tongue, she spit it out.

Gelhard looked on appalled by her disgusting action and grew angry when she slapped the piece of bread out of his hand. His angry retort died on his lips when she said, "Poisoned."

She turned away from the two men, stuck her finger down her throat, and forced herself to purge her insides.

~~~

Talon had just entered the practice field, Wrath and Paine already there along with other warriors when Tilden came running toward him shouting. He could not make out what he was saying until Tilden got closer and began waving at Talon to follow him.

"Poisoned, Hemera!" Seeing the King break into a run, Tilden turned and followed beside him.

Talon could not run fast enough, his heart pounded like a mighty fist against his chest, not from running but from the dread that filled him at the thought of losing Hemera. He heard running footfalls behind him and knew Wrath and Paine followed.

Tilden pointed in the direction of the cookhouse and Talon did not wait, he sped past him. When he rounded the end of the building, he saw Hemera bent over, heaving, and he rushed to her side.

His arm circled around her waist and she grabbed hold of it and brought her head up to rest it back against his chest.

"I did not swallow any of it, but I had to be sure. I could not take a chance," she whispered through heavy breaths.

He felt her hand move to rest below his arm. His heart swelled with gratitude and something much deeper for her for protecting their bairn, should there be one. He turned her around in his arms and she laid her head on his chest.

"It was the bread," Gelhard said the shock of what had happened quaking his insides. "Hemera took a bite, spit it out, and slapped it out of my hand or I would have eaten all of it." *And died.* The thought struck him. She had saved his life.

Talon looked to Nock, staring at what was left of the bread in his hand.

"Who made that bread?" Talon demanded.

"One of the servants, I believe it was Cyril, but I

am not certain." Nock turned to the group of people who huddled near the cookhouse. "Cyril, come here."

A thin young man, his hair cropped short around the sides, defining him in service to the King, stepped forward cautiously. He held his hands clasped tightly in front of him and stopped not far from Nock.

"Did you make this bread?" Nock asked.

Cyril shook his head. "It was Opia."

Nock shouted for Opia to step forward and a young pleasantly plump lass with a pretty face hurried over to Nock. "Did you bake this?'

She shook her head. "Cyril did."

Talon looked to Paine. "I will not waste time while they accuse each other. Fetch your wife."

Paine nodded and went to do as the King ordered.

"Have the servants return to their duties," Talon ordered Nock.

Nock was quick to obey.

Talon looked down at Hemera and before he could speak, she said, "I am not leaving your side."

He did not bother to argue with her, since he felt she was safer by his side than anyplace else.

Talon had learned to watch others around him while focused on one person. He saw how still Cyril remained and how Opia kept glancing around anxiously.

"He is too still, too confident," Hemera whispered.

Most would have suspected Opia since she glanced about as if she was ready to run while paying no heed to Cyril. Not so Hemera. She saw that Cyril stood much to still, not displaying a bit of concern. Even innocent people grew anxious when standing in question before the King.

Opia stepped forward. "Have her touch me first. You will see I am innocent."

It took only a moment, but to Hemera it seemed like forever as she watched in horror as Cyril drew a knife, Talon shoved her behind him, and Wrath rushed forward, stepping in front of the King just as Cyril lunged with the knife, driving it into Wrath's shoulder.

## Chapter Twenty-four

Hemera stood shocked at the scene in front of her, everything happened so fast that she was not sure what happened at all. Wrath remained on his feet while Cyril lay on the ground blood pouring from his neck. It was not until she noticed the dagger in Talon's hand, blood dripping from the blade, that she realized he had been the one to slash Cyril's throat.

Opia stood screaming, her wide-eyed stare focused on Cyril.

"Silence!" Talon yelled and Opia clamped her mouth shut, though her eyes remained wide with fear. "Go fetch the healer," Talon ordered and Opia nodded and ran off crying.

Hemera had regained her senses and hurried around in front of Wrath, who to her complete amazement was still standing. When she came around in front of him, she saw that the knife had remained embedded in him. She was relieved to see it had penetrated the leather strap that crossed his chest before settling in his shoulder, which explained why he had remained on his feet.

"You need to sit," Hemera said.

"After I make certain the King is secure and safe," Wrath insisted and went to step around her.

"You will sit now," Talon ordered and pointed to a bench that sat against the cookhouse wall. Wrath looked ready to argue and Talon was quick to stop him.

"Your King commands it."

Wrath nodded and Hemera walked alongside him as he took reluctant steps to the bench. She was worried for her sister's husband. All wounds, even the smallest, turn fatal, if not tended properly.

As soon as Wrath sat, his hand went to the hilt of the knife to pull it out.

Hemera grabbed his hand. "Not yet. Wait for the healer."

"Bethia will not have the strength to pull it out," Wrath argued.

"But she will have the wisdom to be prepared if the wound should need immediate searing," Hemera said.

Wrath's hand dropped away from the handle and he and Hemera turned at the sound of his name being screamed.

"Wrath!" Verity ran straight for him and he hurried to his feet with a grimace, the sudden movement having caused a shot of pain to stab at his wound. It pained him even more to hear the fear in his wife's voice and see her eyes pool with tears.

Hemera got up from the bench and wanted to give Wrath a nudge to sit back down, but it would be useless. She saw that he waited to take Verity in his one arm, extending it out to welcome her and assure her that he was fine even if he was not. He would not have her worry over him and Hemera admired his courage and that he worried more for her sister than himself.

Verity gasped when she saw the knife in her husband's shoulder and Wrath was quick to coil his arm around her waist and draw her against his side.

"I am fine. There is no need for concern," he assured her.

"We will see about that," Bethia said as she took hasty steps toward him, Opia following behind her. "Now sit and let me look at you."

Paine and Anin arrived and while a worried Anin rushed forward to comfort Verity, Hemera saw how Wrath gave Paine a nod and he turned to speak with the King. She had often seen the many silent signals Wrath and Paine had exchanged between themselves and with Talon as well. They were like brothers the three of them, but battle did that to men, drew them closer.

Bethia determined it would need searing as soon as the blade was pulled out.

Verity was not happy to hear that Wrath intended to have Paine do it and in the torture chamber.

"Bethia will see to it in our dwelling," Verity insisted.

Bethia was quick to agree with Wrath. "Paine would do better with this than I would."

"Then it is settled," Talon said, ending the disagreement as he approached.

Verity wore her worry heavily upon her, her face grim, and still fighting her tears. "Then you will rest in our dwelling."

"That he will," Talon said, making it clear that Wrath had no choice in the matter. "I will have a word with Wrath." Talon kept his voice low after they all moved a distance away, affording him privacy. "You have seen for yourself what can come of a wound such as yours even after searing. Rest and heal. I fear a battle may be brewing and I need you at your best."

Wrath understood the wisdom of his words and nodded. "I will do as you say, my King."

"You did well, Wrath, you saved my life," Talon

said.

"You would have easily saved your own life if you had not taken that one moment to protect Hemera. You care for her deeply, *far more deeply than I think you even know*." It was an observation and one Wrath wished he had been wise enough to see sooner.

*Tuahna.*

Was that what Wrath was implying? It was not a word he had ever expected to say to a woman, let alone feel for someone and it was not spoken lightly. Few people would admit such a deep feeling, for it was believed to bind two people forever. He never thought of feeling that strongly for any woman. Yet as he had seen the knife plunging toward Hemera, a fear so strong had struck him that he had responded without hesitation and with no thought to his own life.

Annoyed and not yet prepared to admit to anyone, even himself, that he could possibly care that deeply for Hemera, Talon ordered, "Go and see to your wound."

"Paine! Broc!" Talon shouted. "Finish taking care of this, then meet me in the High Council Chambers. You as well, Gelhard."

All three men nodded, though Talon paid no heed to their responses. He walked over to Hemera, took her hand, and was about to walk off when Hemera stopped him with a hard tug.

"I would prefer to be with my sister. She needs me."

He stepped closer to her. "Wrath needs her right now. You may visit with her later."

Hemera turned to see Verity focused on her husband, not having left his side as they made ready to make their way to the torture chamber.

Talon took hold of her chin and turned her head to face him. "I need you where I know you will be safe—alongside me."

Seeing her sister with thoughts only for Wrath, Hemera did not argue, though she asked, "May I have a moment with my sister?"

Talon nodded and released her.

Hemera went to Verity, her hand going to rest on her shoulder and giving it a squeeze. "I will see you later when all is done. If you need me, send someone to get me."

Verity nodded and whispered, "Later."

"Wrath is not only strong, he is stubborn and—"

"Aye I am strong, stubborn I am not," Wrath said so seriously that Verity and Hemera laughed.

Talon watched the exchange between the three. They laughed easily and cared for one another with the same ease. Being King did not afford him such ease, though he had found a comfort with Hemera that he had not expected. He stretched his hand out, letting her know it was time for them to take their leave and she left her sister's side and hurried to him.

Hemera took Talon's hand and almost sighed with the strength and warmth of it as his fingers closed around hers. A slow tingle made its way through her as they walked together to the feasting hall. She was glad for the silence between them. It allowed her to enjoy this strangely intimate moment with him. It was almost as if they were forever linked together and not because their hands were joined, but because they truly were one and always would be.

A sudden swirl of wind whipped around them and had Talon coming to an abrupt halt to take Hemera in his arms and shield her with his body.

Hemera buried her face against his chest and smiled, not only pleased to be wrapped in the strength of his powerful arms but to hear clearly the message on the wind.

*Tuahna.*

The word sent a shiver deep through her and Talon's body closed tighter around her.

*Tuahna.*

She felt it and sensed that he did as well and she raised her head to look into his eyes and she saw it there, bold, bright, strong, and shocked at the discovery. She watched as his lips moved to speak and she felt in her heart what he was about to say, what she never expected to hear from a man.

"My King, hurry, before the rain is unleashed on you," one of his guards called out.

A splat of rain hit Hemera's cheek and broke the intimate bond between them.

Talon hurried her to the feasting house, out of the rain before it fell in earnest. Once in the High Council Chambers, Talon released her and walked away to pace alongside the table. He rubbed at his chin and along his jaw, trying to make sense of what he had felt only moments ago and continued to linger in him. It had come upon him as suddenly as the gust of wind, shocking him, and yet he had felt himself revel in it, embrace it, and never wanting to let go of it.

*Tuahna.*

He never thought he would feel that way about any woman, but then Hemera was not any woman. She was *his* woman. There and then he pledged to himself that nothing would stop him from making Hemera his wife.

He stopped pacing and turned to look at her. She stood not far from the closed door, her head tilted and her glance drifting off as she was wont to do when her thoughts took hold. Thoughts that held more wisdom than most could understand. Talon waited for her to speak

It was only a moment later that she said, "Someone fears something."

"There is always someone fearing something," Talon said and took her hand and led her to the table to sit.

Hemera shook her head as she sat on the bench to the right of where Talon took a seat at the head of the long table. "Why would there suddenly be an increase in enemy incidents?" She shook her head again. "They have become impatient, almost as if time was running out for them."

It was odd how she thought the same way he did. The exact thought had crossed his mind. What was happening that seemed to make his enemy suddenly impatient?

"Had the bread been intended for you or me?" Hemera asked, her brow narrowing as she considered her own question.

That was another question that had come to mind and disturbed Talon and one he intended to get an answer to.

"You will know soon enough when you have Anin touch Nock."

He had to ask since she seemed to know his mind. "Do you read my thoughts?"

"No, that is Anin's gift, though I have come to know you better since my arrival here and even better since we have shared more time together." She laughed lightly. "But then you are King and there is not much people do not know about you. Of course some may be more tale than truth."

He leaned closer and gave her a light kiss and he felt a slight tremble run through her. He was pleased that such a faint kiss could stir her and he had to chase away the urge to ignore all else and carry her off to his sleeping chamber and finish what his kiss had started. Or was it to satisfy what his heart felt?

"It is not fair that you should know more of me than I do of you," he said, realizing this was a chance to find out more about her. "Later you will tell me more about your time with the Northmen."

Talon was glad Gelhard's arrival robbed Hemera of a response, since she appeared ready to protest. They would talk later. He would make sure of it.

Hemera thought Gelhard would protest her presence in the High Council Chambers, but he said nothing. She understood why when shortly after Anin arrived escorted by Tilden. Hemera was not surprised to see Broc lead Nock and a teary-eyed Opia into the room.

Talon gave a nod to Anin and Tilden remained by her side as she approached Opia.

"I did nothing wrong, my King," Opia sobbed.

"Then you have nothing to fear," Talon said.

Without being ordered, Opia stuck her arm out and Anin took hold of it. She did not hold it long.

Anin turned to King Talon. "She knows nothing and has done nothing wrong."

Opia wept with relief.

"It is good to know you are loyal to your King,"

Talon said.

"Always, my King, always. You saved me and my mum from certain death during the war to unite the tribes and we both will be forever grateful."

"Go and be with your mum for the rest of the day. You can return to the cookhouse on the morrow."

"I am most grateful, my King," Opia said, wiping away her tears and followed the guard who stepped up to escort her out of the room.

"I am loyal too, my King," Nock said and held his arm out to Anin.

Anin rested her hand on his arm and it remained there longer than it had on Opia's, making Talon wonder what Anin was learning.

"He is innocent of poisoning the bread and loyal to you," Anin said, looking to Talon.

"You took longer with him. Why?" Talon demanded when she said nothing more.

She hesitated a moment, looking to Nock as if for permission to reveal what she had learned.

"He has no say, you will tell me, Anin," Talon commanded, his powerful tone leaving no room for disobedience.

"I have nothing to hide," Nock said with a respectful nod at the King.

Anin did not hide her relief at Nock's words and she felt more comfortable saying, "He is not happy in the cookhouse."

Hemera's words came back to Talon. *I do not think Nock likes his task as cook.*

"Is this true, Nock," Talon asked, wanting to hear it from the man himself.

"Aye, my King," Nock said with a nervous tremor.

"Choices were given when chores were handed out," Talon reminded him.

"He was not given a choice," Anin said.

"Why not?" Talon asked of Nock.

"It was late in the day and I was not asked. The person told me I was to be in charge of the cookhouse."

"Who told you this?" Talon asked, having given specific orders that each person was to be given their choice of chores, if possible, or at least close to what they believed would suit them best. It would make for a more satisfied and productive village if people did what they favored.

"I do not know who he was. There were so many unfamiliar faces when the stronghold was just settling in."

"What task were you seeking?" Talon asked, recalling those chaotic days when his reign was just beginning.

"Metal work, I am good at it," Nock said, raising his head in pride.

That disturbed Talon. Why would Nock be given a chore so far removed from his skill? "Is there someone in the cookhouse that could take your place?"

"Aye, my King. Barkell enjoys working in the cookhouse and often tells me what I am doing wrong. He would serve you well as would others there, though there are a few Barkell would dismiss if given the chance."

"I will visit with your staff on the morrow and see what changes can be made," Talon said and gave a nod to the guard at the door.

"I am grateful, my King, so grateful, and I will serve you well," Nock said, bobbing his head and followed the guard out.

Talon did not want to turn and look at Hemera. He knew she would be wearing a smile and he knew what she was thinking. *I told you Nock was not happy in the cookhouse.* He turned to her anyway, but instead of a smile, she wore a frown and he wondered why, though not for long. More than likely her thought mirrored his and she wondered over why Nock had been placed in the cookhouse.

Paine entered the room and went to Anin. "You should be sitting." He turned to Talon. "My King—"

"Anin has done well as usual and may leave," Talon said.

Tilden stepped forward and Anin went to protest an escort. One look from her husband and her words died on her lips. Though, she turned to the King. "Would it be permissible for Hemera to join me and see how Wrath fares?"

Talon could almost hear Hemera in his head, pleading with him to let her go. He turned to her and the pleas he heard in his head were clearly visible in her eyes. "You will return here after you are done."

"As you say, my King," she said with a nod.

"You may go," Talon said. A sudden tug grabbed at his heart as the door closed behind her. Only a moment from his sight and he missed her. He was as besotted as Paine and Wrath and that would not do. He was King. He pushed Hemera from his thoughts or so he thought. She returned before he could address the men in the room and remained there, refusing to leave. Annoyed that he no longer had control of his musings, he spoke abruptly. "We have much to discuss."

## The King & His Queen

~~~

It had been a long day and Talon was glad when he and Hemera were finally alone in his sleeping chamber.

"I am relieved that Wrath's wound is not as bad as I first thought," Hemera said, a long yawn following her words. She discarded her garments as she continued talking. "The knife struck his leather strap and gratefully it did not penetrate his flesh as deeply as first thought. He was lucky. The wound was seared, though it will barely be noticeable with his body drawings." She walked over to Talon, scrunching her brow.

He tossed the last of his garments aside just as she came to a stop in front of him. He rubbed at the tight wrinkles between her eyes. "Something troubles you?"

"I am curious," she said and her fingers went to trace the body drawing on the side of his face. "Why only this drawing and no other?"

"The old woman who did the body drawing in our tribe claimed I was destined for far greater things and when the time was right, she would give me the body drawing I was meant to have. It was when fierce fighting broke out among the tribes that she came to me and told me it was time. She explained that I needed only one drawing and it had to be on my face for all to see. She also told of how I would sweep across the land and unite the tribes, gathering them together as one force against foreign invaders and how I would ensure that Pict blood would forever claim this land." His hand went to rest on her stomach. "The start of that legacy may well reside in you."

"How could that be when I am not queen?"

"It is a Pict woman I need to wed and you are

Pict."

"You cannot mean to make me your wife," Hemera said, taking a step back away from him.

She did not get far, his hands settling at her waist and giving her a gentle tug, drawing her closer to him. "To be a Pict King, my children must be born of a Pict mother. You are Pict and you were born of a Pict mother, were you not?"

Hemera nodded.

"You are also from one of the oldest tribes, the Alpin Tribe. You would make a fine queen." She drifted off in thought and he wondered why. "Is there reason for me to think otherwise?"

"Several reasons," Hemera said to his surprise, "the most important being that many will think me a poor choice to be queen and that will only serve to embolden your enemies."

"I alone choose my queen and the people will learn soon enough what a wise choice I made in making you my queen," he said, tucking her closer against him and feeling her shiver ripple over him. He scooped her up in his arms. "You are chilled."

The strength of his powerful arms and the heat of his hard body flamed the spark that had already burst to life inside her and she whispered, "Warm me."

He lay down on the sleeping pallet alongside her, settling his naked body around hers. "I will do more than warm you, after you tell me what other reasons you believe will prevent me from making you my queen."

She remained silent and Talon smiled and brought his lips down on hers and teased her with gentle kisses that promised so much more. "See what you will miss if you do not answer me."

She sighed. His warmth, the comfort of his powerful arms, and his arousal nestling hard against her had ignited her passion as soon as he had wrapped himself around her. She rested her hand to his cheek. "Can we talk of this later? I need you so much right now." She pressed her finger to his lips when he looked as if he would argue.

Talon took hold of her finger and kissed it before moving it away from his mouth. "Tell me one, just one reason."

"After you warm me, I promise," she whispered and brought her lips to his, her kiss not gentle.

He grabbed a handful of her hair and pulled her head back, breaking their kiss. "I will hold you to your promise."

"I will keep it, but at this moment I need you more than ever."

Her aching need flamed his need that had been tormenting him from early on and he was soon lost in the sweet taste of her lips once more, though their kiss was anything but sweet. It was hungry and demanding as were their hands that roamed eagerly over each other.

She surprised him when she shoved him onto his back and slipped over him and began to work her way down along his flesh with kisses and nips, and he savored every one of them.

Hemera wanted to taste all of him, know every part of him, and save it to memory. Should one day come that she was no longer with him, she would have the memories to cherish. She favored his alluring scent and savory taste. For some reason, she was reminded of the scents of the forest, the pungent pine, the musky soil, and the fresh smell of the foliage after a rain. She would never be able to walk in the woods again without thinking about Talon, but then he was never out of her thoughts.

She continued kissing down along his body and when she got close to his manhood, stiff and ready for mating, she felt a pain pierce her heart. If separated, she would miss mating with him, but more so she would miss the closeness she shared with him, sleeping nestled in his arms, or the way his fingers closed possessively around hers when he took hold of her hand.

Hemera continued kissing him, not realizing tears had sprung to her eyes and that one spilled over and fell on Talon.

Talon groaned with pleasure, not something he usually did. He always contained himself, never letting a woman know how she affected him, but then no woman affected him as Hemera did. He was lost in an exquisite pleasure he never recalled ever feeling. Hemera was different than other women in so many ways and he would never let her go. *Never.*

His pleasure was suddenly disturbed. Was that a drop of wetness he felt? He waited and not long after he felt it again, then again.

Was Hemera crying?

Talon reached down and grabbed her, hoisting her up beneath her arms and brought her to dangle over him face to face. He got upset as soon as he saw her tears. "You are crying. Why?"

Hemera brought her hand up to her one eye and wiped at it, a look of surprise on her face. "I am crying."

"Why?" Talon could not keep the concern from his voice. "I do not force you to mate with me."

"It is not that. I want to mate with you. I cherish your touch, your taste, you slipping inside me." She could not stop more tears from falling.

"I have never seen you cry," Talon said, a fierce pain striking his heart and turning his concern to anger. He did not mean to sound harsh when he demanded, "You will tell me why you are crying."

*Tuahna.*

The word tolled in her head like a bell that refused to stop ringing. That was why she hurt so badly when she thought of never seeing him again. She had not only lost her heart to him, she had found with him what most people never find. *Tuahna*, a caring so strong, it seeped down deep inside to remain there forever.

The word slipped from her lips softly at first. "*Tuahna.*"

"What did you say?' Talon asked, struggling to hear her.

A heavy sob rose up as she once again said, "*Tuahna.*" She did not stop this time, she said it again and again. "*Tuahna. Tuahna. Tuahna.*" Another tear fell, splashing on Talon's chest. "I never thought I would ever feel *tuahna* for anyone. But I do for you, and I so fear being taken away from you."

Her words shocked Talon, though it was more the intense joy he felt hearing her say it that had stunned him. He had never felt so pleased, not ever, but her last few words stirred his anger.

He brought her down on his chest and took her face in his hands, wiping at the tears on her cheeks with his thumbs. "No one will ever take you from me. I will kill anyone who tries. You are mine and always will be."

Tears continued to glisten in her eyes. "They will come for me."

"They have tried and failed. They will never get you."

"I am glad you know what I feel for you so that if—"

"You will tell me often, for I enjoy hearing you say it," Talon said, preventing her from saying what he refused to hear, that if anything should happen to her at least he would know how she felt for him. The thought of her gone from him was a thought he refused to consider. It would not happen. He would not let it.

Talon eased Hemera onto her back, his hands going to either side of her head to support his upper body as he hovered slightly over her. "No one will take you from me. I will remind you again and again. You are mine and always will be. You will be my queen."

He kissed her and all thoughts and worries slipped away. They mated slow and easy, savoring every kiss and touch and when he finally slipped into her, she eagerly welcomed him and they finished together as one, bursting in a climax that completely exhausted them both and soon after they fell asleep wrapped tightly in each other's arms.

## Chapter Twenty-five

Talon woke to find Hemera gone and quickly donned his garments to find out where she had gone off to. He had expected her to be there in his arms when he woke and he was more than disappointed to find himself alone.

They had fallen asleep soon after coupling and he was pleasantly surprised when she had aroused him awake. He had enjoyed hearing her whisper *tuahna* to him several times during and after they mated. He could still hear her voice now, whispery soft in his ear, and gooseflesh rose along his bare skin. He would never grow tired of hearing her say it. It filled him with a comfort and peace he never knew existed, a peace that he found only with Hemera.

He was still trying to comprehend it, still trying to accept how he felt, still trying to grasp that he felt for her as she did for him.

*Tuahna.*

He shook his head. He had never thought it possible, never thought he would find something so special, so rare with anyone. Though, Hemera was not anyone... she was his future queen.

Talon left his sleeping chamber, intending to find Hemera. They had never gotten to talk last night and he had wondered over her reluctance to do so and how she always avoided talking about her time with the Northmen. It had him believing that she was hiding something from him, but what?

When Gelhard seemed to step out of nowhere in front of him when he entered the feasting hall, he remembered he had things to deal with this morn, the cookhouse problem being only one of them. Still, he would know where Hemera was before he did anything.

"Hemera?" Talon asked, expecting Gelhard to have an answer.

"She rose early and I walked her to her dwelling along with one of your personal guards who remained with her," Gelhard informed him. "I asked her how she knew the bread was poisoned."

Talon headed to the High Council Chambers, while Gelhard followed alongside him continuing to talk.

"She told me it had been the smell and taste that had warned her. I asked her how she would know the smell and taste of poison. *Instinct* was what she told me, though for some reason I felt there was more she was not telling me. Naturally, I will do my best to see what I can uncover."

Talon took his seat at the High Council table and after taking one look at the bowl of gruel placed in front of him, he pushed it away. "Bring Nock and Baskell to me. It is time to make changes in the cookhouse."

"They are on their way," Gelhard said and a knock sounded at the door.

Talon was again reminded why he had chosen Gelhard as his High Counselor.

After only talking to the two men for a few moments, Talon could see that Baskell was suited for the cookhouse far better than Nock.

"You still do not recall who appointed you to the cookhouse, Nock?" Talon asked, continuing to wonder why the man had been placed there.

Nock shook his head. "No, my King. I believe being sent to the cookhouse after I requested metal work so surprised me that I remember little else of that time."

"Your chore from this time on, unless I say otherwise, shall be with the metal workers. Go join them now." Talon looked to Gelhard. "I assume it already has been arranged?"

Gelhard nodded. "It has, my King."

Nock thanked him profusely and hurried from the room.

"I expect improvements not only to the food, but the cookhouse itself, Baskell. Are you up to the task?" Talon asked.

"I am, my King, and I am eager to get started. Your meals will be much improved as will the running of the cookhouse," Baskell said. "I will implement new rules once I return to the cookhouse."

"I am pleased to hear that, Baskell, though what concerns me is that poison had been brought into the cookhouse without anyone's knowledge. Does no one oversee the making of the meals?"

"Not to speak ill of Nock, for he is a good man, but he paid little heed to what went on in the cookhouse. He allowed far too many people to come and go who had no reason to be there. I had been pleased when Hemera took Nock to task for how poorly he maintained his duties. I had hoped he would listen to her suggestions, but to my disappointment he ignored them. Things remained the same. It really was no wonder the poison found its way so easily into the bread."

"It was that easy for Cyril to poison the bread?"

Talon asked his annoyance sparked.

"Far too easy for him or anyone else since many of the workers brought things to the cookhouse that they had foraged in the woods, then used without Nock's knowledge."

"Does Ebit not supply you with enough of what is grown that the workers forage in the woods for food?"

Baskell seemed hesitant to answer, then he spoke up. "The cookhouse share of the harvest from Ebit has been less and less lately, since his crops have been less plentiful than they once had been. It is also what caused Nock to look elsewhere for food staples and foraging was one way he could get more."

"Why was I not informed of this?" Talon asked his annoyance mounting.

"Ebit told us that you had been informed."

Talon's annoyance switched swiftly to anger. "You will come directly to me with any problem. You will also keep me apprised of what goes on in the cookhouse. Is that understood, Baskell?"

"As you wish, my King."

"We will talk soon. Your task is heavy, go see to it," Talon said and dismissed the wiry young man, then turned his attention to Gelhard.

"This is why you need a queen," Gelhard said. "The cookhouse is for her to oversee."

"It is a king's duty to make sure there is enough food for his people."

"I will get Ebit," Gelhard said.

Talon stood. "No, I will go speak with Hemera."

"She is not queen," Gelhard said his brow pinched tightly.

"No, but she warned the soil would not accept the

seed and if it proves true, we will have a weak harvest and little food for when it grows cold again. I will not take that chance," Talon said and went to find Hemera.

~~~

Hemera smiled, dusting her hands of dirt, pleased that her garden was finally ready to seed. The soil was moist from the rain that had not lasted long yesterday. It had made the earth easier to work with and the seeds would do well when planted.

"I will have a fine crop to harvest," Hemera said, looking around to find that Bog was gone. He had arrived shortly after she had started working in the garden and she had talked with him the whole time. She had wondered why she had seen so little of him of late. She got the sense that something was troubling him and reminded him with a hug and a kiss that she was there if he needed her.

She dropped her head back and was pleased to feel the sun linger on it. The sun would remain longer and longer in the sky each day, nourishing the seeds so they would grow.

"Seeds." She reminded herself and turned to fetch the seeds and her smile grew when she saw Talon approach. She did not wait, she hurried to him.

Talon halted his steps and braced himself to catch Hemera against him, when all of a sudden she stopped abruptly before reaching him.

"I am covered in dirt," she said, raising her dirt-covered hands as proof.

"And still I want you," Talon said and reached out, grabbed her arm, and caught her in his embrace as his lips came down on hers. Her lips were warm, moist, and welcoming as was her body that pressed invitingly against his. He wanted to linger there and lose himself in her, a dangerous thought. He reluctantly moved his lips off hers, kissing along her cheek until he reached her ear and he nipped at it as he whispered, "You tempt me, woman."

"My sleeping pallet is but a short distance away," she murmured and tugged playfully at his ear with her teeth.

He had not meant to speak aloud. "Ebit can wait."

Hemera stepped out of his arms so fast that Talon almost stumbled.

"What is this about Ebit?" she asked, staring at him anxiously.

"Later," he said and went to take her hand, but she slipped from his grasp and he scowled.

"Is there a problem? I warned him of the soil. If he is not careful, he will have a poor harvest."

That he needed to be reminded of his duties had his scowl deepening. "Ebit is the reason I came to find you." He held his hand out to her and he closed it tightly around hers when she took hold so there would be no chance of her escaping him again. "I have learned that the planting fields are not producing the fine harvests that they once did and I want you to take a look at them, speak with Ebit, and suggest anything that would help."

"Of course I will," she said and tugged at his hand to get going. Hemera cast questioning eyes at him when he did not move.

"When we finish—"

Hemera smiled and as if it was meant to be a

secret, she whispered, "We will return here, for there is something in my dwelling I wish to give you."

"What is it?" he asked, a spark of passion flashing in his deep blue eyes.

"Me," she said softly and tugged at his hand once more.

This time he went with her, eager to be done with Ebit and return to her dwelling.

~~~

Ebit was not happy to see Hemera and even less pleased to learn the King was now aware that the fields were not producing well.

"We had far too much rain one time and hardly any the other, and far too few seeds another time," Ebit said, trying to offer reasons for the poor crops.

"Excuses," Hemera said. "You ask too much of your soil or you keep weak seeds when they should be discarded. She bent down and scooped up a handful of soil from one of the planting fields and held it out to Ebit. "Can you not feel that the soil struggles? You cannot keep taking from it and give nothing in return. It needs to be fed just like you and me."

"That is nonsense. Soil does not need food," Ebit argued and looked to the King. "She makes no sense. I have tended soil and plants longer than she has. I know what I do."

"What you do is threaten the food supply of the stronghold, if you continue to treat the soil and plants as you do," Hemera accused.

Ebit went to protest again, but held his tongue when the King raised his hand and turned to Hemera.

"What needs to be done to see that the harvest is an abundant one?"

"My King," Ebit said, attempting to protest again.

"Hear what Hemera has to say or risk losing your seat on the High Council," Talon warned.

"You need to plow new fields, nourish others, and get rid of the weak seeds or they will only produce weaker seeds until there are none left," Hemera explained with enthusiasm.

"Again nonsense," Ebit argued. "A seed will grow with sun and rain to nourish it. It needs no more."

Hemera shook her head. "A seed needs more. It needs to be planted with care and tended with just as much care as it grows so it will blossom strong. I would say let me plant half the fields and you the others, so that you may see the difference, but I fear there will not be sufficient food when the cold comes again."

Ebit drew his shoulders back and his chin went up. "I will take that challenge and win."

"You take such a challenge when your harvests have been less than abundant? It is not only the stronghold we feed but other tribes that are in need, and what of your lies?" Talon asked, attempting to keep hold of his anger. "You fail to report how poorly the harvests have been. I hear it from others. You have done well in destroying my trust in you."

"You have much to concern yourself with, I did not want to add to your worry," Ebit said. "And poor harvests are to be expected now and again. This harvest will be an abundant one and will make up for the others."

Talon took a sudden step toward Ebit. "You do not decide what I concern myself with. Your task is to provide me with the truth so that I can make wise decisions in regards to the people. You have failed to do so."

"I meant no—"

"I do not care what you meant," Talon snapped harshly. "You will follow what Hemera tells you or vacate your High Council seat."

Ebit was quick to reply. "I will do as Hemera says, my King." He turned to Hemera, his tongue curt. "Where do we start?"

Talon reached out and jabbed Ebit in the chest so hard he stumbled back. "Keep that tongue sharp and you will lose it."

"Forgive me, my King," Ebit said and turned anxious eyes on Hemera.

Talon stood aside, watched, and listened. Hemera did not stare off in thought or hesitate to speak, she spoke with considerable knowledge and he wondered where she had learned so much. Ebit questioned her reasoning on several of her suggestions and Hemera was quick to explain. She talked on and on until Ebit began to show honest interest in her every word. The more Talon watched her the more he believed she would make a good queen.

He remained watching them, signaling his warriors that patrolled the fields to follow the pair as they walked among the seeded rows. He would not follow them, he was King and followed no one, but he made sure Hemera was not too far from him, if he should need to protect her.

Ebit was nodding his head as Hemera and he finished and approached Talon.

"I will get started right away making the changes,"

Ebit said and with a bow of his head to Talon, he hurried off.

Talon took her hand, eager to return to her dwelling and as he walked with her through the stronghold he became aware of how the people stared and turned their heads to whisper, and he realized why. Holding Hemera's hand as they walked among the people was a foreign sight to them. He had never walked with a woman through the stronghold, let alone holding her hand. It was good that he did now, for he wanted all to know that Hemera belonged to him.

He slowed his steps, kept hold of her hand dusted with dirt, and decided to satisfy his curiosity. "How do you know so much about the soil, seeds, and plants?"

She cast a strange glance at him and he thought she might not answer, but when she spoke, he was even more curious.

"You will not believe me."

"Of course I will, I trust you," he said, realizing the truth of his words. He did trust Hemera, more than he ever thought he would trust any woman. "Tell me."

That he had not hesitated to tell her that he trusted her gave her the courage to say, "The forest taught me."

"You have me even more curious now. How did the forest teach you?"

Hemera had never spoken to anyone about it and she hesitated to do so now.

Her silence had him asking, "Do you trust me, Hemera?"

"Aye, I do," she said with certainty.

"Then share your secrets with me, for I believe you have a few. Besides, secrets become burdensome after a while."

Hemera could certainly attest to that and she did something she had not done for what seemed like forever. She opened her bag of secrets and began to let them spill out.

"I was assigned to serve Haggard's family."

Talon was surprised to learn that she served the Northmen Chieftain of the Southern Region, but said nothing.

"Not long after my arrival there, Ulric took me into the forest, ordering me to forage for a plant he favored added to his food. He left me there, telling me he would return for me. He did not return. When it grew dark, I grew frightened, then I began to hear whispers and after a fleeting moment of fear, I realized that the forest was speaking to me, offering its help. When dawn broke, the whispers guided me home." She shook her head. "Not home. It was never truly my home."

They had reached her dwelling and Talon stopped in front of the door, anger marking his words as he said, "You were a small bairn and Ulric left you in the woods alone and unprotected."

That he cared more about her safety than the woods speaking to her warmed her heart. "It was not the only time."

Talon's eyes darkened as he pushed the door open and eased her inside with his hand to her back. "Tell me more."

They sat on the benches near the fire pit and Hemera continued her tale. "The next time Ulric took me into the woods I knew what he intended. Only that time, I decided to remain in the woods for a couple of days and see what else the forest had to say to me. That is how I gained my knowledge, though I never let Ulric know. As young as I was, I realized the more fear I showed him each time he took me there and left me, the more he would take me to the woods. He enjoyed seeing me fearful."

"You tricked him." Talon smiled, proud of the courage she showed when so young and pleased that she had shared her secret with him. "Did he ever discover your secret?"

"He did," she said and her eyes filled with sadness.

"Is that why he took the switch to your back?"

She shook her head. "No, by the time it was discovered, Haggard had so enjoyed the foods made from the plants I collected that he ordered me to continue forging."

Talon leaned closer and laid a gentle hand on her back. "What caused Ulric to beat you?"

She rested her hand on his knee and whispered, "Promise me Verity will never know what I tell you."

"I told you that what you share with me is for my ears alone. I will reveal it to no one. You have my word." He sealed his promise with a tender kiss.

Hemera briefly rested her brow to his. "I am grateful." She continued, glad Talon kept his hand gently upon her back. She needed to feel his comforting touch. "Verity was moved around to serve various families. One family treated her poorly, barely giving her food to eat. I was allowed to visit her only so often, which was something I could not tolerate. I would sneak a visit to her and when I saw how she was suffering, I began to bring her food I had foraged in the woods. Ulric found out what I was doing and with Haggard away at the time, he took the switch to me as punishment."

The anger that had been churning in Talon was about ready to erupt. He wanted to roar with rage for how badly she had been abused. He silently promised himself that he would make Ulric suffer unspeakable pain for what he had done to her.

"What did Haggard do when he returned and learned what Ulric had done to you?" Talon asked.

"He never knew. No one but Ulric's men knew."

Talon's brow drew tight. "How could that be?"

"Ulric took me into the woods to deliver my punishment and left me there with a warning when he was done." She shivered, recalling the beating. Talon's arms slipped under and around her and she found herself sitting on his lap.

He tucked her close against him. "He threatened harm to your sister?"

"He did. He told me he would see that she took a far worse beating than I did. I went to Haggard when he returned and begged him to move my sister and he did. The family she went to treated her much better."

"How long were you in the forest alone?" he asked an image of her suffering there alone with no one to help her, twisting at his heart.

"I do not recall. The only thing I do remember was my dreams. My grandmother came to me in them and seemed to help me. After the beating and with Verity's visions increasing, I knew it was only a matter of time before something dreadful happened to one or both of us. That is when I started planning our escape."

Talon rested his brow on hers. "I will keep you safe. Never will you suffer such horrendous harm again." He kissed her gently. "You are a courageous woman, Hemera, and I am proud that you are mine."

He stood with her in his arms.

"Make me forget," she whispered the memories much too vivid in her mind.

"You have my word on that."

Talon laid her on the sleeping pallet and kept his word.

## Chapter Twenty-six

Hemera stood, rubbing the soil she had scooped up in her hand between her fingers. Her garden was doing well and soon sprouts would burst through the soil and raise their tiny heads to the sun and begin to grow, similar to the seed that had sprung to life inside her.

She pressed her hand against her middle. Time verified what she had known, sensed, from the day she had planted the seeds in the garden nearly a moon cycle ago. Somehow the earth had let her know that she too would blossom and bear a bairn when the ground went dormant and slept.

A smile erupted across her face, turning her eyes wide with joy. She was happy. She would give birth to Talon's bairn. A shadow suddenly dashed across the sun and Hemera shivered. It was not only Talon's bairn she would give birth to, it was the King's bairn as well.

Thoughts of what that would mean had haunted her and she had good reason to wonder. Since the day of the attempted poisoning, Gelhard seemed to have made it a daily task to speak with her. Their discussions would vary, but inevitably they would somehow entail her past, whether about her tribe, her parents, or her time with the Northmen. She had kept her answers vague, which had not pleased him. She wondered if he spoke with her of his own accord to learn if she was fit to be queen or if Talon had ordered him to do so.

She had no desire to be queen, but she did desire

Talon with all her heart. Anger jabbed annoyingly at her at the thought of Talon with another woman. More importantly, there was the bairn to consider. What would be best for him? She smiled and stroked her stomach. She had no doubt that she would give Talon a son.

It was time to tell him. She could keep it to herself no longer.

She washed her hands in the bucket near the door and scooped up the wool cloak Talon had given her. He had also seen that new garments were made for her, two shifts and a fine tunic, a lovely green color that reminded her of the color of the forest.

"Stop dallying," Hemera scolded herself. It was not that she worried over telling Talon, for he waited with hope for the news she carried his child, not that he had ever voiced it. It was the many times his hand would rest protectively against her middle that she knew he was thinking about the possibility of his bairn growing there. He would be more than pleased.

What troubled her was how things would change once it was learned she carried the King's bairn. She shook the troublesome thought away and smiled. The only thing that mattered now was sharing the exciting news with Talon.

She turned, ready to hurry off, and stopped, Bog standing nearly on top of her with something in his mouth.

She bent down and held her hand out to him. "What have you there, Bog?"

The wolf dropped what he was holding in her hand.

Hemera let out a soft gasp. "A wolf pup recently born." She caressed the tiny pup and he barely moved.

"He is ill." She rested a hand to Bog's head. "The pup is yours and you want me to heal him."

Bog gave a soft whine.

"I will do my best to save him, but he is very ill," Hemera said softly.

Bog rubbed his face against her leg, his whine increasing.

"I will do all I can to save your pup," she said and stood, keeping the tiny pup cradled in her hand.

Bog suddenly turned and took a protective stance in front of her, growling, and showing his fangs as if he were ready to attack.

Hemera watched as Talon and Paine approached.

"Bog!" Paine's strong command did little to change Bog's protective stance or stop his vicious snarling.

"Get that wolf away from her," Talon ordered the look in the animal's eyes all too familiar. Warriors wore it when they went into battle ready to kill.

"No! You will leave Bog be," Hemera commanded. "He has come to me for help."

"I do not care what he has come to you for. He intends harm and that I will not tolerate it." Talon turned to Paine. "Control him or I will see him killed."

Hemera stepped in front of Bog and with a quick, sharp tongue ordered the wolf to stay, and he did. "You will not harm him. He does what any father would do when his child is ill. He seeks help." She settled her eyes directly on Talon's angry ones. "Would you not do the same if your bairn was newborn and ill?" She lowered her free hand and placed it against her stomach.

Talon stared at her and when she gave a brief nod,

he felt a punch to his gut and a squeeze to his heart. She was letting him know she carried his bairn.

Hemera held her hand out so Talon and Paine could see the pup. "I fear he will not make it, but I must try. Paine, please get my sister and see that she brings reeds with her and what milk she can find."

Paine stared at the lifeless pup for a moment, then took off.

"You are sure?" Talon asked.

"There is no doubt," Hemera said.

Talon wanted to go to her and take her in his arms and never let her go. Instead, he said, "I will wait here while you see to the pup."

Hemera nodded and hurried into the dwelling, Bog following close behind her. She sat by the fire pit and held the tiny pup close to her chest. She recalled all the forest had taught her about newborn animals needing to be close enough to the mum to hear the steady beat of her heart. Warmth was also important and food. The poor pup was too weak to suckle, which was why she needed her sister to bring what reeds she had. Hemera could feed the pup with one of the hollow ones.

She held the pup close, speaking softly to him as she caressed him ever so gently with one finger while Bog rested his head on her knee, watching...until voices sounded outside the door. He rushed over to it barking, snarling, threatening anyone who tried to enter.

"You are not going in there," Wrath ordered, now understanding why Paine had advised him against walking his wife to the door.

"Do not be foolish," Verity said. "My sister needs my help."

"He is an angry, snarling wolf," Wrath said as

## The King & His Queen

though it would make her see reason.

Verity smiled, patted his cheek, and said, "So are you, but I handle you well and you have never bitten me." Her voice turned to a whisper. "Well, maybe in play."

Wrath glared at her and she hurried away from him and slipped inside the dwelling, the snarls stopping instantly. He heard Paine laugh and he turned, ready to take his anger out on his friend and stopped. The worried look on the King's face had Wrath sending Paine a nod, then gave a nod toward the King.

Paine understood his silent signal and both men went to the King.

"Is something wrong, Talon?" Wrath asked as a friend.

"Get me Gelhard," Talon ordered.

Wrath went off to do as ordered without question.

"We can stand here silent or you can tell me what troubles you," Paine said.

"Hemera will be my queen," Talon said as if he commanded it and was stunned by the rush of joy that shivered his flesh as it ran through him. He may have claimed that Hemera belonged to him but a union would seal that claim forever.

"You cannot mean that. I have yet to learn enough about Hemera to ascertain she is fit to be your queen," Gelhard said, rushing toward the King. "I was on my way here for my daily talk with Hemera when Wrath informed me you wished to see me. She is not forthcoming about herself and I fear she hides something. You must wait, my King. Give me more time to make certain this would be a good union for you."

"I am certain it will be a perfect union," Talon said, declaring it so. "Make plans for the ceremony. We wed at the start of the new moon cycle."

Gelhard shook his head. "You cannot be serious. That is not enough time to send word and have chieftains attend and they will want to attend."

"Gelhard is right," Paine said. "Tribes will rejoice over the news and chieftains will want to take part in the celebration. It will give them hope for the future and weaken your enemy's claim to the throne, especially if Hemera gets with child right away."

Gelhard's head took to nodding with every word Paine spoke and continued as he spoke. "It would secure your rule."

"No rule is secure," Talon argued. "There will always be men and women who seek power and wish to rule."

"A strong monarch with a good heart, wise ways, and with roots buried deep in this soil will make sure Pict blood forever rules this land."

The men turned and looked at Anin.

Paine went to his wife, his arm going around her protectively and she settled comfortably against him as she always did.

"That is exactly what the people want to be sure of," Gelhard said with a firm nod of his head. "The people must know without a doubt that Hemera is truly a Pict and that her blood is of this land."

"You doubt she is a Pict?" Wrath asked.

"I doubt her story that she and her sister were abducted in a raid on the Alpin Tribe. I can find no source who can confirm such a raid existed. Minn disputed Hemera's claim of a raid when they had spoken. She never heard of a Northmen raid on the Alpin Tribe."

"Are you saying that Verity and Hemera are not Picts?" Wrath asked ready to argue with Gelhard.

"I am saying we do not know enough to know either way," Gelhard said.

"I know enough!"

All turned to see Verity approach them, her eyes lit with anger. "My memory does not fault me of that time. I remember well, being grabbed by what seemed like a giant to me and tucked under his arm and carted away to be dumped in a boat that rocked so badly my stomach would not stop emptying even when there was no more to empty. I remember my sister throwing herself on top of me and taking the blow when the giant brought his hand down to hit me because I would not stop crying. When the giant pulled Hemera off me, she kicked, punched, clawed, and spit at him and when his hand slapped her so hard in the face that she fell from his grasp, she crawled over to me and covered me with her body once again. She told me she would keep me safe and not to worry that we would return home one day, she would make sure of it, and she did."

Wrath had gone to his wife as soon as she began talking, his arm circling her and growing tighter around her as he felt her legs go weak.

"There is much about our time with the Northmen that Hemera will not even discuss with me and it pains my heart to know what she must have suffered to keep me safe. She is more courageous than any of you and more Pict than any of you."

Verity let her tears trickle down her cheeks, though she kept her chin and pride high. "I need to get something for my sister since she is fighting to save a life while you bicker out here about her worth."

Wrath's arm tightened around her as she went to step away from him, knowing her resolve was strong, but her legs still trembled. "I will go with you and help."

"Go, all of you," Talon said and waved his hand, dismissing them as he walked toward the dwelling.

"My King," Gelhard called out.

Talon stopped and turned such a murderous scowl on Gelhard that he took several hasty steps back.

"Not a word, Gelhard. Go!" Talon ordered and turned to the sound of snarls and barks. He shoved the door open and was met by a wolf braced for attack.

"Bog!" Paine called out ready to step forward not only to protect the King, but Bog as well.

Anin shook her head. "Let them settle it."

Paine saw that the King felt the same, since he raised his hand for Paine to be silent.

"Move, Bog, now!" Talon ordered.

The wolf's growl lessened but he did not move.

"The King comes to help, Bog, let him pass," Hemera said and the wolf slowly moved away from the door to take a protective stance next to Hemera and his pup, never once taking his eyes off Talon. "Do not come too close to me," she warned Talon when he entered and closed the door.

"Will the pup live?" Talon asked and Bog's eyes went to Hemera as if he understood and he was anxious to hear her answer.

"It is too soon to tell. He was born weak and often a weak pup is pushed aside and left to die, but instead Bog chose to seek help for him. There is little I can do but to keep him warm, feed him, and hope it is enough to grow him strong."

"As you do with our child that grows inside you?" Talon asked, wanting to hear her confirm what she had silently relayed to him.

Hemera smiled and the tiny pup stirred against her chest and she wondered if it was because he felt her heart thump with joy. "Aye, our child nestles safely inside me and will be born when the ground goes dormant and cold settles over the land."

Talon had waited far too long to hear that and he never thought he would be glad that he never heard those words from his two previous wives, but he was relieved that he had never gotten either of them with child. He was overjoyed that a woman of such strength, kindness, and bravery would bear him a child, though most importantly a woman he had lost his heart to.

"I want so badly to take you in my arms right now," he said, taking a step toward her and stopped when Bog's head turned sharply in his direction. "I am more pleased than you will ever know and proud that you will be my queen." He had not expected her smile to fade or for her to drift off in thought at his announcement and it took all his will to remain silent and wait for her to speak.

The pup stirred against her again and she adjusted him in her hand to lie more comfortably against her breast. She had managed to get some milk into him, but he would need more and at more frequent intervals. She had sent Verity to find a thinner, hollow reed so that she could drip the milk more slowly into the pup's mouth and see better how much he actually took.

She sighed and Bog lifted his head off her knee to

stare at her. Her sigh was not for the pup, but what she must say to Talon. She reached out and reassured the wolf with a gentle rub. "Your pup does well so far." Then she gathered her courage and looked at Talon.

He had never known her to struggle to speak and he wondered what caused the struggle he saw in her now.

Before either of them could speak, Bog's ears shot up and he rushed to the door, crying.

Talon opened the door and the wolf rushed out and stood just outside the door, his head up and his eyes and ears alert. Talon stepped out to stand behind him and that was when he heard the lone cry of another wolf.

Bog looked to Paine who had not followed Talon's command to leave and ran to him.

"Take warriors with you and do what is necessary to keep his family safe," Talon ordered and Bog turned and stared at the King for a moment, then took off, Paine hurrying along with him.

Talon returned to the dwelling and made his edict clear. "You will be my queen."

"There are things you do not know about me," she said, sounding as if she was ready to confess something.

"I will have the truth. Were you born of a Pict mother?"

"I was," she said without the slightest hesitation. "But—"

"Nothing else matters," he said, preventing her from saying anything more and not caring what else she had to say. "As long as you are a true Pict, born of a Pict mother then your blood is strong in this land and you are worthy to be my queen."

"My blood does run strong in this land," she assured him.

"Then nothing keeps us from wedding. You will be my queen." He went to her and leaned over her, slipping his hand beneath her chin to raise it as his lips came down softly on hers.

## Chapter Twenty-seven

"I advise you again to postpone this union," Gelhard urged the King, following him into the High Council Chambers. "Let me find out more about her before you do this, before it is too late."

"I know all I need to know about Hemera," Talon said, walking over to examine the small facsimiles of buildings he and Paine had designed in preparation of constructing them on a larger scale. He looked over the replica of the feasting house and his quarters on the second level. He would need to expand it with the bairn on the way and with hopes of future sons and daughters.

"Hemera has changed things here," Gelhard complained.

Talon turned to face his grumbling High Counselor. "Perhaps change was needed."

"Not change that disrupts," Gelhard argued. "She changed how Ebit tends the planting fields and—"

"Ebit confirmed that the fields are doing better than he expected and that in one field the sprouts look ready to break through. He is pleased with Hemera's advice and talks often with her."

Gelhard's brow pinched in annoyance. "Due to Hemera's interference, Bower has altered his bow making—"

"With improved results," Talon said. "My archers tell me that the bows are easier to handle and much sturdier."

Gelhard refused to give up the fight. "The cookhouse—"

"Has never produced such tasty food or its workers been so pleased," Talon said. "Hemera has been good for the stronghold."

Gelhard threw his hands up, though not in surrender. "She had that wolf's pack brought into the stronghold."

"That was my doing," Talon snapped sharply. "They keep to the area of Hemera's dwelling and will leave once their pup is well, and he improves more each day. He is finally able to feed from his mum, though he still needs to grow in strength."

He thought how much time and effort Hemera had given to the pup and was stung with jealousy. He had not seen her as much as he had hoped to since she had taken the pup in several sunrises ago. He had missed her in his sleeping pallet. She had remained in her dwelling since she had to wake several times throughout the night to feed the pup. He had finally gotten so annoyed that he had gone to her dwelling to sleep with her there, though that was not what he had had in mind. Unfortunately, it was what wound up happening. Hemera was so exhausted from having to feed the pup in several short intervals that she fell asleep in the middle of him kissing her.

Verity had tried to relieve her sister, but Bog and the female wolf would not allow it. They trusted no one but Hemera.

Talon wondered why. After all, Paine and Bog were like family. Why did Bog not trust Paine to help?

Gelhard went to protest again and Talon held up

his hand. "Enough. It is done. The wedding will take place soon with a celebration to follow when it grows warmer."

"Why hold the celebration later? Gelhard asked.

"So all can see, my enemies included, Hemera round with my child."

"You cannot be sure tha—" Gelhard's eyes rounded like full moons when he realized what Talon was saying. "Hemera already carries your child?"

Talon beamed with pride. "She does and that is why nothing else matters. She will give me a son. She is sure of it and so am I. There will be an heir to the Pict throne when the cold settles in."

Gelhard smiled broadly. "This is joyous news, my King. I will see to planning a ceremony immediately and I will send out news across the land that you are wed and that the Queen is with child, and will let all know a huge celebration will be forthcoming."

"Hemera was born of a Pict mother. She belongs here as much as we do. That is all that is needed for her to be queen."

Gelhard hesitated before asking, "What if she gives you a daughter?"

Talon grinned. "Then my daughter will rule the Picts."

Gelhard nodded slowly. "I believe she would, my King. Now I must go, there is much to plan." He stopped abruptly. "I almost forgot. I received word that Dalmeny has yet to return from his hunt for the Northmen in his area. Also, would you like me to send word to your uncle Egot about your wedding so that he may attend?"

"No, I think it would be best to keep it quiet until

after it is official and Hemera is queen."

Gelhard's face pinched in thought. "That is true. Once it is learned that she is with child, your enemies may try to harm her." His eyes turned wide. "That is why you do not want anyone beyond the stronghold to know that you wed yet and why you have more warriors watching her."

"I will take no chance of harm coming to her and my child," Talon said.

"I understand and I will send no word out until after the ceremony," Gelhard said. "And forgive me, my King, for doubting your wisdom."

"It is your task to doubt me and to question me. It makes me wiser."

Gelhard raised his chin with pride. "I am honored to serve you, my King."

Talon was about to request that Gelhard have Paine sent to him when a frantic knock sounded at the door.

Gelhard opened it and a warrior all but fell into the room.

He was breathing heavy and looked to have been traveling for a good period of time.

"Help him to sit, Gelhard," Talon ordered but the warrior waved Gelhard away.

"News," the warrior breathed the word heavily.

"Your message serves no purpose if you cannot speak it. Calm yourself, then tell me the news," Talon said.

The warrior nodded and took a few deep breaths before he was finally able to be understood. "Haggard, Northmen and Chieftain of the Southern Region has landed on Pict soil and wishes to meet with you. He is only a few days away."

~~~

Hemera glanced down at her lap, the tiny wolf pup curled in a ball sound asleep. She turned and looked at the other three pups born to Bog and his lady, busy feeding from their mum in the lean-to that once was Bog's. It served the family well until the time came for them to return to the forest. Bog kept guard much like the warrior that watched over Hemera. Between the two, she doubted anyone could get to her.

The sun had not lasted long today and a strong chill filled the air. She sat at the round tree trunk that Paine had fashioned into a table with two smaller tree trunks serving as benches. It was a good place to sit and think and to gain some wisdom from the old tree. It had so many age lines, Hemera marveled over how much the old tree must have seen in its time.

The pup shivered when a gust of wind suddenly whipped around them and Hemera tucked her cloak over him, forming a tent to keep the pup safe and warm.

She ran her hand across the table top and the multitude of age lines. She missed connecting with the trees and the knowledge they had to share. She recalled the fright that had gripped her when Ulric had first left her in the woods that day. Her fear had worsened when she began to hear the whispers. Things had changed greatly since then. She was now grateful for having been left there and given the chance to speak with the trees and the animals. It had felt as if she had finally returned home.

Bog walked over to her and stuck his snout under her cloak. She eased the cloak back so that he could check on his pup. Satisfied, he pushed her cloak with his nose and Hemera once again covered his pup. Bog sat beside her and stared up at her.

Hemera patted his head and rubbed behind his ears. "All goes well, though I cannot say the same for me."

Bog continued to stare, as if waiting for her to continue.

"The only time I have truly felt free in my life was when I was very young. My mum would take me into the woods and sometimes my grandmum would join us. I would have the most wonderful time. I have far too few of those memories or has it been so long that the memories have been lost to me?" She sighed softly. "Now I am to be queen and I do not know if I want to be." She shook her head. "I favor solitude, yet I miss Talon when he is not with me." She rubbed Bog again. "Change comes, Bog, whether we want it or not."

Bog licked her hand.

"I am grateful you lent me your ear, my friend." She went to rub him again when he suddenly backed away and hurried around the table, growling.

Anin soon appeared and Bog ceased his snarling, went to her, got a generous rub and a kiss, then took a protective stance in front of his family.

Anin approached. "I do not disturb you, do I?"

"It matters not if you did, it is good to see you and looking so well and round," Hemera said with a soft laugh.

Anin laughed herself as she caressed her bulging stomach. "If I did not know I was having a daughter, I would swear I carry a son as big as his da."

Hemera stared off a moment, her smile fading. When words returned to her, she said, "You knew I would be queen, yet you said nothing."

"Some things are meant to be discovered, not be foretold. You needed to find out for yourself how you would feel about Talon and the same for Talon. You both were meant to discover each other."

"I thought you felt only the nature of a person, good, bad, trustworthy," Hemera shook her head. "You see far more."

"It has only been recently that I have realized the change. Actually, it was after the time I spent with my grandmother that I noticed it."

"You know more about me than you have told Talon," Hemera said, worry drawing her brow together.

"I spoke the truth to Talon and as I said some things are meant to be discovered, though I would warn not to wait too long, for the time to tell him may come too late."

"Hemera!"

Bog hurried to snarl and snap at Verity as she ran toward them.

"Hush!" Verity warned Bog with a sharp snarl of her own. "This is important."

"What has you running like a mad woman?" Hemera asked, her worry mounting.

"A messenger has arrived with news and a High Council meeting has been called."

"Something must be amiss to have the High Council convene so fast," Anin said.

Verity nodded. "That is everyone's thought and tongues are running wild with worry, especially with no word forthcoming."

"We will know soon enough," Anin said.

Without warning, Verity's eyes rolled back and her

# The King & His Queen

body crumpled.

Hemera rushed the tiny pup off her lap and into Anin's hands and dropped down to catch her sister against her before she hit the ground. "I am here, Verity. I will not leave you," she said, holding her close and chasing the guard away with a wave as he rushed to help.

Bog did not seem to know what to do. He paced in front of Verity and Hemera while his eyes remained on Anin.

"Your pup is fine," Anin assured him and confirming her words the tiny wolf pup gave a soft yelp as if testing his bark for the first time, then settled once again against her chest. She looked to Hemera. "Should we send for Wrath?"

Hemera shook her head and hurried to say, "No. It is best we see what her vision shows her before we let anyone know she had one."

"The King's guard will tell him about this," Anin said, keeping her voice low.

Hemera kept her voice to a whisper as well. "We will hear it first and decide what should be told. As you reminded me, some things are better left to be discovered."

Verity stirred, her eyes fluttering, fighting to open.

"You are safe, Verity. I am here with you. You are not alone."

Verity stopped struggling at the sound of Hemera's voice and after a few moments her eyes slowly opened, then spread wide, and she paled.

Hemera was almost too fearful to ask, but she needed to know. "What is it? What did you see?"

Verity gripped Hemera's arm. "Haggard has landed

on Pict soil. He is here for you."

## Chapter Twenty-eight

Hemera sent Verity and Anin on to the stronghold while she saw to settling the tiny pup close to his mum. The three of them wanted to be there in the feasting hall when the High Council finished and learn for themselves what was going on.

She turned and saw that Gerun had stopped Simca, from approaching. Hemera knew Simca only by sight and what she had heard of her. Not that she paid much heed to what others said, having learned from her own experience of what people thought of her.

She raised a crock wrapped in a cloth. "Opia sent a hot brew for you."

"I will take it to her," Gerun said and took the crock from Simca.

If Hemera was not in a rush to get to the stronghold, she would have invited Simca to sit and share the brew with her. Instead, she called out her appreciation and watched as Simca walked off.

Hemera stared after her, her eyes narrowing as she watched Simca's every step. There was something familiar about her gait. The wind caught Simca's cloak and she was quick to tuck it around her and that was when Hemera realized what was so familiar. Her strides belonged to the person in the woods she had seen wearing one of the King's personal guards' cloaks. Other memories came to mind as well. Hollins had told her that the person who found her would weep and a man would not weep, only a woman. Then there was the time Hemera had seen Simca and Tarnis together and she had ran after Tarnis upon the King's arrival. Had she taken his cloak then? Had she been the one Hemera had followed? Simca also served in the feasting hall, a servant gone unnoticed as all those spoke freely around her.

Gerun interrupted her thoughts when he placed the crock on the table and Hemera lost no time in removing the cover and taking a sniff.

"Is something wrong?" Gerun asked, placing his hand across the top of the crock, preventing Hemera from going near it.

"Aye, there is, Gerun. We should waste no time in going to the feasting hall."

"The brew?" Gerun asked.

"I believe it is meant to make me sick," Hemera said as an icy shiver ran through her. "Dispose of it."

Gerun hurried to see it done, then returned to Hemera's side. "Stay close to me," he ordered and another chill ran through Hemera as she nodded and followed alongside him.

She was anxious to get to Talon and not only tell him about Simca but make certain he was safe. Gerun must have thought the same for he kept a rapid pace. She was surprised when Gerun gave a shout and another warrior seemed to appear out of nowhere.

"Alert the King that there is a problem," Gerun ordered and the warrior rushed off.

Hemera was relieved that it would not be long before they were among the other dwellings, surrounded by people. Unfortunately, it was not soon enough.

# The King & His Queen

Gerun suddenly stumbled beside her. She went to help him and he yelled for her to run.

Too late, she felt the point of a knife at her back and was shocked to see blood pouring from Gerun's back when he fell to the ground.

"I have avoided you, for unlike these fools who think you slow-minded, I know your wisdom surpasses even the King's." Simca poked her with the knife. "Walk with me."

It was not a request and Hemera did what she said.

"I realized you saw me in the woods, though did not know it was me, when you began to pay attention to the King's personal guards' cloaks. It was only a matter of time before someone as tenaciously wise as you would fit all the pieces together and discover the truth."

Simca stopped her when they reached a section of the fence in the far back area of the stronghold and pushed at it with her shoulder. It opened, though not wide. "Step through and do not think to run. My aim is good and you will not get far, though it will take you a while to die from your wound and it would be a most painful death as it will be for Gerun."

Hemera held out hope that Gerun would survive his wound, as for her, she had no intentions of tempting such a dire fate. Besides, she was relieved to enter the forest. It would protect her as it always did.

Simca was close behind her as they slipped out of the stronghold and into the woods.

"I assume that you are bringing me to your chieftain," Hemera said.

"I am bringing you to the true King of the Picts," Simca said and gave her a shove that almost sent Hemera tumbling.

"I have upset your plans."

"You have. The brew would have made you ill and rid you of any bairn that may already be growing in you and put more doubt in the minds of the people that King Talon cannot protect them. A few more attacks by the King's enemies along with the Northmen who have joined us and the people would have been demanding the King's head."

"And your chieftain would rule, without anyone knowing that the attacks and the Northmen's part in it all was his doing. He would be the one to come to their rescue and save them."

"The rightful one to the throne," Simca reminded once again.

"I suppose he will return my brutally beaten body to the King along with dead warriors or Northmen he will claim were responsible for my suffering and death. The people will cheer his victory and be ashamed of their King's failure to protect the future queen and his people, bringing King Talon's reign to an end."

Simca laughed. "That is only part of it. He will show the people the full worth of his strength, wisdom, and ability to rule."

"The people already have such a King."

"A king who harbors his enemies within the stronghold, had them members of his High Council," — she laughed— "and is not potent enough to sire an heir? And with all that against him, what does the fool King do? He intends to wed a woman that had been a slave to the Northmen and is thought slow-minded." Simca sneered. "The fool brings this on himself. He does not deserve to be King."

"What did you do? Prepare a special brew for the

## The King & His Queen

King's former two wives and the women he mated with so that his seed would not take root in them?" Hemera asked, more things making sense the more she talked with Simca.

"Another reason for a change in plans, since I realized too late the King was poking you. We cannot take a chance that you will get with child. It would ruin everything. Though finding your broken body after it has been left a few days in the woods will work well along with an unexpected attack on the stronghold."

Hemera nearly fell when Simca shoved her again. She almost rushed her hand to her middle, worried about the bairn, but caught herself. Simca must not know of the bairn, fearing what the woman or her chieftain would do.

"Move faster, we have a distance to go," Simca ordered, "and do not waste your hope on being rescued. I know these woods far better than anyone and I know where every sentinel is posted. Now hurry, I am glad to finally be rid of this place and able to join the true King."

Hope remained strong in Hemera no matter what Simca said. The woman might think she knew the forest better than anybody, but she was not part of the forest like Hemera. She did not hear the trees whisper or have the animals speak to her, or know its secrets. The forest protected its own and it would protect Hemera and the forest would make sure Talon found her.

~~~

Talon entered the woods with his warriors, rage burning deep in him. Wrath and Paine stood to either side of him, his personal guards flanking them, their anger as palpable as his since one of their own had fallen and was not expected to survive. Orders had been given that they would not return until they had Hemera.

Talon looked down at Bog standing alert between him and Paine. "Find Hemera."

The wolf took off and Talon followed, the others falling in behind and others spreading out along the sides, keeping their King in clear view, no one sure what awaited them.

~~~

Hemera talked with the forest as she kept the rapid pace. She could not allow herself to get too far from the stronghold. Talon would not be that far behind them and he would be wise enough to have Bog help track her. The forest would do the rest. Now, though, she needed the forest's help in escaping Simca before it was too late.

With silent words, she called on the wisdom of the forest and after only a few steps a low-lying fog began to creep past the surrounding trees toward them. In no time, it reached them, hugging their ankles and making it impossible to see where they walked. It was not long before the fog reached their waist.

"Stop," Simca ordered a tremor in her voice and took firm hold of her arm and pointed with the knife. "Over there."

Hemera looked to where she pointed and realized her intention. A vine wrapped around the trunk of a tree and Simca intended to use her to bind Hemera to her so they would not get separated in the fog. It did not worry her. They would never make it to the tree before the fog completely swallowed them.

"Hurry, hurry," Simca urged, tugging her along as the fog raced up around them.

The fog was so thick that Hemera could not see Simca, though she felt her hand tighten around her arm.

"Do not try to run or you will find my blade buried in you," Simca ordered.

"How could I run in this?" Hemera said.

Simca kept walking, unwisely not slowing down, thinking she still headed for the tree and Hemera waited for the inevitable. She did not have to wait long. Simca tripped, going down hard and Hemera took the opportunity to wrench her arm free. She wasted no time in hurrying off, letting the whispering trees guide her, and she asked the wind to take a message to Talon.

~~~

Talon stopped and wanted to roar at the cursed fog that descended on them and prevented any of them from taking another step. Instead, he called out, "Stay as you are."

Fog was one thing that frightened warriors no matter how hard he trained his warriors against it. They believed that angry forest spirits sent it and with it came death. Even Bog stopped and he only knew that because the wolf brushed against him, letting him know he was there. Then he was gone and this time Talon could not follow.

"You have only one choice," Paine said, standing beside him, though Talon could not see him.

Talon agreed, though worried it might not be the

wisest choice. "Call out to her and hope she can do the same." Fear gripped at his insides that he could worsen her situation with his choice, but her situation was already dire. The thought that he could lose her and their child filled him with anger far greater than anything ever had in his life. He had never imagined a woman becoming so important to him that he would do anything to save her.

He would do anything to save Hemera, even relinquish his own life and a King was not to think that way. When it came to Hemera he was not King, he was a man whose heart belonged to her.

*Tuahna.*

That was what he felt for her and had refused to acknowledge.

A lone howl suddenly filled the air, Bog thinking the same as them. The howl came again and Talon could almost feel a heavy unease spread throughout his men. They could not just stand here and wait to see what came out of the fog.

Talon turned to Paine and spoke low so the forest would not echo his words. "Converge." While his order was passed down the line, he turned to Wrath and said the same. He listened as his men stepped closer together, touching shoulders.

*Follow my voice.*

Talon heard Hemera clearly in his head and he did as she said.

~~~

Hemera smiled when she heard Bog reach out to her with his woeful howl. It meant Talon was not that far away, though the fog would have slowed him as well. Bog would reach her even with the fog, though he could reach her much faster without it as would Talon. Simca would have the same advantage, but Hemera was willing to take that chance. After all, the forest would protect her.

*You are safe, my child.*

She smiled at the familiar voice that was the strongest when she was in the woods and never failed to help her, as it did now.

Talon's voice reached her as the fog began to dissipate.

*Do not fear, I am coming for you.*

The fog was almost gone when another of Bog's howl sounded eerily through the woods and Hemera was about to chase after it when she saw Simca running frantically toward her in the distance. Hemera did not hesitate, she ran.

*Chased. Simca.*

Talon heard her and his feet took flight. He was faster than any of his men and soon they were far behind him. He let his feet guide him since they seemed to know where to go.

*Your knife, you fool.*

The sharp-tongued voice had him reaching for the knife at his waist and wondering who had spoken to him, for it was not Hemera he had heard.

The trees began to thin and he caught sight of Bog up ahead and in the distance he spotted a figure, running... and his heart slammed against his chest. It was Hemera. He would reach her on time. She would be safe.

He pumped his legs harder, though they were

already screaming in pain. He had to get to her. He had to. They drew closer and closer. Soon, very soon, she would be in his arms.

Fear slammed into him like a mighty fist when a figure suddenly appeared behind her. The woman clutched a knife in her hand and raised her arm high, ready to throw. Hemera stood between him and Simca when all of a sudden Bog launched himself through the air at Hemera, knocking her to the ground and Talon did not hesitate, he threw his knife and sailed through the air, lodging in Simca's chest.

Bog hurried away from Hemera when Talon reached them and rushed over to Simca to make sure the woman would trouble them no more.

Talon scooped Hemera up in his arms before she even realized he was there and when she did, her arms hurried around his neck, burying her face against his chest and holding on tight.

That was how his men found them, clutched to each other with no intentions of letting go.

Talon could feel her heart pounding against her chest, he held her so close, and he could feel the tremor in her body as it slowed and dissipated. Mostly, he could feel her joy of being in his arms.

"You are unharmed?" he finally asked as his warriors took up a protective stance around them.

"I am, but what of Gerun?" she asked quickly.

"The healer has concerns as I do of you," he said and slipped his hand under her cloak to rest it against her stomach.

"We both are well," Hemera assured him in a whisper, laying her hand over his.

Two warriors stepped aside to let Wrath enter. "We

should go, since we have no trackers out to alert us to anyone else's presence."

"Simca was taking me to her chieftain or the true King as she claimed," Hemera said as Talon helped her to her feet.

"He is here, nearby?" Wrath asked anxiously.

"Simca told me he was a distance away."

Wrath looked to Talon. "How could our enemy be right in front of us?"

Talon and Hemera answered simultaneously. "Our enemy is also our friend."

## Chapter Twenty-nine

"You are saying that Simca put something in the King's previous wives drinks that kept them from getting with child?" Gelhard asked, shaking his head in disbelief.

Hemera nodded. "So she admitted, and it would make sense why the King's previous wives are now with child. She was wise in the way of plants and wise in her deceit."

"Then she was the one to poison the bread," Paine said, he, Wrath, and Gelhard being the only ones permitted in the High Council Chambers upon their return from the woods.

"She was here in the stronghold from the start, working in the feasting hall, hearing things and passing on all she heard and learned to our enemy," Wrath said.

"You rutted with her. Did she learn anything from you?" Gelhard asked.

Wrath rose slowly off the bench and leaned over the table toward Gelhard. "I should kill you where you sit for thinking I would betray my King."

Gelhard drew back away from the man, the blazing anger in his eyes and voice enough to shiver him with fear. He quickly apologized. "I meant no disrespect, Wrath, anything could be passed in innocent conversation."

"Talk was not something Simca and I shared, though she was with Broc and Tarnis as well and who knows how many others."

"Simca worked her wiles well, learning information and no doubt persuading the embittered to join with her against the King. It is no wonder our enemy does so well, having had her among us for so long," Paine said.

"At least now the enemy will lack for information," Gelhard said.

"Unless there are more traitors among us," Wrath warned.

"It is the enemy who is the King's friend that should concern you," Hemera said. "He no doubt has at one time or another spoken with all of you here and as Gelhard mentioned things can be passed in innocent conversation, though if he is believed a friend than far more was probably discussed."

Talon watched how the men who once thought Hemera slow-minded were now paying attention to her every word. Did they finally realize that her strange ways were because she was far more intelligent than anyone could ever imagine? It certainly had taken him long enough to realize it and there was also something else about her he had yet to grasp. In time though, he would.

"It is good the wedding will be private with a celebration to follow when the land blossoms. Otherwise the enemy would probably be in attendance, leaving the King and his queen vulnerable to possible harm," Gelhard said.

"I will wait no more to make Hemera my queen. We exchange permanent vows on the morrow in the feasting hall," Talon commanded and noticed the small gasp that Hemera tried to hide. "Let the news spread through the stronghold that all are welcome to attend and tell the cookhouse to prepare a feast. I want all to know a queen will be crowned."

"Aye, it is wise to wed now. The people will be happy with the news, though..." Gelhard raised a finger. "Excitement would grow among the people if a rumor was heard that the future queen already carries the King's bairn."

Hemera looked to Talon. He reached out, taking her hand that rested on the table in his. "It is time for all to know how proud I am that you will not only be my queen but that you also carry my child, heir to the Pict throne." He gave her hand a squeeze before turning to Gelhard. "Let the rumor be heard."

Gelhard beamed with excitement. "I should start on that right away. May I take my leave, my King?"

"By all means, Gelhard, you have much to do and I am confident you will see it done."

"Aye, my King, I will. I have waited long for this glorious day and news of an heir to the throne." He bobbed his head and hurried from the room.

It was not lost on Hemera that Wrath and Paine were not surprised by the news that she was with child. Wrath no doubt had been there when Verity had told the King of her dream and Anin probably had known before Hemera herself did and had shared it with her husband.

It would seem that secrets might be difficult to keep here and the thought reminded her of something she had to do. "I must speak with my sister."

Wrath nodded. "I agree. Verity would want to hear from you about the wedding tomorrow and the rumor that is sure to spread quickly."

"I also want to see how Gerun is doing and see how the pup fares," Hemera said anxious to leave.

"You are telling me that you will be gone a while?" Talon asked, not caring for the news. He preferred she remained by his side where he could keep her safe.

Hemera nodded, her thoughts heavy.

He saw no smile on her face and it disturbed him. "You do not smile. Do you not want to be queen?"

Hemera stared at his fine features and thought how much she enjoyed looking upon him, though she enjoyed the closeness they shared even more. She had never expected to feel as she did for Talon. She had always thought she would live a more solitary life, mostly because she felt so different, so removed from others. Losing her heart to Talon had changed all that, but being his queen...

"I do not know," she answered truthfully, "though I do know that my heart belongs to you and there is no other place I want to be than beside you—always. If I must be queen to do that, then I will gladly be your queen." She stood, went to him, and as she leaned down to kiss him, she whispered, "*Tuahna.*"

He thought he saw tears glisten in her eyes as she stepped away from him and he reached out to grab her hand, but too late, she already was out of his reach and as she hurried off, she paid no heed when he called out to her.

Hemera wiped at her eyes, refusing to let one tear fall. There was much she had to see done before the wedding and things Talon should know. Secrets she had once promised to keep that now would come to light whether she wanted them to or not.

She headed to the healer's dwelling, first to see

Gerun and upon seeing him, feared he would not survive. His skin was hot and his wound deep and he was not responsive to her voice or touch.

"I am sorry," Bethia said. "I have done all I can."

"You must help him fight to live. You must not let his body become too heated or let his wound grow putrid. "I have some herbs that may help. I will see them sent to you with instructions."

"I am grateful for any help you offer," Bethia said.

Hemera went directly to her dwelling after leaving Bethia and asked Tilden, who shadowed her every step to send for Opia in the cookhouse. She was pleased to see that the wolf's mum was seeing to the pup's care. Now that the tiny pup showed no signs of illness, the mum accepted him into the pack and was seeing that he got fed. Pleased with the pup's progress, she hurried to fill a pouch with a mixture of herbs that she hoped would help Gerun.

She gave specific instructions to Opia as to how the mixture was to be used and after the young woman assured her that she would explain it all to Bethia and help her prepare it if necessary, Hemera headed for Verity's dwelling.

Her steps were slow. She had never thought she would speak to her sister about this and dreaded doing so, but she had no choice. She had to tell Verity, for the truth would be revealed soon and she would have her sister hear it from her lips and no other.

Hemera knocked on the door and when it swung open, Verity threw her arms around Hemera.

"I was so worried about you, but I knew when I heard of your return that you would come to me as soon as you could." Verity stepped back. "Come in. come in.

I have prepared a brew for us to enjoy."

Hemera stepped inside and as she closed the door, she said, "There is something I must tell you, Verity."

~~~

Wrath walked in on his wife and Hemera hugging and crying, he assumed tears of joy at the news that Hemera would be queen. "Delight over the impending wedding stirs outside as well as in here."

The sisters broke apart, though remained beside each other.

Wrath knew his wife well and it was not happiness he saw on her face. He walked over to her, forcing Hemera to step away as he came between them and slipped his arm around Verity. "Something troubles you?"

"No, No," she assured him quickly. "It is all that has happened and now Hemera will be queen. So much change to accept at one time."

Wrath knew by his wife's forced smile that she was not telling him the truth and he was surprised that she would lie to him. They kept nothing from each other. Why did she feel the need to now?

"I will see you at the feasting house later," Verity said as Hemera walked to the door.

Hemera turned and nodded at her and as she spoke Wrath looked on surprised and was more surprised when his wife responded in the tongue of the Northmen.

When the door closed, Wrath turned to his wife. "Your sister speaks the language of the Northmen."

"That should not be a surprise since we both spent

such a long time with them. We were bound to learn it," Verity said.

"She speaks it with the skill of someone born to it."

Verity's head shot up. "Do you think she is not a Pict?"

He did not expect such a defensive tone from her. "No, I simply marvel at her skill."

"A forced skill, and the reason we decided while on our journey here that we would never speak it again."

"Then why speak it now?"

"An old memory brought it forth," she said, sadness filling her eyes as she laid her head on his chest.

Wrath held her close. "Tell me."

"It is a memory better left forgotten."

Wrath wanted to believe her but something warned him against it. Whatever the sisters had discussed here was important and he intended to find out.

~~~

Hemera felt her heart constrict with pain. She should have realized that her and her sister's return home would eventually unlock secrets. Secrets she did not want to face or others to know. She thought of running to her dwelling and doing what she often did...escape into solitude. It had been unwise of her to engage with others as much as she had done since her arrival here. She should have kept to herself, but there had been an eagerness to gain more knowledge of her home and its people. What had it gotten her?

She turned to seek the solitude of her dwelling.

## The King & His Queen

*Stop running from your destiny.*

Hemera almost stumbled, she stopped so abruptly at the scolding voice in her head. Was that what she had been doing? Was this all truly her destiny?

She looked in the distance where her dwelling waited and turned and looked toward the feasting house. She did not hesitate... she ran to the feasting house.

~~~

Talon stood in the feasting hall, looking to see if Hemera had returned yet. It had concerned him to see tears in hers eyes after learning she would be queen and he wanted to know why. He also wanted to know why the sudden need to speak with her sister. Mostly though, he wanted to take her in his arms and hold her close.

"My King," Gelhard said as he rushed toward Talon. "A message has been delivered. Your Uncle Egot and Aunt Ethra will arrive on the morn."

"Egot never sent word he was coming here," Talon said and wondered over the man's unexpected visit. "I am sure you have already seen to having a dwelling prepared for them."

"I have, my King," Gelhard said and lowered his voice. "He was a distance away when Simca took Hemera and he is a friend."

"He is more than a friend, he is family," Talon said disturbed by what Gelhard implied.

"You are right and he is *well-trusted* by us all." Gelhard bobbed his head. "I must see that all is going well for the ceremony tomorrow."

Talon would never believe that his uncle would betray him, though he understood Gelhard pointing out the obvious to him. It was after all Gelhard's task to make him aware of things he would not take heed to. But his uncle had fought hard alongside him in uniting the tribes and had advised Talon often on what was expected of him when he became King. The question still remained. Why was his uncle here?

The door to the feasting hall suddenly burst open and Talon glared as Hemera rushed in, Tilden following on her heels and stopping abruptly when she came to a halt. Her fiery red hair was windblown, ringlets springing out around her face, her cheeks were flushed as red as her hair and... tears ran down them.

She shuddered as she took a labored breath and his heart felt her pain. He raced toward her, pulling her into his arms. She buried her face against his chest as his one arm tightened around her waist and his hand went to the back of her head.

He looked to Tilden. "What happened?"

"I do not know, my King. After leaving her sister's house, she looked as though she would return to her dwelling when she suddenly turned and ran here as if a snarling hound was after her."

With a firm hold on Hemera, Talon ushered her into the High Council Chambers and hastily sat, pulling her into his lap. His worry was in his words. "Do you feel ill? Is it the bairn?" He rested his hand to her stomach as if somehow he could protect the nesting child.

Hemera placed her hand over his. "The bairn is fine and I am well."

"Then what is wrong?" he asked relieved she and

## The King & His Queen

the child were well, though concerned for her tears.

She looked off in the distance for only a moment, then rested her brow to his. "There is something I must tell you."

Talon kissed her gently. "Do you still give your heart to me freely?"

"Without question," she whispered, running her thumb over his lips softly before kissing him.

"Will you continue to whisper *tuahna* in my ear?"

"Until I have no more breath left in me," she said.

"Then there is no more I need to know." He kissed her silent when she went to protest.

Their kiss barely ended when Hemera attempted once more to speak.

Talon pressed his finger to her lips. "There is nothing that will stop me from making you my queen, so do not waste your words."

"After I am queen you will hear what I have to say?" she asked, resting her hand to his cheek.

"Aye, I will hear you then," he agreed and turned his head, letting his lips graze the palm of her hand.

Hemera shivered.

"There is something I have been meaning to tell you," he whispered, his lips drifting to her ear. *"Tuahna."*

She stared at him not sure she had heard him correctly.

He brushed his lips across hers. *"Tuahna."*

A gentle smile surfaced as her heart swelled with joy and a single tear rolled down her cheek.

Talon wiped it away with his thumb. "No matter what happens, no matter what we face in the future always remember that you will forever have my heart.

*Tuahna.*"

Her arms went around his neck as his lips settled on hers and he sealed his words with a kiss.

A knock at the door had them both shaking their heads.

"Enter," Talon said his tongue sharp for the person who dared to disturb him.

Gelhard took a cautious step into the room. "The women are here to tend Hemera."

Hemera turned a confused looked on Gelhard. "I need no tending."

"It is a custom among the chieftains when they wed and has been continued with the King," Gelhard explained. "Verity and Anin await you."

Hearing it was her sister and Anin who would tend her eased her concern some, though she still turned to Talon and asked, "Must I?"

"The people like it when customs are followed."

Hemera stood reluctantly. "I will see you later."

"That is not permitted," Gelhard said. "You will see the King at the ceremony on the morrow."

That news did not sit well with Hemera. She could see that it was not going to be easy to be queen. She smiled, bobbed her head, and said, "Until the morrow, my King." She walked to the door.

"Hemera!" Talon called out, stopping her.

She turned, still wearing a smile.

"Behave!" he warned sternly.

"Always, my King."

## Chapter Thirty

Hemera sat in her dwelling alone. She had chased Verity and Anin away as dusk fell. She wanted to be alone. She shook her head at her paltry excuse. She did not want to be alone. She wanted to be with Talon. It surprised her how much she wanted to be with him and how accustomed she had become to being with him.

She harbored doubts about being queen, but she harbored no doubts about being Talon's wife. She rarely saw him as the King, he was and always would be Talon to her. Talon was the one she would wed. Talon was the one she would spend her life with and Talon was the one who...

*Tuahna.*

Talon felt for her as deeply and strongly as she did for him.

She wished she could go to him now, feel his arms around her, his lips on hers, his touch, she shivered with the thought. She glanced over at her cloak hanging on the lone peg by the door and wondered how she could get past the guard and to the secret passage that would take her to Talon's room without being spotted.

She was about to stand when the door flew open.

Talon stood there, filling the doorway, staring, much like Hemera would often do... only his eyes where focused on her. He wore a long tunic opened down the middle and held closed by a leather tie. His arms were bare, his muscles solid. The dark braids at the sides of his head were pulled back and knotted at the nape of his neck and his deep blue eyes were ablaze with passion.

He closed the door and stretched his hand out to her, and she went to him. He pulled her to him, turning her so that her back fit nicely against the front of him. He lowered his head, and she tilted hers, leaving her neck bare for his kisses that turned her skin to gooseflesh.

"I could not wait for the morrow," he whispered and continued to treat her neck to kisses and nibbles.

She smiled up at him. "And you warned *me* to behave."

He grinned. "I like it better when you misbehave. I half expected you to slip into my chamber through the secret passage. I grew impatient waiting."

She turned around in his arms. "I was figuring out a way to slip past the guard."

"Another reason I came to you instead. I have more than one guard on you."

She smiled, draping her arms around his neck. "You have such little faith in me?"

Talon laughed, his hands going to her backside and giving it a squeeze. "No. I did not want my personal guards to be embarrassed when you eluded them."

Her smile softened while concern grew strong in her eyes. "Talon—"

He silenced her with a kiss. "The only words I want to hear is that you cannot wait to couple with me."

She turned a feigned pout on him. "I have been eager to couple with you since you disappointed me in the High Council Chambers."

"Disappointed you?" he asked as if he did not quite

believe her remark.

She tugged playfully at his ear with her teeth before whispering, "You sent me away when I was aching for you."

A shudder ran through him and his desire spiraled. "I will never send you away again."

"I have your word on that?" she asked.

Her voice was not only filled with desperation but so were her eyes. "Aye, you have my word. *Never* will I send you away. *Never.* Doubt rose in her eyes and it troubled him.

He went to move away from her and she reached out to stop him, but his arm never left her waist. He reached out to open the door.

"Tilden, come in here," he ordered.

Hemera's brow puckered, wondering why he would order Tilden inside.

"My King," Tilden said with a nod and shut the door.

Talon's tone turned solemn. "You are to witness us exchange vows and know this night Hemera became my queen. If anything should happen on the morrow to delay or prevent the ceremony, you will verify that Hemera is already my queen."

"I would be honored, my King," Tilden said, his chest expanding with pride.

Talon smiled when he saw that Hemera looked too stunned to speak. "You will need your voice for this."

His teasing tone and that he would make her his queen this night with only Tilden as witness thrilled her beyond reason. "My voice will ring clear for I am honored to speak my vows with you in this humble dwelling."

Talon walked her over by the fire pit.

Tilden stood on the opposite side and his pride swelled even more as he watched the King take hands with Hemera as the flames danced brightly before them as if joyous to witness this special moment.

Standing close, their bodies whispering against each other, Talon held her two hands in his. "Hemera, you have my heart. It belongs to you and always will. As King of the Picts, I proclaim you my queen from this moment to forever. *Tuahna,* my wife*, tuahna*."

Tilden's gasp was soft, but Hemera heard it along with her own. Never did she expect Talon to speak that word in front of another. It was not something that was done, but then neither was him claiming her queen forever. It meant their vows could never be dissolved. With him doing that, her heart surrendered to him completely.

"My King, I give you my heart freely and forever. I am honored to be your queen and accept all that is expected of me. I will serve you well and I will always stand by your side, from this moment to forever. *Tuahna*, my husband, *tuahna*."

Talon lowered his lips to hers, their kiss sealing their vows and binding them together forever.

Talon turned to Tilden. "You are witness that Hemera is now my queen."

"Aye, my King, and I am proud to have witnessed the exchange and I am proud to be the first to say," — he turned to Hemera—"I am here to serve you, my Queen." He took a step back. "I will make certain you are not disturbed, my King." He turned to Hemera again. "My Queen."

Hemera continued to stare at the door after Tilden

closed it. She was truly queen?

"You are Queen," Talon confirmed, knowing her thought. And it will be your last night in this dwelling, our last time here."

Sadness had her frowning. "I will miss this place. It was home to me after too long of not having one. I planted my garden and looked forward to seeing it flourish and grow and enjoy harvesting it." She stared for a moment, then a soft smile surfaced, chasing away her sadness. "You are my home now." She took his hand and placed it on her stomach. "You have planted a seed that will flourish, grow, and live on."

He pressed his hand firmly against her. "I plan on planting many seeds inside you and see them flourish." He brought his lips to hers and kissed her.

His lips never felt so good to Hemera. It was as if he kissed her for the first time and he actually did, for this was their first true kiss as husband and wife. It sealed their union, bound them together just as their vows had done, just as their coupling this night would do.

He scooped her up in his arms. "Now you become my wife and nothing will ever be able to break the bonds we seal here this night."

*Please. Please let it be so*, she silently pleaded.

When he placed her on her feet next to the sleeping pallet, neither of them wasted time in stripping the other of their garments. Once done, they stood naked in front of each other and Talon's fingertips began to lightly roam over her like a feather teasing the flesh.

"Your skin is so smooth and soft, I so enjoy touching you." When his fingers grazed her middle, he reached for her hand and sat down on the sleeping pallet to ease her between his slightly spread legs. He pressed his face to her stomach and gave it a tender kiss. "I cannot wait to feel him move inside you."

Hemera cupped the back of his head with her two hands, cherishing this moment he paid homage to their unborn child.

"I never thought this day would come," —he raised his head to look up at her— "then I met you, a woman different from others, a woman who challenged me like no other, and a woman more perfect for me than I ever imagined... my queen and the mother of my child." He pressed his lips against her stomach, holding them there as if waiting for his kiss to penetrate her flesh and reach his child.

She seared this moment in her memory, never wanting to forget it and gasped when she felt his fingers make their way between her legs. He stroked her ever so gently and her hands fell off the back of his head to rest on his shoulders—not rest—more grip his strong shoulders. Grip them, she did, especially when his thumb slipped over her thatch of fiery red hair to find the tiny nub that was already sensitive to his touch.

Her legs lost their strength as he teased it and when his tongue replaced his thumb, her legs almost crumpled, but his firm hands cupping her backside kept her on her feet. She dropped her head back and she moaned, enjoying what his wickedly talented tongue was doing to her.

She would not last long if he continued on like this. "Talon, please," she begged and he paid her no mind. "I am going to come."

He stopped and glanced up at her. "Aye, many times this night."

Hemera dug her fingers into his shoulders so hard, she thought he would yell out in pain, but he uttered not a sound. He continued enjoying her, continued bringing her pleasure until finally she cried out, feeling everything shatter around her in a climax that left her unable to stand.

Talon scooped her up and laid her on the sleeping pallet. He spread her legs and dropped down over her, his manhood slipping inside her and fitting them together as one. He teased her toward another climax, but held back on his own. He did not want this to go too fast. He wanted this night filled with pleasurable memories for them both.

He brought his head down near her breast and flicked at her nipple with the tip of his tongue, causing the puckered nub to pucker even more. It also caused Hemera to buck against him, taking him deeper inside her and if he was not careful he would climax sooner than he planned to.

"Come with me," she said, reaching up to wrap her arms around his neck and forced his lips to meet hers. She fed on him, hungry for his taste, eager to have his tongue delve into her mouth as his manhood continued to delve into her. Instinct took over and she wrapped her legs around him, locking her to him firmly. She wanted to feel his climax and have it feed her own.

"Not yet," he warned and tried to break free of her, but her passion had grown her strength and he could not escape her.

"Please," she begged.

Her plea was like a passionate poke that sent an explosive wave rushing through him. He burst in a climax that had him dropping his head back as a lingering moan spewed from his lips, intensifying his climax that seemed to go on forever.

Hemera joined him, her climax feeling like a mighty wave that descended upon her, engulfing her with pure pleasure, until she shuddered with the last of it.

Talon eased himself off her, covering them quickly with the blanket and tucked her against him. "The pup kept you away from me too long. We have lost time to make up for."

Hemera chuckled. "Then you best get some sleep so you have the stamina to last."

"You think you can outlast me?" he asked with a chuckle of his own.

"We shall see, *my King*."

He took hold of her chin. "I prefer my name on your lips when we are alone."

"Is that all you prefer on my lips when we are alone?" she asked with a wickedly innocent smile.

He squeezed her chin. "We shall see where I want your lips later, for now we rest some." Her yawn confirmed his wise decision.

"A short nap, for we must make certain our vows are consummated over and over so that no one can refute our marriage." His warm body had her snuggling even closer against him and his arms closed tighter around her. She could sleep now. She was finally home where she belonged.

He wondered over her worry that they would be separated or that somehow she would be taken from him. It was one of the reasons he had exchanged vows with her. Once their vows had been spoken, they were bound to each other, nothing could break their joining.

# The King & His Queen

So, what did she fear?

Haggard's arrival? Did she think he would come here to demand a slave be returned to him?

He shook his head. That was foolish and Hemera was far from a fool. What then disturbed her?

He felt his eyes grow heavy, the comfort of her safe in his arms, lolling him to sleep, and he surrendered to it.

Hemera woke him, her lips nowhere near his mouth and he quickly took control of the situation. If he had not, it would have been over quickly. Afterwards, they slept again.

Talon woke Hemera the next time and they took it slow and easy, sleep claiming them fast when they were done.

They both woke together the third time and they both yawned together as well. They laughed, settled in each other's arms and went back to sleep.

A rap at the door woke them next. "My King, dawn is about to break," Tilden called out.

Talon hurried off the sleeping pallet and into his garments, worried if he lingered he would not take his leave until well after dawn.

He leaned over the sleeping pallet and kissed her quickly. "From tonight on it is *our* sleeping pallet we share." He kissed her again. "I look forward to exchanging our vows again. Until later... *tuahna*."

She whispered the same in return and watched him leave the dwelling. Her heart soared with such joy that she thought it would burst. She was happy, truly happy, and it frightened her.

~~~

Talon could not keep his mind off his wife. He had stopped himself from smiling several times after making his way out of his sleeping chamber, as if he had been there all night, and down to the feasting hall. Not that many paid him heed. They were too busy preparing the hall for the celebration.

He was about to slip off to his High Council Chambers to escape the chaos when the doors opened and in strode his uncle Egot. He was a good-sized man, thick and solid in body. He kept his hair shorn so that the drawings that marked the top of his head and ran down the sides of his face could be seen clearly. His features were good even with wrinkles that dug deep at the corners of his eyes.

Egot's boisterous voice echoed in the room. "You will take a queen today and I was not informed about it?" He stopped in front of Talon and bowed his head. "My King."

"For good reason," Talon said and stepped forward, his arms going around the man. "It is good to see you, Uncle, and I am pleased you will be here for the ceremony."

Egot gave his nephew a tight hug, then stepped back and resumed his show of respect. "As am I. Who is this fine woman who will be your queen?"

"Hemera, Verity's sister."

"She is the one Minn told me about. By the way, Minn tagged along with us, having been on her way here. This woman, is she not slow-minded? Or so says wagging tongues." Egot said, concern in his tone and his eyes turning wide with surprise when the King smiled. Egot could not remember when last he saw his nephew smile.

"Believe me when I say she is far from slow-minded," Talon said.

Egot grinned, hearing the pride in Talon's voice. "I cannot wait to meet her."

The doors burst open again and Gelhard entered, shaking his head and hurrying over to Talon. "Dalmeny and his warriors are not far off. He will arrive here just before the ceremony. That means more people than expected."

"That is good, more people to help celebrate this happy occasion," Egot said.

The door burst open again and a warrior rushed in and over to Talon. He gave a hasty nod of his head and hurried to say, "The troop of Northmen draw near.."

## Chapter Thirty-one

Hemera was relieved that she and Talon had exchanged vows last night. No matter what this day brought, nothing could change that they were bound together as husband and wife. She stretched herself off her sleeping pallet, having slept far later than she had intended. She was surprised Verity or Anin had not woken her by now. They were to help her get ready for the ceremony.

A shudder ran through her along with a pinch of fear when she stood. She snatched up her garment and slipped into it just as the door opened and Verity entered, more than a pinch of fear on her face.

"Haggard and his men arrive this day." Verity took a breath. "The King has ordered the ceremony to take place earlier than planned. His uncle Egot and his wife Ethra arrived unexpectedly as well as Dalmeny Chieftain of the Imray Tribe with several of his warriors. I have met them before when Wrath and I had gone in search of you. They appear to be good people and loyal to the King."

"Is Minn with them?" Hemera liked Minn when they had met. She was a skilled warrior, though more importantly she was from the Alpin Tribe, the last of the Alpin, or so she had thought until she met Hemera and Verity.

"Minn came with Egot, having been on her way here. It will be good to see her again," Verity said. "Her warrior skills would prove beneficial if necessary."

"If Haggard intended to attack the Picts he would have attacked as soon as he landed on Pict soil. His intention is not war. His intention is—"

The door opened and a swirl of wind hurried Anin in, rushing past her to embrace Hemera.

*Be watchful.*

The soft whispered warning shivered Hemera.

"That wind came out of nowhere," Anin said, settling her cloak around her and shaking her head when she looked at Hemera. "You must hurry and get ready. The villagers already begin to gather outside the feasting hall. Meats are cooking on the spits and brews are flowing freely. And the heavens smile down with sunshine."

Hemera wanted to believe all was good, but the wind had told her differently.

Verity and Anin helped her wash and get ready, fussing over her like two loving sisters and when they stepped back away from her to have a look, tears pooled in their eyes.

"You are beautiful," Verity said, wiping away the tear that had escaped.

Hemera ran her hand over the soft green tunic that draped gently over the long, pale yellow shift. They were lovely garments even her foot-coverings were newly crafted, all fit for a queen.

Verity had fashioned a forest crown for her, the kind she and her sister had once made when they had been no more than wee lassies. It nestled comfortably in her wild red curls atop her head.

"Are you ready?" Verity asked.

Was she? Was she truly ready to face not only her

future but her past? She had to or she would lose Talon and that terrified her more than anything.

Hemera smiled, courage taking hold of her. "I am ready."

*Stay strong. This is your destiny.*

Hemera had never heard the voice so strong in her head and it gave her more courage to face the task ahead.

"I was thinking," Anin said as she draped a cloak over Hemera's shoulders. "I could touch some of the unfamiliar people in attendance and see what I learn."

"No!" Hemera snapped, startling the two women and herself, for she sounded like a queen issuing an order. She shook her head and softened her tone. "You could put yourself and your bairn in danger if you do that. Do not take such a chance."

"Hemera is right," Verity agreed. "It is much too dangerous."

"Talon is a wise King and one who will not take chances with his people. I would not be surprised if he has plans no one knows about, except perhaps Paine and Wrath," Hemera said. "Besides, you had seen what was to be between me and Talon. You must know other future events as well. Does peace not prevail?"

"I have not seen that far beyond. I see the immediate present and perhaps a bit more, and I feel what others feel, but the future is not mine to see."

Hemera smiled. "That can mean only one thing... the future is ours to make."

The three women laughed as they walked off, it soon turning to talk as several of the King's warriors followed their every step.

## The King & His Queen

~~~

"It is wonderful news that greets me, my King," Dalmeny said with a nod to King Talon. "And glad I am to be here to witness it."

"I am pleased to have you here, Dalmeny. You fought bravely during our struggles to unite the tribes and you continue to serve me well," Talon praised the large warrior. He was a hulk of a man more in width than height and the few scars marring his fine features told the tale of his courage. His long dark hair was braided thickly at the sides of his head.

"I would give my life for the Picts." Dalmeny lowered his deep voice that sounded as if it rumbled in his chest. "I have yet to have any success in discovering who leads your opposition and aligns himself with the Northmen."

"There is time for us to speak of that. Today is for celebration."

"As you say, my King, but I heard Haggard and his fierce warriors are on their way here. Surely that does not bode well."

"If Haggard wanted war, he would have started it by now," Talon assured him.

"Then what does he want?"

"We will find out soon enough," Talon said, his glance drifting to Gelhard talking to Minn and the smile he wore when he first approached her now turning to a frown.

"My woman is not with me. Is there any willing ones available while I am here?" Dalmeny asked, looking around the feasting hall with a curious eye.

"Wrath," Talon called out and Wrath turned from

talking with Egot and approached. "See that Dalmeny finds a willing woman."

Talon walked away, hearing Dalmeny tell Wrath about the woman he enjoyed the last time he was here.

"Dark hair and a body a man could enjoy. Her name escapes me, but then—Simca—that was her name."

Minn gave a respectful nod to the King when he stopped in front of her and Gelhard. Minn was a true warrior as vicious as a man and besting many a one. She was tall, her body solid, though with curves that left no doubt she was a woman. She had sharp, attractive features and her long, dark hair was braided on one side of her head.

"I am glad to be here for this special celebration," Minn said, "and proud that an Alpin, one of my tribesmen, will be queen."

"I am pleased you are here, Minn, and we shall talk later, but right now I need to speak with Gelhard," Talon said, dismissing her.

"My King," Minn said with another nod and walked away to join Wrath and Dalmeny.

"Minn has told me—"

"I will not hear it," Talon ordered, his voice low, though harsh. "Nothing will interfere with this celebration or prevent it. Hemera will be my wife and nothing—*nothing*—will change that. So celebrate along with us or take your leave."

Gelhard held his tongue, though he would have preferred not to. "I am honored to celebrate this joyous occasion, my King,"

The doors to the hall opened and Hemera entered and all eyes turned on her.

## The King & His Queen

Talon's heart lurched in his chest upon seeing his wife. Never had he known a more beautiful woman, not only in features but her nature as well. She might be different, but she was so much more than people thought her to be and he was lucky to have her as his wife.

He stretched his hand out to her and she smiled and hurried over to him to take tight hold.

He leaned down and whispered, "There is nothing to worry about. We are already wed."

Her smile grew. "And glad I am for that."

Talon turned to Gelhard. "Let us see this done so we may celebrate."

Gelhard led the King and Hemera to the long table at the far end of the feasting hall and gave everyone time to assemble around the tables and along the walls eager to witness the ceremony. Verity went to Wrath with tears in her eyes, happy, though worried for her sister and Anin walked over to Paine, slipping into his protective embrace. Many took hold of vessels, ready to raise them in honor of the King and his new queen.

Talon and Hemera stood behind Gelhard, their hands still joined tightly together.

Gelhard stepped forward. "This day will live long in Pict minds and hearts, for today King Talon takes a queen. Let it be known that King Talon has chosen this woman Hemera to be his queen and Hemera agrees to serve the King well. The King and Hemera will now exchange vows that will seal their union and claim Hemera Queen of the Picts." Gelhard stepped aside.

Hemera could not stop the slight tremble that ran through her and she was relieved when Talon took both her hands and held them firm in his. He eased her to take a step forward and turn so they were facing each other and he spoke in a loud commanding voice.

"Hemera, you have my heart. It belongs to you and always will. As King of the Picts, I proclaim you my—"

The door burst open and several of the King's warriors entered and behind them followed Haggard, the Northmen and Chieftain of the Southern Region. He was a tall, bulky man, though solid, and his flaming red hair matched his long beard that had two braids starting at each side of his mouth trailing down his chin to join with a single, longer braid.

He pushed past the King's warriors and with a gruff voice demanded, "What goes on here?"

Talon took a hasty step forward, his nostrils flaring along with his temper. "I warn you once, Haggard, make another demand and your warriors will be taking your body home."

Haggard gave a barely noticeable nod.

"Since you are here, you are welcome to join in the celebration and witness my wedding."

Haggard's red bushy brows looked as if they joined together over his eyes, his scowl ran so deep. "Who is this woman who will be Pict queen?"

Talon reached out to Hemera and she took his hand and stepped forward. "Hemera of the Alpin Tribe."

Haggard's face burst red with anger and he sputtered as he spoke. "You will not marry Hemera."

"You have no say here, Haggard, so hold your tongue or lose it," Talon threatened and felt Hemera's hand begin to tremble. He stepped closer to her and eased her against his side.

"This wedding will not be and you will take your

hands off my *daughter*!"

Gasps flooded the feasting hall and whispers soon followed.

"Silence!" Talon ordered with a curt shout and the room stilled instantly.

"Come here to me, Hemera," Haggard ordered.

"No," Hemera said quickly. "I am finally home on my mother's land and here is where I will stay."

"I am your father and you will obey me," Haggard demanded.

"Hemera obeys only me," Talon said and thought better of his words since Hemera rarely obeyed him.

"I will not give permission for my daughter to wed you," Haggard said, sputtering his words again, his anger so strong.

Breaths were held, eyes turned wide, and all waited for the King to speak, for without a father's permission a woman could not wed.

Talon's arm went around Hemera. "You are too late. Hemera and I exchanged vows last night and sealed our union."

More gasps and rushed whispers rippled through the feasting hall.

"You lie!" Haggard shouted.

"Tilden!" Talon called out and the warrior stepped forward to stand beside Haggard. "Tell everyone."

Tilden raised his voice for all to hear. "I witnessed the King and Hemera exchange wedding vows last night and stood guard outside the door to Hemera's dwelling afterwards. The King did not leave until the sun peeked on the horizon."

"It does not matter, the union can be broken," Haggard argued.

Tilden shook his head. "It cannot. The King claimed Hemera his queen from the moment he spoke his vow until forever and Hemera spoke the same words as well. No one can undo what has been done. They are joined until death."

Haggard's hand went to the hilt of his sword at his waist and Tilden rushed to step in front of the King while his other personal guards stepped forward, along with Wrath and Paine. Haggard wisely moved his hand off the handle of his sword.

"We will talk," Talon said and turned to Hemera. "You will wait with your sister."

"No," she said softly. "I go with you."

Talon kept his voice low. "This is—"

"About me and I will be part of it."

"Hemera is a true Northmen, she speaks her mind to her husband," Haggard said with a boisterous laugh that shook his thick body.

Talon turned to Haggard. "You admit then that Hemera is my wife."

Haggard stopped laughing, his eyes flaring in anger once again.

Hemera would not embarrass her husband—the King—in front of Haggard and the people. "I will wait with Verity while you speak with my father." She brought her lips near his ear, though it looked to all that she kissed his cheek, and whispered, "I tried to tell you."

Talon pressed his cheek to hers and whispered, "You are mine and always will be and nothing else matters." He kissed her cheek and turned to Tilden. "Do not let her out of your sight."

"As you say, my King," Tilden said and remained

# The King & His Queen

close to her side as she walked past her father.

"You will be coming home with me," Haggard said as Hemera passed him.

Hemera smiled. "I am home."

Talon walked over to Haggard, his face showing none of the rage that swirled inside him. "You will not speak to my wife without my permission. Follow me."

Wrath and Paine fell in behind Haggard and the King's personal guards trailed behind them. When Wrath and Paine went to follow the two men into the High Council Chambers, Haggard objected.

"Do you fear being alone with me, Talon?" Haggard challenged.

Wrath spoke. "Our King fears nothing, but you will give me your weapons if you wish to speak to the King alone."

Haggard looked to Talon.

"Wrath is commander of my personal guards, I would obey him since his strength and impatience is well known," Talon warned.

Haggard grumbled as he handed over his sword and two daggers and the door finally closed on the two.

Talon did not take a sit. He looked directly at Haggard and said, "Tell me how Hemera came to be your daughter." He was surprised when Haggard's face softened.

"I found with Bera, Hemera's mother, what I never thought I would ever find. You Picts call it *tuahna*, something she said to me often." Haggard sat as if the memories had grown him weak.

Talon took his sit at the head of the table and poured them each a drink from the large vessel.

Haggard cupped his hands around the vessel Talon

handed him, though he did not drink from it. "I met Bera on trading day when the Northmen sailed to the Pict land far north from here to trade their wares with your people. If you think Hemera is beautiful, you should have seen her mum. I could not stop staring at her and being a young warrior I could not stop thinking of mating with her."

"You took her against her will?" Talon snapped.

Haggard shook his head. "No, it was not a thought. I knew upon seeing her that I did not want that between us. I went and spoke with her. She was fluid in our language from trading with us. I remember that first day well. I found excuse after excuse to speak with her until finally she asked if I would like to sit and share drink and food with her. I thought my heart would burst while my stomach churned." He laughed. "Never had I felt such for any woman."

"I understand."

Haggard looked at Talon. "You care for my daughter?"

"I would give my life for your daughter."

Haggard drew back in shock. "You are King. You cannot do that."

"Aye, I am King and I can do what I please and it pleases me to shield my wife from harm."

"That is foolish," Haggard said, shaking his head. "You have no heir to take the throne."

"There will be one soon enough and more will follow. Picts will always rule this land."

"You sound sure of this and yet your two previous," —Haggard glared at him—"my daughter already carries your child?"

"She does," Talon confirmed, "though it has not

been announced yet."

"That changes things."

"I thought it would. And if you are the wise ruler I believe you are, then you will see that this can benefit both our people. But before we discuss that, tell me what happened that Hemera wound up with you and was treated like a slave."

"Hemera was no slave." Haggard grew silent for a moment. "Bera and I lost our hearts to each other, but my father refused to accept it when I asked for permission to wed her. After that I was prevented from seeing her. I sent a message to her through a friend, but she was not at market nor did she ever return there. It was not until much later that I learned Bera had given birth to a daughter and that she herself was dead. I discovered that a close friend of hers claimed the lass as her own."

"So Hemera and Verity are not sisters?" Talon asked.

"They are not and yet they are, for Hemera fought like a wild beast to keep Verity safe." Haggard took a swallow and wiped his mouth on his sleeve. "The warriors I sent were unsure of which lass was my daughter, though if the fools had any sense they would have known the one with hair flaming as red as mine was my daughter. Unsure, they took both."

"So you raided a Pict village to get your daughter?"

"There was no raid. I negotiated with the village for Hemera. Unfortunately due to my warriors' lack of wise judgement, they took both lassies and that caused Verity's mum to scream in protest. She tried to tell my warriors it was Hemera, but they did not listen and from what I was told there was a bit of a scuffle."

A scuffle to the Northmen meant a good fight and Talon began to realize that Hemera had believed the Northmen had raided the village and that would explain why Minn knew of no raid on the Alpin Tribe. His curiosity had him asking, "Why did you not return Verity? Why keep her as a slave?"

"It took me a short time to realize that my daughter was much like me. She would not easily obey, but she did when I threatened harm to Verity. I hoped with time, Hemera would come to see that I cared for her and while I believe, or want to believe, she has, it is nothing compared to the bond she has with Verity. And I could not take that away from Hemera." Sadness filled his eyes. "When my people began to call her dim-witted, I knew better. Her mum was the same way, appearing slow-minded when actually her wisdom surpassed the wisest of men."

"I have come to learn the same myself."

Haggard nodded. "I am glad to hear that. I miss my daughter and the challenging talks we shared, though I was not surprised when she fled. I expected one day that she would do just that... return home."

"Where she belongs, and do you know how badly your son Ulric treated her?" Talon asked, trying to keep hold of his temper that simmered within him.

"They did not get along. Ulric did not like that he had a sister who was part Pict. I did my best to keep them apart."

"He beat her unmercifully, the multitude of scars on her back evidence of it, then he left her in the woods, no doubt to die, but she lived," Talon said his tone filled with venom.

Haggard stared at him, his mouth agape.

"You did not know."

Haggard shook his head, words failing him.

"Ulric deserves to die for what he did to Hemera."

"He is my son—"

"And Hemera is your daughter born of the woman you claim to have cared for like no other," Talon challenged.

"My son is my heir and I must protect him. I will agree and praise this union between you and Hemera, if you give me your word that you will not harm or kill my son. We can also discuss a more favorable trade agreement now that we are family."

Talon did not hesitate to agree to his terms, knowing he would find a way to see that Ulric got what he deserved.

The two talked and Haggard shared many memories of his daughter with Talon.

"I gave Hemera two weapons to help protect her, courage and strength. I explained they were her shield and her sword and that she should always keep them close," Haggard said.

"I can assure you that she does," Talon said with pride.

"I think my daughter may do well with you," Haggard, said raising his vessel.

Talon raised his as well. "She will. You have my word."

They drank, toasting their agreement.

They walked to the door, but before Talon opened it, Haggard stopped abruptly.

"Something else you need to say?" Talon questioned.

A smile surfaced on Haggard's face. "You do not

know who Hemera is, do you?"

"She is your daughter," Talon said, the corners of his eyes wrinkling as he tried to make sense of what Haggard implied.

Haggard laughed. "She is that and more, but I will let you discover for yourself." He opened the door and shouted as he entered the feasting hall. "We celebrate the union of my daughter Hemera and King Talon."

## Chapter Thirty-two

It was not until after vows were exchanged, toasts made, and songs sung in praise of the King and his new queen that Hemera finally got a somewhat private moment with Talon at the head table. Food and drink flowed in abundance along with robust laughter and merriment, affording them time to speak.

Hemera turned to her husband. *Husband*. It was still difficult for her to grasp, to believe it was real. That Talon and she were joined as one. Her heart fluttered at the thought, but her insides churned as she spoke to him. "Upon my arrival here, I feared to tell you of my father. I feared you would return me to him."

Talon went to speak and she placed a finger tenderly to his lips.

"Please, I must say this," she begged softly, and he nodded.

She dropped her hand away and Talon caught it in his, entwining his fingers with hers and pressing their locked hands against his chest.

"I had thought after I made certain Verity was safe and protected here that I would take my leave, for I feared my father might come for me. But this place creeped into my heart and the longer I remained here, the less I wanted to leave. When you kissed me, it changed everything. I never meant to keep my secret from you, but then I never meant to feel as deeply as I do for you and never did I think," —she touched her brow to his—"*tuahna*, my husband *tuahna*."

Talon eased his brow off hers and ran a gentle finger down her cheek. "It does not matter, wife. There was nothing you could have said or that anyone could have done to stop me from making you mine now and forever. We were destined for each other."

Hemera smiled, her fears vanquished, her heart full, and hope for a blessed future restored.

"You cannot keep her all to yourself," Egot said, stepping around the table to sit next to Hemera.

"You old fool, leave the young ones alone," his wife Ethra scolded as she approached the table.

"Quiet, wife, I am sure the new queen would like to hear about when the King was a lad and refused to listen to anyone who gave him an order."

"I would very much like to hear it all," Hemera said, turning to Egot with a generous smile.

"Be careful, Uncle, or I will have a few tales to tell myself," Talon warned teasingly.

"I will hear them," Ethra said and sat beside the King.

Talk and laughter filled the air and as time passed those who had joined her and Talon would leave and others would sit and visit with the King and his queen.

Hemera sighed when Verity finally took the seat beside her and Talon got lost in a conversation with Wrath.

The sisters joined hands, squeezing tight as if nothing could separate them, as they had often done when they were but wee bairns. Especially on the night the Northmen had come for them.

"I remember the night we were taken more clearly now," Verity said, "Mum screaming, Da trying to stop them from taking me, yelling it was you they wanted, then him falling to his knees when a Northmen hit him. I knew I could not let them take you, at least not alone. You are my sister."

Hemera threw her arms around Verity and they hugged tight before easing apart.

"I remember now, how you begged them to let me go as we were carted off. That it was you they wanted," Verity said.

"But what no one knew was that you told them it was you they wanted, confusing them and making them take us both." Hemera shook her head.

"I could not bear to think they would take you away, that I would never see you again. But what hurt me most was that you would be alone away from all those who cared most for you."

Hemera watched a tear fall from Verity's eye and she gently wiped it away, feeling her own tears building. "You suffered helping me."

"And you suffered protecting me, but we survived." Another tear touched Verity's cheek and Wrath was suddenly at her side.

"Tell me your tears are ones of joy," Wrath said as he hunched down beside his wife and took her hand.

"They are," Verity said and looked to her sister. "We are truly home."

Talon leaned over his wife's shoulder to say, "And here is where you will stay and together we will watch our bairns grow strong along with the Pict Kingdom, forever to rule."

"I believe our daughter agrees with you, my King," Anin said with a laugh as she approached with Paine. "She has yet to be born and she kicks and punches like a warrior."

"A true Pict," Talon said with pride.

"A word with my daughter," Haggard more demanded than asked as he approached the table.

Talon looked to Wrath and Paine and the two men escorted their wives away.

"Have your say," Talon commanded.

Haggard made another demand. "I will speak to her alone."

"Never will you speak to her alone." Talon's commanding tone made it clear that he would not debate the matter.

"Say what you will, Da," Hemera said as Talon's arm went around her.

Haggard stepped closer to the table. "Your mum touched my heart like no other woman could. When I learned she had died, I believe my heart died with her. Then I learned she had given me a daughter. Bringing you to my home was a way of having her with me once again."

"If that is so, then you should have protected Hemera better," Talon accused and was surprised at his response.

"You are right." Haggard nodded and looked to his daughter. "I favored you over my other children and they knew it, especially Ulric. I had thought of returning you here to your mum's people, but I could not bear parting with you. As I watched you grow strong and defend Verity, I knew one day you would leave. I am grateful for the time I had with you and proud to see the strong, courageous woman you have become... in spite of me."

Hemera tried to feel for her da, but his heartfelt

words did little to erase the memories of what she and Verity had suffered. "We will talk one day, Da, but not this day... in time."

"I look forward to it." Haggard went to turn away and stopped. "I am sure your grandmother will make herself known soon. Tell her she was right. I was not the right man for her daughter." He looked to Talon. "Hope the old woman does not feel the same about you for her granddaughter."

Talon did not have a chance to ask Hemera about her grandmother with Broc approaching the table in quick strides.

"I must talk with you, my King," Broc said.

Talon saw that Wrath and Paine were already headed toward the High Council Chambers as well as Gelhard. He stood and went to summon Tilden but his uncle Egot was suddenly at his side. "Something seems amiss. Go. I will protect your wife."

Hemera stood and rested her hand on her husband's chest. "Go do what you must and worry not about me."

Talon brushed his lips over hers. "I will always worry over your safety. Stay here until I return."

Hemera nodded and watched the King hurry to the High Council Chambers, concern for her husband heavy in her heart, for just as he would worry over her, she would worry over him.

"Sit and I will tell you more about Talon," Egot urged.

Reluctantly, Hemera took her eyes off the High Council Chambers' door that had closed behind her husband, and she sat. Soon Egot had her laughing.

Not long after Minn approached the table with

Dalmeny. Hemera had met the warrior briefly after the ceremony. They joined Egot and shared tales of Talon.

Hemera kept glancing toward the High Council Chambers door, anxious to know what was happening and grew even more worried when Minn was summoned to the High Council. What could they want with Minn?

Her thoughts were distracted by shouts and she looked to see that a warrior, not one of the King's warriors, was arguing with a Northmen. It took only a few more angry words for fists to fly and chaos to ensue.

Dalmeny stood before Egot could and grabbed Hemera's arm. "I will get her to safety."

Egot shoved Dalmeny's arm off Hemera. "I gave my word to the King. I will see her kept safe. Go see to stopping this brawl."

Dalmeny disappeared into the melee while Egot kept Hemera tucked behind him, throwing a punch or two when battling warriors almost collided with them. Hemera stretched her neck to see that Verity and Anin had wisely moved away from the table to brace themselves against a wall out of reach of the chaos. Once Egot got her to the steps, he rushed her up them to the second floor and into Talon's sleeping chamber.

Before he shut the door on her, he said, "Open this door for no one but me or Talon."

Hemera nodded and stood by the door, listening to the chaos below. It was not long before she heard her husband shout, "Enough!" Deep silence followed.

That was when she heard the creak. There was no time to turn and see who it was. She called out to Egot just before she felt a blow to the back of her head and darkness engulfed her.

Egot turned around and opened the door. "Hemera!"

He was met with a knife to his gut.

## Chapter Thirty-three

"What goes on here?" Talon demanded, his eyes instinctively searching the feasting hall for Hemera and his concern grew when he did not see her at the table where he had left her.

Wrath and Paine sent quick glances to their wives and both women nodded, letting their husband's know they were unhurt.

"Whoever started this step forward *now*!" Talon demanded.

A Northmen warrior stepped forward without hesitation.

"There is a coward among us?" Talon called out and no one moved.

The Northmen looked around. "I do not see the warrior who started arguing with me for no reason."

His words alarmed Talon and he called out, "Where is Hemera?"

Verity stepped forward, raising her voice to be heard. "Egot got her safely to your sleeping chambers."

Talon did not hesitate. He took quick strides to the steps, people hurrying out of his way, and took the stairs two at a time. Wrath and Paine followed close behind.

Fear slammed into Talon like a mighty fist as soon as he entered the room and saw his uncle on the floor, his hand covered in blood as he hugged his side.

"Who?" Talon demanded, dropping down beside

his uncle, while Wrath hurried to call for the stronghold gates to be closed and the healer to be fetched.

"Hemera?" Egot asked with a groan.

"She is not here," Talon said. "Who did this? Who took Hemera?"

"Impossible." Egot cringed in pain. "I stood guard at the door and no one passed me." He shook his head. "I did not see who did this." He cringed again. "Forgive me, my King, I failed you."

"You did not fail me, but you will if you do not fight to live, Uncle," Talon ordered.

Ethra hurried into the room and her hand flew to her mouth to cover her gasp when she saw her husband. She lowered herself down on the floor beside him. "You old fool, what did you do now?"

He clung tightly to her hand when she curled hers around his. "Quiet, woman, and stay with me, for I want no other beside me if the spirit of death takes me this day."

"The spirit of death has to get past me first," Ethra said.

"Then I will surely live, for death would not want to deal with your nagging tongue." Egot groaned.

"Then my tongue will not stop nagging you."

"It never does. No wonder I live so long," Egot said, tempting to smile through his pain.

That was the last Talon heard as he slipped through the door in the wall, Paine and Wrath following in surprise.

Once they reached the bottom and stepped outside, Paine hunched down to examine the marks in the soil. "Single prints. He carried her." He stood. "How could he know of this passage when Wrath and I knew nothing of it?"

Talon shook his head. "That is of no importance now. Hemera must be found. Have the stronghold searched thoroughly and get the tracker here to see if he can follow."

Paine nodded and reluctantly left the King.

*Stay alive, wife, I will find you.*

~~~

The pain woke Hemera. It radiated in the back of her head and down her neck. She went to reach her hand up and fear struck her hard when she discovered she could not move. She felt it then, the rope around her body, keeping her arms tight at her sides. It wound down around her to her ankles like a snake that refused to let go. She did not have to open her eyes to know she was tied tightly to a stake, but she opened them anyway.

It took her a moment to focus and when she did, she saw Dalmeny standing a short distance away, smiling.

~~~

Talon had donned the garments he hunted in, a black leather tunic that fell just above his knee and dark leather foot-coverings. Leather straps crisscrossed his chest and back, the two back ones holding the sheaths that held his two swords. He had tied his long hair back at the nape of his neck with a leather tie and his face wore the mask of battle... he was ready to kill.

Verity approached the King as he stood outside the

stronghold gates waiting for word that tracks had been found.

"My King," she said and his head snapped to the side to look at her.

She hastily took a step back. It had been said that when the King went into battle he could kill the enemy with one look. Seeing him now, she believed it.

"What is it, Verity?" Talon asked impatiently.

Verity wished she was not so afraid of the King especially now with him being her sister's husband. She swallowed her fear as best she could and said, "Please, my King, I beg you, please bring my sister home safely."

His features softened, though only for a moment. "That I can promise you, Verity."

Wrath approached and Verity hurried to hug him tight, then stepped back. "I will wait with Anin in the feasting hall. The King will bring my sister home to me."

Wrath turned to Talon as his wife rushed off. "You were right. It is Dalmeny. He cannot be found. When did you realize it?"

"Too late."

"You cannot blame yourself. None of us saw it," Wrath said. "Not even Minn who saw him every day, not until things began to surface. And why even think it could have possibly been Dalmeny when he had fought so bravely beside us?"

"I should have known. I should have seen it sooner. I heard him ask you about Simca and if I had paid heed to it, I would have recalled he had sought her favor whenever he visited here. Minn recalled as well, his favor for Simca. And while he had respectfully addressed me as my King, he told me he would die for the Picts. Never once did he say he would give his life to protect the King. But it was the secret passageway that confirmed it for me. I remembered the old warrior who built it was Dalmeny's uncle."

A shout rang out, drawing Wrath and the King's attention.

"Several different tracks have been discovered in several different places," Paine informed Talon when he reached the King. "It is meant to confuse and divide us."

"They plan to separate you from us," Wrath said to Talon.

"When that happens, you know what to do," Talon said and the two warriors nodded.

Broc hurried over to them. "Dalmeny's tracker wishes to speak with you."

"After you bring the tracker to me, send word to the tribes that wait in place and inform them of Dalmeny's betrayal. Have them sweep the land from where I have had them waiting to the stronghold for Dalmeny's warriors and any Northmen that may be among them. The traitorous band is probably on the move, with plans to join Dalmeny and make it appear as if he saved the Pict people. Do not let the band reach Dalmeny."

"All is in place, my King. The traitorous band has no chance against the hoard of Picts that will descend on them," Broc assured him and with a nod took his leave to fetch the tracker.

"We need to be cautious," Paine said, moving to stand next to Talon, his voice low. "You cannot walk into a trap alone."

"You and Wrath must be cautious as well. Dalmeny will know that you follow, want you to follow and he will have warriors waiting to make certain you die. He will leave no true friend of the King's alive. You will keep a good distance from me and dispose of any threat."

"And you will wait to confront Dalmeny until we meet up with you," Wrath ordered.

"Tell me, Wrath, Paine," Talon said, looking from one to the other. "Would you wait if it was Verity or Anin held captive? And do not bother to tell me this is different, that I am King. I am a husband fearful of losing his wife and unborn bairn."

Wrath and Paine remained silent, since there was nothing they could say to contradict the King.

Talon gave a nod and Wrath and Paine looked to see a short, wiry warrior walking toward them with Broc.

"I am Dalmeny's tracker and a skilled one. I believe I have found the tracks you should follow. They resemble more closely the tracks leading from the back of the feasting hall. Though, I would caution that the other tracks not be ignored."

Talon looked from Paine, to Wrath, and Broc and gave orders he knew would not be obeyed. "Follow the other three trackers. I will go with this tracker."

"No," Wrath said, stepping forward, knowing he would be expected to protest. "I go with you."

"Dalmeny warriors would gladly protect the King," the tracker offered.

"I cannot spare you, Wrath. You must lead a search party. You will follow the command I gave you."

"As you say, my King," Wrath said looking

annoyed, which he was. He did not like the King being alone with Dalmeny's men, but he and Paine would rectify that soon.

They all spread out and entered the forest, going in different directions. Clouds had moved in overhead, though no storm brewed and a chill filled the air. Since there had been no sign of horses' hooves in any of the tracks, it had been decided to follow on foot so they would not miss any vital signs.

Talon followed not far behind the tracker. As they got deeper into the woods, Dalmeny's warriors began to fan out away from him while the tracker made the excuse that he had to scout ahead. Soon Talon was alone.

He heard the howl of a lone wolf in the distance, if it was a true cry, and was reminded of Bog. He would be here helping if he was not off settling his new family deep in the woods.

He stopped, when he heard another lone howl. Was it in answer to the other? He remained still and listened to the forest, waiting to hear what else it had to tell him and hoped he would hear Hemera call out to him. It took only a moment for a sharp wind to whip around him.

*Talon.*

It was Hemera.

Talon gave a quick look behind him. Wrath and Paine were there somewhere. They would do what was necessary and so would he.

The wind whipped at him again.

*Talon.*

"I am on my way, Hemera. Stay strong."

## The King & His Queen

~~~

"You are finally awake. Good, for the King will be joining us shortly," Dalmeny said as he walked toward her.

Hemera stared at him, scrunching her brow.

"I forgot you are slow-minded in understanding things." He shook his head. "Why the King would wed you is reason alone he is not fit to be King. I was meant to be King."

Hemera remained silent, though inwardly she begged the forest to keep Talon safe, especially since he was entering a trap and she was the bait.

Dalmeny paced slowly in front of Hemera. "I am wiser, stronger, and more capable of being king than Talon. He is too easy on the people and does not demand enough from them, and he needs to conquer the southern region or dal Gabran will conquer us. When I am King, things will change and the Picts will rule this entire land and woe to those who try to take it from me." His eyes turned angry. "Talon also needs to pay for my sister's death."

Hemera tilted her head in silent question, thought thinking it would make sense that Simca was Dalmeny's sister.

"No one knew she was among you and fed me information or that she kept any fool woman who mated with Talon from getting with child." Dalmeny stopped pacing. "Simca did well. and I will revenge her death and see that our plan reaches fruition in her honor." He walked up to Hemera and grabbed her chin roughly. "And I will see that you and Talon suffer unmercifully before you die."

Hemera continued to stare at him, saying not a word.

"Have you nothing to say?" Dalmeny demanded, releasing her chin with a sharp shove.

She held her tongue for a moment, until the sharp pain that shot through her head eased. "You were in the feasting hall when Egot took me upstairs to Talon's sleeping chamber. You did not have enough time to get through the fighting and up through the secret passageway. Who was it that took me?"

Dalmeny laughed. "You ask me that and not how I knew of the secret passageway."

"The only way you could have learned of it is from the person who built it, which means you were close to him." She shook her head. "Though, I cannot see this man betraying the King after he went through so much trouble of building the passageway all on his own."

Dalmeny responded out of sheer surprise that she had realized that. "My uncle built it and I learned of it as he lay on the battlefield wounded and mumbling, thinking I was Talon. When I finally understood what he was saying, I made sure he would speak of it to no one else. I did not even tell my sister, knowing one day it would be of use to me and me alone." He smiled. "That day finally arrived and I shared my secret with another." He stepped aside.

"It is good to see you again, *sister*," Ulric said, stepping out from behind a group of trees.

"I go about Talon while you speak with your sister," Dalmeny said and disappeared into the woods.

It had always seemed strange to Hemera that Ulric's hair coloring was closer to Verity's than to hers, bold like the sun, his beard a bit darker with braids running through it. His features were not as striking as Talon's, but there was something about them that drew the eye or perhaps it was his eyes as blue as the summer sky that captivated women. He was tall and slim, his body defined with muscles and he was strong, exceptionally strong. She had seen him squeeze the life out of a man with one hand.

"Da has made peace with Talon. He will not be pleased with what you do here," Hemera said as Ulric approached her.

"Da is a fool." Ulric stepped close to her, his breath heavy on her cheek. He grabbed her neck and gave it a threatening squeeze as he whispered, "And when this is done, I will not only be Chieftain of the Southern Region, but also conqueror of the Picts. The fool Dalmeny will never see it coming."

He released her and when Hemera's throat eased from the pain, she said, "You will never defeat Talon."

"I thought that once, then you came along and a wise King turned into a fool." Ulric planted his nose so close to hers that they almost touched. "You, my dear sister, will not only be the fall of the King of the Picts, but the entire Pict Nation."

*Stay strong.*

Hemera's heart beat so loudly upon hearing the voice in her head that she was not sure who had spoken, but she held fast to the encouragement and continued to silently reach out to the forest for help and strength.

"You are wrong, Ulric. You will never defeat Talon, King of the Picts."

The light suddenly faded and Hemera and Ulric cast a glance upward to see that a large, dark cloud had drifted overhead, robbing the forest of light and a slow creeping fog began to spread along the ground.

"The forest does not like what you do here," Hemera warned.

"The forest has no say, you fool," Ulric said but cast a wary eye at the encroaching fog and the dimming sky.

A rustle in the bushes had him turning and reaching for his sword. He dropped his hand away when he saw it was Dalmeny returning. His scowl told Ulric that something was wrong.

"The fools lost Talon," he said with an angry growl.

Hemera kept herself from smiling. The forest had heard her and was keeping her husband safe.

The fog grew thicker, rising up and swallowing the trees and making it impossible to see beyond them.

Dalmeny and Ulric cast cautious and anxious glances as the fog rolled over their feet, but rose no higher. It was as if the fog purposely left them visible while devouring everything around them.

Hemera could not help but add to their unease. "Talon will be here soon and he will kill you both."

Ulric landed a blow to her cheek that sent her face jerking to the side.

A raging roar poured out of the fog. "For that and all the other evil you have done to my wife, you die an agonizing death."

## Chapter Thirty-four

Ulric and Dalmeny went for their swords as Talon emerged from the fog, the heavy mist retreating slowly behind him as if bowing in homage to the mighty King.

Talon was a sight to behold. His dark garments made him appear as if the earth had spewed him from its dark depths, and a flicker of fear sparked in Dalmeny and Ulric's eyes. Hemera shivered herself, especially seeing Talon's two swords gripped tightly in his hands and his deep blue eyes swirling like a mighty storm about to break loose. There was no denying he was ready to kill.

"Release my queen," Talon demanded his voice as strong as thunder.

Spittle spewed as Dalmeny spoke his anger was so tangible. "She is not fit to be queen or you King." Dalmeny raised the point of his sword to Hemera's throat.

"Are you too cowardly to face me without the threat of my wife between us?" Talon did not wait for a response. "You are a coward and a traitor and I will see you dead for what you have done."

"Let us see who the coward is," Dalmeny challenged, lowering his sword and stepping away from Hemera. "Come get her... if you can."

Warriors poured out of the forest and down from the trees, ten in all, blocking Talon's path to Hemera. They were large men, many of them thick with muscles and some with several scars, meaning they were all seasoned warriors.

Talon laid eyes on each one of them. "Drop your weapons and surrender and I will not kill you."

They all roared with laughter, except one.

"You were warned," Talon said and with the lithe swiftness of a wolf ready to attack, he charged at the warriors. The first two ran at him as well and when they looked about to collide, they swung their swords. Talon dropped just before the sharp blades reached him and their own blades struck each other, felling them both. Talon was up on his feet before the next two reached him and the ones behind them were not far off. He was on the one warrior before he could raise his sword. He sent him stumbling into another warrior and as the two fumbled apart, Talon drove his one sword through them both, swinging them around and sending them into two other warriors. He finished those two off with quick thrusts.

The last two warriors hesitated, not a wise choice. Talon let out a roar that tore through the forest, the birds taking fearful flight while animals scurried to find shelter. He charged at the two men who swung their blades in fright instead of precision. With arms crossed over his chest, the sharp blades not far from his own neck, he once again dropped to the ground, though this time he swung his blades and sliced the warriors' legs with such powerful blows that he nearly severed one leg completely. He was on his feet in one fluid motion, his swords dripping blood as he held them down at his sides and approached Dalmeny.

"Any closer and my sword cuts her just enough for you to watch her die slowly," Dalmeny threatened,

# The King & His Queen

nicking her neck with the point of his sword.

Hemera felt a dribble of blood, but her worry was not for her. She needed Talon to know how important it was for this land and its people for him to live and rule. And if it should prove necessary, he had to put that above all else... even her. "You are King, my husband, and that is more important than anything."

Talon's fury had never raged as hot as it did at that moment. She all but told him her life was unimportant compared to his, as if he should forfeit her life so that he may rule. "Hear me well, wife, *you* are all that matters to me."

His heartfelt words brought a tear to her eye and it spilled over and ran down her cheek to meet her gentle smile.

"Let her go. I will not warn you again," Talon threatened.

Dalmeny snickered. "I will—"

Talon was a blur to Hemera, he moved so swiftly. She jerked her head back and squeezed her eyes shut as soon as she felt the blood spray her face. Dalmeny's agonizing screams made it impossible to keep them closed. She opened them to see what had happened.

Dalmeny was on his knees, his head dropped back, screaming to the heavens as he cradled his one arm, his hand dangling off his wrist having been nearly severed off completely.

Another blow from Talon's sword and Dalmeny's hand fell from his wrist and rolled to a stop not far from him.

"Finish it!" Dalmeny screamed in agony.

"Not until you confess the names of every single traitor involved in your betrayal," Talon said. "Only then will you die."

"I will never tell—"

Talon's sword was swift, leaving a gash in Dalmeny's arm. "You will tell me or you will face a torturously slow death." A hard whack with the hilt of his sword to Dalmeny's head had him dropping to the ground in silence.

"I am glad you did that. His screams were growing tiresome," Ulric said, having stepped a distance away.

Talon turned his sword toward Ulric.

"I would think twice of harming me. My father would not take kindly to it," Ulric said, his tone full of confidence and his arms folded across his chest as if in defiance.

Talon spoke not a word to him. He slipped his one sword in its sheath at his back before turning to Hemera and slicing the rope down the side, freeing her. He stepped closer as the ties fell away. His one arm caught her to rest against him, her limbs so numb she could barely stand on her own. He held her close, his heart pounding like an intense war drum against his chest, relieved he finally had her safe in his arms. He never intended to let her out of his sight again. He almost laughed at the impossibility of that task, but for now he would let himself believe the unlikely thought and ease his worries.

Hemera rested her head on Talon's chest, relishing the pounding of his heart that belonged to her, the comfort of his strong arm that hugged her close and that he—the King—cared deeply enough for her that he would give his life. Not that she would ever let him.

His hand pressed lightly just below her waist. "You are unharmed?"

"We are good," she whispered, "now that you are here."

"She has survived worse," Ulric said.

"At your hands," Talon accused.

"She grew stronger because of it."

"Then you should grow extremely powerful by the time I get done with you." Talon raised his sword, though kept hold of his wife. "Your father does not know you are here, does he?"

Ulric's hand moved to the hilt of his sword. "What difference does that make?"

"All the difference," Talon said. "Haggard would never know what happened to you if you simply disappeared."

"Northmen who survive the search for those who helped Dalmeny and they will tell my father I was here. He will then know it was you who took his son's life and he will go to war with you." Ulric grinned and nodded at Hemera. "Until we meet again, *sister*."

Talon felt the shiver that ran through Hemera and he wanted Ulric dead for what he had done to her and the torment he was causing her.

Her husband's eyes warned of another impending storm and every muscle in his body grew taut in preparation. With some of the numbness having faded from her limbs, she was able to raise her hand and rest it on his chest. "Let him be. It is not worth it. One day he will get what he deserves."

A gruff voice drifted out of the fog. "That day is today."

The fog that had begun to dissipate returned, growing heavier around them.

Talon closed his fingers more tightly around the

hilt of his sword and kept his arm firm around his wife.

Ulric drew his sword, his knuckles turning white, he clutched it so tightly.

A crackling laughter sounded and an old stooped woman, leaning on a staff a good head taller than herself emerged from the fog.

"Grandmother," Hemera cried out with joy and, with weak steps, hurried to the old woman who held her arms out to her. "I have missed you so much. I was hoping you would find me." She hugged her grandmother with what strength had returned to her, happy to once again be in her arms.

Talon stared speechless.

"Have you lost your voice, you fool? You certainly did not lose it the last time we met," the old woman scolded, looking to Talon.

Hemera turned to Talon, her smile wide. "You have met my grandmother?"

Talon was trying to comprehend what he was seeing and what it meant. "Your grandmother is the Giantess?"

Ulric started laughing. "This short, skinny, old crone is your fabled Giantess?"

The Giantess patted Hemera on the back before easing her away. "Go to your husband, my dear granddaughter."

Hemera was reluctant to leave the old woman, it having been too long since she had seen her. But when she felt Talon's hand slip in hers and close firmly around it, she turned and stepped into his powerful arms.

"You better treat her well or you will deal with me," the Giantess warned and reached out to poke him with her boney finger. "I will be watching."

Talon fought the urge to say something to her, but being well aware of her powers, he wisely held his tongue.

The Giantess turned to Ulric. "As for you—"

Ulric burst out laughing. "What are you going to do, old woman, hit me with your staff and warn me to behave?"

Talon could not help but smile.

The Giantess shrugged her shoulders. "As you said, I am a fable and what can a mere fable do?" She rubbed her chin. "Let me show you." She raised her one hand slowly while she began to chant.

Ulric shook his head. "As I said, *sister*, I will see you again."

Talon's smile faded, hearing Ulric's threatening tone.

Ulric grinned at Talon, pleased that he was leaving him unable to extract revenge while letting the King know he had not seen the last of him. He turned to leave and stumbled, falling to the ground. He sat up, his brow narrowing at the vines that had wound around his feet. He went to cut the encroaching vine away but before he could, it curled rapidly upward around his legs. He went to raise his sword, but a vine suddenly coiled around his wrist, squeezing so tightly that it forced him to drop his sword.

He turned angry eyes on the Giantess and with a flick of her finger the vine rushed up his whole body, wrapping him tight and leaving only his eyes and nose to be seen. She stomped her staff on the ground and a length of vine shot out and wrapped around the bottom of it.

"I will release the fog so your warriors can find you," the Giantess said to Talon and once again raised her boney finger at him. "Remember, harm my granddaughter in any way and I will harm you far worse." She turned a smile on Hemera. "I will visit soon and we will spend time together. You have learned well your heritage, but there is more for me to teach you."

She disappeared into the fog, dragging a struggling Ulric behind her, his eyes pleading for help until he could be seen no more.

~~~

Hemera sighed, glad the long, eventful day had finally come to an end and she and Talon were alone in his sleeping chamber. She sighed, pulling the blanket up around her.

Talon turned away from the fire pit when he heard her. "Something is wrong?"

"Aye," she said with a spark of teasing in her eyes, "you fail to keep me warm."

He approached her slowly and Hemera could not help but admire his naked body, and know that every night from this one on, he would sleep beside her.

"How warm do you want me to make you, wife?" he asked, yanking the blanket off her and covering her with his body.

She winced when his one leg touched hers and he was off her in a flash, stretching out beside her to examine her leg.

"I forgot about the rope burns you suffered," he said and also gave a look at the burn on her one arm.

"My own fault. I tried to wiggle free before I realized how tightly I was tied." She pressed her hand to his cheek, his warmth tingling her palm. "I am glad it is over."

"There are still things left to do. I cannot leave the Imray Tribe without a chieftain for long."

"Minn," Hemera suggested. "She would make a good chieftain."

He pulled the blanket over them when he felt her shiver. "We think alike, wife."

"Then there is my father. He will demand answers about Ulric."

"I will be truthful. I kept my word. I did not harm Ulric." He ran his finger faintly over her lips and she shivered, though this time not from a chill. "There will be little he can do to prove otherwise without implying that his son was here to start a war."

"I am pleased to know that Bethia has hope of your uncle surviving, though I am sorry that Gerun did not. He saved my life."

"He did his duty and he will receive a warrior's burial and his family will be well cared for.

"You are a good King."

"I do not think the Giantess would agree with you."

Hemera sighed. "I only heard my grandmother called that once when I was very young, but my mum told me I needed to always remember it. That I could reach out to my grandmother if ever needed. She would always help me."

"Why did she not come get you after your mum died?"

"There are times my grandmother hibernates. It is vital to the well-being of the forest and the land. By the time she found out it was too late, though it helped when I realized I could reach out to her through my thoughts. She helped me to survive, helped me to learn. My grandmother's roots go deep in this land as do mine. It was one reason it was so difficult for me being away from here. The Northmen's forest treated me well, taught me much, but it too knew that I needed to connect with my roots to flourish, knew I needed to return home." She smiled. "I was pleased that you had met her."

Talon cringed. "It was not exactly a cordial meeting."

Hemera laughed softly. "Grandmother has more of a caring heart than she shows."

"Her heart cared not at all for me."

"Now that you are my husband it will be different," Hemera assured him.

He shook his head. "I do not believe that."

Hemera poked at his chest playfully. "You will see. Grandmother will grow to care for you."

Talon shook his head again.

"She will," Hemera insisted and her hand went to rest on her stomach, "especially when our bairn is born. You want Pict blood to forever run deep in this land and my grandmother wants this land to forever flourish with her roots that have fed this soil long before man laid claim to it. And I would not be surprised if my grandmother had a hand in bringing us together."

"If that is true I am grateful, for I do not know what I would do without you by my side," Talon said and kissed her softly. "You are mine. Now and always."

## Chapter Thirty-five

*Winter*

Hemera looked up at the heavens and smiled as the delicate snowflakes kissed her face. The snow would turn heavy soon and coat the land with its pristine beauty.

"A few moments more and we return to the stronghold," Talon said concerned with the snow that had begun to cover the ground and how rounded his wife was with their child. Any day now their bairn would be born and he wanted Hemera tucked in the warmth and safety of their home.

Hemera breathed deeply of the cold air as she stroked her large stomach. "It will be a heavy snowfall."

"All the more reason for us to return now," he said, stepping in front of her and resting his hand on her stomach and being reminded of the nights she slept in his arms and he would feel his child kick inside her. They had created a life together, a future that would live on far beyond them.

Hemera took another deep breath.

"Your sister and Anin will be expecting you at Anin's dwelling for your midday visit. You know how much your sister's son, Shand enjoys seeing you. And how Areana, Anin and Paine's daughter, favors you.

"And I know how you find reasons to cut my visits

to the forest short," Hemera said with a delicate laugh.

"You grow close to your time and I worry," Talon admitted, patting her stomach, "over the both of you."

"Why do you have my granddaughter in the forest while it snows when she is near ready to give birth?"

Talon turned to glare at the Giantess, annoyed how she suddenly appeared anytime she wished, and he let her know it. "You cannot just suddenly appear on my land without notice."

"You attempt to command me, you fool? This land belongs to me and always will. You make a home here because I allow you to live here."

Hemera laid a hand on her husband's arm and gave it a squeeze, then turned a smile on her grandmother. "And we appreciate your generosity, Grandmother. I am here with the snow falling on me because Talon indulges me. I wanted to spend time here, so our bairn would connect with the earth."

"He can connect later," the Giantess snapped. "You need to be inside where I can tend you."

"I have a healer," Talon argued.

The Giantess jabbed Talon in the arm. "I will deliver my grandson and the six that will follow in the future."

"Six?" Talon's glare was one of shock. "Hemera will give me seven sons?"

"And a daughter, though she will spend much time with me."

Hemera smiled, watching the two argue as another pain washed over her. She was glad she was here in the forest. It comforted her, welcomed her, and let her know that all would be well.

"If I give permission," Talon said.

"I need no permission from you, you fool," the Giantess said.

"Watch who you call fool, *crone*." Talon warned with a sharp tongue.

"Crone?" the Giantess said, her face scrunched in anger.

Hemera suddenly gasped in pain, her hand rushing to her stomach.

Talon scooped his wife up in his arms. "I know it would please Hemera that you tend her birth, but you will keep your harping tongue silent or I will turn it silent."

"You dare threaten the Giantess?"

Talon kept walking, cradling his wife close against him. "I threaten Hemera's grandmother who feels she can demand me, the King."

Hemera let out a soft groan and Talon's eyes immediately filled with pain.

The Giantess kept step with Talon as she said, "You suffer with her."

"Always," Talon said. "We are one and always will be."

The Giantess nodded, a grin spreading across her face. "I knew you would be the one for my granddaughter. You did not fear me. You challenged me and though you did not win—"

"I won, Hemera is mine," Talon said, as if declaring it law.

The Giantess smiled. "That she is, you foo—"

Talon turned a warning glare on her.

"Hurry, *Talon*, and get her to your sleeping chamber where she can be comfortable and deliver your first of many sons."

"As you say, *Grandmother*," Talon said and hurried along.

~~~

The snow covered the ground several times over before Hemera finally delivered Talon's son, heir to the Pict Kingdom. His was a large bairn with a sprinkle of dark hair, and his cries were heard throughout the feasting hall while vessels were raised to toast the new heir to the throne. A worthy name would be chosen for him, though the Giantess had already bestowed a name on him—Bram—and claimed it would not be changed. It was meant for him.

Talon sat beside his sleeping pallet, watching his wife and newborn son, cradled in her arm, sleeping. Hemera had delivered their son easily with mostly moans and groans and barely a scream or two, which had torn through him and caused him excruciating pain. He hated to see her suffer but she had been courageous and talk would spread about the Queen's bravery.

A shiver stirred Hemera and Talon hurried to the fire pit to add more wood. He turned to find Hemera easing herself off the sleeping pallet, leaving their son to sleep. She walked over to him and his arms went around her as they always did. When he closed them around her, he could feel her body sigh with relief and he, himself, felt whole again.

Talon did not want to let her go. There in his arms was where she belonged, but she had only delivered their son. "You should rest."

Hemera met her husband's eyes filled with fatigue and she ran a gentle finger beneath each of them. "The birth tired you."

He took hold of her hand and hugged it, bringing it to rest against his chest. "Not as much as you."

"You are pleased with your son?"

"More pleased then I could ever make it known."

"Grandmother?" she inquired cautiously.

"She is in the feasting hall bragging about her grandson and out drinking my warriors," Talon said, shaking his head.

Hemera was left with a smile after her soft laughter faded and a yawn quickly followed.

Talon lifted her gently in his arms and commanded, "You will rest."

"Only with you beside me," she said and pressed a soft kiss to his lips.

"Alongside me is where you will always be. I will have it no other way. You have my heart forever." He brushed his lips over hers and whispered, "*Tuahna*, wife, *tuahna*."

## THE END

## Titles by Donna Fletcher

**The Pict King Series**
The King's Executioner
The King's Warrior
The King and His Queen

**Macinnes Sisters Trilogy**
The Highlander's Stolen Heart
Highlander's Rebellious Love
Highlander: The Dark Dragon

**Highlander Trilogy**
Highlander Unchained
Forbidden Highlander
Highlander's Captive

**Warrior King Series**
Bound To A Warrior
Loved By A Warrior
A Warrior's Promise
Wed To A Highland Warrior

**Sinclare Brothers' Series**
Return of the Rogue
Under the Highlander's Spell
The Angel & The Highlander
Highlander's Forbidden Bride

The Irish Devil
Irish Hope

Isle of Lies

The King & His Queen

Love Me Forever

For a complete list of Donna's titles, visit her website… www.donnafletcher.com

# About the author

It was her love of reading and daydreaming that started USA Today bestselling author Donna Fletcher's writing career. Besides gobbling up books, her mom generously bought for her, she spent a good portion of her time lost in daydreams that took her on grand adventures. She met heroes and villains, and heroines that, while usually in danger, always found the strength and courage to prevail. She traveled all over the world and through time in her dreams. Some places and times fascinated her more than others and she would rush to the library (no Internet at that time) and read all she could about that particular period and place. After a while, she simply could not ignore all the adventures swirling around in her head, she had no choice but to bring them more vividly to life, and so she started writing.

Donna continues to daydream, characters popping in and out of her head wherever she goes and filling her with tales that keeps her writing schedule on overload. You can learn more about her on her website.

Donna enjoys living on the beautiful Jersey shore surrounded by family and friends and a cat who thinks she's a princess, but what cat doesn't, and a dog who bows to the princess's demands.

Printed in Great Britain
by Amazon